PRAISE FOR *SHAME AND THE CAPTIVES*

"Keneally's gift, and his blessing to the many hundreds of characters he has created, is always to find the extraordinary within the ordinary. . . . With a virtuosity he has rarely matched, [this is] another of Keneally's grand entertainments."

—*The Australian*

"He weaves his magic and the reader falls under his spell. Keneally negotiates the separate and intertwining narratives with his usual elegance and skill."

—*The Guardian*

"A fine novel that asks challenging questions about death, about the cultural differences of East and West, about cruelty and mercy, about ideals and violence. . . . That the novel feels authentic owes much to Keneally's way of fleshing out a character, his skill at dramatizing the war of weapons and points of view, and the unflinching vision that portrays humans at their worst, and on occasion their best. . . . Prepare to be amazed."

—*South China Morning Post*

"Gripping. . . . A remarkable achievement."

—*The Scotsman*

"This is historical writing at its best. The details of life in both the prison camp and the civilian/military personnel in Gawell are based upon research into a similar prison break elsewhere during the war. This is a must-read for those who enjoy well-researched and atmospheric novels of World War II. The reader can feel the shame felt by the Japanese prisoners, and their preference for a merciless death to the humiliation of imprisonment. An exceptional story, highly recommended."

—*Historical Novel Society*

PRAISE FOR *THE DAUGHTERS OF MARS*

"Poignant . . . masterly . . . epic . . . [Keneally] has rescued forgotten heroines from obscurity and briefly placed them center stage."

—*The New York Times Book Review*

"A burly, captivating saga of Australian nurses on the front lines of World War I. . . . Inscribed with the stately, benign authority of an eminent tale-spinner."

—*The Wall Street Journal*

"Magnificent . . . a stunning performance, full of suspense, searing particulars, and deep emotion. . . . The huge talents of Thomas Keneally are everywhere on display."

—*The Guardian*

"*The Daughters of Mars* is the work of a master storyteller, sharing a tale that is simultaneously sprawling and intimate."

—*NPR*

"[A] poignant novel."

—*The New York Times,* Editor's Choice

"May be the best novel of Keneally's career . . . a book that aims for, and achieves, real grandeur."

—*The Spectator,* One of the Best Books of 2012

"An epic, sweeping book."

—*Los Angeles Times*

"Extraordinarily moving. . . . Keneally is a master of character development and period detail. . . . Fans of *Downton Abbey* and *Gallipoli* alike will find much to admire in Keneally's fast-moving, flawlessly written pages."

—*Kirkus Reviews* (starred review)

"Superbly exciting to read. . . . An unmissable, unforgettable tribute."

—*The Times* (London)

"Not only is *The Daughters of Mars* one of the most ambitious novels in a career that stretches back to 1964, but it might even be *the* best. . . . The result is something few other authors would aim for, let alone achieve: genuine grandeur."

—*The Telegraph*

"A big and brutal book, a new prism through which to think about World War I . . . breathtaking . . . magnificent and almost magical. There are moments of joy, of pleasure, that make you look up from their page for a while to arrest and savour their sensation."

—*The Australian*

"Expansive and brilliant . . . a masterpiece that is sure to rank among Keneally's best works."

—*Bookpage*

"Greatly detailed . . . boasts authentic characters set in equally authentic locations."

—*Booklist*

"Like the warriors of Homer's *Iliad,* Keneally gives readers a sense of the vast and continuous casualties dealt by war and reminds us that each soldier was once a boy armed with little more than a pitchfork."

—*The Missourian*

"Keneally has summoned all of his ample talent to write a sweeping novel of World War I."

—*Pittsburgh Post-Gazette*

"By Page 6, readers can put up their feet and relax. They know they're in the reassuring hands of a master storyteller, and a fascinating read lies ahead."

—*San Jose Mercury News*

"A bravura piece of writing."

—*The Seattle Times*

ALSO BY THOMAS KENEALLY

Bettany's Book

Office of Innocence

The Tyrant's Novel

The Widow and Her Hero

The People's Train

The Daughters of Mars

NONFICTION

Outback

The Place Where Souls Are Born

Now and in Time to Be: Ireland and the Irish

Memoirs from a Young Republic

Homebush Boy: A Memoir

The Great Shame

American Scoundrel

Abraham Lincoln

The Commonwealth of Thieves

Searching for Schindler

Three Famines

Australians

FOR CHILDREN

Ned Kelly and the City of Bees

Roos in Shoes

SHAME AND THE CAPTIVES

A Novel

THOMAS KENEALLY

WASHINGTON SQUARE PRESS

New York   London   Toronto   Sydney   New Delhi

WASHINGTON SQUARE PRESS
An Imprint of Simon & Schuster, Inc.
1230 Avenue of the Americas
New York, NY 10020

First Washington Square Press trade paperback edition December 2015

WASHINGTON SQUARE PRESS and colophon are registered trademarks
of Simon & Schuster, Inc.

For information about special discounts for bulk purchases,
please contact Simon & Schuster Special Sales at 1-866-506-1949
or business@simonandschuster.com.

The Simon & Schuster Speakers Bureau can bring authors to your live event.
For more information or to book an event, contact the Simon & Schuster Speakers
Bureau at 1-866-248-3049 or visit our website at www.simonspeakers.com.

Manufactured in the United States of America

10 9 8 7 6 5 4 3 2 1

The Library of Congress has cataloged the hardcover edition as follows:

Keneally, Thomas.
  Shame and the captives : a novel / Thomas Keneally. — First Atria Books
hardcover edition.
      pages ; cm
  1. World War, 1939–1945—Prisoners and prisons, Australian—Fiction.
2. World War, 1939–1945—Prisoners and prisons, Japanese—Fiction.
3. Prisoners of war—Australia—Fiction. 4. Prisoners of war—Japan—
Fiction. 5. Escapes—Australia—Cowra (N.S.W.)—Fiction. 6. Australia—
History—20th century—Fiction. 7. Cowra (N.S.W.)—History—20th
century—Fiction. I. Title.
  PR9619.3.K46S53 2015
  823'.914—dc23   2014034535

ISBN 978-1-4767-3464-4
ISBN 978-1-4767-3465-1 (pbk)
ISBN 978-1-4767-3466-8 (ebook)

Author's Note

Where the Tale Comes From

The outbreak of Japanese prisoners from a camp on the edge of the New South Wales Central West town of Cowra occurred when I was nine years old and while my father was absent, serving overseas. Without him to stand on the threshold of our house and repel this outburst, it seemed, even in the suburbs of Sydney, a terrifying business—an invasion from within the heartland. We did not understand its motives, which lay beyond the horizons of our culture and imagination. We judged them to include the intent to do unspeakable damage to women, children, and men, in that order.

To thwart such malice, people armed themselves. A great-aunt of mine, her menfolk away, shared her bed with an ax in a town near Cowra. Farmers, if they needed to go briefly away from their farmhouses, left behind a rifle for their wives to protect the hearth and their own person.

Over time, a more accurate picture of the motives of those who broke loose would emerge, and can be garnered from the experts, books, and documents I acknowledge at the end of this narrative.

The truth is, though, that I have not created exactly the set of events that occurred in Cowra during the outbreak of August 4–5, 1944. I did not want to offend those who lived through that night, and the days before and after, and though—above all—I have tried to read as exactly as I can the cultures of both sides to the calamity, this is not what is called a roman à clef, a novel in which every character is meant to stand for and reflect on a real human, living or dead. My characters are not designed to reflect any virtues, sins, follies, fevers, and acts of courage evident in any of the real actors in the Cowra outbreak. The details we have are not sufficient to fill out all the characters, in any case. And combining and enlarging details is something the novelist has to do—it's part of the job. It can be apologized for, but not avoided.

Yet, using the context of a prison camp set on the edge of an Australian country town, I have tried to write a parallel account, or a tale provoked by the events that unfolded in Cowra in 1944. I have placed similar events in a fictional location named Gawell, for which I ask the pardon of the citizens of Cowra and the spirits of those obliterated in the fury of that night. My story is like a sibling version of the Cowra one—related strongly by DNA, and the same in many regards, but in others bearing different names and features.

For example, the full moon plays its part in the Gawell outbreak, as it did in that of Cowra; the climactic night was one of fierce cold in the case of the real and the fictional towns. Yet Alice Herman is a creation and did not exist outside this narrative's limits. The same can be said for the Italian prisoner Giancarlo Molisano. (We know, however, that relationships similar to theirs occurred at the time.) A novelist, Major E. V. Timms, was in command of an Italian compound at Cowra. But the fictional Major Suttor, who writes morale-boosting radio serials and commands Compound C of Gawell Camp, is not meant in any way to mirror E. V. Timms's life, actions, motivations, and preoccupations. Nor is my commandant, Colonel Abercare, crafted to reproduce the character and events of the actual commandant's life. There *was* a Korean informer inside Cowra, but he was not the Cheong of my account. There was a Japanese prisoner who sought to warn the garrison, but he was not the man named Ban in the tale as I tell it.

Yet I hope there's a truth in this fiction, in its imagining of motives, and in the actions of these characters—that they do represent in feeling what happened in those times. Fiction has always tried to tell the truth by telling lies, by fabrication. Through fictional Gawell, I am in my own way trying to interpret the phenomenon of Cowra and the great forces of intent and contrasting views that were let loose and illuminated by the outbreak.

These sorts of disclaimers often accompany novels, and the novelist can be fairly accused of claiming the best of both worlds. If so, I hope that readers of this novel feel they are getting the best of both worlds too. For whatever the liberties that have been taken, this is a great story, made only in part by me but, above all, by the events that took place in August 1944, in a township far from the battlefronts and from the main discourse of the earth.

When Aoki got down from the truck and presented himself at his mother's house, he was pleased to have the village that now lay around him validate his memory of it, to have his childhood and youth reabsorb him, altered and limping as he was. He did not make a noise but waited by the door. Here he was all at once outflanked by a terrified shrilling from his wife, who happened to be coming up the path from the fields. Turning, he saw the screaming, instantly familiar woman, her mouth livid amidst the shade of a conical straw hat. There were flecks of mud on the hands and wrists she raised and on her hempen overskirt. His mother appeared at the door now, summoned by the screams. She looked aged yet, like the village, continuous with all he had once known, and almost intolerably and too-suddenly present. His similarly too-real wife flung herself at him from the side, his mother, howling now his wife had ceased, from the front.

"I must bathe," he told them.

"Your father is dead," his mother told him.

The women tested out his substance and could not stop exclaiming at his resurrection but seemed to want to prevent him from entering the house. His wife rushed inside. His mother hushed him and held him back from following. His wife emerged with an engraved stone tablet, the death memorial tablet from the house shrine. His return could be confirmed only by evicting it. He saw his name marked out in red paint on black stone. She dropped the tablet to the damp ground before the house and went to the side of the garden for a mattock and, with this implement, began work on his memorial, splitting and then fragmenting the stone, howling with each stroke. When that was done she threw the mattock away and rushed to embrace him forcefully again. He felt revivification surge in him.

His family and his wife's were summoned, and had all gathered by late afternoon. His wife now produced a tall funerary urn sent her by the government. It purported to hold his ashy bone fragments. But obviously, she said, it must contain another man's. A cousin had brought shochu, which he brewed himself, and had drunk a few cups of it, and declared, "At least we should look inside."

Aoki's wife asked, "Why disturb the urn?"

"Well," said the cousin, "they might have put a slip of paper, or some other clue to identity in there. His uncle, his mother's elder brother, was voted the proper person to intrude, and reverently and solemnly opened the urn, cracking the hardened wax that sealed it. The lid removed, he peered inside. He then shook the thing. It rattled. Bone fragments? He reached in and extracted a handful of gravel. He held his hand up with the stones visible in his palm. He invited his father's brother to feel inside. His paternal uncle, frowning, brought out gravel, too, and now delved deep inside and still found only small chips of stone. The uncles looked at each other with a fierce, indefinable grievance in their eyes. Then the maternal uncle began to laugh, close to hysterics. "They sent gravel," he hooted, and laughter became general, and a few cousins said dark things about authorities who would treat mothers and widows with such deceit.

The two uncles took the urn to the door and flung its gravel, a handful at a time, into the garden, dispersing it like all the other lies of failed government.

This act was the cue for him to explain himself to his clan, and so he began. Veteran cousins could have posed a challenge to credibility, but those who had served outside the country were dead, except for one young man struck dumb on Saipan and dependent on his parents to guide his movements.

Waiting for shipping to become available to take him home, Aoki had rehearsed this tale for more than a year, and he could not deviate from it, since it had in a way now become as true as himself. As a solitary soldier, with an abiding wound in his lower leg, and survivor of a slaughtered section of men, he had been bypassed by a fluid jungle battle in New Guinea and found himself amongst the savages. These were people, he explained, who wore headdresses of the more vivid feathers, but also tusks of pigs implanted in their septums. Amongst them he prepared for his final resistance. But he waited and waited. The war had moved thoroughly on, and months and longer passed, and he was lucky that, reconnoitering a track one day, he ran into a handful of other holdouts. They made their way with native guides, by way of the tracks not used by the enemy, down into the kunai grass coastal plain and through swamps to the coast. The country was full of battle wreckage, but even its dead were already buried, and from there the holdout party took a native boat and so fetched up on the coast of New Britain. Found by an officer in a small truck, they were told that sadly the Emperor had ordered surrender. Hence, amongst them, Aoki came to Rabaul, to wait for a ship home. The wait was very, very long.

When they were alone, she said to Aoki, "You were surrounded by those black savages . . . All that time you had in the jungle . . ."

Her voice fluted uncertainly, and she did not want—after such a length of separation—to offend him or start an argument. He knew she was asking him about jungle women, though, and wondering, had he succumbed to them?

"I was still a soldier," he declared softly, deflecting the inquiry.

She said nothing. She wore a blue silk nightgown, and he the green, high-necked pyjamas she had bought when she'd first heard of his survival. They were fabrics unfamiliar to him. A hateful silence threatened to break out. He heard her silk gown moving with a whisper, like barely heard surf, and he knew he should not let the silence grow. He addressed the issue obliquely. "And I was outside their life—like a ghost. They were terrified of me. They still pursued their own grudges against each other as if I weren't there. They fed me purely for the sake of their superstition." His belly was liquid with desire. She was still so beautiful with her slightly wasted face—the woman who had succeeded the girl he'd met before they had sent him to China. He had been lucky to find her, to have been chosen by her, given that awkward ancestral stoop he had, even as a young man, and his taciturn ways. A lot of people had told him that at the time.

"You have to remember," he said to fill the void, "that the women of New Guinea chewed betel nut and it stained their teeth dreadfully. They gave off a smell no one civilized could have tolerated. They coated themselves with pig fat to ward off malaria, and let it stay there, no matter how rancid it got."

He lay still and tense and let the details settle in her mind. It was mainly true, he believed, from what he had observed of natives during his last campaigns. The native women did coat themselves with pig fat, he had seen it on the hillsides behind the beaches. And so now he lay in green cotton exaggerating the native women's repulsiveness. In any case, after the soldiers had rounded up their men as porters, the women had vanished into mountains on unguessed-at paths into great, misty thickets of jungle.

"No," he told her softly. "I was true to my vow." He sounded to himself like a liar. There had, in fact, been a Chinese woman in Rabaul, but that had been more than four years ago. There had been China itself—better forgotten.

And yet somehow and with merciful suddenness, it worked a wonder. She undid a sash and unleashed from her nightdress her

breasts. And though he had poisoned the air of the room with his fic-
tions, he could not prevent himself from answering her gesture, from
turning his eyes full on her. Within the limits of his everlasting deceit,
he answered the unnegotiable kindness of her breasts.

And now he could never reveal any hint of the reality of those
shadow years, or plead he had done the best, to the point of comedy,
to end himself and validate that shrine. He *had* limped into the enfilading paths of machine guns and failed to be reaped. While steeling
himself to be strangled with honor from a tree, on a barbarous ridge
in a country of absurd people, accident *had* let him down, and lanky
alien soldiers with voices like crows *had* arrived and retrieved him
as if he'd committed a mere misdemeanor. He had stood before a
military inquiry that had every reason to demand his life, and it had
grotesquely failed to. Those details were not for his kin and not for his
wife, repossessed now in her divine shell of satin skin.

PART I

AUSTRALIAN SPRING AND SUMMER 1943–44

1

On an unexpectedly warm day in the second October since her husband's capture, twenty-three-year-old Mrs. Alice Herman saw—from the veranda where she sat sewing buttons on one of her father-in-law's shirts—an army truck pull up in the middle of the rutted clay and gravel road outside the Hermans' place, three miles west of Gawell. She believed at first that the truck had simply broken down. But it had a purpose. Four guards with rifles alighted, and then six of those others—prisoners in their deep-red shirts and trousers— were ordered down from the back. They were instantly fascinating, with their subtle contours, even in the different way they jumped, stood, and moved. They were beings from the other side of the veil of what was understandable, of what could be condoned or countenanced. Even without their repute as frenzied warriors, the perilous difference of their blood was proscribed in the canons of White Australia. A person at a safe distance couldn't avoid gawping at them.

Certainly the Mussolini-loving Italians from the same Gawell Prisoner of War Camp weren't as interesting. Even in Alice's girlhood, there had always been an Italian family or two in each country town. They tended to sell fruit. The Italians in Gawell Camp were not only more numerous, they were also scattered as laborers on farms all over the place. Duncan Herman, her father-in-law, had applied to a place called the Control Center to send him one. But Italians surely lacked the novelty value of the Japanese.

There were, by contrast, only perhaps a thousand of these Oriental exotics over there, three miles off in Gawell Camp, and they were normally kept out of public sight. So they were an astounding apparition for a woman like her, one dedicated to a life of near drudgery, cooking and pickling, bottling fruit, feeding chickens, milking, churning butter, and—in season—lambing. Since the rouseabout who had lived in the shearers' quarters had joined the militia, Alice had been assigned to these tasks by national necessity. She did not wish to go home to her parents' place to fulfill similar work and attend to her querulous mother as well. She stayed on the Herman farm, of which her absent husband was son and inheritor.

The second reason the men engrossed her attention was that they shared with her husband, Neville Herman, the condition of being prisoners. Though they might be so removed from jovial Neville by layers of oddity, their captive state was a reproach to her. She had barely known her husband as an abiding presence before he was gone. She felt this was her fault, since she had married him as an opportunity and without certainty. It had also been such a short marriage—they had barely got beyond much playfulness and one or two lesser flashes of irritation. As for the physical side, she felt there hadn't been enough of it to impress her body with memory and ache. She knew the wives of other men now held by the enemy, and could sense the more strenuous, sinewy bonds of their marriages. She might have been like them had she and Neville lived together for a year, instead of for a brief season of what seemed sport. Sometimes now Neville seemed more a story than a man: nearly got away, poor Nev. A victim of the code of mateship. And so even with these prisoners down on the road, she had a mad suspicion she could, by observing them, learn something of Neville, and that she had a duty to do that.

Neville had sat a time on the shores of Crete with thousands of others who had missed the last friendly ship, or been considered ineligible for it. He had then joined some comrades on a Greek vessel called a caïque and sailed eastwards to Chios, off Turkey. Men were taken off Chios at night by further small vessels, which made for Alexandria—so a friend of Neville's who'd got away in that manner had told her in a letter. Neville had given up his place on a vessel to a man with pneumonia, the letter writer said. Duncan had believed that outright, but Alice—for reasons she couldn't define—wondered whether it was the truth or a consoling lie. Not that Neville wasn't a good enough fellow for that to be true! In any case, the Germans had occupied Chios while Neville was still waiting there.

"At least he gave it a go," said Duncan of Neville's escape to Chios. "He didn't sit on his backside and just wait for the buggers to drive up in trucks."

At the end of Neville's Greek adventure, after marches and steamer and train journeys, which he'd described in a letter, he'd ended in a place in the east of Austria named Eichberg. That was where the food parcels she got together were sent, via a Red Cross address in Sydney. In his most recent letter, which had arrived in July, he had praised the last parcel and said that it was good, after the winter, to be let out to the farms, even if it was only for the day. These details were too sparse; her imagination could not get purchase on the life he led, and she gazed at the prisoners, as if they could give her a clue.

The laborers on the road in their russet-dyed uniforms whom Alice now observed were said to belong to an army who "gave it a go," as Duncan had said of his son. That was why there were only a thousand of them in Gawell, and a scatter elsewhere in the countryside. They were said to choose mad last stands before surrender, and were not as reasonable—once things became impossible—as Neville had surely been on Crete and Chios. It was a matter of gratitude he was not one of *their* prisoners but a captive at least of the European army.

On close study, she could see that two of the six men unloaded on the road were older, nearly as old as the guards. The rest of them were young—just boys, even if, judging by the news from captured areas, boy-faced monsters. They showed no interest as an army dump truck ground up the road and backed itself towards her father-in-law's fence. Its tray rose and gravel fell from it with chattering brevity. Then, with tray lowered again, it charged away as if it had urgent business on similar roads.

It left behind the vehicle that had delivered the prisoners and their guards, with one set (the guards) possessing only four old rifles from another war, rifles of the kind Duncan himself owned. Six shovels were now thrown down on the road by the unarmed driver of the first truck, and the prisoners were ordered by gesture and loud, English-language urgings to pick up the bloody things. They did it without rush, keeping close to the line between obedience and surly delay. A guard tramped around the road indicating surfaces and dips and ruts where the gravel was to go. It was hard to believe, though, that the road past Herman's farm was going to benefit much from that dumped gravel. The six prisoners were not moving to the heap with any pressing desire to mend the surface. But the guards went on yelling, raising and lowering their rifles as if they were dumbbells, suggesting the pace of work. The strangers began sullenly to spread the gravel. Even the slow grind of the shovel blades into the heap of stones sounded contemptuous. The same with the prisoners' movements to potholes, where they dropped the gravel like men who wanted it to be as small a remedy as possible.

The driver, meanwhile, with a peculiarly military lack of interest— that princely boredom Alice had seen in underemployed soldiers before—got back into his cabin and drove the truck into the shade of a tall peppermint tree, and then turned off its engine. He got out and sat on the running board and smoked a cigarette. The empty cicada-shrilling day, peopled by middle-aged guards and indolent captives in burgundy-dyed shirts and trousers, seemed to Alice to be ripe for intrusion by someone active and purposeful. Could it be her?

But it was more appropriate and obvious that she ought to stand up with her sewing and back away towards the door into deeper shade, as if with the intention of going into the kitchen. To hide was as natural as to gawp. Those gentlemen over there, or their compatriots, were the violators of Chinese women and impalers of children in Nanking. She had seen it all in newspaper photographs, hard to look at but impossible not to. What in God's name, it had been asked at the time and ever since, would they do to white women and children?

She noticed now that the guards had taken to the shade of some red gums on the far side of the road. Things seemed finely, even dangerously, balanced out there. There was a dormant risk the laborers might rush on the guards with their shovels, which possessed in sharpness almost as much efficacy as the rifles. One attack by the captives and one rifle seizing up might lead to the guards being battered and slashed. And who'd be next? The Hermans, and her, in particular: Duncan, her father-in-law, was not in close reach, but out on the tractor scarifying his fifty-acre paddock. But the guards seemed lazily alert. In terms of escape, there was nowhere the men could travel, and no way they could conceal who they were in a landscape where anyone except whites and blackfellers stood out.

According to the pattern of her daily tedium, she had a stew on the stove, and she regretted having to go to attend to it now. Even on the hottest days, except at times of exceptional demand on his attention (lambing, haymaking), her father-in-law ate a substantial midday dinner. So at last she turned and made it in through the door, up the hallway, deposited her mending on a chair in the lounge room, and went to peel and boil potatoes. They were far too outlandish to fit into the torpor of an accustomed farm day. You could not avoid knowing they were *there*. Able to judge boiling times to a nicety, she went out again to check on these unknown quantities and see if they were still there. A westerly had begun to blow and she knew that if she stepped off the veranda the sun would descend on her like a doubled-up form of gravity. The wind nudged her cheek and brought her a conviction again that in some ways she could not explain.

It was definitely more than a desire to see something novel and unsteadying up close, though it was that as well. But it was also that their drudgery might run parallel to Neville's in another place. Occasionally heard Methodist sermons on matters such as the parable of the Good Samaritan suggested to her, and even raised an instinct in her, that to succor men so strange might earn succor for poor barely known Neville when he was marched out to work on harvests, as a recent rare letter had told her he did. In seeing them, she believed, she did in a way see him, and gain memory of him.

Back to the kitchen she raced and fetched from a box by the dresser the remaining leftover lemons from the two trees in the informal orchard beyond the back gate. She began to slice the fruit, squeeze it out, pour the juice into jugs, go to the ice chest, chip ice off the ice blocks, put it all in the jug, mix in sugar—a reckless amount of her ration—add water from the kitchen tap with tank wrigglers in it, and stir it all up. She did not want her father-in-law to come in and see her behaving like this, so it must be done briskly.

When the juice was made up, she found a tin tray, placed six glasses on it—five for the guards and driver and one for the prisoners to share—and the jug, and then set off down the hallway, across the veranda, and out into the cloying solidity of air. The density of the heat on her forehead made her feel a certain clarity, and seemed to prove to her that she was doing the right and humane thing. And it was only October. This was going to be a terrible summer. She put the tray down on the earth so that she could open the gate to the road, and was aware that the guards were watching her already through their sun-narrowed eyes.

She picked up the tray again, carried it through, set it down not far from the new gravel heap, and closed the gate. Then she retrieved her cargo of minor mercy and made her way to the first two guards resting in the shade of the red gums.

"You beauty!" one of them said, seeing the jug of lemonade and rising awkwardly from his haunches.

They were weather-beaten men, lacking the bloom that Neville's face had had when he'd gone off to the Middle East. These ones were exactly like the questing men who'd come bearing swags of few possessions to her parents' farm near Coonamble during the bitter years, before war had taken away the young and brought a kind of rationed prosperity. "It's a pretty fierce day," she told the two men. She poured each of them a glass of her lemonade and told them she hoped it was sweet enough. She visited the other two guards at their post under the further tree, and the driver, who had wandered over.

"Do you mind if I give the prisoners some?" she asked them.

The aging soldiers looked at each other.

"Maybe that's too kind, missus," one of them said. "We'll sling them a bit of water later."

"It's very hot, though. In anyone's book."

"Yes, but look, love, the only reason they're out here is that they're the beggars who encouraged others not to work. So the colonel told them they had to work or their baseball kit would get taken off them. Lost cause, if you ask me."

The truck driver said, rising, "God knows, they're doing bugger all, if you'll excuse me, miss."

"My husband's a prisoner," she told them, though she knew her argument was risky to enunciate. "I'd like to treat them well in the hope he might get treated well."

"You can't be sure it'd be reciprocated, love. Not if he's a prisoner of theirs."

"I'd like to give them a drink each unless there's a rule against it."

One of the guards sighed, left the shade of the red gum, his rifle at the slope, and gestured to the prisoners. The six men, strung out between the gravel heap and the needful holes, put down their shovels. The other sentries took a more professional hold of their weapons. First Alice laid the tray on a tree stump, then poured six glasses, though five of them had already been drunk from. She did not know if she wanted to wait long enough to watch them drink one at a time. She offered the tray to the nearest prisoner.

He was one of the younger ones. He had very startling wide-set eyes and handsome features, to the point of prettiness, and he made a minute bow with a few seconds of half smile on his lips.

"Watch out for him," one of the guards called. "He's a flash pilot. Only thing is, he crashed."

The guard uttered a momentary laugh. The young man seemed not to recognize the taunt. The prisoner stared at her with such a limpid-eyed directness she was forced to look away. It seemed the result of something that would not be soothed in her that made her avert her eyes in a landscape that belonged to her and not to him. She became convinced he would refuse to take the glass, that he would embarrass her in front of the guards. She was surprised by the small noise of his picking it up and turned her eyes back. His style of accepting the glass, of bowing and of drinking, was to Alice like the practices of a religion she had never before encountered. When he was finished, he bowed to her and replaced the glass on the tray. By then his other companions were accepting glasses, though none of them quite matched him in bearing and ceremony.

Alice had a chance to study them as they drank. Apart from the handsome boy, there were three narrow-mouthed kids who were not expressive at all, but who nonetheless made quick bows of the head when accepting the lemonade. Then came a stooping older man with a limp—as she'd observed—who obviously considered refusing the glass and delayed some seconds before seeming to find the frost on its flanks too great a temptation. His long face was a hard map to read. Last of all was a thin man about the same age as the lame one, and wearing a judicious sort of frown.

Alice felt she was learning little by reading these mute prisoners so intently. She realized she would have welcomed sneers or leering since that would have, by contrast, made Neville somehow realer, more sharply seen. But they were prisoners in a different way from Neville. They were here and could not be interpreted. Neville was in another hemisphere yet his nature was formulated—not least by the tale of his capture. Neville wanted liberation. But what did these men want? They did not even take her lemonade with any outright gratitude, though the temperature was as high for them as it was for the other men.

An untoward sadness seized her. She felt cheated that she had studied so hard the faces of those she had been merciful to and had learned so little. She was consoled to some extent because she knew she had defeated their understanding too. But it was mercy without the reward of knowledge, a gesture that didn't earn enlightenment, a mere dimple in the day's argument between guards and shovelers.

They put the glasses back on the tray after they were finished. The guards moved in and reclaimed the day for labor, ordering the six prisoners to take up their shovels. And although these people had at one stage of their history owned every island in the Pacific except this one, the biggest and driest, here on Herman's Road they were like wisps of men. She and they were ghosts to each other, and nothing had been learned for Neville's sake.

Duncan Herman was a wiry fellow, smaller than his absent son, who had inherited his build from his late mother. Duncan was one of those fellows who had always been baffled by women and maneuvered edgily around them with a gruff jollity. Now, as a widower, he had that same wary manner towards Alice. It was obvious he would never remarry; Alice had overheard him murmur to another farmer he'd met on the street in Gawell, "I've retired from the business of women." In his system, you tried things once and if they ended halfway badly you did not attempt them again. It was an agricultural attitude and on the level of farming had proved fairly reliable. He held no rancor against the human race—he just didn't need it greatly.

Duncan's wife had developed consumption and been operated on and put in a sanatorium in the Blue Mountains. The expense had been a burden, but Duncan had met it for two years. It was on a day after he had visited her that Mrs. Herman had died unexpectedly of a stroke. Neville had been eighteen at the time and knew that Duncan carried a vague sense of blame, convinced that a woman was a set of symptoms which in Mrs. Herman's case he had somehow set off.

Not long after Alice had met Neville at the dance in Gawell, where she had been visiting a girlhood friend, he had told her this, because—typically of a country town—there were gossips. Alice should understand, Neville insisted, that because his mother had been a town beauty, scandalmongers had talked with pursed lips about the tragic contrast between her as a girl and as a woman, and somehow had found his father to blame for the difference. But it was just really bad luck, said Neville. Okay, a bit of a mismatch, but made in good faith. None of it was Duncan's fault—according to Neville. His father was a brick, a true gentleman. Farm work had been hard on Mrs. Herman, of course, but no harder than on other women. But it did show you that farmers should marry farmers' daughters. Your average mixed livestock and grain farm could be a shock to a town girl. For it had hidden tests.

Neville was a different creature from his father. Already a recruit, and possessing the faint glamour of warriorhood, he had an arduously brilliantined head of dark hair, which somehow touched Alice, not for the reasons he would have wanted it to, but because of all the solitary effort he put into it. He had a glimmer of unmeasured possibility in his eye, and that, too, seemed poignant to Alice. It would need a great deal to happen to him before that glint of hope was snuffed out. It seemed to be great days for marriage. Soldiers' girlfriends were becoming engaged, it seemed to Alice, as a gesture towards morale.

When Neville asked her about ten o'clock on a Saturday night during a School of Arts dance, acceptance had seemed unavoidable. It was well-known from the flicks and radio serials that a soldier needed the solace of a remembered girl to soothe the harshness of army life, and on foreign fields a wife's name and picture and letters to provide him with certainty and wisdom and discretion.

"I don't want to have to chase any Pommy girls," he told her. At that stage he thought his division would be sent to England. "They wouldn't be a patch on you."

The very ordinariness of his sentiments had, in the circumstances, more force than if he'd quoted Wordsworth.

He was considered A1 by the army, which had condemned him to the infantry and only occasional leave; and she knew what a mixed farm was, and how to be of use on one—marriage would be a matter for her purely of changing locations from Coonamble to Gawell.

When he was home on leave, Alice and Neville married. Her mother had met Neville earlier and liked him but thought the marriage ill-advised given the state of the world—as well, Alice thought, for other, unstated reasons, whose aroma her mother had the power to release into the air rather than going to the trouble of defining them.

Alice judged her marriage a matter of sensible decision as well as infatuation. She thought sometimes that she had decided to fall in love with this young soldier, who wore a uniform which, like everything about him except his good nature, put him at a remove from his father and at a brave distance from the family tragedy. Her mother asked her if she knew the story of Neville's mother. "Don't be angry with me," she said in a way that always and infallibly angered Alice. "You have to be careful in case he inherits that personality his father has. His father's a hermit, and his mother had bad lungs. You don't want the situation to come up where Neville goes all glum himself and keeps you and your kids secluded on the farm."

Alice and her mother had always irritated each other, sometimes severely so. She was a blunt woman whose opinions Alice's father went to some trouble to avoid challenging. She had warned Alice about a certain bush type—the narrow and mean-fisted contrarian, and his joyless spite. But Alice was willfully certain Neville did not fit the category. Yet she knew her mother was correct in another sense in her doubt about the marriage. During the engagement, Alice was more excited, skittish, and feverish than at any other time of her life, and she realized she was enacting a version of something she had seen at the Rialto Cinema—the breezy, happy engaged girl over whom no cloud hangs. There was something in it all she herself didn't quite believe. Whether she loved Neville or not was a mystery to her. His announcements of love were compelling, however.

As for the risk of Neville becoming Duncan, she thought the contrast between them was extreme. Neville liked the picture houses, too, and said he'd come to town every night if he could. He had at least half a dozen close men friends from school and had been a good dancer at the Bachelor and Spinster Ball. He'd even brought other soldiers home with him on leave and showed Alice off to them. Her mother had come with her to the Hermans—Alice couldn't very well prevent it—and in the lounge room Neville had played the gramophone and the soldiers had taken turns dancing with Alice and her mother. Neville wasn't jealous, either, if a visitor danced with Alice. In fact, occasionally he'd chase up a few Gawell friends to play mixed doubles, Alice partnering the other fellow. Nature seemed determined not to repeat in him the characters of his parents, but to send him off on a new and healthier tangent.

Before a child was conceived, Neville was convoyed off to Egypt. That had been two and a half years before she served the lemonade to the unreadable presences on Herman's Road. Before Neville went, there had been a little time to raise questions about fertility, but they would not be answered until she saw him again. She had always calmly seen herself, without desperate yearning, yet of her essence, as an eventual mother—but, given the circumstances, the eventuality was to be delayed. Still, she could imagine children hanging from a tree like fruit, or riding together, burlap bag for saddle, on the old plough horse Duncan kept.

2

The young man, led by desire for the farmer's wife and by what he was sure was witchery to drink lemonade rather than defy thirst, went in the camp by the name Tengan. He had been a prisoner for more than two years. As he remembered it years past, in blue dawn, far to the northwest of the target, all their cowlings and propellers had been blessed by a priest and, insofar as it counted, deities were called down to loose their favors on fliers and machines. Tengan, a city boy, was sceptical of religion but was conservative enough to feel that to ignore the ritual might bring misfortune.

The first light had promised the finest of tropic mornings, like a day three months before when the aircraft from his carrier had cracked open the sky on the enemy's holy day, and descended towards hapless airfields and ships, dominating the air and flaying the earth which—until then—another empire, the hubristic American one, had assumed was their own. That day had been just short of a jaunt. One of them had said so in the crew room after a jubilant return.

But—as they had been frankly told in flying school—they must realize they rode through the sky propelled by a fallible engine, and sitting in a barrel of volatile fuel with two temporary bombs and a permanent cannon strapped to it. So, though in the past months their missions had proved favorable, and had included unopposed strikes against the Dutch in their supposed Indies, it was appropriate to welcome any ceremony, any cry of good luck, whether from priests or deck crew.

Tengan had not flown in China or acquired the languor and seen-it-all coolness the older fliers had. He needed to compensate, too, for his slightly girlish eyes, fine-drawn features, and sensitively wide lips, so difficult to maneuver into the ferocious slit most could manage for photographs sent home. Some severity of gaze was, however, not hard for him to adopt, because he did have a streak of zealotry in his temperament, quite irrespective of any training. He was also squadron wrestling champion. Without his knowing it, the aircraft commander on his carrier wondered whether Tengan's earnestness would survive exposure to the fallibility of some of his officers. The young pilot had not yet seen much fallibility.

This morning he lifted his plane off the deck in a state of ecstatic fervor. In a bright corner of the air, five thousand meters above a smooth sea, the aircraft of their fleet began to assemble in a series of large Vs. Tengan took his place by his officer's wing. For two hours, they flew an uninterrupted course through skeins of clouds, which might later assemble to make an afternoon storm, and over a brilliant ocean. Then they crossed a blue slot of sea separating the two large islands that served as a marker to the target. Soon enough the mangrove coast came up beneath them and they began their descent. They swung to starboard over a great lagoon, and then banked over immense vacancies of yellow and red clay on which spaced trees made shadowings like a scatter of commas. They would sweep in a semicircle over this scrubby, inner terrain and then, unforeseen, take the port from the south, inland side.

The low-slung town and angled harbor emerged as if from the earth ahead. It was—at first sight—an objective lacking in grandeur. But according to the pronouncement of both Tengan's captain and admiral, it was a key to the expanding world they sought. Darwin shared this with Shanghai and Manila, Honolulu and Singapore.

Flights of heavier aircraft stayed high, while other squadrons like Tengan's came down to less than five hundred meters. Tengan followed his officer to that lower altitude, and then lower still. The port with ships was sighted ahead and this side of it, the airfield Tengan's squadron was to assault. Breaking from the surface of the airfield were a few gusts of antiaircraft fire in sparse and futile black vapor. Tengan saw hangars and, wheeling on tarmac, planes intending to rise to the combat. Two hundred meters above the field he released one bomb and could see the upturned faces of men serving a small gun with almost piteous purpose. Ahead of and below him, an enemy pilot in an opened cockpit raced his plane down the field, determined to come up and make some answer to the interlopers. Very nearly as a cure for the man's innocence Tengan fired his cannons on him, and as the pilot, doomed and honorable, eked his plane a few meters into the air, both he and it were consumed by a frightful orb of fire.

Through the rim of its smoke, the vapors of the incinerated hero, Tengan climbed a little now to skim along the town's main avenue and its modest official structures. These were to be left to the latecomers. He and his fellows had a further assigned task related to the port. Tengan saw that an earlier bomb had cut the pier in two. Men ran on hectic tasks or in frenzy on either section of it, and he fired his cannon at them. A moored ship was burning and now edging away from the wharf. He did not feel exultant but merely a calm, professional, and almost religious gratification as his cannon splintered the wharf and terrorized men hunched by the railway lines that ran along it, some being driven to jump into burning water.

A few seconds later, past the wharf and above the harbor, he was all at once not as easy at heart as his godly situation should have allowed him to be. In the noise and rage and columns of flame lay some dissonance or sudden handicap. It preyed on the part of his mind that was not already taken up with a last duty—to attack one of the enemy's warships, which was beginning to move in the harbor but too slowly to fulfill its ambition for the open sea. The release of his second bomb caused him to bounce upwards, and he pulled casually on his controls to see what good he'd done and believed he saw that one of the projectiles had entered the ship's afterdeck and might destroy its steerage.

However, he couldn't know, and now he had a new urgency to reach a more reflective quarter of the sky, in which he might have time to consider his instruments. But low to the water still, a further enemy fighter presented itself to him, a less pliant machine than his, straining for height too steeply, its pilot so ill trained that he offered his entire flank. Would it continue to be so easy; would the enemy always present themselves like lambs? He suffered a further background disquiet because of a vaguely heard difference from the normal register of his own engine. He hoped on that basis that he was not himself a lamb. It took three seconds to transform the sacrificial aircraft ahead into a sphere of flame through whose edges he rode unscorched.

He was able to reach a thousand meters, but something in the mechanism prevented him from more than that. Nonetheless, now he had leisure to regard his instruments. They gave grounds for his suppressed concern. Oil and manifold pressure had risen to an undesirable level. His oil was overheating. Yet he had felt nothing—no shock in the plane's structure to explain what he was reading. The contemptibles at one of the aerodrome machine guns! Under the governance not of their own skill but of some malicious and ironic spirit, with their ill-aimed and antique weapons, they had lodged a small round somewhere critical in his engine.

The rule for such unsatisfactory instrument readings was that he must attempt at once to reach any of the fleet's carriers. A desire to turn and expend a portion of his fuel on assessing the scope of the damage done to the port couldn't be entertained.

It became clear to him that he was not ordained to reach his carrier, and there arose the question that would never allow him peace. Why was it he, out of an entire air fleet, who must be so humiliated in this bright segment of the limitless sky? He observed the embargo on radio transmissions, even had he been able to inform his mother vessel. The two large islands barely separated by a channel, which had served as a marker on the way in, presented themselves again to him. From his faltering altitude he could see a low area between hills at the western end of the bigger one. On that ground only occasional scrubby trees grew. It provided a credible landing place. Even such a dedicated flier has his preferences for death, and Tengan preferred to be incinerated with his aircraft rather than sink down with it, or float unobserved and abandoned in the sea. So he would land on that low ground.

He brought his fighter in a broad turn to align it with the geography. He lacked the hydraulic pressure to lower his wheels. Otherwise he was able to land perfectly, nose up, tail down, as in the manual. The force was ferocious, nonetheless, and he could not prevent his face from smashing again and again against his gun sight. But the punishment did come to an end and left him conscious. His impulse when the facial wounds began to throb was to leave the plane according to orders, to separate himself from it in the hope it would not easily be found, this sophisticated machine whose secrets of range, weight, composition, and armament would fascinate the enemy.

In a haze of concussion, clearing his face of blood to enable vision, he climbed a hill and came down its more wooded side and found a stream from which he drank deeply before vomiting. He was hot and sweating a great deal, and became aware he still wore his flying suit. He shed it and tried to cover it with stones and branches. He retained his holster and pistol but now he was dressed in shirt and pants of tropic weight.

The coastal passage and the further island could be seen from here. He moved towards the coast, where a reconnaissance float plane might see him. It proved, of course, a longer walk than he thought and the coastal thickets held him up. The stream he followed ran down into tangles of estuary mangroves, which did not offer a passage onto the beach. He sat and vomited again and lost consciousness while leaning against a rock. He had time before oblivion to extract his pistol and cradle it between his thighs.

He woke in the night with his facial cuts stinging, but he was not a young man who expected mercy, and he rose up by moonlight and continued his descent towards the beach. He found himself instead in another sump of earth and facing further mangroves, and weariness overcame him again amongst crooked trees. He slept more and was roused in early daylight by the shrilling of some species of women. He reached for his pistol but it was not there.

He had dropped it, he realized, at his last resting place. He walked away, and in a small opening amidst the trees saw an elderly savage woman minding three baby savages, while their mothers were off amongst the trees gathering something, he could tell, and laughing and squealing.

The elderly woman stood with one of the infants in her arms and the two others around her feet, playing with roots and pebbles. Tengan saluted her and understood that to do so was not utterly rational. He put his hands out for the baby, which struck him as an exquisite, small anthracite artifact. The elderly woman, eyes wide, let him take it from her. But she wailed at a great volume and a young woman appeared, fearless, and snatched the infant back from him. He bowed to her, saluted, and turned away.

Now that the women savages knew he was in their vicinity, he was impelled to walk as far as he could. He met another watercourse. Hours were consumed fighting through it, and then withdrawing and trying to penetrate from another point. Night found him still wrestling the coastal mangroves, and when he paused he heard the savage voices and a song again. He drank some brackish water from a pool in the ground and gave up and turned back into saner country, where there were clearer streams and more negotiable forest. When he saw a campfire in a clearing, he lay down within sight of it and yet again fell asleep, but on dry earth and lulled by the tribe's conversation.

He woke both thirsty and needing to urinate. While he was attending to that he felt a prod in his back so fierce he was nearly toppled. He turned and saw that one of the savages had his pistol. There were a number of young males with him, carrying long, thin clubs that looked weighty. They escorted him through the bush away from the channel he had wanted to reach, and came within a half hour to a building in which a white man in a half-military uniform was eating a plate of porridge. The man picked up a rifle, pointed it at Tengan one-handedly. Tengan bared his chest, inviting the man to shoot him, but was ignored. The man with the rifle went to a radio at one end of his hut to make a transmission. Then the savages gave Tengan water and tied him by the hands and the ankles, using a thin but dense-fibered rope. Eventually, a launch arrived with soldiers in their wide-brimmed hats. So they took him back by water to the port he had bombed.

He told his captors there that his name was Tengan—the name of a classmate he had admired and even envied—and kept his real name, Okabe, a secret. That way it was harder for them to tell what prefecture he came from, and what unit, and who his family really were. Tengan, with its reference to the tiger, suited his attitude, which was to try to compensate by ferocity for his bad luck and obloquy.

Then came a plane journey, during which his two guards made motions that they might throw him from the transport aircraft in which he sat wearing cuffs and anklets. He encouraged them to do so by smiling at them. He was in principle willing them to do it. His father, an accountant; his mother; his elder brother, a civil engineer working on fortifications; his elder sister, the schoolteacher—all would mourn him as much as if his crash had been fatal. They would be advised by the military to despair of him, and he did not wish to dishonor their tears by turning up at a future time of liberation.

His face was dressed in a hospital, and two intelligence officers—

both of them seemingly philosophic souls—took him for strolls inside a compound, trying with their small gift for language to get information from him. One even played him at badminton.

After two long railway journeys, the second in a train full of Italians, from whom he was segregated with guards in his own compartment, he reached Gawell. It was late in the year. He and a handful of other captured airmen were permitted to live amongst the Italians, who called him Numero Uno and observed that he was impressively austere and churlish. He tried to ignore the guards' and sundry Italians' sexual endearments, mainly fake and derisive, but sometimes grounded in authentic lust, and came to communicate with some of them in a halting patois of Italian and English and Japanese. He spent time with one of them—an amiable fellow—exchanging cultural information and trading this or that word. This Italian's name was the near-unpronounceable Giancarlo Molisano. Giancarlo seemed amused by Tengan's air of melancholy and disdain. Tengan, said Giancarlo, reminded him of Dostoyevsky's relentlessly gloomy brothers, the Karamazov boys. It was clear that nothing could be given to the Japanese pilot to appease his aloofness and nihilism.

"War end," Molisano told him, "you go home."

"No," Tengan asserted. "War end, they shoot us all." Surely they could be depended on for that much. Tengan restated his conviction. "Japan win, *they* shoot us all."

"I ain't think so," Molisano told him and shook his head and was amused. *Amused!* He was sanguine about living on unsoured by the repute of having been a captive.

Ultimately, there could be no true meeting of souls between Tengan and the Italians. He harbored despair at any idea of a future homecoming, while the Italians spoke endlessly of theirs. Some of them seemed not to care if their army must be defeated along the way.

Later, as more of his nation was rounded up in New Guinea—in

Buna and Gona, in Salamaua and Wewak and Hollandia—Compound
C at Gawell was built and filled with Tengan's compatriots. Tengan,
as a former pilot, asserted status amongst the compound's population
of Japanese. His spiky behavior, admired by some, grew from the very
circumstances he kept secret from others—that he had been taken
prisoner by savages, towards whom his feeling of repulsion grew as
he recovered from his concussion. He had not charged either the revolver or the rifle. His being taken by savages and by the man with
the radio and then by the launchful of soldiers could be explained by
someone merciful as the result of shock and brain bruising. But he
was not willing to be merciful to himself, and so had to adopt this
strict attitude in Compound C to counter his fear that his fellow prisoners would hear he had been captured by people marginally human.

3

The site chosen to house the Gawell Prisoner of War Camp was a sloping plateau east of the town, screened from it to the west by grassy hills and congregations of granite boulders and outcrops, and fringed by wide-spaced white and red gums and other eccentric, angular, sharp-elbowed, erratically designed, continuously bark- and leaf-shedding antipodean trees, reminiscent of no other vegetation the inmates would have seen where they came from. The trick of releasing a potent eucalyptus smell by crushing the leaves of these trees became a recourse for prisoners with colds but soon lost its novelty. The subtle pungency of the native pepper tree was notable at first but soon taken for granted. For the vegetation was not considered to meet the aesthetic requirements of flora. From occasional angles, some of the farmland around the town could be seen from the place, the pastures often brown from lack of moisture in summer and because of the frosts of winter. But it was by design that the camp would not be able to see the town itself, nor the town itself the camp.

Gawell Camp had begun as one large compound, a one-quarter slice of what was envisaged to become eventually a giant pie. Soon enough, though, with more Italians arriving by way of camps in India, and a continuous trickle of Japanese from advances made by the forces of light in New Guinea and the Solomons, it grew to four compounds, four equal slices of the pie, within a perimeter that was circular, or close enough to it—subtly twelve-sided to aid supervision and to facilitate lines of fire in the unlikely event of an outbreak.

The location was spacious. There were nearly thirty sleeping barracks in each, placed as far as could be managed from the outer strands of wire. An orderly hut, a recreation hall, a mess hall, a bakery, latrines and shower blocks, and in two of them a large clinic or small hospital tended to make each compound is own self-contained planet. There was room for sport to be played, or for men to congregate if they chose, within good sight of the garrison for formal or informal meetings, for open-air lectures and concerts.

The camp was bisected down the middle by a road called Main Road, with strong, tall gates at either end. Main Road, for example, separated the Japanese warriors of Compound C from the Italians in Compound A. Halfway down, Main Street was crossed by a laneway, similarly diametric, named Kelly's Lane—to honor a famous Australian bandit from the last century. Across Kelly's Lane from the Japanese prison lay the second Italian compound, D. The fourth slice was Compound B with its Japanese officers and former, aged Japanese merchants from the South Seas or Australian ports, along with Taiwanese and Koreans, and Indonesians, who hated the Dutch and might connive therefore with the Japanese who occupied their country. Compound B was a place of internecine assaults, the Koreans fighting each other or fighting the Taiwanese. More twenty-eight-day detentions were earned there than in any of the other quarters.

It was the Italian compounds that would come in time to take on more of the character of work camps for former combatants, for whom there existed no available shipping home. By the summer that would take 1943 into the New Year, Italy had not only surrendered but had itself declared war on Germany, and the fervor of the *camicie nere*, the devoted Fascisti inside the Italian compounds, had shrunk. There were still, nonetheless, residual knots of devout Fascists in both Italian compounds who held out hope that their leader and his German allies, in concert, would endure in the north of the Italian peninsula. But they were outnumbered by the hundreds who did not believe anymore—or who had never believed—and hoped, if it had not already happened to them, eventually to be allotted to farms up and down the inland of New South Wales.

The camp commandant wouldn't have minded if the growing Italian appetite for getting along as amiably as they could with the garrison authorities would wash across Main Road and Kelly's Lane and sedate the prisoners of Compound C, which remained the most unpredictable and surly in the camp, potentially a place of serious conspiracy, hard to interpret. For that reason it was hemmed in on its outer side by a considerable outlay of wire—three tall fences on the outer skin, and cruel coils of wire on top of the middle of the three fences. The other, inner perimeters of the compound, which ran alongside Main Road and Kelly's Lane, were straight and double-lined with wire. Here, through gates in Main Road, idiosyncratic Compound C was entered, and from when it was first peopled, members of the garrison entered it with caution and tentatively. For Compound C contained those who were the enemy in the profoundest sense, and would have been the enemy even on cultural grounds, let alone because of their invasions.

Major Bernard Suttor was its commander. He was above all a writer for radio, but also, which seemed to count more with his officers, the Gawell garrison battalion's sole published novelist. This meant little to him, and he counted his radio work higher, but he knew that the names of radio writers failed to register with the public. And admittedly his novel, *A Blue Mountains Affair*, had got him his real job in radio. Radio was his cup of tea, and paid superbly by contrast with literature, which he had been happy to abandon to the talented and deluded and impoverished. He had never finished another book, but he'd written millions of words for radio, and he considered that his sole boast.

Early in the war Suttor had served in his hometown's part-time militia and had attended their annual camps, but he was considered too old at forty-four years to accompany the young who were being sent off to save the known world in New Guinea. At the time of his appointment to manage the Japanese captives in Gawell in late 1942, the proposed camp was still being built and was as yet a single wired-off compound. Suttor had merely a handful of Japanese captives to administer. There was plenty of time for him to go on writing his most successful serial, *The Mortons of Gundabah*, the tale of a sturdy family in a town of Suttor's invention.

The air of seemingly unexplained hostility that emanated from Major Suttor towards the Englishman Colonel Ewan Abercare, his superior and the camp commander, derived—the colonel himself guessed—from his attempt, mild in his own eyes, to suspend Major Suttor's association with commercial radio for the duration of that gentleman's duties at Gawell prison camp. At their first meeting at what the military called Lines of Communication Headquarters, Abercare had made the suggestion, or more exactly taken it as a given, that Suttor would now relinquish his scriptwriting, as famous as the programs he wrote might be.

At once Suttor identified Abercare as an adversary. This was partly Suttor's temperament and partly the solace the damn radio thing gave him. Vacuous as his serial might be, it was not too much to say it was the light of his days and was even his religion. Determined to defeat Abercare on the issue, Suttor enlisted to his side the management of the radio network he wrote for, who then approached the great journalist Keith Murdoch, placed at the apex of the Department of Information, who said he believed Major Suttor's serial essential to national morale, subject to review. The judgment gave Suttor glee. Though one side of Suttor's nature shied from unnecessary conflict, another—as he knew in his moments of self-perception—made up its mind about people very quickly. Not only had Abercare slighted his serial, but he was also the sort of aging and lusterless military man Suttor hoped to avoid becoming. So he had decided to treat Abercare forever with little more than a polite distance.

The officers' mess was a poor imitation of what Abercare had known in India, yet he understood he was working with rough material and must be tolerant for the sake of peace. The mess was simply a barrack room featuring two long tables, and generally there was only a scatter of officers along both. The cook could do a passable but overcooked roast, and steak and chops likewise. He put a tang of curry powder in the stew at Abercare's insistence. His cooking seemed a reflection of the few Department of the Army photographs adorning the comfortless timber walls. At one end was an inadequate fireplace, at the other a bar manned by an orderly and a shell casing which, when occasionally rung, meant an officer, perhaps for his own birthday or to celebrate the birth of a child, was—again an Australianism—"shouting" drinks for everyone in the mess. Most officers drank beer with their meals.

There was not much mess solidarity. Some of the officers had rented houses in town, and dined—or as they said—"ate their tea" there, or else at hotels, or at the houses of friends. Abercare indulged himself occasionally in that regard, accepting an invitation from Dr. Garner, a respected physician. Abercare had met him when the doctor was called to the camp to consult on illnesses or injuries amongst the garrison troops or prisoners. Then, occasionally dignitaries from town, the mayor, clergymen, lawyers, or doctors, were invited for formal evenings, where officers' attendance was compulsory. The visitors did not wear dinner suits nor did the officers don more than full uniform jackets and pressed trousers.

But Abercare felt it was his duty as commandant, despite Suttor's subtly hostile manner, to keep this overcasual mess alive. There, one night when Suttor had drunk whisky, he answered with enthusiasm some questions raised by an older lieutenant, who declared himself a great barracker for the Mortons and their mythical town. This man was a pallid supporter, though, typical of garrison personnel: he had been a corporal in the earlier war and would soon be retired with a failing heart.

Abercare was present at the time of the lieutenant's praise, eating dinner and obviously listening. Suttor confessed that he knew the Mortons so well now that it took him only about four hours to write a week's worth of scripts—five fifteen-minute episodes. As for his near-forgotten mystery novel, which was also praised, Suttor reiterated his earlier perceptions about literature: only those with inherited wealth and no need to work could be novelists. Whereas radio was steady—although at times you flinched to hear some of the creaky lines you'd been guilty of.

Then Suttor said, with a particular edge to his voice, "Besides, Colonel Abercare wouldn't like me writing novels on the job."

Why drag me in? Abercare wondered at the time. "If you want to write a novel, Major, I suggest you do so. I mean, if a chap can get by on six hours of sleep, as many chaps can, there's nothing to stop you spending an hour or two here or there on a new novel. How many hours of a day does a novelist need to write?"

"How long is a piece of string, sir?" Suttor asked in belittling politeness, and deniable malice. "It varies from person to person. I can generally write a thousand words an hour if I find that much time. But finding the time beforehand to come up with the material, and making it good—that's the rub."

There was, Abercare thought, emanating from Suttor the old antipathy between regular soldiers and citizen warriors. In no country was it so reflex as in this one. In Britain the regular officer was an object of respect. In this rougher bush version of Britain, the bearing and very habits of military gesture, and forms of addressing other men and officers, were options for mockery. The regular had to prove himself to the citizens, and amongst the rest—to the clerks, and the writers of radio serials.

At headquarters in Sydney, the chief-of-staff of the garrison forces and the lines of communication throughout the region had told Abercare that Suttor's son, David, had been taken prisoner when Singapore fell. (Suttor had never himself told Abercare.) This, headquarters believed, given their assessment of Suttor, made him more suited to the special balance and tact required for the management of a proposed compound dedicated to "Japanese Other Ranks." Suttor, in their view, would have an investment in being moderate towards an enemy who held the destinies of more than twenty-five thousand Australian souls, including his own son's, in the palm of an unpredictable hand.

There was a further thing Abercare believed Suttor irrationally resented about him. Suttor's file showed that he had married an actress, and when Abercare had made a remark on that—to him—exotic reality, Suttor had become surly to an extent that Abercare had made inquiries of headquarters. Suttor's wife, Eva, was in a sanatorium in Jervis Bay, he was told. Abercare would have liked the chance to utter a few words of fraternal commiseration to Suttor—for he was in no position to feel smug about wives—but he knew that would be misinterpreted.

Apart from his hostility, Suttor was an efficient and dispassionate officer, who seemed to Abercare to have less rancor for the dozens, and then the hundreds, of Oriental prisoners eventually arriving at Gawell than he had for his commanding officer.

At another dinner in the mess, Abercare attempted to mend his fences with Suttor.

"I got a copy of your book from Gawell Shire Library recently," he informed Suttor. It was the case, though he had not enjoyed it much.

"I am amazed they still have it, sir. It's older than Herodotus."

"But an interesting premise, I think. A modern murder involving a grievance that began with two convicts in colonial times. First class altogether!"

It had been a melodrama—both the modern, overblown characters and the historic ones, the tempestuous daughters of the first settlers bringing livestock over the mountain road, past the blazing eyes of Britain's worst transported felons. But Abercare did not wish to point out literary faults, on which—God knows—he was no expert.

"Oh, if only the reading public had agreed with you!" said Suttor, and then began a critique of his own book. "A gentleman convict falls in love with the commandant's daughter and there is a child. On one level, doomed love, and on the other the descendant of the illegitimate child killing the descendant of the convict. Tra-la-la! You'd think people would gobble it up, wouldn't you? Maybe they would have if the publisher had ever let them know the book was there."

"But . . . I was interested . . . Penal times are a natural interest of yours?"

"I think I might have made a good gentleman convict myself." There was almost warmth in the answer.

"Well, there's a certain irony, don't you think?" Abercare ventured. "That you should have this interest and are now earning your own living from guarding prisoners in the twentieth century. May I ask you, as an ignorant Englishman, were there many escapes from the early penal settlements?"

Suttor said, "It was generally impossible for people to get away. That was the attraction of Australia to the imperial authorities."

"Ah," said Abercare. "May I say, a fortiori Gawell?"

Suttor would not concede the point. "But you can't depend on the fact that prisoners know a place is unescapable. Some Irish convicts got away into the bush in the belief that China was just beyond the Hawkesbury River. Passions and delusions enter the equation too."

Abercare said, "In any case, the Italians don't seem to want to get away. Not passionately, anyhow. And they're supposed to be masters when it comes to passion."

Suttor was determined not to succumb to Abercare's rosy view. He said, "I concluded from reading the *Historical Records of New South Wales* that no one can predict what might seem to be rational to a prisoner. To be a prisoner is like having passed through a mirror."

"Nonetheless," Abercare persisted, not—he hoped—without good humor, "perhaps the Italians can be depended on to have motives we can understand. Even the devout Fascists. They seem to put all their energy into persuading their padre to let them sing the Fascist anthems at Mass. They give us the utterly reasonable impression they still want to be leading a tolerable life by the war's end—even if that's not for another ten years. And at risk of the virtue of the ladies of Gawell Shire." He was referring to the use of Italian prisoners as farm laborers and hoped for a laugh from Suttor. But Suttor had made up his mind, and it didn't come.

"The Italians," he conceded, "are a different story. But they tell us damn all about the crowd I'm in charge of."

"Yes," agreed Abercare. "But we'll keep the lid on them, won't we? Kindness, distraction, containment." And a conspiratorial light blazed keenly and melodramatically in his eyes.

What an ass! Suttor thought.

But Abercare was not a fool, merely an Englishman trying too hard with colonials. He said, "In spite of their contempt, they must know their cause is lost."

Suttor hurried to rebuff this, just for the sake of it. "Do you really think they believe the newspapers we send inside to them?"

"Perhaps not. But remember, when we first came here, they looked to the skies, expecting to see their own aircraft. They imagined their carriers off the coast. Well . . . simply from my own observation, they don't look at the sky in that way anymore."

Suttor snorted. "But that hasn't made the buggers more tractable."

Abercare knew he would not be permitted to win.

He said, "I suppose we'd have to be one of them to know what their convictions are now. As distinct from playing a role. Excuse me, Suttor."

And he went, according to the spirit of his normal duties as senior officer, to visit the other table, where someone happened to be telling a story about Yanks and Kings Cross harlots.

4

The pilot sergeants such as Tengan who arrived early at Gawell were small in number, like any aristocracy. As well as Tengan, in its early days the camp held four members of a reconnaissance plane's crew who were found floating near Timor and had passed themselves off at first as merchant seamen; also two fighter pilots who had been found at sea near the Solomons. Amongst them Tengan behaved in his lordly manner because he felt he had most to hide and, publicly, most to expiate, given that humiliating number of his, 42001—the year he had been taken prisoner, and the fact he was the first to have been captured.

The men who could best resist the arrogance of the fliers were the other two members of the compound's council—the triumvirate, as Colonel Abercare called them—elected by the compound population. They were older men, accustomed to composure, and they called themselves Aoki and Goda. As senior sergeants in the infantry, they had both learned to be taciturn. Aoki was tall and bowlegged and rather stooping—perhaps congenitally, perhaps from two unextracted bullets in his upper leg. Anyone watching him would not necessarily have guessed their influence on his gait, attributing it perhaps to arthritis. He was aware of his wound, however, and of the limits it put on the time he could stand in comfort and his capacity to move promptly. Aoki's careful movement helped to endow him with what the young thought of as an air of sagacity. He had joined the army for a span of three years after a bad farming season in 1930—he foresaw it as a brief and financially necessary interlude in his marriage and career. He expected to be stationed somewhere from which he could visit home. But then came the invasion of Manchukuo (which the world at large knew as Manchuria) and he was designated a permanent soldier.

Aoki believed the lanky Goda, a China veteran like himself, to be a man of excellent counsel. Goda was about the same age as Aoki, somewhere in his midthirties, maybe even forty. Goda, like most of the inmates, avoided talking about his family. But Aoki got the sense somehow that his comrade was something of a patriarch, with an indefinable number of children. Goda had let slip that he'd had a job as an insurance clerk once, but he admitted little other than that. He had never gone to the trouble most of the others did of explaining how they had been taken by the enemy; how it had been beyond their power to resist, or had occurred when they were not conscious it was happening. No explanation from the insurance assessor. Generally he had a reserve most men did not broach. In peacetime he would have cast a calm, judicious eye over building collapse and flood and fire. Goda was like a rudder, Aoki felt, between the polarities of Tengan and himself, between Tengan's positive hunger for ultimate elimination and his own more regretful acceptance of it as a mere duty. Goda did not seem frightened of Tengan's handsome young ferocity. There was something, however minor an impulse, in Aoki that sought Tengan's approval. It seemed unlikely there was anything like that in Goda.

Aoki's capture had occurred when his ship had exploded nearly two years earlier, and he was hurled on a high trajectory into the Bismarck Sea. No steel fragments had entered him, and he'd landed in the sea with as much vigor left as he'd had before the blast. He saw the enemy's planes machine-gunning lifeboats, and clumps of men in the water, and expected the same himself. But no. He was pulled aboard an untouched lifeboat, which drifted with thirteen men through the night and up past a reef onto the shelving beach of an island.

He had come through China unmarked in any way considered serious, and to him that prompt current sweeping them to the island was the continuation of a glut of good fortune. There, a little off-shore, they holed and sank their lifeboat, and slept.

Still resting behind the beach in early light, they saw an enemy patrol arrive by amphibious craft with the apparent intention to hunt survivors. They believed the enemy was not interested in shooting to wound and did not take prisoners. There must have been an instinct in some of the survivors from the boat to hide deeper in the island, but the place was small and could be easily scoured. Better to go down showing some spirit.

As the enemy, once landed, divided their tasks and took their first purposeful steps in three directions across the wide beach, Aoki and his companions in the fringes of the jungle divided into two parties, and he—in whispers—assumed command of one of them. All his fellows whom the sea had cast up were enthusiastic for the demonstration that the presence of alien patrols offered them. Other issues were overshadowed by their purpose of exonerating themselves and avoiding seizure. At a count of ten, they charged out of the undergrowth in their two screaming phalanxes with sharpened bamboo stakes in their hands. Aoki himself, leading, shrieked as he ran, and felt subsumed by the combined severe purpose of his men, and exultant in the way he had sometimes felt in earlier campaigns.

The enemy reacted inevitably with their small automatic guns and their rifles. Around him other survivors of the sinking fell down, silenced. He ran on unscathed and neared one of the others, a man so close that Aoki could see the sweat on his young face. This soldier deliberately shot him twice in the leg. In the enemy soldier's mind, Aoki knew this was an exercise of mercy and contrary to the rules, and he deplored and despised it. He was kneeling, half-keeled sideways, in the hope the youth might decide to do better work, as others of them had done with their targets. But the alien soldier assured him, "Doctor! Hospital!" He believed Aoki's gush of tears and tormented face had to do with pain, as if Aoki had not undergone such a long tutelage in dealing with it.

"You runny shit!" he called the soldier, through tears.

He had left his hair and finger clippings back in Rabaul to be sent to his wife if he did not return. They would confirm his death, and they committed him to it. But he had run into a child who would not grant the extra bullet. "You huge runny shit!" he cried out, weakened by loss of blood.

Four lethally wounded men of Aoki's party implored other enemy soldiers to finish them off, and those soldiers, more reliable members of the enemy army, did it. But where was the consistency in that? A true army could be depended on to conclude their work. These men were unpredictable, as capable of fury as he was, but without any pattern of resolve. Contrary to the assurances his officers in Rabaul had given him, some shot to kill, some to wound. They lacked a spiritual pattern and a defined military purpose. They were despicable.

Three captured and undamaged survivors were required to dig ten graves, and no more chances of martyrdom were offered, no matter what insulting or imploring gestures Aoki, from his position on the sand, and the gravediggers made. As Aoki watched them, his wound was inexpertly dressed and he was dragged across the beach onto the steel floor of the landing craft as a prize for intelligence officers. He was now malignly immortal, he felt. The odds had cursed him. The enemy planes had obliterated his convoy and shot nearly all the survivors floating in the Bismarck Sea. Except those in his boatful. And now the pattern had been repeated on land.

• • •

Traveling in the well of the landing craft back to some main island, he was taken thrashing and struggling into a tent and etherized by force, orderlies with their sour sweat holding him down by arms and chest. He woke at night in a shrilling of frogs and insects to find his wound dressed and painful, and by his bed an enemy officer and a Chinese translator. They would be, he knew as he fought the ether nausea, very interested in his name and place of birth and his unit. He chose the names of two dead friends, gave one as patronymic and the other as personal name. So he became Aoki. The officer had his own form of cunning, though, and wanted to talk through his Chinese interpreter about the crop cycles where Aoki came from and then asked about rice-planting rituals. It was a way they thought they had of finding out your province. The first of June, rice planting started, said Aoki to satisfy him. With women wearing straw hats and decorated kimonos, dressed like princesses and ankle deep in water.

The officer then said assuredly, "So your village is near Hiroshima?"

Aoki managed a face of contempt stoked by the pain of his wounds. "I am from Etajima Island, you idiot!" he falsely informed the Chinese translator. "Tell him!"

The intelligence officer and his translator visited Aoki a number of times, and Aoki came to respect both of them a little. The officer even went walking with Aoki as his wounds healed, and they seemed—as far as they could manage—to talk about normal things. The officer had a child. Aoki had not been blessed with one, but said brusquely he had two. Slowly Aoki's defiance transmuted itself into something subtler, more subterranean, more appropriate to his essentially genial nature and his purpose. You didn't need to confront these people all the time. You could deceive them better by a neutral or even half-polite tone.

• • •

They sent Aoki on a southward-bound train with fifty others who had turned up from the wreckage of the destroyed Bismarck Sea armada, and when they reached a city they locked them in a closed hospital ward. One day, he looked in the mirror and found that he was sleek as a neutered tomcat. It was their bread—it contained a different starch from that in rice. It loosened the muscles of men's bodies, weighed down and muted them.

Now, in the beginning of the southern hemisphere summer, the party was sent further south, in carriages with unopened windows. One flask of water lay at either end of the compartment. There were four guards at either end, too, as if protecting the water from those who would try to seize it. A young marine named Hirano had vomited and seemed to suffer from heat exhaustion and an embarrassment at this apparent weakness. Aoki found the sentries did not maintain any appropriate policy of preventing him going to fetch water for the boy by reaching down the glass decanter and pouring the fluid into a small metal cup. He took it to the young man and told him to sip it, and although at first the marine resisted, he gave way to Aoki's rank in the end. When the cup was empty, returning to the decanter Aoki quenched his own thirst.

Immediately the carriage divided into two camps—those willing to drink and those who would not do it for stoicism's sake, or because they despised mercy, or from a belief that the guards had put a sedative in the water to make their charges more tractable on the journey. Aoki's reassurance after an hour or so that he still felt wide awake did nothing to dent the resolve of the stoic party. He understood that to go thirsty by an exercise of will was for some of them a way of striking back. It made them more cheerful. Wherever they send us, he thought, there will always be this division between us. Two ways of negotiating the phenomenon of capture, accepting occasional comfort on the way to one's extermination, as most men would, or engaging oneself in relentless rejection of every minor solace, which he knew would be the choice of some.

On arrival at Gawell Camp, Aoki and his fellow captives were greeted by an enemy sergeant who, Aoki observed, had the soulful, unrequited look Russians have. Indeed, as they left their bus from the railway station and stood in a drizzle of rain, the man greeted them in faintly Russian-accented Japanese. He had, he said, studied the roll of names that had come with them. He immediately recognized two of the false names the prisoners were using as being those of generals who had humiliated the Russian Empire in the war of 1905. "That's been tried before," he told them.

He had them marched to the office of the commandant, a square-faced officer who had once been handsome. They were made to stand to attention while he inspected them, a process that seemed to have more to do with assessing their hygiene than with any military purpose.

Now, in Colonel Abercare's office, they heard through the mouth of the Russian émigré in his ill-cut uniform that the commandant had some excellent advice to give them that he would translate. The colonel spoke for a time and then stopped. The Russian took no notes, perhaps because he was familiar with the content, and began when the colonel stopped. He identified himself as Sergeant Nevski.

"The colonel wants me to say," said Nevski, "that he is well aware your nation used to frown upon soldiers who became prisoners. By now, however, there have been so very many of your fellow countrymen taken prisoner that the old warrior rules have been revised. Imprisonment is no longer considered, either on our side or on yours, to be shameful. And self-harm would these days be seen by your captors as cowardly, the act of men who cannot deal with living in Compound C. There are thousands of our people in your prisons, and we on this side are proud of them, not ashamed. Because we know they used every endeavor to fight before yielding."

The colonel peered and nodded as if he understood the Russian.

"The same can be said for you," the Russian continued. "You should be proud of having done your duty, not ashamed. There is a new world coming, and those extreme military codes are now obsolete and do not serve as a useful guide. You will be well fed, your complaints will be sought and acted upon, and when the war ends you can return to your people with honor. In the meantime, do your best to pass the time. Find a hobby. For time will pass one way or another, tediously or well used."

Then the commandant turned to the guards who were with Aoki's party and told them to march away the prisoners. It is easy, Aoki thought, for those who lack any military code to speak of honor as extreme.

The party first met Tengan in the orderly hut inside Compound C. They had entered the gate warily, fearful that by malign chance there might be someone there they knew, and thus they would be more acutely judged by eyes accustomed to the same landscapes and nuances of language as their own. Aoki would see the same caution in other, later-arriving men who turned up in the bus with the painted-out windows from Gawell railway station. Men with similar accents were particularly edgy with each other, since they were sure that each of them knew the same units, and in some cases the same dead men, and that those men, once evoked, would be a judgment on their captive condition.

Tengan, his flier's insignia attached to his makeshift hat, saluted them, but exercised what he considered his duty as an aviator of being cold to them. One of Tengan's assistants, a loud, jovial sapper, handed out their deep-dyed clothing with a black "PW" imprinted on the back, and did not himself seem driven by any duty of hauteur. He issued them a heap of five blankets each.

"Take the blankets," Tengan growled at them. "You'll need them for the colder nights."

So it seemed that this aviator had already experienced a winter here. Aoki also observed that the prison uniforms he and his party received were much darker in color than Tengan's. In the mess he would dare, on the strength of his superior rank, to approach the table occupied by the fliers and raise the issue. Tengan told him, "There are ways of making them much paler over time. Undoing the work the enemy put into them." With an almost boyish enthusiasm, he told Aoki to instruct his party to launder their uniforms with a mixture of soap and ashes to bring about a bleaching process. It was apparent he saw the job of lightening the color of the uniform as an arm of warfare, an antidote to the passivity and opprobrium of imprisonment.

In his time in Compound C, Aoki would encounter many such gestures. In the first place no one who possessed an infantry cap wore it. Instead, men spent a lot of time cutting out the canvas from their sport shoes to make replicas of a campaign cap—a symbolic gesture in that they refused to wear their own hats in front of such a pathetic enemy, at the same time as they dented the enemy's supply of canvas.

Men would rip their blankets and wear holes in them by rubbing them against cement floors in the shower block and cook house, all with the same manic purpose of being able to ask for a replacement and thus dig a little deeper into their foe's wool supplies. They snapped their toothbrushes in two for the same motive. They scraped their safety razors, supplied by their captors with the intention to thwart use of the blade for self-harm, up and down walls to render them blunt and make their replacement necessary. Aoki wondered whether this was a kind of group madness, substituting the true battle against enemy flesh for one against lesser fabrics.

Aoki, because he was a veteran of many years' service and was amiable, was quickly elected hut leader, as was Goda of another hut. One of Aoki's hut mates was the young marine named Hirano, who was characteristic of what could be called the "ultras," the dogmatists or the party of certainty, the unflinching group of which the aviator Tengan was the high priest. That is, they were the ones who at the least pretended that dying at the hands of the enemy was their constant thought and their chief agenda item.

Other men were more ambiguous and could accept that some secretly wanted to survive. But Hirano was typical of the party of certainty in that he had been much influenced by his captain's behavior when things had become hopeless at Buna, on the north coast of New Guinea. Trapped in a small pocket near the beach and about to be driven out onto the open sand, they had heard an enemy officer call on them to surrender. He shouted that he would count to ten to allow the captain time. The captain stepped out of the palms and into the waist-high grass, carrying a small flag above his heart and clamped on top of his unit patch and held it there as a target while the officer counted. When the officer was close to ten the captain cried out, "Here!" and drew a pistol. So they shot him through the heart, and the other men rushed to his flanks, without rifles since they were without ammunition, and exposed their own chests. But that day, since they were victorious now, it was the way of the enemy to take prisoners, out of a sort of contempt for how withered and segmented their opponent's front was. Hirano, kneeling beside his captain's body, from whose back wound a fistful of flesh and bone and membrane had been ripped by the bullet's exit, became a prisoner.

Hirano was excited now by a further intake of prisoners into Gawell Camp. A serious mass of men was being assembled in Compound C, he earnestly told Aoki one day in the mess. As if the new inmates were in fact reinforcements. Compound C was a force now, said Hirano, a full-strength regiment. At a suitable moment, he said, the regiment might be unleashed.

Aoki had heard similar, overly simplified sentiments from others and he became fed up with their stridency, even if he had reconciled himself to the idea that he must not survive to take home to his wife and family his crimes and his shame.

"Look," he told Hirano, "we're prisoners, but that *doesn't* mean we're nothing when it comes to simple enjoyments. Even a nothing must live till the end—as well as can be managed. Trying to be warm in winter, cool in summer, even feeling joy in a show of color in the sky. We know they'll probably shoot us when it suits them. So wait for that."

It was a common and comforting belief in Compound C. The garrison would shoot them all when Japanese forces landed on the coast. As a corollary to that doctrine, the inhabitants of Compound C would not go quietly but resist with staves and baseball bats and knives. The only blot on the dogma was Aoki's own experience—the youth who'd shot him *in the leg*. In the end, could the garrison also take such halfhearted options?

"Play a bit of baseball and badminton," he advised Hirano, "and relish what's left. No one says you can't have a bit of fun. That's my advice. There are enough misery faces around the compound."

Hirano said, again too fervently, "If they won't end things for me on the day we win the war, I'll hang myself. I'll join the shadows where all the other victors wait, because there aren't any misery faces there."

Aoki got unreasonably annoyed by the raw child-infantrymen like Hirano who hadn't been in China. To him, China was the test, and the islands of the South Pacific an arena for latecomers and amateurs and the partially informed.

"Until that time," said Aoki, "there are all your living comrades wandering around in the dust here who aren't shades. Do you ever think of women? You're not dealing with ghosts here yet. You're dealing with men with cocks. Have you seen them hang round that balladeer character Sakura, the one they call Blossom? Do you think that's because his costumes are so well made?"

Sakura was a sapper, and a professional female impersonator according to the comic-erotic tradition. He, or as the men usually said, "she," was a great favorite as a performer, and in other ways, in Compound C.

"So just stop glowering," Aoki continued, "and live until it's time to die. They haven't had enough provocation to turn on us yet. The savage spirit is there in them, and events will bring it out in the end."

5

A week after the recalcitrant Japanese had made a show of shoveling gravel, Alice watched as a truck delivered Duncan's Italian to the Hermans. Since she expected to see a short, swart peasant with variable agricultural skills, her interest was not at the peak it had been in her previous encounter with prisoners.

Duncan had received a telephone call only the day before from the Control Center to tell him of the prisoner's imminent arrival. Since then the idea had grown in Alice that she might learn something useful from an Italian laborer. You could talk to an Italian. The axiom was common in the town. "The dagos are no problem." They were Europeans. Close enough, anyhow.

Now Duncan sat on the veranda, smoking and waiting for the truck, and as he watched the gate, Alice observed him. When the camouflaged two-tonner came in through the front gate of the farm and pulled up outside the farmhouse, its canopy was off and Alice could see half a dozen prisoners sitting in the back. A two-door black Ford, with a pointed grille that seemed sharp as a knife, came onto the farm behind the truck and also pulled up. The sergeant from the Control Center got down from the front seat and met up with an elderly but vigorous man in a dark suit who had disembarked from the Ford. They advanced through the garden gate towards the farm-house. The civilian was the Swiss general practitioner from Bowral, who had been given the job by the Red Cross of occasionally escort-ing prisoners to the farms to which they were assigned. His duty was to ensure that the farmer maintained certain standards of treatment of the laborer he was receiving. Duncan warmly shook both men's hands as they reached the veranda. Duncan said he'd be grateful for the fellow.

"Here I am," he said, "two big sections of pasture for sheep, and three paddocks for wheat and cereals. Just under three thousand acres. My daughter-in-law's done a lot, a real brick, and I have to hire others when I can. But to have a man full-time . . ."

He was so conscientious about this negotiation that he had placed a fountain pen and a bottle of ink, ready for use, on the table at which he had been sitting. The men handed him their two sets of papers, the government's and those of the Red Cross, for his study. He in-vited both of them to sit while he studied the papers page by page, the sergeant explaining Control Center clauses, and then the elderly gentleman speaking of the Red Cross's concerns.

The prisoner had by now been ordered by the driver to jump down, and was standing with his knapsack on the packed earth out-side the gate. The men still on the truck and bound for other farms yelled their Italian badinage in Duncan's prisoner's direction, and the prisoner, carrying his jacket and wearing maroon shirt and pants, smiled briefly, and briefly again, making a gesture that signaled he preferred they should keep things down and not make trouble for him.

Alice, meanwhile, unseen, confirmed by further study that the man was angular and fairly tall by the standards Gawell imagined Italians to be. So the idea of short, compact peasant power was gone. A belt around his waist gave some style and shape to his slim hips. She knew his labor would earn him a certain number of pounds ster-ling per month, but the government, not Duncan, paid that. As for

Duncan, she knew he got a small extra ration of petrol to take the Italian to Mass on Sundays.

At last Duncan completed his man-to-man transactions with the sergeant, who said that Duncan should always call the Control Center, not the camp, if there was a problem with the dago. The Swiss doctor made a final explanation of the obligations Duncan took on in employing the Italian. Everyone stood, and Duncan shook hands again with both men. Beyond the garden gate, the elderly doctor spoke earnestly to the prisoner, shook hands with him, went back to his car, and followed the truck out of the farm onto the Gawell Road.

Alice saw Duncan go out and introduce himself to the prisoner, saying loudly, "Herman. Mr. Herman." And then in basic and emphatic English, "You work on farm before?"

She heard the young Italian say, "*Si*, I work on farm. But *meccanico* . . . mechanic . . . I do it most."

"Mechanic'll be handy," said Duncan, and proposed he show him his quarters. "Follow," Duncan said. The young man, perhaps around the same age as her, Alice could see now by advancing undetected up the hall to the doorway, picked up his knapsack and carried his jacket slung over his shoulder, moving casually behind Duncan in a way that was brisk and yet rhythmic. His gait was in a style somehow removed from Australian modes of walking. She would come to think that he moved as if he were aware of the labor that had been required of his ancestors, and was keeping a private amount of it in store for his successors.

Duncan meanwhile looked less comfortable about the whole business, and more eager to please, than the prisoner was. But that was Duncan for you. Both men moved towards a screen of lemon-scented gums.

The absorbing sight of the Italian revived at once the question pushed on her at get-togethers of POWs' wives, mothers, and fiancées: would there be a swap of prisoners between the enemies? It was a hope raised in occasional circulars she received. There seemed always, whether at the Gawell meetings or in the circulars, to be Red Cross reports of promising debates between the German and the British governments through what were called "Swiss interme-diaries."

She had been hearing about it for more than a year now. And if the Swiss were successful, she felt she would need to relearn who her husband was, this enthusiastic boy and returning ghost. She seemed at times to know only a few strands of his nature—the dancer, the tennis player, the man of average, well-meant jokes, and oiler of hair. Sometimes she was more angry than admiring of his sacrifice on Chios—"Listen, mate, put him aboard, and I'll catch the next one. Come on, I'll be jake." She was bound to the man of that gesture by the three-year-old echo of vows she had uttered in the Presbyterian Church in Gawell, in a time when she seemed to herself now to have been vain and shallow, and before there were wars and reckless cam-paigns, and any Italians and Japanese in the camp near town.

She returned down the hallway to the kitchen. Since the prisoner did not look like she had assumed he would, she was more stimulated than she expected by the question of who this young man might be, and whether he might be useful or passive, clever or a dullard.

It was half an hour before Duncan came back from settling his Italian into his accommodation in the shearers' quarters. For a great deal of that time she had been able to see her father-in-law through the kitchen window, strolling about between the hut and the fruit trees as a kind of unarmed sentry, undecided as to whether to leave the prisoner to his own devices or not. She could not see, of course, if the Italian stayed inside his room or sat on the shearers' quarters' ve-randa, watching Duncan watch him. Now, coming back to the house, Duncan stopped at the veranda where Alice was hanging tea towels.

"By the way," he said, "I showed him the shearers' long-drop lava-tory out the back there. He'll be using it, not ours."

She ignored this remarkable detail of Duncan's attempt to create a regime.

"I've got your afternoon tea ready, Duncan."

She called him "Duncan" at his insistence, but rarely, because it offended some sense she had that he should merit more reverence. "Do you think I should take him some tea now?"

"Well," said Duncan after measured consideration, "I reckon you could. I'd come with you, but . . ."

She said, "No, you sit and enjoy yours. I'll handle it. They say the Italians are harmless."

She went inside with Duncan, poured boiling water into the teapot, and cut fruitcake for him. Then she fetched the same tray she'd served the lemonade on and considered it a second, wondering whether to put the Italian prisoner's tea in a pannikin or a china cup. She grabbed a china cup in the end. She wondered whether Duncan might think this was too premature a kindness.

She said, "I always hope that some German or Italian woman on a farm will give Neville a china cup to show him he's human. That's all."

"Fair enough," said Duncan, easily persuaded to be lenient. She put cake on a plate and added that to the tray, and started out from the back door carrying it. She felt she was engaged in a great inquiry. She was about to encounter and weigh strangeness.

When she got down to the shearers' quarters she saw the man in the burgundy shirt and pants busy inside, disposing his clothes in a doorless cupboard; hanging up the overcoat and jacket it was still too warm for him to need; and placing on a pine table, made from a butter box and set by the window, an Italian–English dictionary and a book in Italian entitled *I Promessi Sposi*.

Alice announced herself from the doorway. "Tea!" she called. She stepped into the room, into the same shadows as he occupied. This was a further adventure for her, as everything is in the first meeting with novel people. She peered around. No smell of sweat from him yet. He had washed to come here, she thought. There was a vegetable and benign musk emerging from him when she'd expected something ranker, hungrier, and tigerish. Duncan would make him sweat soon enough, though. Out in the paddocks.

She made to place the tea down on the primitive table, and he moved both books and put them on his bed.

"Well," said Alice, who had no practice in remembering non-British names, "what is your name again?"

"Giancarlo Molisano," he told her too quickly for her to get it. Yet it sounded a melodic name on his lips. He clicked his boots in a way suited to a ballet, not like the Nazis in the pictures, softer and with less invasive intention. Then he stood to attention and saluted for just a second.

"Could you say it slowly please?" she asked. "Slow-ly. And louder."

"Gian-car-lo Mo-li-sa-no," he repeated. Alice said, "John-Carlo."

"Yes," he said. "Sound like John, Missus 'Erman." He was content with the approximation.

She said, "I'm sure we can get you a little table and chair for the veranda so you could sit out there if you want. For the moment there's tea and some cake here."

"Kike?" he asked. The manner of his confusion interested her—the concerted seriousness of the face, the way the arched black-brown eyebrows set themselves in interrogative lines above his large, active eyes. His mouth, too, was long enough to allow the lips to express a knot of puzzlement at the center.

"No, no. Ca-a-ake!"

It became apparent what she was saying and he nodded.

"The stupid question," he said, condemning himself.

"No, it isn't. It's accents, that's all. Let me pour you some tea."

She did it as they both stood. He didn't want milk or sugar when she asked him about them. Strange, he didn't want sugar. But a welcome response, given the stuff was rationed. She slid fruitcake from a dish on the tray to his saucer and handed him the lot.

"Wife of boss?" he asked, nodding at her.

"No. I'm Mr. Herman's daughter. Daughter-in-law, in fact."

"Daughter?"

"In-law. I am married to his son, Neville."

He understood and showed it by saying, "Missus 'Erman" softly, nodding.

She thought he had a measured voice compared to hers. Compared to everyone she knew. It seemed to move in meters, like Shakespeare.

"You have what you need in here?" she asked.

"All A-1," he assured her. "All sweet."

He must have learned those terms from the guards, she thought. But still he did not touch either the cup or cake, and seemed to wait for permission.

"Go ahead," she told him firmly.

He nodded to the tray she had already put down.

"For you, signora?"

"No, I've had some."

But he seemed still to wait for instructions. "Look," she said, "I'll leave you, and when you're finished, bring the tray . . . the tray there . . . up to the house. To the back door there. Gate's always open."

She edged out of the door and indicated the direction of the back door. He nodded again, and she noticed how the bones showed through the flesh of the tops of his hands when he flexed them for the small task of lifting the cup.

"*Grazie*," he called to her, "Missus 'Erman."

"And don't forget," she said, enjoying giving him orders. "Bring it back to the kitchen door. The other side of the break of gums and through the fruit trees."

"Sure thing, signora," he murmured.

An Americanism. She could bet he got "all sweet" from the garrison and "sure thing" from the American films shown up there at the compound.

She couldn't stay any longer and still maintain her hauteur and her authority.

Later, without ceremony, when he'd moved his chair and table outside onto the shearers' quarters' veranda, she delivered his evening meal, which Australians—without any sense of contradiction—also called tea. She did it without ceremony and with just a few words.

The next morning, a hot one again, Alice found Giancarlo Molisano already milking the cow, Dotty. Duncan must have told him to. He brought the full bucket to the door and she took it, with no more than a thank-you, and poured it into the separator and began to crank the handle. It became obvious, though she did not yet say so to Duncan, that it would be most convenient if the Italian had his breakfast on the veranda, instead of her having to take his porridge and cream and his bread down to the shearers' quarters. But it was somehow not time for such a suggestion yet. Things were not to be rushed.

So she carried another tray down to him this morning, and found him sitting on the veranda by his pine table. Although he stood in a courtly manner, she put down the breakfast with barely a word and went away. She was making up, of course, for having talked at length yesterday. She thought if she began a conversation, it would run on too long, and there was the question of what Duncan might think. She also enjoyed making her own mysteries to keep the Italian wondering. She didn't know who he really was yet, and she should work him out before he worked out Duncan and her.

6

By 1943 Ewan Abercare had few illusions left that this war was going to elevate him to general rank. He realized by now that he was one of those men of limited gifts who might be asked to make a stand somewhere; to go down with a battalion or company whose faces he knew. Or else he could be charged with administering some distantly placed garrison. He had never been to the Royal Staff College, after all. Yet commanding Gawell Camp, which had turned out to be his military inheritance, had not been part of his revived if modestly hopeful imaginings when the crisis in the Pacific had first begun.

Abercare's orders and instincts at Gawell were to keep the inmates if not in a state of happiness, at least in a state of dull acceptance, occupation, or languor. Indeed, their languor was desirable. The Geneva Convention—so he was told—was to be his bible and text. As with the true Bible, like many of the faithful, Abercare felt one careful reading sufficed. After that, largely familiar with its clauses, he put it on the shelf beside the unread texts on military law. The Convention, after all, was merely applied decency.

Visits from the Red Cross delegates, most commonly from the immigrant Swiss general practitioner from Bowral, and from officials

at Sydney's Swiss consulate general who worked for the Japanese bureau of the Swiss, never found serious flaws in his management of
Gawell, or in his subordinate Suttor's administration of Compound
C. Abercare received regular delegations of committees elected from
amongst prisoners, compound by compound, and generally was able
to agree with their requests or reach a compromise. His job was thus
a matter of maintaining stability. It had nothing to do with the normal
military issues of advance or retreat.

A little Department of the Army booklet on the Oriental enemy's
military culture and another on their culture in the broader sense,
along with directives from garrison headquarters in Sydney, were
Abercare and Suttor's chief guides to Compound C. Abercare was
issued with a similar book on the Italians, but they did not mystify
him as much. For example, the booklet from the Department of the
Army counseled that "the Japanese have been trained from childhood
to spit on any mercy extended to them by white hands. Though our
own code of decency compels us to act with moderation and even to
extend treatment to their wounded, in their mind all such niceties are
contemptible." But if that was the case, then why were his written
orders, repeated in many directives from Lines of Communication
Headquarters in Sydney, to extend not only neutral treatment but
every leniency to the inhabitants of Compound C? The army seemed
to want them cosseted. He liked to think that as a civilized officer he
would have behaved in that manner in any case, but as so often with
Compound C, all official advice came to contradict itself in the end.

Abercare, ruling the camp with a light hand as instructed, explained with marginal honesty to others, "My wife's health is such
that she cannot stand the extremes of weather of a place like Gawell."
Hence he lived in camp at one end of a hut in the officers' quarters,
which allowed him a sitting room, a bedroom, and a bathroom. He
found it all soulless, and as hot as the bedroom was in summer, it
was bone freezing in winter. This bachelor's accommodation lay in
the lines of his headquarters' company. He had three companies all

spread around the perimeter. From the side windows of his office in the north-end administration hut he could look down a gentle slope to the seemingly unbreachable and lacerating fences of Compound C.

Colonel Abercare, his officers, and the garrison were fortified by the knowledge that down the road, three miles north in a direct line, lay an infantry training camp. It possessed its core of veterans who had fought battles both in deserts and jungles, and eighteen-year-olds innocently anxious—with that anxiety without which wars could not be fought—to taste the conflict before it was resolved. There was an arrangement in place, early prepared and now in filing cabinets in either camp, which decreed that should there be an outbreak at Gawell prisoner-of-war camp, two rifle shots and three red flares would be fired into an atmosphere generally noted for clarity rather than fog. The young infantry novices from the training camp, and the warriors who taught them, would then be deployed to help the garrison contain the attempted escape or to search out escapees.

This plan, as all such arrangements, had become blurred with the passage of time. Officers had forgotten whether it was three red flares or two. And they'd also forgotten where exactly the flare pistol and the flares were kept.

Between them, the three companies who guarded the camp, and the young men and battle veterans of the training brigade, were extremely welcome to the cinema owners, the pubs, the sly grog shops, the starting-price bookmakers, the ministers of religion—whose congregations were pleasingly enlarged—the milk-bar owners, and even the jewelers of Gawell. To get to the Saturday-evening pictures reservations had to be made, and for some actors, including Merle Oberon and Errol Flynn, you'd better make your bookings on the Monday morning or you stood no chance of getting in the following Saturday.

The garrison was warned about spreading any gossip about the prison, or any other speculation, when they were in town on leave.

Two factors, as Abercare knew by instinct, made this naïve advice. One was that the men of the prison garrison lived a tedious existence and, even before they had properly begun to sip their schooners, sought to build up their own importance with tales of the surliness and danger of the prisoners, particularly those of Compound C. Similarly, the young men from the training establishment, who were insulted all day by their instructors, could be heroes only at the bars of the Royal, Hibernian, Commercial, and Federal hotels.

The fable of explosive peril from within Compound C became well established in the gossip of the town, and on the basis of the persiflage and bulldusting of guards, the town—unlike Colonel Ewan Abercare or Major Bernard Suttor—believed from the start that one day there would be an outbreak from the camp. Indeed, some townspeople enjoyed the shiver of peril that ran through them at the idea and distracted them momentarily from the ennui of their homes in Gawell's streets.

Major Suttor, as commander of Compound C, had—like his colonel—been informed already that the prisoners in there felt a level of dishonor at their capture.

Dishonor. Suttor was sure his son felt none, amongst all else that the poor little bugger might be feeling. David Suttor had been the victim of the incompetence and hubris of his generals. Major Suttor would wake at night sweating with rage at what had befallen his son, and grieving for the powerless feelings the boy must suffer. The young men in the infantry training camp over there, on the far side of town, got more instruction these days than his son had ever got before being dumped on Singapore's bombed and blasted wharves and being left to wonder what—apart from submission—his orders were. No shame for him, then. Just calamity.

As well as the literature supplied to Suttor to help him understand his prisoners, a visiting intelligence officer, Captain Champion, had assured Suttor of the infamy his inmates felt, as had Sergeant Nevski, the Russian immigrant who was the interpreter in Compound C. "It's not only that they feel their shame," Champion told him. "They feel they *must* feel it. They owe it to each other. No one fellow in there ever says, 'Hurrah, I'm alive!' Except in his inmost soul."

Suttor placed a lot of reliance on Sergeant Serge Nevski. Some years since, Nevski had taught literature classes in Harbin in the Japanese province of Manchukuo. As a young graduate, he had adapted himself to the new educational reality when the Japanese had marched into the region. Nevski had advanced within the university but had become a target for Japanese security police at the height of the last summer of world peace, after the Russians had invaded Manchukuo from Mongolia, fighting some successful engagements. Even though Nevski and his late father had originally fled to Manchukuo to escape the detested Stalin, Nevski found himself now treated as the enemy. After his flat had been smashed by Japanese police searching for suspicious materials, of the kind they hoped might prove him an enemy agent, he had acquired false papers, which identified him as a Pole, and traveled by train to Shanghai.

He had lived in that exquisite city in an apartment in Little Vienna, a largely Jewish sector in the International Settlement, working as a Japanese tutor for wealthy Chinese and Americans, who knew they would soon need to do business in that language. He left on an American steamer bound for Australia two days before the Japanese marched into the streets of the settlement.

Nevski had been given a temporary lectureship in both Slavonic and Japanese at the University of Melbourne and had almost certainly foreseen his future as tranquilly involved with the small groups of students who were interested in these disciplines. Then he had been conscripted into the Australian military forces.

Now, Suttor thought, Nevski was probably the best educated man in the Gawell garrison. He certainly bore an air of having descended to a menial job, and harbored that common Russian demeanor of intense and dolorous disinheritance, which Suttor had also seen in the Muscovites who ran those coffeehouses in Kings Cross that were popular with the actors and writers he knew from his radio days. And that's what the irreplaceable Nevski had now diagnosed in the captives in Compound C: a burden of mortification. This explained why, unlike the Italians, and even the Koreans, neither of whom were Nevski's business, the prisoners of Compound C always showed an aggressive laziness when taken out on work parties. They would not let themselves be accused of doing anything to improve the fabric of their captors' world.

Colonel Abercare and his headquarters were wondering by the end of 1943 whether it was worth going through the paces of exacting labor from them at all. After all, most of the other prisoners were said to welcome the chance to get beyond the fences. But apparently not these jokers! Not these men whose army had advanced close enough to take their tens of thousands of prisoners, to be repelled in the last of the Pacific's archipelagos, and to be prevented thus from taking on the arid steppes or the lush southeast of Australia, in whose wheat belt sat Gawell. If it were decided to suspend their work parties, it could save a lot of trouble and be presented as a punishment, an imposition of well-earned boredom.

In the meantime, if humane tradition and the Geneva Convention did not require the continuing good treatment of the prisoners in Compound C, wisdom did. In that spirit, Major Suttor had supervised the delivery of netting and timber poles for a structure like an Olympic hammer-throw enclosure, but in this case to enable baseball to be played. Baseball bats, gloves, and balls were delivered in cases of two dozen, procured from the American supply base in Sydney. Suttor, who had been until a year or so ago a serviceable early order batsman in the Crows Nest Second XI, had never seen this kind of equipment in his life, except in American films about miraculous triumphs by low-rated teams. The rules of the game his prisoners began to play in the compound, in teams applauded by hundreds of their brethren, were as opaque to him as Sanskrit. But so be it. It puzzled him that the inhabitants of Compound C should be so keen on the great summer passion of their chief enemy, of the America they had sought to supplant as rulers of an entire ocean. It was as if they wished to conquer not only the prodigious Pacific but to claim an entire enemy menu of sport as well.

Boxing gloves were also delivered at the compound gate in the avenue that bisected the four compounds, and liniment for wrestling, for which these men had an obvious passion. Volleyballs and their nets and uprights were passed into the fences as well. Cards, Go, and mah-jongg were provided. By regulation each man was to receive five cigarettes per diem, and those who did not smoke and used them for gambling on those games were tolerated.

All these goods and materials were collected without apparent gratitude by a delegation of the prisoners at the Main Road gate into Compound C. Lack of apparent gratitude was a code of conduct with them, given that they could not, or refused to be, consoled. They saw their imprisonment as so mean, their captors so contemptible, their status so reduced that they had no reason to celebrate the small mercies of boxing gloves.

It was inevitable that Abercare and Suttor would receive complaints from the compound leaders on a number of matters—about the European-style flush toilets, for example, which the prisoners argued were bad for gastric health. (Nevski told Abercare that urban Japanese actually thought upright toilets fashionable, but this did not temper the force of the complaint.) They were dubious, too, about the health results of showers, as distinct from the deep baths Nevski told Suttor were the Japanese norm and in which men communally fulfilled the important purpose of scrubbing each other's backs. But the army hygiene experts had recommended these arrangements as the best for maintaining camp health, and Suttor told Nevski to tell the compound leaders so. The ruling confirmed to the inmates of Compound C that they were prisoners of a barbarous people of utterly unpredictable intent.

Nevski quickly became the conduit between Suttor and Abercare and the complaining triumvirate of Tengan, Aoki, and Goda, who represented the thousand men of Compound C. This display of democracy surprised Suttor, but not Nevski. The inmates seemed to keep excellent and nonpreferential rosters to do kitchen and garden duties. Since it was their own garden, they were willing to work in it, though not, of course, in the great garden beyond the fences, Australia. Having elected each of their hut and section leaders (a section being half a hut, since a wall was placed in the middle to baffle drafts) to act as a sort of legislature, they voted individually on issues such as what demands to make of Abercare and Suttor. And from a catwalk near the outer fence, you could—in good weather—see them divide themselves up equally into baseball teams, or elect sporting or cultural committees.

Nevski interpreted these mysteries for Suttor. Their captives' pride, their good order, their energy and despair seemed to Suttor a combination which in young men was poignant, as is the case for all young men caught on the hook of their culture. In the meantime, the major was pleased that he did not, at least, have to deal with the officers in Compound B, who were rarer captures. They were said to be leftovers who had avoided the entrenched necessity to sacrifice or disembowel themselves. Intelligence had heard from private soldier captives that many of their officers had said good-bye to their diminished units as the beachheads had shrunk to patches of swamp and palm and sand, and had formally washed and then killed themselves. Or else there was the option of the hopeless charge. The officers in Compound B had sidestepped both these imperatives, though they would have told you with some truth that they were sick or wounded at the time.

One of them yelled incitements to resistance whenever he saw work parties from Compound C assembling in Main Road. But most officers seemed muted and somnolent, involved passionately with mah-jongg, flower cards, and Go. Their rebellion seemed restricted to being deliberately and insolently late for roll call. Some were getting plump for lack of physical exercise. If active at all, they chiefly applied themselves to bullying and sodomizing the Koreans and Formosans, army servants and dogsbodies, captured in the field along with their masters.

As for Compound C, it was essential to Suttor that when the Swiss rapporteurs visited Gawell, they could send a glowing picture to the authorities in that North Pacific archipelago of Japan, the counterweight in the northwest Pacific to Australia's mass in the southwest, of how well their children in captivity were being treated. Thus, in a way, it gratified him that in administering Compound C, he was sending signals to the barbarians for his son's sake.

7

Suttor had seen the bags of mail addressed to prisoners in the Italian compounds arrive, toted by groaning garrison soldiers into the office of the Italian censor, Lieutenant Danieli, the son of Calabrian raisin farmers in the Riverina, who had supplemented his dialect by reading Italian novels and such copies of *L'Italo-Australiano* as came his way.

Danieli would remove the stamps from the letters, as ordered (did Headquarters sell them?) and read the letters for censorable bursts of raw Fascist sentiment. If there had been any in the earlier days of the Gawell POW camp, there was very little enough now. Letters to the Italian compounds were growing less political in that sense, and the normal tone was now leftist or social-democrat talk, or simply plain curses against those who had put the letter writers in their present purgatory on earth, in the contested ground of Italy, amidst battle and resultant ruin and hunger.

Major Suttor, even though he had no direct command of the Italian compounds, was curious enough to ask Danieli about this correspondence.

"All the writers complain about is hunger and girls wearing short dresses and flirting—or worse—with the Allies," he told Suttor.

"Ah, no new Roman Empire?"

"I'd reckon," said Danieli, "that people from Rome southwards have forgotten all that guff."

"I wish some of that crowd in Compound C would forget their guff," said Suttor with a sort of bewildered longing.

Obviously there were a few men in the Italian compounds who still believed that their Duce and the Fascist vision would prevail—*Fascisti* fighting along with their German brothers in their enclave in Italy's north. But their power was in decline and the Italian priest, Father Frumelli, by now had been able to act on his convictions and ban the singing of the Blackshirt hymn "Giovanezza" at the end of Mass. When the camp had first been established, there were fist-fights and, on two occasions, knife fights between the *Fascisti* and self-declared disbelievers, including some Communists—the *Fascisti* thereby asserting their philosophic dominance. But the disbelievers were legion now. Indeed, some of the prisoners had sent Abercare letters offering themselves for military service with the Allies, whom their official government had now joined. The expectation of these letters, which seemed in part sincere and were certainly eloquent, was that somehow equipment and scarce shipping would be quickly provided to get them from one end of the earth to another. Some of them asked frankly for precombat leave in Italy, during which they would amaze families with tales of their imprisonment, their work on Australia's acreages, and the nature of farmers' families in a land as distant as you could get.

By comparison with the two Italian compounds, mail for and from Compound C was very small in quantity. The Italian compounds' massive incoming mail, for example, was bulked out by occasional letters to each prisoner from His Excellency the Apostolic Delegate in Australia. But there was no spiritual leader to write to the men in Compound C.

Nevski was the man employed in reading the mail from people in Japan, and their letters generally said that they had heard their son, lover, husband was dead, but the Red Cross had given them hope by notifying them that their beloved one might be still living and breathing in a far-off nation. The writers of some of these hopeful letters seemed to believe—heretically in military terms—that existence was more important than blood offerings. The correspondence often contained further news of weddings and dead uncles and crops or air raids—just in case it reached a surviving soldier.

These letters were delivered to the triumvirate of camp leaders at the gate of Compound C, for they were often addressed to names not on the prison camp register, so many of the inmates having assumed false names. But since the Red Cross had their suspicions about assumed names, the mail was still passed on. In a few cases Nevski, having made a list of Compound C addressees, was able to observe as unobtrusively as possible who the camp leader gave the letter to, and so discover a man's true identity, and place it on the nominal role as at least an alias with whom the Red Cross might try to communicate.

Most of the mail to prisoners in Compound C went unanswered by the men to whom the letters were addressed. As Sergeant Nevski knew and warned Abercare, the addressee prisoner often handed his letter to his hut leader, who wrote back under a fictional name, so that his own shame would not be exposed, and told the parents, the lover, the wife, that their man had been killed while bravely confronting his captors, and that the Red Cross had therefore sadly passed on incorrect information. Thus, by conviction or under pressure from their military peers, prisoners decided that their people should not know of their location.

Living in easygoing Aoki's hut, for example, were some young fanatics of whom Tengan would have been proud and who seemed to Aoki to be even more extreme than the young marine Hirano, to whom Aoki had brought water when the boy was sick on the train south. A youth named Omura, a wireless operator from a ditched reconnaissance plane, seemed to be a true nihilist. He was more profoundly serious than Hirano, for whom, Aoki believed, severity was either a pose or an attempt to fill the nullity of prison days with something of overarching nobility. Then there was a young soldier named Domen, who sang in the most heartbreaking tenor, and a younger kid named Isao. Aoki managed a friendly association with these four strident youths, who all bore watching. Aoki and Goda wanted to lead a relatively tranquil life in Compound C until the right moment came to embrace the end, at the hands of the garrison or, if not that, at one's own. That remnant of time still left could be compromised, as could the chance for final gestures, by some premature action by such men as these, something that might result in the compound being broken up and part of the men being shipped away.

And though he was an older man, considered by all to command his own soul, and though he and Goda had privately traded jokes about Tengan's reaction to the farm-woman who had recently offered them the lemonade, Aoki found he was not immune to the opinion of these stringent young men. They sat and watched him, with the greatest grave respect, as he sat, in turn, at a card table and answered the requests for information. Aoki felt it was correct to make an offer to all men that they could accept the letters from home, taking them to themselves for a while and cherishing them. But even that was more painful than comforting for the individual. And as for any individual answering a letter—it would be a false mercy to incommode and disgrace their families with the news that the child whom the family had ceremonially mourned, lived on in disgrace.

The eyes of young militants like Hirano watched Aoki as if he were not aware of this reality or the imperative duty it placed on him; as if he had not uttered it before; as if his old-soldier idea of waiting for the end in whatever social and physical comfort he could manage made his principles shaky. He felt like saying to Hirano, "Don't glare at me, Private. I've got it under control." But they knew he had talked it all over with taciturn Goda, as if there were anything to discuss, as if there were some softer, unwise option the two older men would settle on. In fact, Goda had similar plans as Aoki for dealing with the unwelcome letters. That was to answer every one of them in terms that denied the son's or husband's presence there, to cancel a clan's cheap hope but reaffirm its more substantial honor. That was in the end the best thing.

Nevski was not surprised that the letter should be unwelcome. The nihilism of Compound C had been clear from the beginning, even if it did seem to take Abercare and Suttor by surprise every time. Each man was given Red Cross postcards when he was brought to Gawell, according to Article 36 of the Geneva Convention, to allow him to send his family the news of his capture and state of health by ticking certain boxes. In the middle of the previous winter Serge Nevski had told Major Suttor that all these postcards were falsely addressed, to streets and towns that he knew, from his Japanese gazetteer, were fictional. They included addresses such as "Triumphant Monkey Hole in the Wall" and "Shitdrip Alley."

Abercare asked headquarters whether Sergeant Nevski should himself answer the inquirers and tell them the truth. Headquarters, however, declared that this might have unexpected results—that accusations could come back that mail from Japan had been tampered with.

There were a few prisoners, as Nevski and Suttor discovered, who managed to keep their letters and did reply to them: one was exotically a Presbyterian and a widower. There were a handful who wrote letters secretly and slipped them to guards. Nevski would read the pathetic confessions of such men. "I am a prisoner and alive, and was captured all unknowing while suffering from wounds/beriberi/malaria/scrub typhus."

It was rare, though, that a clandestine message emerged from Compound C. Nevski did not send on the false letters written by Aoki and other hut commanders. He let them accumulate in his office. One misty Tuesday when he needed to go to town to buy a birthday present for an émigré friend working in Sydney, he took the letters with him and climbed through barbed wire into someone's paddock, and burned them under a gray sky, beneath which the smoke of these incinerated lies could be mistaken for a mere vapor. For Nevski the ashes were a small sacrifice to honor those earnest kin still seeking their lost ones. With the hut commanders' lies consumed, modest and unsated faith could go on keeping its corner at Japanese hearths.

8

Major Suttor wrote chiefly in the evenings in his small living room, off his bedroom, in the officers' quarters within the garrison lines of Gawell Camp. On still nights or when the wind was right, he could often hear the music from the Japanese and Italian compounds. The Japanese were closer and he had become accustomed to the more plaintive airs, suited to life behind wire, that they often played. Instruments had come to Compound C by way of a Japanese cultural group that had been formed in Sydney before the war. There was a sort of guitar, a rectangular board with a set of strings stretched across it. There was also a haunting flute, a sinister-sounding drum, a kind of lute, bamboo pipes, and a bugle. Not all was plaintive. Some of the music from Compound C could sound very jazzy—or jazu, the prisoners called it—but tending to the blues. They played songs you could tell were more ancient, too, some of them doleful, and these, to Suttor's ear, emerged like an unintended confession of the folly of the war.

It was not all grim stuff, though. There were nights when the recreation hall in Compound C rocked with laughter.

Someone was being satirized—General MacArthur, Colonel Abercare, he himself, Nevski. Then there were nights when Compound C went quiet after dark, emitting only an occasional yelp or shout, or short spates of laughter or fury. It was then that the further-off Italian songs could be heard, sometimes accompanied by a full band—jaunty stuff convinced either of the hilarity of life or of the total validity of love. The Italians sang every night, and their music provided the accompaniment to Suttor's devotion to *The Mortons*.

His life in Gawell would seem to some people lonely. He, like Colonel Abercare, lived all the time in camp, except for leave. It was said the colonel was looking at houses to rent in town in the expectation his wife would join him soon, but Suttor knew his would not. Eva Suttor had been an actress in Raymond Longford's early silent films, and adored for a time. She'd continued acting for the screen after their son was born, and was still a yearning virgin in the eyes of picturegoers. Australians said that her longing and blazing eyes were better than Lillian Gish's, thus indulging the national myth that Australians could outdo Americans, whether it came to racehorses, boxers, or actors, but that they were willfully ignored by the world because they were at its end.

Eva and Bernard Suttor had married in 1923, and it had not been easy since. During their life together, she accused him of coldness, and, as time went on, he recognized the validity of the charge. He was a cold man at core. But he also came to see in her what he could not believe he had not seen when they'd first met—the influence of her alcoholic father, the melancholy of the mother. She had frequently threatened him with knives, even with the boy, David, the infant who was the future prisoner, in the kitchen doorway watching. When he thought of his son now, he saw that spectating waif.

It was an omen of his child's imprisonment, since a small boy cannot escape from a household, however questionable the elements out of which it is constructed might be.

Eva had found herself unsuited to motherhood and had doused her misery and fueled both her depression and her occasional peaks of manic and unreliable affection for the child with any liquor she could find. Interestingly, she had an especial appetite for rum, the drink of farmers and shearers and stevedores, but she added milk to it as if that endowed it with innocence. It couldn't be said that she did not love the child, but unevenly—sometimes with an intense and proud indulgence, sometimes with a blazing petulance which might even be called cruelty.

Years ago she had gone to a hospital in Sydney and been given shock treatment, and when Suttor visited her she would beg him to rescue her from it. He worried now that there had been vengefulness in his insistence, echoing the doctor's, that staying there was essential for her health. Later, she was moved to a sanatorium down the coast.

Then he had taken what some might have thought of as further revenge by going to work in America for a time. But she had remained ill and became markedly worse after the capture of her son. Suttor dutifully and cautiously visited her as irregularly as he could get away with while maintaining some passing repute as a husband. His excuse was that he was likely to be blamed for indifference whether he went there weekly or monthly. Even the nurses took a vaguely chastising air with him, though that had softened a little now in view of his military duties. The word had got around, too, that he was still doing service to the nation as writer of that national favorite and cultural glory *The Mortons.*

For two years he had pursued an affair with Marcia, the girl who did the voice of Nellie Morton. At the start of his infatuation, he would turn up to recordings and stand in the booth with the producer simply to listen to Marcia's velvety voice. She was an amiable, earthy, practical girl, and ever afterwards, when he thought of her and of arriving at her flat on summer evenings with the glint of the harbor stinging his eyes, the memory of her was associated with blatant sunlight. Inevitably, their affection and hunger for each other diminished over two-and-a-half years. He wondered now if she had kept the affair going because she feared she would lose lines if she ended it.

When a friend invited him to New York in the year of the Munich Crisis to write a nationally broadcast serial named *White Man of the Congo*, both Marcia and he knew that this was a natural close to their affair. He had made a lot of money in New York, but there was David, just finishing boarding school, who could not be required to live alone and like a freestanding bachelor yet. His son wanted to stay close to his flawed mother, but then contradictorily wrote to neutral New York that he had enlisted in the great struggle, and Suttor feared David would be consumed in another European war.

Suttor came back across the as-yet-unthreatened Pacific early in 1941, and himself enlisted—out of patriotism, of course, but also to find a new life. He was shunted into a garrison battalion, and—given that the enemy failed to invade as some men, including himself, had silently hoped they would—thus to the witheringly tedious military business that garrison life involved, until he was offered his position at Gawell.

After the novelty of his outlandish prisoners in Compound C had worn off, the major found that he was stuck with paperwork and routine. In fact, the only drama in his situation was provided by the idiosyncrasy of his prisoners and his attempts to read their motives. But familiarity with this chore, and their determined churlishness and muteness in his presence, eventually seemed to complement the rote work of administration. He wrote reports for Abercare and for Sydney headquarters, and requisitions for equipment and supplies. He issued detentions for grosser acts of rebellion, insult, or assault upon authority. He needed to attend a daily meeting of the colonel and the other compound commanders, and of course receive delegations from the three Compound C leaders, whose ways, expressions, and postures he got to know well. There were also issues to do with the company of the Australian garrison he commanded—drunkenness, insubordination, neglect. He did not like to be a schoolmaster and depended on his orderly sergeant, an old regular, for advice, and on Nevski. He attended roll call at 1600 hours after making an inspection of the compound from outside the fence. All this made a busy day, two-thirds of which was repetition and fuss.

It was a pathetic boast, and he made it purely to himself, that his most enthusiastic hours were invested in the utterly fictional *The Mortons*. The Mortons were Suttor's forte and his vocation, but they also allowed him to visit a more kindly planet with a better climate. It was in his characters that he transformed himself into the dutiful husband and the warm soul. It was in them that he was solaced. He had created them himself and had been writing them into being since 1933 with a while off when he was in New York.

The period in which he'd begotten them had been a time of bad and risky days, when there was a chance of a civil war being waged by the not-so-secret secret armies of the pastoral and commercial gentry against the "Communists"—anyone who was actively discontented. None of this shadow had, however, fallen across the Mortons. There had been a reference to the Depression in one episode, when Mr. Morton's job was under threat, but Mr. Morton had sympathized with his boss's struggle to keep the stock and station agency, for which Morton was accountant, going. There was no class warfare. Boss and hired man were fellow passengers in the one boat heading in the one brave direction. The agency had been saved by an emporium owner from Sydney. Capital to the rescue! A proposition that could not be believed outside a serial.

At Kings Cross parties in Sydney, when challenged by leftist friends in the radio business who wanted him to admit through his prodigiously popular characters that capitalism was the problem, Suttor argued that such friendships as those between Morton and his boss were more common in bush towns than in a mass industry in the city. But the truth was he wanted it that way. The Mortons' world was one in which no laissez-faire indifference to the masses (such as the masses were in the fictional town of Gundabah) existed.

In that world, too, men became soldiers to save the Empire and precious Australian things—wattle; cricket; dinky-di, honest women.

Men enlisted early in the war, too—they weren't cynical leftists who waited for Hitler to invade Russia. The Morton son, Trevor, late of the Gundabah butter factory, had been a Spitfire pilot in North Africa, and then Britain.

In *The Mortons of Gundabah*, betrothals might be unwisely entered into, but they were called off in time. No one ever married the wrong person. Falls of livestock prices would be remedied in the next few episodes by an unexpected rise. Failure of rain was followed by splendid downpours within little more than a week's worth of writing. In *The Mortons*, no one ever had adulterous affairs or visited prostitutes. The oldest profession, like Marxism, had no place in Gundabah. The Mortons' daughter, Nellie, was, of course, a virgin, and had been since 1933. The passage of time affected only the wider world, making it older and older, and more and more vicious.

The serial, like all such entertainment, was subject to an advisory code. The Morton women, for example, mother and daughter, discussed how to design and wear austerity dresses, which fully satisfied their desires for fashion and which they wore with the awareness that the silk they were sacrificing would go to make Trevor's parachute, or the parachute of some other noble youth. They loudly disapproved of women who bought hosiery on the black market. Under the urgings of the code, Suttor made Mr. Morton use his petrol sparingly.

In his other and staler reality, Suttor had become now, without too much guilt, a man of casual encounters, restricted to leave in Sydney and gin-struck evenings with old flames from the Fellowship of Australian Writers, who, being Depression-era leftists, often ended up at the close of their lovemaking chastising him for his total lack of political insight. He didn't go to the radio studio anymore when he was in Sydney. He had lost interest in the recording process, and long since found radio producers to be annoying filters of his work. One of them, a youngish, shortsighted but unassuming sort of fellow, blithely changed lines. If Suttor ever challenged him, he would tell the actors to change them back, while muttering, "No offense, Sutts. No offense."

In the end, Major Suttor decided that listeners enjoyed the thing no matter what was done with it, as long as it was not totally usurped, which the management would not allow to happen. In any case, these days his visits to Sydney were too intermittent to guarantee his supervision would make much difference. He never listened to episodes himself. His comfort was totally in writing it. And if this was propaganda, he wished he could be allowed to write it full-time. For, after all, this was not like Dr. Goebbels's propaganda. This was holy propaganda. The mother of the child with the rash was Suttor's wife, perfected. The soothed child was his son, now saved by calamine and blessed with an invulnerable future. And all the others—the father, the cop, the alderman—were the wise he wished he were numbered amongst.

Some stringed instrument would peter out in Compound C; some Italian song parodying love would end with a mandolin twang. He would hear the boots and gruff commands associated with changing the sentries. Sedated by *The Mortons*, Suttor slept.

9

Eventually Alice had the chance to read the documents Duncan had signed when the Italian had first arrived. Copies of them stood in a place of solemnity—the polished table in the lounge room. The prisoner's number was 411729. His name was Molisano, Giancarlo Benedetto. His place of birth was an unimaginable town named Frattamaggiore in the province of Naples, and the date of his birth was June 18, 1922. His marital status was single, and his next of kin was his father, whose address was Sant'arpino. The date of his capture was March 5, 1941 (hence, she presumed, the "41" with which his number began), and his "place of arrest," to use the same quaint term his papers did, was Benghazi, Libya. His military service was recorded as having been with the 86th Regiment of Infantry (Abruzzi). She would discover in the end that Abruzzi was not his home region, but she knew by now there was no rationality to the military. He had been held in Africa and elsewhere until he'd arrived in Australia on the ship *Brazil* eighteen months past. His civil occupation was mechanic, and his religion was listed as Catholic with a question mark beside it.

Further, his personal description gave his height as 5 feet 8 and his weight as 135 pounds. His eyes were brown—though Alice had thought them darker—his hair dark brown and his complexion fair but tanned. He had no distinguishing marks. Thus he came to Duncan's farm as intact as he had been at birth.

When she undertook to sweep his room while he was out with Duncan, she came across his prisoner-of-war identity card, and within it his thumbprints and his description again, and a full-face and profile picture. She found herself studying this young profile. For some reason, it occurred to her abstractedly—not, she could swear, as a thought connected to that particular Italian—that she had not been held by a clear-faced young man for three years, and everyone, the whole of her known world, considered that this was as it should be. She absorbed the fresh yet knowing face; its combination of willingness and steadfastness and wariness. Yet, as everyone would have said, not steadfast in battle, this Giancarlo. Because he had surrendered at Benghazi, as had some thousands of others of the garrison. Neville had been there, victorious. Before the stupid Greek campaign.

At the breakfast table Duncan said to her, "I've got fifty lambs to load up. I'll get the Italian to help. That'll show me what he's made of. Then you'd better make up a few sandwiches." As an afterthought he said, "And a sandwich for me to give Mussolini too. He can eat it after we've finished the muster. Then you'd better come into the saleyards with me. We can leave him here and try out how trustworthy the blighter is. Before we take too many risks."

She would have preferred to stay and go down to the shearers' quarters to investigate further the otherness that had entered their lives. It was of immensely more interest than the sheep-stinking saleyards. But that would have been out of order and untoward. She began to get the evening meal ready, since she'd be gone that afternoon. Meanwhile Duncan fetched his dogs and the Italian, and they mustered the lambs from the past season. Duncan was wonder-ful with dogs and at the subtleties of commanding them by varieties of whistling. And with that help and that of the Italian, he would drive them to the mustering yard and up a ramp leading into a large cage, exactly measured, which sat on the back of his truck. When the lambs were loaded, Duncan waved good-bye to the Italian and col-lected Alice from the farmhouse for the journey to town.

Duncan declared on the way to town that this fellow seemed a fairly able sort of bloke. But then he said, "We'll see. We'll see."

Alice continued to take the prisoner his evening meal on a tray at dusk, for Duncan—tolerant boss though he was—was still making up his mind about Giancarlo's suitability for the farmhouse table. Giancarlo was generally sitting outside, by his door, smoking the same sort of thin, self-rolled cigarettes Duncan himself smoked. He would rise to bow and then receive the tray with formal thanks. She liked this ceremonial acceptance of the tray. It added an element of grace to her plain and torpid days.

At the table one night with her father-in-law, Alice suggested it might be useful to teach Giancarlo some further rudimentary En-glish.

"I could get him a school reader," she said, as if the purchase were hypothetical and she weren't utterly determined to do it. "I could get him one of those kid's primers from the bookstore."

"You reckon he can read to begin with?" asked Duncan.

"I reckon he can if their school system's anything like ours."

"Fair enough, then," said Duncan. "It'll make it easier for me to talk to him anyway."

"I'll just read with him for half an hour," said Alice, as if she wanted to guard her own time from intrusive and lesser duties and might have trouble finding the time. "After knock-off."

"Listen, I'll shout the book," Duncan said. "You shouldn't have to pay for it out of your POW allowance." The government sent it to her with sparing gratitude, a month at a time. But in the light of this offer, it had to be said Duncan was not as tight-fisted as many farmers—as her own father was, for that matter. Frugality and meanness were not the same thing. Duncan had a reputation for being a man who would invest for a return and had the intelligence to see that Giancarlo's improved English would help the running of the farm. And the running of the farm was Duncan's entire world.

"Another thing," he said, as if he had been waiting for a pretext. "We could invite him to dinner. Say on Wednesdays. That might teach him something too. Maybe just to use a knife and fork."

She suspected Giancarlo had much to teach Duncan and her, rather than the opposite. But in any case, both prospects—lessons and Wednesday dinners—filled her with a pleasant feeling that utter monotony had ended.

Duncan claimed he was slowly improving Giancarlo, or assimilating him. To fit him out for work around the farm, Duncan had given the Italian a larger hat and one of his own sweaters. Some days later Duncan awarded the man some pants, and from that day Giancarlo did not wear burgundy on the farm and could not be distinguished by sight from an average farmhand working on his own behalf. Neville Herman's farm clothes, of course, lay untouched in Alice's bedroom. It seemed a blasphemy to give the Italian any of those.

Duncan's friendliness towards Giancarlo was a result of the Italian's industriousness. When the cutting of the cereal hay and wheat began, she brought the men their noontime sandwiches carried in the basket of her old bike. She had seen Giancarlo on the running board of the tractor Duncan drove, looking back like an old hand at the hay baler rolling behind and dropping its square packages of fodder across the paddock. He continued to attend to the milking of the Jersey, Dotty. Looking up from the stool, he would give Alice his long-lipped smile. "The bucket, she's full." She would have liked to have been in a position to give advice on his method with Dotty, to create a distance of instruction and authority and so protect herself. But there was nothing she could manage to say.

So teaching him English seemed a most sensible thing. On the Friday just two weeks after the beginning of Giancarlo's service at the Herman farm, Duncan and Alice left the farm again in the Italian's care, this time with more confidence. They drove to the stock and station agent's, where Duncan intended to top up his depleted super-phosphate fertilizer at a time of year when it generally got cheaper, which—along with the government bounty on the stuff—made it a good deal indeed. Alice left him to his business of purchasing and loading and walked down William Street to March's Western Stores to buy new ribbon for trimming one of her perfectly good old hats whose brim had become frayed.

Then, at three, for Neville's sake and for the sake of her marriage as undernourished and spectral as it had been rendered by absence, its substance being all in the future, and an honest hope of hearing some news or of extending solace to other women, not least those with children, who seemed each to have an acuter sense of the man she was missing than Alice had of Neville, she attended the Friday meeting for wives and mothers of prisoners of war at the School of Arts. One of the other motives for attending involved a sense of obli-gation to the indomitable Mrs. Cathcart, who had founded the group. The purposes of these meetings were said to be to fortify the souls of the women who were afflicted by their men's absence, to revivify memory, which was in the process of eroding, and to share any news that came by way of governments or the Red Cross—letter or post-card. Those who attended were invited—but only if they wished—to place in a box silver coins or even ten-shilling notes for wives who were having a hard time, and that, too, was why Alice came now and then, to make appropriate contributions.

She had been a loyal attendee of these events for the first two years but, like others, recently had begun to lose faith. Early on, there had been all manner of hopeful rumors. They had all evaporated.

Alice occasionally pleaded the demands of the farm. Mrs. Cathcart, though, was different. She could not be stopped. Her husband had been a notable fighter pilot who had been shot down near Brussels, and she had the qualities of an ace herself. She administered the Cathcart property, which was larger than the Herman place by some thousands of acres. She had also what many of the women perceived as an advantage in that her husband was a prisoner of Europeans, not of the unreadable Orientals. For many of the wives and mothers of those held by the Japanese had received, the better part of a year after capture, only the most rudimentary cards from their men, of the ilk: "I am well and a prisoner. I am in good health and well-treated but a bit busy but thinking of you." There was too little to discuss in such messages to shed light.

Early in the existence of the group, women had been encouraged to read out edited sections of their husbands' letters from German prison camps. But the letters from Europe, intermittent though they might be, were so much more numerous than the ones reaching women from Asia, and remained so proportionally numerous as the months passed, that the practice was abandoned as too painful. Wives like Alice, whose souls were wavering as 1943 neared its end, were shamed by Mrs. Cathcart's cheerfulness, and temporarily exhilarated by her ceaseless questioning of governments and agencies, and her ferreting out of new information about the kindly involvement of the Red Cross and Swiss legations in camps throughout the world, though that always seemed less significant after you'd left the meeting than it did during it. It was hard to fly the flag for months on end if you had to live on a wives-of-prisoners' allowance. It was even harder to fly it with sufficient conviction when you were the as-yet-childless wife of a dimly remembered and briefly held husband.

There were a scattering of children around the meeting room on this occasion. Alice was drawn to a three-year-old named Bunny and praised her dress and bounced her on her knee. Bunny's father had been shot down just three months before, on one of his first missions, in a bomber over Europe. Holding the child—indeed, before she even had begun to hold her—she felt a movement in her own stomach for all the world like some kindly, warm animal turning itself about there. It was pleasant, it was doleful, to hold the child so intimately, and a delight when the infant fell into afternoon sleep in Alice's arms, which continued to harbor the girl. In the child's trustful limpness, she felt a foretaste of her own motherhood. It seemed to her inevitable, and with that inevitability Neville's presence seemed more palpable. She could hear him whistling a dog and dropping boots on the back veranda and preparing to enter his kitchen and say something habitual. That was the problem. She did not know what that habitual utterance would be. Habit had not had time to form.

Mrs. Cathcart called the meeting to order. She and her regulars quickly disposed of apologies and the last meeting's minutes. The child slept on, a pleasant, honeyed weight in Alice's arms. Older children played hide-and-seek around the sandwich table, or galloped round the outskirts of the chairs set out for the women.

Today there were about eighteen wives and mothers, because rumors of prisoner exchanges were in the air. Mrs. Cathcart read a report from the Red Cross journal that told of a meeting in Geneva between German and British officials. The Red Cross had also made approaches to the Japanese Foreign Office and Ministry of War. The talk thus far between the various enemies had been about the exchange of civilian internees rather than captured troops, but—said Mrs. Cathcart cheerily—the proposition of exchanging military prisoners was an item on the agenda for the next meeting in January.

Bunny stirred in Alice's arms. There was again a corresponding movement within Alice. But the image that was evoked at the mention of these negotiations in unimaginable Switzerland was not entirely that of Neville but, more prominently, of the Italian. He might be exchanged too. Neville for Giancarlo?—now that should be a delight for her. Yet she found she couldn't be sure it was. Her mind was distracted by this impropriety of choice as she heard, as barely more than background, Mrs. Cathcart comfort the womenfolk of prisoners-of-war of Japan with news that, through the Red Cross once more, Japanese civilian internees were indeed to be exchanged forthwith for British and American detainees in Japan. Yea, even the gates of Gawell might be opened to let the Japanese civilians go home under some flag of exchange.

There was tea after the meeting. Women thanked Mrs. Cathcart in brittle excitement. Bunny woke and started chasing after older girls. After one quickly drunk cup, Alice excused herself. She had more errands about town. She strode off to Oxley Street, where the newsstand sold schoolbooks. Here, she acquired two readers for children: *Don and Jane Go Shopping* and *Don and Jane Go to the Country*. Full of pedagogic fervor, she bore them home with the grocery shopping.

The following Monday, when Duncan Herman came into the house at the end of the day, Alice went down to the shearers' quarters and sat with Giancarlo at the pine table outside his window and gave a forty-minute lesson. She was conscious of the time allotted, and determined, for the maintenance of some instinctive standard, that it should not be longer than that time. She sat at his shoulder, a little to the rear of him, with the books on the table, and pointed at words as he read: "After they came home from school, Don and Jane went shopping for their mother."

This came out with all sorts of added vowels—the mystery of Italian pronunciation recurred again and again as he paused for a moment or two over sentences.

Don—obviously so named to honor the great Australian batsman Don Bradman—sounded in Giancarlo's mouth like Doan. That was to be expected, she knew. She did not try to correct him unnecessarily. For though she was there to teach him English, she was also *not* there to teach him English, but to learn from him something she still could not define. After two, nearly three years of her father-in-law's company, she had a hunger for the company of a man, someone who had not resigned yet from the business of being one. Not a spent force of a fellow like Duncan, as decent a chap as he was.

She sensed that she required conversation with a young male, even if it did involve negotiating a wall of language. But even given that, now and then a handclasp of shared understanding could be achieved—relief from the fully shared but dead-plain discourse with Duncan and from the hours of servitude.

"Is this of any use to you?" she asked, pointing to the school reader. "Is it all too simple?"

She could not help suspecting all the time that he was more subtle in a way she would have had to come from his world to gauge.

He assured her with a doleful face. "Is all good to know," he insisted. "Is *all* good."

"But are Italian towns," she asked helplessly, scrambling for detailed news, "like our towns? And Italian children?"

"All the same," he assured her softly. "All the same Don and Jane."

But she could somehow tell there were broad differences he could or would not describe. She would have been delighted to comprehend what they were. He could sense disappointment.

"No footpath," he contributed. "The road." He laid his left hand flat, palm down. Then he made his other palm vertical beside it. "And then the wall. No good for Don and Jane."

He made a sound like an approaching car. *"Barp! Barp!"*

Altogether, she'd learned next to nothing from this, except that he was willing to try to placate her. Once she realized she could not get very far with her kind of direct and even childish quizzing, that she would hear from him in better form what he desired to tell her on his own account, the lesson began to improve.

Leaning forwards, she could see that Giancarlo approached the labor with an unseamed brow and without a learner's frown. She was easily convinced, given his finer features, that it was not the uncreased nature of stupidity. It couldn't be . . . Could it? . . . That he was patronising her, and did not need the class? *Don and Jane Go*

Shopping was quickly dispensed with. In the second book, Don and Jane went to the chemist for medicine for their sick uncle, the farmer. Until now Giancarlo had managed the names of all the animals, the horse with the ghost of an "a" at the end, the goat, and the rest.

"Chee-mist?" he asked with that earnestness of his.

"Keh-mist," she said. "Medicines."

"Medico," he said.

"No, a shop. The chemist makes the medicines for people."

"Farmacia," he said. *"Farmacia.* Keh-mist."

"Pharmacy, yes. A chemist's."

She had seen Americans call it "drugstore" in the motion pictures.

"My father—*mio padre* . . . he is a *farmacista.* He has a *farmacia* in Frattamaggiore."

She had read that town name in his papers.

"Is it a big town?" she asked slowly in children's reader–like words.

"It's—how to say?—the whole *distretto?* Twenty thousand . . ." The word "thousand" sounded lyrical in his pronunciation.

A song dedicated to the constituent hundreds.

"My father," he said, "a man with education."

"Were you *forced* into the army?" she wanted to know. "By Mussolini? Or did you join because you wanted to?"

In an early letter from the desert, Neville had said they were conscripts. That's why they weren't so interested in dying.

Giancarlo said, "If a man healthy, he can't say, 'Mussolini, I don' wanna.' So . . . Libya. In Benghazi I repair the Breda guns."

"Brayda?" asked Alice.

"Breda. Machine gun. *Rat-a-tat.*"

He put his head apologetically to one side and seemed to know that his part in preparing these life-reaping machines might not be popular with her, and indeed she asked, "But you didn't like Mussolini?"

"Abbasso il Duce! I am *anarchico. Mio padre* . . . father. He's *socialdemocratico.* Come Labor Party! Mr. Curtin!"

"You know about Mr. Curtin?"

The much-loved prime minister of the Commonwealth, with his soft, weary features and his frown of endeavor.

"From the *Herald*. They give us *Herald* to show us bad news from Italia. I know this Mr. Curtin. Good fellow. *Socialdemocratico*. As my daddy."

"Your father," she insisted. "Children say 'daddy,' grown-ups say 'father.'"

"My father," he said obediently, making a wry mouth. "Mussolini don't like *Socialdemocratico*. But up in camp there now they all say they hate Benito. You go into the Compound B and the Compound D and they all tell you they done never like Mussolini. But they much lie. They some still like him. Not the same as before. When Benghazi fall . . . the *Fascisti* say to us, you are disgrace to surrender . . . they like Mussolini a lot then! They think then he still win the war, and *l'Impero italiano* and all that horsefeathers."

"Where did you learn a word like 'horsefeathers'?"

"*Cinema*. Marx Brothers."

And he made an elegant gesture with his right hand, clearing that issue out of the way.

"Your English is coming on," she said.

"Coming on?" he murmured doubtfully.

"Getting better," said Alice.

"No, not so good," he said with his half-committed smile.

"Well," she said, "Rome wasn't built in a day."

She realized the dictum was absurd to his ears and shook her head. "That's just a saying," she assured him.

"Roma wassa not built in a day," he repeated twice. The laughter between them was confident. She knew it was something like this, reaching over the line of language to find another person, not a student. Besides, Alice knew she'd been naïve with her Don and Jane primers. It was a wonder he hadn't been offended by them. She removed them from the table and placed them beside her on the chair. His command of the language seemed at least as serviceable as that of the Italians who'd run the fruit shops in town before the war started—the ones who had been briefly interned and who had then returned to take up business again. Duncan thought Giancarlo needed English classes. Yet now the prisoner seemed to be unveiling the range of his English to Alice. Might he have done it innocently, speaking in one or two words to try to please Duncan, attempting not to be considered a smart aleck, or—more than that—trying not to break the unspoken compact by which it was assumed in the bush that Italians *could* manage only one or two words of English at a time.

"So," she pursued, "you mentioned something elsewhere. Something between Curtin and Mussolini? You said that's what you are. Like John Curtin."

"No. I am *anarco-sindacalista*. You know *anarco-sindacalista*?"

"No, I don't have the foggiest idea what that is."

"The 'one big union,'" he said. "All men and women together. The state . . . it'sa no good for the real people."

She wondered if he really meant this—that the state was no good to anyone. She'd never heard anyone ever propose it wasn't. "You're messing around with me, aren't you? There's no such thing as this one big union? If there were no state, we wouldn't be able to fight the Japanese."

He smiled mildly and his eyes glimmered. "If there is no *stato giapponese*, no need to fight the Japanese."

"But you fought for the state of Italy?"

"Because I don' wanna go to prison." He laughed outright now and shook his head. "So . . . I am a *prigioniero* anyhow. But better here than a Mussolini gaol. Signor Duncan better than Benito." She knew guiltily that wherever Neville was, he wasn't smiling as complacently as this Italian, and that the contradictions would not be sitting as easily with him as they seemed to with Giancarlo. She did not like to think this Italian was having an easier time of it than Neville. "We are well treated," Neville had written in one rare letter earlier in the year. But was he required to? And did he enjoy the ease of soul that Molisano did at this moment?

"Do you know what?" she asked. "I think you are a cunning man."

The frown that came on was chiefly in his eyes; his brow remained smooth and seamless. It was as if he was trying at that moment to prove that what people said about Italians was true. That they tried things on, saw how far they could confuse people.

"Do you know what 'cunning' means?" she asked. "It means deceitful . . . telling lies."

He raised his hands palms up as a protest.

She said, "You are telling us stories to suit your case."

He seemed mildly offended, but there came no grin of repentance, of a man caught out in a lie. In fact, he bowed his head a little and looked at her from beneath his brows, to assess whether she was playing with him or not. He was affronted so subtly that no reasonable person could have called it insolence and rung the Control Center with complaints. His mild but complicated pique fascinated her, sent a pulse of curiosity that urged her to press her case against him.

She said, "It suits you to talk about how there should be no state now that Mussolini's on the way out. But did you say anything about that when you were in Benghazi? Before the war really got going?"

She laughed then, not totally indulgent. His concern at being found suspect made her recognize that she had power over him, and how odd that was, since in a lifetime she had never had power over any other man. She wondered what to do with it. She wanted to be moderate. She thought so, anyhow. It was the decent thing to be.

But other undefined impulses, ones she thought of as beyond her nature, but powerful ones anyway, crowded in. To somehow impress herself on him from above, without proving any "niceness" first, without painfully and by the long rigmarole of bush etiquette proving her fitness. To be more blatant and casual with him than in her accustomed world, where women presented themselves like job applicants. To be blunt, as men were with each other, and if he didn't like that, to find some alternate path of brisk contact, something candid beyond anything she'd ever done.

How could she tell what that was?

"I'm just mucking around," she explained quickly to Giancarlo, doing her best to get back to known ground. "Teasing."

"Teasing," he nodded. He waved his head from one side to another, as if to gauge whether teasing was safe.

10

Tengan, the naval aviator, the first prisoner of all and so a figure of ambiguous authority, moved like a man of martial purpose. His zeal had been dented by his ill fortune; nonetheless he maintained it and sought means to let Compound C know his vigor was still in place. Aoki thought Tengan wasn't a bad fellow and even had the capacity to be flexible, but he seemed to feel bound to manifest his unyielding esprit.

At a meeting of the council of three in Aoki's hut, the mats and mattresses on which men slept now rolled up against the unlined timber walls, Tengan, for example, declared that he was against baseball and wanted it banned. Not, he said, that he had anything against the game itself. It was baseball within Compound C that took on a malignant character.

"I played badminton," he told Aoki and Goda, as if that proved what a jovial man he was. "In Brisbane, when they held me there. But only so I could watch my enemy. The baseball they let us play here is designed to make us content when we shouldn't be content. So that the camp officers can look down from the towers and say, 'There they are, happy with themselves. What a consolation!' Baseball makes it possible for the enemy to gratify himself with our behavior."

Goda, who had become, as much as it was in his nature to be, Aoki's familiar, clinically and with a citified confidence raised the issue of mental and physical vigor, and the way both could be revived on the baseball diamond. "The boys can't just sit in their huts sulking and wasting away," Goda grumbled as he accepted a small gift from Aoki, a thin-rolled cigarette, packed into the Zig-Zag brand of papers they were happy to receive from the captors.

Tengan declared he wasn't saying that. There were other pursuits. For example, wrestling was a different matter, said Tengan. "Men can exercise their bodies and souls in wrestling. Brother to brother, man to man. And it's not like baseball—it's not some kind of communal drug."

Goda cried out from his place that he respected Tengan's argument in principle, but a decree outlawing baseball would be bitterly resented. Aoki was surprised that Goda cared about the resentment of men, but he might fear it more as something that frayed their souls rather than a factor that might see him fall as a member of the council. Tengan and his stridency seemed potentially dangerous. Goda moved that they should put it to a vote by the hut and section leaders. For this accorded with the spirit of democratic process.

Tengan's proposition would get some support, Goda and Aoki knew. One part of it would come from the strict logic of his case. Some of it would come from his authority as a flier, and the respect that aviators garnered from the young ultras, even the army men. Tengan had thundered through the sky, and reduced to submission the earth ahead of the infantry. He had done this before their enemies had even understood the winning equation between the armies of the air and the armies of the earth. Tengan might have fallen from the sky, and so be a fallen god.

The hut commanders were notified to meet in Tengan's hut to decide whether the issue should be submitted to the prisoners as a body. When they gathered, sitting at card tables or on mats, Tengan spoke first and explained the false balance of soul deriving from baseball. This time he seemed to be a margin more nervous, plucking once or twice at his maroon-dyed tunic. He mentioned that solidarity was torn into fragments by distracting men into baseball's internal groups—the northern half of the compound, for example, against the southern half. When the game was over, and one team yelped and the other sloped away, what had been proven, except disunity? And then it was an opiate and a distraction, designed to drug the prisoners into accepting their condition.

Still he explained himself with some primness and delicacy, like a junior headmaster, and a man trying out ideas rather than wed to them. He was not making a killjoy denunciation of baseball as if it were some evil in itself, he declared. If played, for example, by the army in the field, that would be a different matter.

There were occasional groans and grunts at all this rectitude of his, but he was not speaking to the groaners and the grunters. He was speaking to the more clear-thinking of the young men, and he knew that he was exactly right on this issue.

And he had a further argument not yet unveiled with Aoki and Goda.

"Our guards fancy they are being very benevolent to us," he said, "letting us play baseball. I have seen them point it out to the visiting Swiss. "Look, we've gone to that trouble for them. Please mention in your report how earnest we've been." Should we allow them to preen like that? Wouldn't they be confused if we returned all the equipment to them? And confusing them . . . isn't that one of our chief interim tasks?"

His tone was moderate but his eye gleamed as he made this last point, so appealing to some of the young intractables. Yet once more he managed to sound more questioning than dogmatic or fanatical. As Aoki and Goda did not want to oppose him or this group of young men too frontally, he also understood that he could not afford to alienate the two older men of the other hut commanders—as muddled as their consciousness seemed—without risking his place in the council.

The discussion began. Omura, who belonged to Tengan's elite bloc, declared he could see Tengan's point. Just the same, couldn't it be argued that their captors were trying to make them content and forgetful in other ways as well, by supplying them with musical instruments, by allowing plays to be performed, even by the scale of rations? Omura thought that at least in part the captors treated them well not just because they wanted to sedate them but also because the prisoners made them uneasy and that the duty to keep them uneasy was not dependent on refusing to play baseball.

With Omura (who, in turn, despite respect for Tengan, wished to remain hut commander) respectfully adjusting but in reality rebuffing Tengan's argument, Tengan could see the prestige of his premise beginning to collapse, and a little more quickly than he had expected. He had expected to lose to woolly minded infantrymen, but not to receive the first dainty blow from one of his fellow aviators.

A crusty hut commander named Kure, who had led a determined-to-die unit in a breakout charge at Buna and—the usual story—had been concussed and wounded by the burst of a grenade, didn't like Tengan and spoke more dismissively.

"It's not the fault of the men in my hut that they're prisoners," he said. "Let the poor kids have a game of baseball! An hour or two of relief from the reality of their situation." Besides that, he argued, the divisions created by baseball weren't real—they were felt only for an hour or so, and then the game and the score faded in memory.

And then Kure put the knife in. The infantry were used to trusting each other in mind and body, he said pointedly. Maybe someone used to the solitude of a cockpit didn't have the same sense of his fellow men.

That was it. The hut leaders were so quickly convinced of the mental and physical value of baseball that all but two of them voted for it to continue in the compound. Tengan had prepared himself for defeat, but not to this extent or so promptly. To shore up his stature, he announced, "I accept that the majority has spoken, and as I am not a fanatic, I concede the ground."

He knew that he must do something to restore himself and hoped he could achieve that by some extent through wrestling. For he was, in all senses, a champion of wrestling. This Kure fellow—he wouldn't waste time resenting him.

11

Alice would sometimes see Giancarlo from the kitchen window, especially when he went scouting amongst the peach and nectarine trees outside the garden fence. He seemed to love the fruit, and Duncan had given him permission to pick it. He would part the leaves with patience, and tenderly feel whatever was attached.

He had made a difference to her laborious routines. He locked the calf away at night and continued to be up to milk Dotty in the morning, when, from the long habits of early rising, she came out to the shed and watched the process as if inspecting it for technique, but still saying nothing. He collected the eggs as well and took them in a bucket to the back door, knocking to say what was obvious—"I have eggs, Missus 'Erman."

The first time she got back from her afternoon lesson and tea party with Giancarlo, she had gone at once and looked up the meaning of the word "anarchist" in the dictionary beside the Bible in the rarely used lounge room of the Herman farmhouse. There was a confident definition there and yet she had never known there were such people. Surely there were none of them in Australia. She put out her hand to the upright piano as if the world had shifted a degree or two off axis. States make war. Therefore, no states, no war. Absolute rubbish. Yet it was somehow a decorative credo in Giancarlo's case and made him larger in her imagination.

The lessons continued. In the kitchen one night, Duncan Herman was still studying yesterday's *Herald* as she came in, but then he got up with an uncharacteristic suddenness to wash his hands at the kitchen sink.

"Spending a bit of time with young Johnny, were you?" he asked, frowning, but concentrating on the soap in his hands.

"Another English lesson," she said quickly. "You know, he's better at it than we thought."

Since, thank God, he was too uncomfortable about having challenged her to raise his eyes, Duncan did not see the blood in her face.

"Do you reckon you ought to give it a rest?" asked Duncan. He began wiping his hands thoroughly and this action, too, commanded his full gaze. "Seems to me he can manage to hear what I say all right."

"I lent him one of Mrs. Herman's novels," she admitted, as if zeal to instruct the Italian was thus proven. "I wouldn't be surprised if he manages to read it. I agree with you, Duncan. He's speaks English better than we thought he would."

Duncan looked up at last. She was pleased that she had by her tone appeased him. "That's right," he admitted. "Is he coming up to tea tonight?"

"Well," she said, "it's Wednesday. Didn't you invite him for Wednesdays?"

"That's right," Duncan admitted again, and finished drying his hands and returned to his newspaper.

And when it was time, she went outside and clanged the bell that hung from the upper part of the veranda, to signal Giancarlo.

"Have you finished that bottle of red plonk I gave you, Johnny?" asked Duncan genially at the table. Duncan had bought the bottle of red wine from a pub in Gawell as a reward for good work. And clearly he expected a bottle of wine to last as long as one of whisky.

"I finish her, Mr. 'Erman," said Giancarlo, smiling. "I don' want she turn to vinegar."

Alice decided not to correct his pronouns.

Duncan laughed, without ill feeling. "Well, I've got to say, you're pretty good at excuses, Johnny."

She wondered whether this was, by some accident of wisdom on Duncan's part, a knowing gibe. But his face now crinkled in innocent delight at his own gift for teasing, and she saw at once what Duncan had been worried about—not that she was beguiled by Giancarlo, but that Giancarlo might learn more English than would suit Duncan as the boss; that giving Giancarlo an equality of grammar would somehow undermine Duncan. It was the upper hand Duncan desired to keep, and Giancarlo knew it. It was why by instinct his speech became more halting, more confused, with Duncan.

Giancarlo's eyes, moving about in answer to Duncan's sally about wine and excuses, hooked onto Alice's. Duncan went on stuttering with laughter over his lamb chops and doing difficult surgery on them, excising the maximum from the bones. It was frugality, not gluttony, that made him do it. But Duncan's application to this work allowed Alice and Giancarlo to gaze more directly than they had ever before had a chance or the bravery to. It seemed to her that a mass of news of a kind she had not received or transmitted before flowed out as if on some sort of radio beam: her uncertainty, her fidelity, her loss of wifehood, her sense of command over Duncan and over him. And by the same apparatus was returned her way his political doubts, his hatred of imprisonment, his sense of being Duncan's subject and friend and never quite either, his fear of her and his want of her and his fear for his parents living amidst Italian battle fronts. It took perhaps twenty seconds as measured in metered time.

Giancarlo showed signs of discomfort for the rest of the night. He was distracted when Duncan spoke to him about the differential on the truck and questioned him about the quirks of engines.

Giancarlo's knowledge, uttered however haltingly, did seem considerable. The benefit of the *liceo scientifico* he'd mentioned to her.

"What's the problem, Johnny? You're looking pretty down."

"Down, Mr. 'Erman?"

"Sad, maybe. Worried."

"I don' like say . . . Your son is in prison. So you worry for him. I worry something else."

Alice was transfixed. She hoped Duncan would blunder on.

"Yeah?" asked Duncan. "What's that, then, Johnny?"

"It's in *Herald*. The enemy give up Napoli. The fighting in my country now. My father, mother, brother—all there. But maybe *i tedeschi*, the Germans, all run through Frattamaggiore. No fight." He gestured with his hand to signify a withdrawal. "Back and back to new line, I hope."

"We hope too," Alice told him. Hope was in fact ardent in her. "We hope your family's all right, Giancarlo."

The meal ended. Giancarlo, anxious about straining his welcome, rose and wished them a good night, carefully enunciated in English. Duncan, in his slippers, went into the lounge room to listen to the news on his big, mahogany cabinet of a wireless. Alice washed dishes abstractly, in a ferment of anticipation. For the first time in her life, she had entered that unpredicted state where there is no history, and in which even the succulent, breathable air seemed to reassure her that her fever would be understood by those who knew the truth, and even applauded. Her intoxication glittered with its own morality so much higher than any accustomed commandment.

She also understood instantly that she could not wait on a word from Giancarlo. He was the prisoner. She was not a prisoner. She was not on any probation; no language was barred to her; she had the space and the sudden, unexpected ability to act. She had not ever been encouraged to feel such authority, this prerogative that seemed larger than pastures and more significant than all the palaver of sheep, wheat, superphosphate. Her authority in the matter, she was sure, had already been established at the table, and not least in the twenty-second spate between the two of them, while Duncan looked elsewhere, benumbed. And Giancarlo feared for his parents and must be consoled for their peril.

Before going to bed, however, she recognized herself as the victim of a malady and tried to give the images she retained of Neville a chance to reassert themselves. She had a sense of flailing at something impossibly remote—a hook could not be attached to it or a familiarity reestablished. She found with fear and bewilderment and a lot of exhilaration that her sense of what was ridiculous had utterly gone. It was not ridiculous to wear a nightdress, a man's plaid dressing gown, and gumboots at three in the morning, to drop from a windowsill, and flank the house in a night on which only the most insomniac insects still chirped. A mild southwesterly evoked a few seconds of lazy movement in the garden shrubs. She moved through the fruit trees, around the screen of eucalypts, to the shadow of the shearers' quarters' veranda. It was a few seconds from the place of her drudgery and daily boredom, but now of a different order of things. She felt the entitlement to turn the plain door handle. Then she was inside, closing out the night. She was not in total darkness—starlight and the moon, she saw, gave a small luminescence to the rough curtain over the window.

She said, "Giancarlo," and he woke in alarm and sat up.

"Missus 'Erman?" he asked in a voice husky from sleep.

"I thought I ought to come here," she told him. "You're not in a position to come up to the house."

"What do you say, missus?" he asked.

"Don't call me "missus" ever again," she told him. "Call me Alice, for God's sake."

But she knew she was setting him a hard task.

"Except maybe in the house."

There was little light, some would say none. Without permission, she sat near the end of the bed. Who had she become? To do that with plaid gown and a nightdress coating her determination. Becoming accustomed to the darkness, she could see a singlet on his upper body, but bare legs. She reached for his wrist. She had never done this before. Her wrists had always bided the touch of other people.

She saw the sudden childlike luminosity of his eyes. She could see he thought everything was dangerous now. There was no move he could make to satisfy her. Underneath it he wanted what young men want, but that wasn't the point anymore.

She held his wrist and raised it. Her left hand was on top, clasping, and her right was like a clenched heart in his palm.

"Missus 'Erman," he said. "Alice. Mr. 'Erman, he's a boss and he's the kind boss. I get sent right back too. I don' want to get sent back to Compound D."

She could sense a torment in him—it was broader than simply being sent back. He did not want to lose his way. Suddenly, she let go of his wrist. It had been right to take it but was not right now. It was a kind of bullying.

"I'm sorry, Giancarlo," she said. She got up. She wanted to flee. "This is your room."

"No," he said, trying to encompass all the perils and guilt, and again not managing to. "Not my room. It's yours, Missus and Mr. 'Erman's. Mr. 'Erman . . . he's a good man to me. And you . . . a good woman."

St. Alice, the frigid widow of Herman's place!

"Good night, Giancarlo," she said, and she got up and charged through the door. In the altered moonlight, making for her room again, she was ridiculous. Giancarlo must think she was mad. He'd been here a mere seven weeks. Seven weeks isn't enough to justify this lunacy.

Her face blazed when she heard his boots on the veranda the next morning, bringing the eggs. She heard a somber, "Eggs, missus."

She gathered herself, hooded her eyes, and assured herself her face was empty of any statement, including shame. She stepped out, and he placed the wire handle of the bucket in her hand. It was close to Christmas and the promised heat of the day breathed on her from over his shoulder.

"Thank you," she somehow muttered, to open and end the transaction. She turned to take the eggs inside, but he murmured, "Missus. Alice." There was a content in his two words whereas she'd tried to take out all the contents she could from hers.

He said, "You are the most good. You don' know it, the good and beautiful, you are. I was sap." (American slang again, Alice thought.) "I was drongo." (Australian.) "I was bloody yellow." (Some war film?)

That's how it was established, on the edge of a bush Christmas.

She said, as the demented always do, "No one will find out." That night during her visit, he told her, "I have nothing here to protect," waving his hand briskly across his pelvic area, implying she could face the risk of a child. But there was the fact she had not conceived in her brief time with Neville, though they'd expected she would as a national duty and so she might have the comfort of a soldier's child in his absence. Neville had confided quite gently and without apportioning blame that he didn't think it was his deficiency—his father had had a kid. So it was pretty much established to be her. What had been a domestic misfortune in the making then, became another kind of fortune now.

"I don't have babies," she told him.

"Still," he told her, as if he knew the male and thus the female mysteries. "I know to be careful. *Bella!*"

She did not want the debate to go any further. She stood up and took off her upper garments. And indeed it didn't.

12

"*D*earest Emily," Ewan Abercare wrote to his estranged wife.

*I received by way of Cecil a kind invitation to join you and
your sister and him at Tathra for Christmas. Since I know
he would have asked you about your feelings on my visit, I
am overwhelmed by your kindness, and of course Cecil's and
Florence's as well.*

*I would love to get away from here—the heat is withering
even by African and sub-Continental standards. The whole
country's shrieking with cicadas and the grass has dried to straw,
and yet farmers tell us it's a good season. But I'm desolated to tell
you I can't leave. Some hundreds of Italian prisoners have arrived
here from camps in India. The reasons have something to do
with the idea the British had that Italian prisoners might work
on Australian farms, whereas they were more confined and of less
use in India. To relieve the pressure I've managed to negotiate
with the Control Center that a further fifty of our longer-term
resident Italians be distributed to farms near and far-off.*

*The added work—and you have no idea how much
paperwork even a single prisoner involves—means I can't*

*leave Gawell for the holiday season, but if Cecil, with your
agreement, will permit me to visit in the New Year, I would be
unutterably grateful. I am desolated not to be with you for the
festival. May I wish you all a very Happy Christmas and dare
subscribe myself*

*Your loving husband,
Ewan*

But almost as soon as the fifty-two Italians went off in Control Center
trucks, seven other prisoners returned from farms—six with fevers,
one rendered catatonic by loneliness. In addition, a certain Gabri-
ele Basile came in one hot day after walking off a farm at Orange
on his own authority. A court of inquiry was held under Abercare
and he was sentenced to twenty-eight days' detention in what even
the Japanese called the "hoosegow"—the detention cells in his compound. A Private Giovanni Verano was meanwhile returned to camp
by the farmer he'd been assigned to. He had refused to work. Benedetto Pachessa was returned because he had gestured with a pitchfork towards his employer. Once again a sentence of four weeks, but
Abercare intended to amnesty him for Christmas. Private Alberto
Marangoni had been brought back by truck from Oberon's Control
Center. He had left the shed where he and another prisoner slept,
and crossed into another farm and slept there. Marangoni, when he
was brought to Abercare, showed a half-healed wound on his lower
arm. The prisoner he'd worked with had inflicted the wound and
had threatened to kill him. What was the cause of the problem, he
was asked, and the answer was, "Songs." Songs were a big issue with
Italians, especially if they were political. The "Internazionale" could
indeed provoke a wound. Abercare could gauge the fear in Marangoni, and dismissed the charge and sought another farm for him by
way of the Control Center. Abercare was asked, too, to approve the

transfer of one Corporal Marco Barbetta, newly arrived from India, from Compound D to A, where he could enjoy the company of Alessandro, his cousin.

Correspondence and report writing on these and other issues blocked out Christmas as Abercare was put to the considerable paperwork of confirming these small but frequent shifts, punishments, and leniencies. Some Red Cross parcels were also referred to him for his ultimate inspection, often on fatuous grounds, by the major who ran Compound A. The officer concerned was wary that hardcore *Fascisti* or simply criminal elements might forge cans of tinned tomatoes and sausages into weapons.

And, above all, to be carefully studied, were reports from Nevski and Champion on the abiding mysteries of Compound C.

Was there a certain relief in Abercare that he would not face the test of Emily at such a high season—that he could spend the day with his town friends Dr. and Mrs. Garner, Garner being one of the more venerable physicians of the town and one who sometimes visited cases in Gawell prison camp?

The recklessness in him that had driven off Emily had occurred far enough away, in Queensland. Perhaps where she was now, in the far south of New South Wales, it could be slowly accommodated and forgiven by her. But Christmas was a dangerous feast, when resentments lay close to the surface. It would be better if he went to see her at a more neutral time.

Some years back, the better part of three, in fact, Abercare, after his life in the army in India, had taken up fruit farming in the Darling Downs. The Australians sold remount horses to the army in India, as well as the idea that Australia was a good place for British officers from the army in India to retire to. He had not known, though, that the idea of being a gentleman farmer in the English manner was one not quite understood, or even viable, on the Darling Downs. He brought with him his wife, Emily, a lean, handsome woman whom he had married in India, after their first meeting in Kenya over a decade past, and who was pliable enough to take on a new country, having come from a family like his own—the kind that spent so much of their lives in British outposts. Emily and her sister, Florence, came from a gentrified but now fairly impoverished Lancashire Catholic family. In their girlhoods, they had shared Mass with the Irish working class of northern England and the Irish soldiers of British garrisons in Kenya, Rhodesia, and India.

On the Downs Abercare had joined the local militia unit, and there his welcome from other part-time officers had at least been sincere. A calamity was considered imminent then. Czechoslovakia lay in the balance, and Nanking had fallen to the barbarians. Through the disasters of the early war, amidst far echoes but disturbing ones for this southernmost region of Britannic zeal and hope, he and other men awaited full-time postings and did not receive them until intelligence arrived of coming, surprise, assaults in the Pacific and Indian Oceans. He had been confident that Emily and a manager could run the fruit farm, but by the time his call-up to a training battalion came, he had already committed that awful bush folly of his, that adolescent wantonness.

All the region he and Emily had settled in when they came to Australia knew the wife of the storekeeper in Elgin. Her name was Nola Sheffield. She was perhaps fifteen years younger than her husband, and it was said the couple was unhappy. It was true that the husband seemed to lack faith in anything except groceries and hardware. Patches of stubble lay on his long face like ash. When Mrs. Sheffield, a woman in her prime, served customers, particularly ones she did not know, she moved behind her counter with a strange, slatternly undulation Abercare found memorable and alluring. Everyone called her by her first name, never by her married title. She was Nola, childless and recently wed, out of pity on Sheffield's part or otherwise, in a town where most girls married at eighteen or nineteen. Hence rumor proliferated. That she had had a child in another town. That she was very simpleminded. That she was very clever and had gone to a private school in Brisbane. On his visits to the store, Abercare certainly found her a village phenomenon, quick at mathematics, at pounds, shillings, and pence.

Whenever he left the store, Abercare found himself indulging the sharpest memories of her walk and intimately remembered details of her body and face, her mouth like a crushed rose, and every subtlety of resentful movement.

As Nola got to be familiar with the sight of Abercare, her demeanor as she approached him up the length of the counter was warmer, and involved an almost expectant smile.

"The usual, Colonel Abercare?" she would ask. Like other men in Elgin, he looked for omens in that simple exchange. "How is Mrs. Abercare?"

He was returning in his Morris car, one dim spring Sunday evening early in the war, from a weekend of militia training. It was a period just before the Japanese crisis, when the military had decided they would require his full-time services at some stage but not quite yet. And, despite the farm, a military renewal was what he hoped for. Then he saw a woman's figure in Wellington boots and with a burlap sack over her head and shoulders as protection against the rain. The woman wore a light summer dress of floral print that was soaked. It was Nola Sheffield, he could tell as she turned to the sound of wet tires on gravel. She faced him with a tear-bruised face, with the rain cascading from its planes. Her lip was also darkened and swollen and divided by a small, sharp-edged cut.

"Mrs. Sheffield," he called, half-abashed in case she was ashamed to be seen like this. "Might I help you?"

With dark, outraged eyes, she was inspecting his uniform, which he still wore in full—Sam Browne belt and service ribbons and all. Somehow he could see her decide that his shell of office did not fit hers of misery. She wanted to be alone in a landscape that suited her grievance.

"Thanks," she said, having decided to treat him as neutral. Her tone became pleasant, but you could tell that alternative tones lay banked within her. She conceded a wet smile beneath her burlap hood. "That's a pretty nice uniform you have."

"Oh," he said, boyishly delighted. "I've just been at weekend maneuvers. Chocolate soldier stuff!"

He could tell she wavered.

"Look, get in, please. It's ridiculous to get so wet."

He wanted to know, but couldn't ask, why her husband had hit her. Who else would have? She got in beside Abercare. It was done lithely. He could smell the wetness of her clothes and the cleaner, cold odor of her saturated flesh.

He put the car back in gear. "Look, I can see you've had a bit of an accident. Would you like to come home, and my wife can give you some tea and sort out some dry clothes?"

And I'd have had you beneath my roof and could watch how you sat at my table. The table had been cold since Emily had grown discontented in this place, and it was worse because she didn't say so. Nola Sheffield would make the table radiant again.

She said woodenly, "Do you mind just dropping me at the park in town?"

"Well, it's not my business. But you'll get wetter still."

"No," she said, "there's picnic shelters there. I just want to have a think. I like parks a lot. They give you a bit of time."

She gave a small, tentative smile that caused a definite movement of something within him, a jolt. The quaintness and the beauty.

"All right," Abercare conceded. "I'll turn the car around."

"Oh," she said, feeling her lip for a second, then—in a sort of stoicism—at once withdrawing her finger. "I hadn't thought of that. Sorry."

But he was already grinding the shuddering Morris into the turn. He decided to be adventurous. "I hate to see you bruised like that."

She said nothing. He'd reached the limit of what was permitted to be said, at least for now.

"I have time for you, Mr. Abercare," she said then, plainly and without emphasis. "You're a different kind of man than they are around Elgin."

"I wouldn't say that. I'm a pretty standard-issue sort of fellow." He put some effort into not glowing with delight. It had struck him by now, though, that if she were observed sitting in the park, he would be observed dropping her off there. Nonetheless, he continued up the rain-slicked gravel road and reached the slumped old houses on the edge of the town and so rolled past pubs and shut drapery shops and the long front of Western Stores to the comfortless park beyond.

"Thanks a lot," she told him and got out.

He knew there was something off-balance in her. The elements did not add up to a whole. She got out into the stubborn downpour. She put the wet burlap over her head again. By the time he'd backed and forwarded a few times and turned the car, he saw she had taken up a seat in a picnic shed.

When he got home, he told Emily all about it, as a sort of expiation, though he didn't know for what. It did not prevent Nola Sheffield and her remembered bruises seizing him by night. In a dream he took this exquisite and baffling creature, his intentions almost as pedagogic as lustful, to an indefinite city.

An uncle of Abercare's died in Scotland, and he received news of a small inheritance from a solicitor in Edinburgh. There were papers enclosed that needed to be signed and notarized, and he was on his way to Stanthorpe on a cranky branch line, in a carriage infested with coal dust from an ancient and inefficient locomotive, to attend to that business. Ninety seconds before the train left, the storekeeper's wife, Nola Sheffield, appeared at his carriage door in a straw hat and a floral dress like the one she had worn in the rain, and stepped up and made her way down the central aisle. She was carrying a middle-sized "port," as Queenslanders called a piece of luggage. He rose to take it from her and say hello and place the bag on the wire rack overhead.

Nola Sheffield permitted this gallantry and thanked him. He turned away to find a seat at a distance from her.

"You're welcome to sit across," she told him, pointing to the seat opposite her.

"That's very kind," he told her, and as if it could be done by will-power, struggled to prevent an excess of blood from coloring his face.

Her features were healed and her eyes had lost that look of universal disappointment. She told him she was going to visit a sick aunt in Stanthorpe who had had a stroke. She would be staying with her cousin, who was minding the aunt.

"What will the store do without your gift for mathematics?"

"Oh, I reckon it will get on all right. True, I got the arithmetic prize in high school, but then my father needed to pull me out."

"And why did he need to do that?"

"My brother was drowned. Dad wanted the help. I was glad to get away from geometry."

"But you're so good at numbers," he protested.

"They're easy," she said. "You can see them in your head."

"Geometry has its uses, believe me," he assured her, and sounded to himself as if he had the arrogance of geometry at his fingertips. He stopped himself talking about its utility in navigation and artillery.

"Everyone says you were a soldier in India," she observed.

"Well," he told her, "Kenya and Ceylon for a little while too." He had met Emily in Kenya, having lingered there during a home leave. He had intended to spend as much time as he could in London and Edinburgh, visiting his widowed mother and members of the family, and going to the country houses of the parents of fellow officers for parties and shooting and fishing weekends. Instead, he let his ship leave Nairobi and delayed a month for Emily's sake, courting her with a passionate respect. He remembered the Muthaiga Club, its pink walls and the casual dusks, the endless evenings and the sweet eternities of conversation with her in the garden, and a torrent of kisses beneath sharp stars towards the end of his stay. He'd written to her from England, once he got there, telling her that he had been given a passage which did not take in Nairobi and asking would she come to India at the end of his leave to marry him. Now he felt a moment's bewilderment that all of it could have ended up in Elgin—all that pleasure taking, all that glut of color, all that sumptuary excitement and transimperial passion.

"And what was it like?" asked Nola.

"Oh," said Abercare, "India was peaceful, strangely."

He told her of the few months he had spent campaigning in Waziristan. A chap preposterously called the Fakir of Ipi had got the local people stirred up. "All I had to do was guard the roads with my fellows and make an occasional search through the villages, looking for arms. Apart from that, it was a wonderful life altogether."

"How was it wonderful?"

"Well, normally we only worked about four hours or so a day."

"Four hours!" she said and whistled under her breath.

"Yes. The rest of the time we played polo or cricket, and sometimes we went on tiger hunts. And then there were mess dinners and balls. The wives of Indian rajas and nizams were there in the most astonishing gowns—swathes of golden cloth and the most beautiful rings and bracelets. When I was young, I thought it would last forever."

The train pulled into a station, and one sullen and reclusive farmer entered the compartment and, as the train moved, showed his determination to check every paddock between there and Stanthorpe in case it carried more pasture than his.

Nola leaned towards Abercare. "The only wonderful thing that's happened to me is that I saw a marsupial lion once. I can't tell too many people, my husband says, or they'll think I'm soft in the head. They're supposed to be extinct, see. Anyhow, I saw it when I was young, about twelve. I was with my father up Crohamhurst way, where the bush gets so thick that you can't see the sun. How does anyone know whether—in bush like that—the lions are there or not, living in the shadows?"

He leaned forward too. He had a sense that she thought this her central secret, and that to give it up was a serious gift.

"How long would you say it's been extinct?" he asked. "Thousands of years, isn't it?"

"No. Sixty years. Sixty years ago someone saw one, and they believed him because he was a scientist. I saw the stripes—because they have stripes, you see. They started behind the shoulders, and thinned out and vanished."

It was, he thought, a mature summary. It also had the delightful weight of something confidentially shared. At the local School of Arts at Elgin, she went on, she had heard a professor from Brisbane speak about the creature. The lion's Greek name meant "pouched flesh eater," she said, as if those words were riveted in her brain. Its large head gave it a strong bite. And when it caught other animals it killed them by dropping on them from trees. Its natural enemy, as it turned out, was the giant goanna, which, thank God, was definitely extinct.

She went on at a slightly manic length, which he afterwards saw as a sign that there was no center to this girl, that her knowledge and her soul were scattered. But at the time of his enchantment, it was what she had to give him, and she gave it in full. "If there is a lion in the bush, then it can't be alone—it must have parents, and perhaps there are four or more of them out there, males and females. Trouble is, there are only four nipples in the pouch, so if more than four are born at the one time, it's bad luck for the weakest one." They arrived in Stanthorpe in what Abercare thought was a half hour but was in fact over three. He offered to carry her relatively light bag, but she declined. He asked if she needed a taxi, but country people rarely took them and so she said she could walk—it was less than a mile. He found himself walking with her into High Street. Before the stores and hotels began, there was a public garden. She said, "Sometimes I go there, too, and sit about for a while. The picnic shelters."

Was this some sort of invitation?

"You really do like parks."

"Well, you're pretty safe in parks," she told him, looking at him directly, in a way that inflicted delight and incredulity on him.

They came to his hotel. She had to go straight on, she told him. He watched her go. After leaving his bag in his room at the hotel he went out again and walked down Connor Street to a solicitor's office, where he had the inheritance documents notarized—a tedious business following the methods inherited from Britain. The rigmarole done, he accepted the man's congratulations on the modest but far from unwelcome legacy. He took the documents back to the hotel but then, in a fever of possibility, walked two miles, eschewing the chemists' shops in the middle of town, to find a suburban pharmacist, and from him received in a brown bag a small supply of condoms, just in case the marsupial lion had been Nola's mating display.

Back at the hotel he dined in late dusk. "Getting an early night?" a waiter asked him.

"Might go for a spin round town."

"Good luck seeing anything of interest," the young man told him.

Outside, it was properly dark now. The streetlights penetrated only fragments of the place. An occasional light from a house in the backstreet combined with wood smoke and the odor of plain, muttony food to make you think a town like this had been here, fixed in manners and aroma, for centuries instead of a mere eighty, ninety years. The street was vacant of witnesses as he turned into the park and walked down paths amongst floral beds and then amongst the little cluster of picnic huts.

He heard her call. "Mr. Abercare." She sat within one of those small cubicles, in a corner.

"Ah," he said, mimicking the last shreds of ordinary, falsely surprised social greeting. As remembered by Abercare, their plain, conspiratorial sentences were enchanting. His blood went hurtling through his body. After a while they moved out of the strict confines of the picnic table and lay on an embankment, where he gallantly spread his coat. Her dress seemed light and enabled him to reach her breasts and shoulders and belly and thighs beneath. Whether she was one person or two, he wanted possession and if asked then would have given his life lightly for that. "A moment, Nola," he pleaded, and artificiality blighted time as he paused to roll the condom onto his prick, a process about which she seemed patient.

Some sense of transcendence took away the indignity of his exposing his middle-aged arse to the night and entering her. Nothing abashed him, and her cries seemed to have nothing to do with the trivialities of his belts and buckles and imperfect flesh. In the moments after climax he felt a sudden tide of reality, and he returned to his normal habits, and advised her to go home to her aunt before they did each other greater damage. But the disabling passion rose again in him before he'd finished uttering the advice. He had a second to think before his thighs followed their own intention.

Then, towards ten o'clock—the first time he had consulted a watch—he was sated enough for reason to have its last say. He would love to meet like this again, but he was married and she was married, too, and from what he could judge there was a risk of damage being done her if this ever became known.

"I've heard that talk before," she told him, half-amused, because she did not believe that the wall he was erecting would stand. "Men never say any of that at the start, when they want a girl. It's always afterwards."

"You should go first, Nola," he told. "I can watch from here so that you get out safely."

On his way to the street he nearly tripped over a couple clenched together on dark grass closer to the gate.

He returned to Elgin and from his mixture of wisdom and cravenness he avoided the store. He saw Emily off on an already planned long train journey to visit Florence in New South Wales, beginning with that archaic regional locomotive, on its creaking regional rails, on which he had conversed with Nola Sheffield.

The farmhouse was lonely when Emily went off on her trip. He had never greatly liked it—its rooms had always seemed grim in a way that could not be remedied by mats or prints or vasefuls of gardenias. He liked growing apples and stone fruit, though, and the previous season had been a good one, with plenty of workers willing to come in and help, and occupy the shanties out beyond the orchards. The thick-forested mountains to the northwest also invigorated him: he liked the sunsets mediated by a ridge line and the upper branches of trees.

He went to the store, and after each visit Nola would meet him by dark in the park at Elgin. He had become addicted to copulation al fresco.

The better part of a month passed and Emily was due home when, one late afternoon, as he came in from pruning a row of plum trees, he saw Nola on the road, approaching along the dirt track with the same sturdy stride with which he had seen her advancing, bruised, into the downpour on the day he'd given her a ride. He waited, mesmerized by her progress. She opened and closed the main gate and came tramping on towards him. He moved to meet her on the gravel path to the front steps.

"Nola," he said. But he couldn't very well say, "You ought to go back. I'll drive you."

"It would be good for us if we went away," she told him. "Elgin isn't the world."

So he had his wish, and it terrified him.

"No, Nola. We can't do that. You're a lovely girl but I have to take you back home. The end of town then." Because she was shaking her head. "I don't want to get you into trouble with your husband."

"Bugger my husband! I'm not going back."

Panic swelled within Abercare.

"It's the end, Nola," he cried.

"You didn't tell me there'd be an end."

"No. I should have. Look, let me take you back."

They were still on the path to the front door, and the absurdity of the whole business threatened to abound when a column of dust advanced down the road from town. Nola was silent as the drone and shudder of the truck grew in volume. Then he understood: She knows this isn't a passing truck. This is her husband's truck, with "Elgin Store" in white on both doors.

Sheffield descended from it to open the outer farm gate and then drove through and closed it, then drove up the track and parked in front of the garden and got out—a gray, ageless man who wanted to strike both Nola and Abercare.

"She's not to be touched, Mr. Sheffield," declared Abercare. Sheffield laughed like a man who would never learn to laugh for jollity. With amazement, Abercare heard himself threaten Sheffield with prosecution for trespass. Nola moved in, pushed her husband, slapped his face, and Abercare and Sheffield were tussling and trading ineffectual blows. In the hubbub of the threats and the banging of his blood, in the shrieks of Nola, in the baying of Sheffield himself, they had not seen the postal contractor, the man named Allen—beloved in the district because he was as good as a newspaper delivering mail farm to farm—enter Abercare's property. It was only the surprising cry of brakes that caused them to stop a moment.

"Bloody hell!" said Allen, taking in the scene.

• • •

Returned unwitting and weary from the long journey to the south coast of New South Wales, Emily was welcomed by Abercare with edgy joy, as if his connection to an ordered world had been restored. But he knew she would hear and so that evening he told her. She was silent. It did not seem anger, so it was all the more punishing. She was calculating what to do as well, in a desperate way.

At first she was pointed out as an object of muttering pity at Mass and in the main street. She did not dare enter the Sheffields' shop and drove as far as Applethorpe for household stores, and everyone knew why. She must have heard at some stage that her husband had been interviewed by the sergeant of police, though Sheffield had dropped the charges of assault for fear of enhancing the ridicule he, too, was suffering. Back home, on the afternoon of the brawl, with Nola pleading behind him, Sheffield had gone into his yard and fetched the rifle and threatened her with it, before going to the doctor's and unsuccessfully asking him to commit her to an asylum.

This poured another element into the brew of rumor and yet was still no defense in Abercare's case. Hadn't fornication, or, more accurately, adultery, ever occurred before in the boundaries of Elgin? But he had committed too extreme a sin. He had done what they all wanted and fucked Nola, and that fed their outrage more intensely.

Nola vanished from town, was seen at the railway station and in the carriage on the regional rattler going south.

"I should abominate the betrayal, Ewan," a superrational and coldly charitable Emily said at one time, as if with a terrible self-knowledge. "And by God I do! But there's the damage to my vanity, too—to my standing. It compounds everything. It shouldn't, since these are fatuous opinions. But they've left their mark. It's the pressure of them, all around, from every direction." She decided to leave the farm, refusing to give him any idea of her destination. She liked Brisbane, and he imagined her taking an office job there, if one was going, for she had typing and shorthand. Or she might join Florence again.

Abercare himself was by now so aware of the amusement and disdain of men and women acquaintances in the street that he felt a rural excommunication. He found he abhorred the loss of social standing and had never loved Elgin or his farm enough to stay there as an object of gossip. He had received notification that he was to stand by for active service. That much, given the war and his experience, was true. He put the farm up for sale, received derisory offers, and at last sold it for a halfway reasonable price to a farmer who had not yet heard the story.

Abercare went to live for a time in a boardinghouse in Saint Lucia in Brisbane, and got a job as an insurance salesman. Emily was indeed working as a typist in the city, Abercare found out by consulting a private detective. He consulted the private detective again and gave him Nola's name. Abercare was told that Nola Sheffield was living in a flat in Kelvin Grove and working as a shopgirl at McWhirters'. He went to the address after work and as he approached he saw Nola emerge from a building accompanied by a man of middling years in a splendid suit. She was handed into a sedan.

He realized he had hoped to resume with Nola, and as the car took her off into a summer night he began whimpering, trying to stop his mouth with his fingers and wailing "Nola" through them. She would not need his concern anymore. He need no longer speculate on the permanence of the marsupial lion, nor of the bewilderment and grief of the girl, who had so swiftly made another version of herself and no doubt had other potential versions available within her.

The great Japanese aggressions of December 1941 saved him. No one amongst the military officers he met seemed to have heard of his small-town scandal, and it lay below the level of interest of an embattled nation.

In Brisbane he was appointed CO of a training battalion of militia camped on the city's edge, soldiers of the country's secondary but suddenly full-time force made up of marginally competent raw youth and much older men. They served as temporal brackets to the great conflicts in another hemisphere. They were too old in some cases, too young in others. They were the understudies to the true fighting force, which in those days operated in Africa and Syria, Greece and Crete, and they were exempt by law from being sent to such distant places.

But now they might be asked to step forward if all this newspaper talk of Japanese imminence was accurate. They could be sent to the scatter of Australian-owned archipelagos in the southwest of that supposedly peaceful ocean. Abercare—he knew this himself—was unlikely to be sent with them, even though he had at first returned to the military scene with ideas of the chance of expiatory valor, and of cutting, in his wife's eyes and in the world's, a better figure—that of a fiftysomething-year-old veteran with gifts still to be deployed. He had, within months of their initial estrangement, sent Emily a photo of himself in uniform—taken by a street photographer in Brisbane— that turned out well enough but was not too vainglorious. "This is where your foolish husband finds himself," he had written. "I wish every second of the day that you are well." More sentiment than that would have been a provocation even to a temperate soul like Emily. He found his behavior with Nola incredible now—the acts of another man.

He and Emily met for tea in Brisbane. She told him she was a typist, residing in a boardinghouse, though she had the means to rent or acquire a place of her own. Their conversation was painful. She said, "I know I must be lenient, now we're away from that terrible place. But I'm just not good enough to manage it. I understand, Ewan, that this is as much my fault now. I'm hurt, but that's not an excuse. The onus is on me as well."

And she meant it. So he couldn't get angry when she seemed to condemn him to a long reconciliation.

Afterwards, perhaps a month or so later, a functional letter from her arrived, hoping he was well and informing him that she had decided at her sister's urgent invitation to live for the time being with her and Cecil on the farm in New South Wales.

Yes, thought Abercare, but it's remote. It will be like living in a nunnery.

13

Two soldiers of the garrison who had managed to get leave that Christmas were Private Eamon Cassidy and Corporal Warren Headon. They were hut mates, but not close friends. Cassidy, after all, was not an easy man to get to know. Though obscure fellows, they were not without aspirations and they were members of a theoretical machine-gun crew.

There was meant to be such a weapon, Machine Gun A, located near the Main Road gate. But it was a phantom, an empty space by the wire, which had never been supplied. Headon, with the self-importance of an unsatisfied soul, had taken it as a duty to instruct the fairly pliable Cassidy on the use of their nonexistent weapon from a Vickers machine-gun manual supplied by Major Suttor. Sometimes Suttor would suggest Headon and Cassidy familiarize themselves with the manual and they would sit together in the guard hut peering at it as Headon informed his companion of the gun's wonderfully crafted and divinely complex parts, and the secrets of its smooth operation.

Headon was a good soldier. He had been an expert on the Vickers gun for perhaps a quarter of a century. He'd first fired one in the rear areas of Belgium at the close of the past Great War, and had more

127

recently admired the mechanism while serving in his militia unit in the scattered bush on Sydney's outskirts. The rites of soldiery, the prime condition of kit, were the male morality of his clan—an English immigrant family who had occupied modest army ranks for over a century and a half in a number of imperial locations from Egypt to Bengal.

Secretly, Corporal Headon regretted Cassidy's undramatic plate of a face, apparent stupidity, sparing talk, and temperamental indifference to the ceremonies of mentally assembling a Vickers. They seemed to bespeak his own misfortune—which was that he had lived a boring life, one that could be summarized in too few words and that generated too few anecdotes. He had never married—he knew he was shy in that regard, but had no idea that his didactic tendencies, bordering on a taste for the harangue, drove girls away. He was forced to keep silent when men from the campaigns of Palestine or France or Belgium compared the damage shrapnel had done to their legs or necks or shoulders. He had still been training in the lines when the Great War cranked to a close; he envied other men their wounds. And in this present world conflict, he was a prison warder, and gunner of a phantom Vickers.

Headon had gone home the previous September to see his mother and married sister in Sydney, and when he had taken the tram back to Central Station to catch the train to Gawell, he'd given way to an impulse to stand at its back window and flash a Morse code farewell at them through the rear windows. His sister had written and said they had laughed themselves sick at his acting the goat like that. In fact, under cover of apparent humor, he had been really displaying to the women his soldierliness. He had wanted them to admire, not laugh. He wanted to be seen as a man who knew mysteries, not as someone just showing off.

Headon looked on his Christmas homecoming with indifference; Eamon Cassidy with eagerness. Despite the double-barreled Celtic plushness and piety of his first and second names, Eamon was, as

Headon had observed, an unremarkable human. Years before, Cassidy's parents had crossed from Ireland of the Sorrows as deck cargo, and then traversed the north of England so that his father could work in the Tyneside shipyards, where Eamon also had begun his working life. His father had been a Cork man with no love of Empire, although he had been involved in building a number of large ships for the greatest navy on earth.

At the time of Eamon's first arrival in Sydney in 1923, his search for accommodation had taken him to a terraced house in Newtown, whose door was answered by a fine, mature woman with questioning, dark eyes and a bun of black hair. Her name was Mrs. Maddie McGarry. In the late high summer she wore a blue and white tissue-thin dress. She showed him his room. By the standards of his cramped childhood it looked very welcome, and there was a picture he recognized on the wall—Our Lady of Perpetual Succour. So they were Catholics.

He made an extraordinary decision, given the sobriety of his character. He would take this room whatever she would charge. He would take extra work to pay the rent if he needed to.

"Well," she said, "you don't look like a pisspot or a gambler to me. And I can't very well ask for a reference from your parish priest! Come and have some tea."

She took him into the kitchen, where a thin man sat reading *Smith's Weekly*, an irreverent tabloid. The man looked up. He had a nose they call aquiline, but that was helped by the fact that the other planes of his face had shrunk away. At the sight of Eamon, the surprise of a strange face, he began to cough painfully and put aside, unlit, a narrow cigarette he had rolled. Mrs. McGarry took no notice of the paroxysm and began filling a kettle. The man was introduced by his wife as Pete.

"You Irish?" Pete gasped.

"No, I'm what they call a Geordie. Irish parents. But I'm a Geordie."

Pete said, glancing at *Smith's Weekly* again, "I know what a Geordie is. If you like, I'll take you down to the Sandringham for a drink later."

"I don't mind a drink when someone invites me," said Eamon. "I don't mean I can't pay for it myself. I'm all set for a job just now. I'll happily shout you one."

Pete laughed and, of course, as Eamon already seemed to know from its first notes, the laughter faded away into coughing of such ferocity that Eamon lowered his eyes with a sort of reverence. Brave enough to look up at last, he saw Mrs. McGarry smiling at him from the stove.

"A person doesn't get much blushing around here," she said. "It's not a suburb for blushers."

Within this simple opening conversation between him and Maddie McGarry, a pattern of connection grew. On the way home from the pub, Eamon paused for one of Pete's coughing spasms. When it passed, Pete stood up straight with tears in his eyes. "This makes Maddie crazy," he said, thumping his own chest and with half his voice. When the whole of it returned, he said, "I sleep out on the back veranda so as not to disturb her."

By 1943, Eamon Cassidy had been involved in Maddie and Pete's welfare for twenty years. For he had become Maddie's lover after meeting her one evening two months into his tenancy, twenty years past, in the hallway as she came from her bath. It was about eight o'clock on a summer's night, but Pete was already in his uneasy bed on the veranda. It had become an obsession with him, being out there, she would explain to Eamon later when they were in bed. "And why did it become an obsession?" she asked. Eamon, circling his fingers gently on her right breast, knew he was not meant to answer.

"Not entirely for his lungs," said Maddie, "but because he really has some fear from back then—all to do with being trapped inside."

Eamon was at first uneasy about his gradual taking on of Pete's role with Maddie. He sometimes resolved during his hours at work that he would leave the family behind, the beautiful hungry wife and the noble, suffering husband looking for a night breeze that would console his lungs and his fear of being buried alive. But his arrival home always brought a call from one or other of them. Pete would shake his head over the sacking of Jack Lang, Mussolini's unimpeded grab for Abyssinia, imperialist armor vented against peasant spears, Franco's advance to the Ebro River, iron-ore shipments to Japan, the Anschluss.

Eventually, Pete acknowledged the reality one dusk as they drank tea. "About Maddie," Pete had said. "I know, son. Do you think she'd keep me in the dark? She isn't dishonest. When I remember what it was like before, and I try to reopen this box where it all was, some high explosive or other bangs it shut."

In that one conversation, Cassidy was transformed from lover into a family man. He brought his pay home for Maddie to distribute from a commonly held fund, into which her own part-time pay went. Eamon's engineering shop closed about the time Franco won, and Hitler banged the table asking for Czechoslovakia.

By 1943, his aspirations were chiefly civilian: to eventually get away from the army to mind what you could call "two old friends," if you wanted to simplify matters. When he was home on leave, he saw the shadow over Maddie's face—a tower of hard years had cast it on her at last. He did not like her blood-pressure level or the tremble in her hand, the tentative way she reached for things, this woman who had always been definite.

So when he got on the train that Christmas at Gawell and left Headon's phantom machine gun behind, he was a man who had ailing and dependent elders waiting for him.

14

On Christmas Day Duncan rose at the prodigiously late hour of nine o'clock. Coming into the kitchen, he told Alice, "Woke up at dawn but went on pretending I was having a good time lying there. Have you wished Johnny a happy Christmas yet?"

"No," she said. "I might go down later."

She wiped the morning's sweat off her cheek. It was already fiercely hot, the oven range radiating inside the house and, she could almost imagine, outside in the country itself.

"You're looking tired, Alice," said Duncan.

Duncan was a babe, with the mouth of a babe as mentioned in the Bible. No evil came from that mouth. She had not been to see Giancarlo since the night she had invaded his room, but thought of him kept her awake, she who had always been drugged into profound sleep by the languor of her days. Now she did not know whether to deplore or welcome Duncan, a fellow so deficient in suspicion.

"A man should go to bloody church on a day like this," said Duncan, sighing with mock self-reproach. "But you need a wife to get you there on the big days. On just about any day, for that matter. Look, I bought you this, Alice."

He handed her a canister of Yardley's talcum and two bars of Pears transparent soap.

She thanked him at length. She made a fuss because she felt he deserved it, and she kissed his pate with its reddish, balding hair. The simple offer of this unwrapped present, the thought of him buying it for her, made tears push behind her lids. She took her present for him from the dresser and gave it to him. Rum-flavored tobacco and a book on North Africa, where Neville had spent time before gimcrack generals and gear and aircraft had let him down in Greece. And then handkerchiefs and a woollen vest with an accompanying card. Duncan opened the package and lifted the items one by one, exclaiming at his liking for the patterns on each handkerchief. "Must have used half of your coupon ration," he said in wonder.

This simple man, so easy to deceive, so willing to see no signs but those in weather and livestock. Her mother-in-law, she thought, must have sometimes silently screamed at the limitations of her husband. She wondered whether Neville would end after all as calm, straightforward, and childlike as Duncan. Not likely, though, since Neville had some of his mother's sharpness to him.

"Do you think we maybe ought to wait to fetch Giancarlo up until towards lunchtime?" she asked, to show herself, and whatever unseen powers observed her, that she could wait so long. She was busy on the cloth-wrapped plum pudding, just testing it for moistness, putting it on the sideboard for final boiling later in the day, and placing the chicken and vegetables ready to roast in the oven.

"I hope Neville's having a bit of cheer," said Duncan dreamily.

What sort of Christmas did prisoners have in that unimaginable camp where he was? She agreed with Duncan. Maybe by next year . . . But then what? she wondered. Neville's joy at homecoming running up against my hollowness. He'll deserve better than that.

"The room looks good, though," said Duncan with reviving liveliness.

She had decorated it with all the resources and imagination to hand. There were arches of crepe paper over both doors and ribbons of colored paper strung above their heads at the level where the picture boards would be in other rooms. She had also found a couple of Chinese lanterns, which her late mother-in-law must have bought, when she was searching for novels for Giancarlo to read.

She decided that roasting a chicken in a fuel oven was a delightfully distracting exercise, even on a day like today when sweat ran out of her dark hair and down her temples. There was something to be said for becoming engaged with the heat. It made you feel as if anything undesirable was being purged from the blood. There was the joy of the penitent sinner earning merit in checking the oven now and then, and in seeing the Christmas chicken turn golden and then tend towards brown, and in turning the spuds and the pumpkin and the onions. Before she knew it, she was mixing gravy and standing it on the stove. And now it *was* a decent time to go and fetch Giancarlo.

While Duncan was poring over photographs in the North Africa book she'd given him, she took from the cupboard her present for Giancarlo, a red-covered copy of a Galsworthy novel she'd found in town. This Italian would soon be better read than any of the Gawell yokels. She pushed her way to the shearers' quarters through the scalding sou'wester. She found him sitting reading at his small pine table on the veranda.

Seeing her approach, he stood up and she noticed, not for the first time, that curious boyish downiness on his cheeks, which took a certain angle of light to spot. She could see, as he looked up, the second of joy and uneasiness she created in him, as if he *were* an utter servant.

She came up to him and he stood up in that altered air that Christmas Day possessed, because of the enchantment it had for a person as a child.

"*Buon Natale,*" she said in a low voice.

He had taught her that in the past week. It came with a layer of new vowels she had not previously known.

He said, "Even *anarchici* say *Buon Natale*." He lowered his voice even further. "I say it to you, Alice."

At this soft utterance, she suffered again an impulse to demonstrate her love to the outer world, to show the supervisory sky above them how with one lesson of the flesh he had enlarged her experience beyond all that had been blushingly taught by her mother and earnestly applied by Neville. But she was saved from that by the fact Giancarlo wore Neville's old pants—Duncan had relented for the sake of fit—with Duncan's old collarless shirt, and these inhibited and confused the impulse and provided necessary second thoughts. She hoped these second thoughts would last out the day, and would rescue her more permanently.

Giancarlo put his head back and yelled across the wheat paddock where the robust crop would give them all plenty of post-Christmas labor, and out into the sheep pastures, *"Happy Christmas!"* Crows and cicadas answered with their scathing respects.

"This is my Christmas present," she said, giving him the book.

"Wunderbar," he said, and winked. "Is much too kind."

"It is far too kind," she corrected him for the fun of it.

"Eet is far too kind." Then he repeated it in a lowered and reverent voice. "It is far too kind."

He began to inspect the pages. He raised the book a little to the sky, wanting to hail it in blistering air.

"Beautiful," he said. "I take 'er inside for now."

"You'll take *it* inside. I am a *her*, but a book is an *it*."

"I notice the difference," he murmured, no fear left in him now, and with his lips formed into a shape of a genial hook capable of catching fabrics and souls.

"I come back," he promised.

His absence was itself a temptation to go in through that open door. But he was back in twenty seconds. He had grown solemn.

"I am not very kind—I cannot get you a gift of any present." She waved the oddity of the sentence aside.

"I have to hurry and look at the chook," she told him, and hastened off ahead of him through the gums and past the fruit trees, through the always opened gateway to the back garden, and up to the veranda by way of the path amongst shrubs.

When Giancarlo entered the kitchen in his edgy, orphan way, Duncan called, "Here he is. Happy Christmas, Johnny!"

"And *Buon Natale*, Mr. 'Erman."

Duncan raised his glass as if toasting. "You might be a Fascist bugger, Johnny, but you're *our own* Fascist bugger." Alice saw that though Duncan had had only half a glass of Dinner Ale to celebrate the day, it had brought out in him a vocabulary he didn't normally use.

"*Morte al Fascismo!*" said Johnny, beginning to smile. "*Abbasso il Duce!* To hell the *Fascisti*! Mr. 'Erman, I wish your son he soon get home."

The wish sounded sincere. His eyes had not consulted Alice before uttering it.

"Would you like a Dinner Ale, Johnny?" asked Duncan. "But hang on, I got you this."

He went to the cupboard and hauled out another bottle of red wine. He shook it around to prove its fullness. "Your plonk rubbish."

"Ah," said Giancarlo. He contemplated the bottle, and she knew what he was thinking—a momentary shame. Then he said, with that expansive shy smile, "Thanks a lot and very kind, very kind. I goan have the plonk rubbish, Mr. 'Erman."

"Grab a glass for yourself, Giancarlo," she called, since her hands were full. As he poured himself red wine, Alice arrived at the table with all the chicken and vegetables on the carving dish.

"There are a lot of people in the world," said Duncan with a sudden onset of sadness, "who don't have a meal like this before them today."

But the solemn pronouncement did not dent his appetite.

• • •

At the end of the meal, which both men praised throughout, the pudding was served. Alice sat down, her hair limp on her forehead, and sipped a shandy of Dinner Ale and lemonade. All was normal as, earlier in the day, she had hoped it would be.

Duncan belched softly and said, "Don't you blokes sing all the time, Johnny? Why don't you sing us one of your dago songs?"

"Mr. 'Erman, I don' have a Caruso voice."

Yet Alice could sense the music pressing up the column of Giancarlo's throat. He was willing to sing but was uncertain. Did he think of Neville, too, and doubt if Neville was being allowed to sing?

"No," said Duncan, "don't be shy, Johnny. Spit it out." Giancarlo glanced at Alice for just an instant, checking where she stood on this issue of a song. Then he declared, holding up an index finger, "I know the one song. She's the song from Naples." He had learned to say the English version of the city's name from reading Duncan's copies of the *Herald*.

"Not 'Giovanezza,'" he continued. "No Blackshirt rubbish."

"No Blackshirt rubbish!" said Duncan, echoing Giancarlo and enjoying himself intensely and raising his beer glass like a carouser.

"This one, 'Tiempi Belli.' 'The Beautiful Times.'"

Giancarlo had a pleasant tenor, which he directed in considerable part to Duncan, but, being a performer, he smiled at Alice, too, as if at an audience member. You could tell this lively and sometimes wistful song was one he had learned in a time before soldierhood, prisonerhood. It was more comic than tragic, more bouncy than mournful. Giancarlo waved his head from side to side as verse upon verse rolled unhesitatingly from his mouth. Occasionally, for a line or two, he would clap his hands. Duncan followed his example.

With his song Giancarlo weaved a skin of innocence over the day. Duncan's beery innocence, Giancarlo's innocence infected her and promised to give her back the calm, charted world.

But by night the calmness evaporated, though this time she left her room and then the house by the saner means of the front door, skirted the house on the side removed from Duncan's bedroom, and arrived at Giancarlo's in a broad flanking movement by way of the farmhouse outskirts.

15

A Korean prisoner, Cheong, happened to be amongst those from his compound enlisted to load bags of harvested wheat onto trucks at farms around Gawell in the high days of the summer. They had been the best days Cheong had had since he had been taken prisoner. They had given him a chance through willing labor to show the authorities that he was not at one with the sullen occupants of Compound C, and such a demonstration was important to him. For Cheong was a nationalist, a Korean separatist. He'd been given a Japanese name—Kagome—but he tried to insist other Korean prisoners call him by his real family name.

Alice noticed how energetically the Koreans who came to the Hermans' farm worked under Giancarlo's supervision. These broad-faced men laughed genially at the Italian's commands, which were uttered in a wild combination of Japanese and English. She was relieved for Duncan's sake that over the previous weeks rain had not turned up to harm the crop, that the harvest was in, and in a good year, in a war market.

Cheong was aware of the crinkled old farmer's pleasure, and it enriched his own. The beautiful dark-headed woman—how sad if she were the old man's wife—would bring them a lunch of bread and canned meat, delivering it by bike over rutty tracks. Cheong thought the woman's arrival, her placing of the tray on a table improvised of hay bales, the removal of the cloth from the tray to reveal food were rituals that outweighed greatly the near tastelessness of the bread and the salt of the briny meats.

He had not been long captured at that time. He had been pleased to assert his right to surrender following a charge by his sergeant and the section to which he was servant. In his compound, and even amongst the temporary wheat-bag haulers, many of his Korean compatriots who were young and of short service in the army had not fully lost their Japanese martial gloss. He was a member of a small group of rebels who dissented from the general acceptance of the imperial aims. But those others of his race at least *pretended* to have shamed themselves by surrender. They had not been bullied by their NCOs in Java and Rabaul and New Guinea for as long as Cheong had been there. Besides, a Korean nationalist and secret rebel as was Cheong thought of his *own* coming war—one not against Britain and America and their white armies, but against those pseudo-Asians of Japan who had recruited and used him; against this empire so eloquent about their fraternity towards Asia that they were willing to kill Asians to prove it. He had also by the time of his surrender seen so many Japanese officers gut themselves and soldiers clutch unpinned grenades to their breasts that he knew their cause was absurdly lost, and he was pleased to know it.

Cheong, when captured, had without compunction or shame given the American intelligence officers his Japanese and Korean names as vengeance for the bullying of his regimental sergeant major. From that day he considered himself an insurgent who intended to drive his Asian masters out of the occupied peninsula that was his homeland by loading wheat, felling occasional trees, making and repairing roads. The garrison only rarely had a problem with the Korean work parties, and Cheong was gratified to hear the camp garrison's NCOs report that fact to the officers in command of the prison camp.

When he and his friend Rhim, a Korean military cook, had first arrived at Gawell, they had seemed slated to be sent to Compound C, until their "military standing had been verified," the translator said (whatever that meant). But, in fact, after one night they were moved to join their countrymen in the perhaps less dangerous and certainly more mixed Compound B.

In Compound B Cheong and Rhim met others of their countrymen. This was not like a homecoming. Not all of them were Korean nationalists by any means; some were proud of their part in Japanese military operations. There were occasional vicious brawls, but Cheong and Rhim saved weeks of cigarette rations to acquire knuckle-dusters manufactured in a small illegal workshop under the stage of the recreation hall and were considered hard targets by the Korean loyalists.

They all worked on that farm together, though, and the appearance of the woman with the tray seemed to Cheong a pledge of their coming unity, for they had all studied her with the same intensity, and all their blood had stiffened with hopeless temptation.

He was disappointed when in the Gawell autumn his time working on farms was foreshortened—a blister on his hand from loading hay bales grew septic. He was sent to a doctor inside the Japanese camp who drained the pus. Then, with his hand sulfa sprinkled and bandaged as a certificate of his helplessness and a guarantee against bullying, Cheong set out to reconnoiter his masters' compound in a way he had not felt confident enough to do in his first visit there.

He walked around the huts depending on a well-rehearsed hangdog gait, which had been one of his staple answers to beatings and other chastisements from bawling Japanese officers or noncoms. Thus, close to invisible—or at least he hoped so—he passed with a seemingly naïve face amongst the prisoners of Compound C. He observed them sitting and standing in clumps by the steps of their huts. He observed some men at wrestling practice, some playing baseball, and some working—according to a roster drawn up by the hut commanders—in the vegetable plot.

As he walked along with his stupidest face and bandaged hand, Cheong heard and saw an older man, a sergeant, lead a section of recently arrived men around the corner of a hut, so that they were on the blind side of the gate that led into Main Road. Because it was his nature, Cheong settled himself around the corner of the hut in morning sun and, obscured thus by the angle of the building, listened to the discussion while he fiddled with his bandages as a pretext for lingering.

The sergeant began by discussing the regiment the newcomers belonged to, because, as he said, he'd served under their colonel in Manchukuo. The colonel was gone? he surmised.

There was the usual shamed silence. Compound C men did not like to reminisce. The new prisoners declared the normal story: The colonel had led them against a machine gun, waving them along with his empty pistol. Machine-gun bullets had cut him in two. None of the bastards, Cheong noticed, ever mentioned fright or kneeling weeping or pissing themselves as the enemy surged on and left them behind to be captured by a later wave.

Now Cheong heard the senior man say, "Don't despair, then. You won't be here forever. There will be a night, believe me! And very soon, after the moon wanes. It's a certainty. We can get through that wire—we have the means to do it."

They asked a few questions. Wire cutters? they asked. Living ladders made of men willing to impale themselves? The senior man waved aside these matters of detail. They had no need for this information yet, he said. "The garrison troops are older men and toothless old bats. They won't get all of us, and then, if we overran them, we could get their arms magazine. And then we could really do some damage. Because over there, we know, nearer to the town, is a training camp full of young boys, great lumps of mutton-fed idiots being trained to invade our homeland. They're virgin yokels and their souls are unformed."

Cheong wondered how the fellow knew that—about their souls.

"So those of us who don't fall in the outbreak can fight a final battle outside, against those oafs, old and young."

The new prisoners made joyous noises of assent, which Cheong did not fully believe in. They thanked the old prisoner for this message of hope. But Cheong was sure some of them, however willing they asserted themselves to be, must retain an appetite for a reasonable life, and must ask themselves why, if the senior man was so avid for death, he didn't slice himself up tonight with the cutlery in the mess.

The senior men told the newcomers that in preparation they should do their best not to be lackeys but to be cooperative with the prison guards, to give off an air of having submitted, and to amuse themselves visibly with baseball, wrestling, badminton, and theatricals.

Cheong finished his fake business with the bandage. Nothing further was happening to gratify his interest. The wind nudged at the corner of the hut, gusting him along, and so he presented himself at the gate into Main Road, to be taken back into a compound which, for all its fistfights between Formosans and Koreans, and Koreans and Koreans, was less plagued with lip service to the glories of self-destruction.

PART II

AUSTRALIAN AUTUMN 1944

16

Tengan's position on baseball had not been utterly opportunistic. He was the champion of wrestling in two senses—his undented belief that it was appropriately individual, appropriately martial; and that it required for victory not only physical force but spiritual preparation. It required a warrior, not a sportive cast of mind. He kept himself to a stern regimen, not smoking, avoiding the camp liquor they called "bombo." He was not unhappy that it gave him respect. To be the Compound C wrestling champion was a useful enhancement of the moral standing he wished to maintain until the culmination.

The camp wrestling championship had been spread over the last weeks of summer and into early autumn, and Tengan had with some ease defeated all old and new hands who'd presented themselves. In half his matches the referee did not have a chance to wave his fan at Tengan's opponent, to yell the formal encouragement, "You are still in it!" before Tengan had managed to hustle the other wrestler from the square. These opponents exuded self-doubt from the time they presented themselves, seemed at some level of their spirits to beg for an early humiliation, and thus deserved only a few seconds' tussle.

Others demanded, by the wounds they had received in battle and recovered from, to be treated more tenderly and technically. He could sense, but was unwilling in some cases to exploit too suddenly, an imbalance between the elements of strength within a mind and the unchosen weakness of a body. He who had suffered only face wounds, of which he carried barely a scar, could not help but respect the more serious approach to death these men, recovered from severe wounds, had made, and which had left them impaired. He let them grapple with him and sway him past his apparent point of balance. He smelled their sweat, blended of camp ennui, memory of defeat, of insignificance on the face of the earth, that a successful wrestling move might allay. He allowed them to try to haul him over their shoulders by an arm drag, an act of ambition that was beyond their means, and then flattered them by stretching his arm in the direction of the ground as if he would soon need it for support. He'd do all that a few times, and then, as if he had tapped an unsuspected well of new strength, would pitch them slowly over, yaw their shoulder down, and make them reach for the steadying and forbidden earth, as the umpire waved his wooden quasi fan and yelled, "You are still in it!"—even though they weren't. The opponent would grasp the gravel, at which the referee would scream, "You have done it!" and raise his fan to signify Tengan's victory.

The winner of the B pool, whom Tengan must now face, was a husky young man named Oka. Oka had suffered no battle wounds, other than from malarial mosquitoes. He was in prime health and possessed the sort of mental strength enjoyed not by deep thinkers but by men of simple elements.

Behind the main assembly hall some months before, Tengan had begun a utilitarian affair with Oka during a performance of *The Reed Cutter*, in which they had both had minor roles. Oka delivered his lines woodenly but had a pleasant voice. Tengan himself was only a middling singer but knew he had feminine looks, something he needed to rise above as a pilot but which, when they were made up for theatrical purposes, he could rather enhance.

It had somehow been all the more erotic, having organized the meeting on the less lit end of the recreation hall, to grasp each other in the dark and, with the noise of the play and the audience behind them, to locate each other under the heavy costumes. This affair of convenience lasted a few weeks because Tengan went through phases of fastidiousness when he could not convince himself of the appropriateness of sex between soldiers. Despite Oka's enthusiasm, sometimes bolstered by bombo intake, Tengan would not have chosen his company had he been a free man. Oka had, for one thing, called him "pretty"—that forbidden term—and this large man-child was doing more than just neutering a need—within the limits of his imagination, he was making a serious alliance of the flesh. Whereas, were Tengan given the chance to marry, he would never have troubled a male again.

Hundreds had watched the elimination rounds, and the entire camp—except those in hospital with a recurrence of malaria, colds, and aftereffects of wounds—turned out for the final, which took place around a square drawn in dust and four-and-a-half meters long on each side. It was contested on a late-autumn Sunday amongst an audience that seemed at peace with itself. Almost directly north of Gawell, but thousands of miles removed from it, an island named Saipan, in the Marianas, considered to be the doorstep of their nation, was preparing itself for a massive enemy attack, but Compound C was not aware of this, and would have considered, in any case, that America was engaged in a fatal overreach in trying to strike so far north.

Before meeting Oka and the crowd outside, Tengan, in his now-empty hut, took off his deliberately bleached jacket and pants, his sweater and woollen underwear and, still wearing his shirt, tied on his wrestling loincloth. Hearing the crowd milling by the wrestling arena, he knelt in the middle of the hut to meditate. To allow the wrestler to perform well, the mind needed to be cleared of fear and ambition. The ferocities later to be directed at the opponent should not be anticipated, but be retained for later release. Tengan now mut-

tered the invocation to his forebears so that they might imbue him
with their strength—the same strength they had given him to become an aviator rather than a mere infantryman or sailor. His father,
an ironworks manager and well-liked fellow, arose randomly to mind.
A wrestling aficionado himself, in a small way, more a spectator who
drank rather than an athlete who fought. That the father would approve of the coming encounter distracted him. Tengan soothed that
irrelevance away and reached for the necessary null, unitary thought
out of which strength arose. Then, settled in soul, he emerged barefoot from his hut.

Around the square, men stepped back as soon as they saw his arrival and made a channel down which he passed towards the referee.
In the center, he made a respectful bow to this officiator, a man of
nearly sixty years who had come in from the civilian compound to
adjudicate the match. He had been, until the outbreak of hostilities,
a merchant in Samoa and a wrestling aficionado, even if a provincial
one. To fail to show him supreme respect was to create a weakness in
oneself, a germ of defeat.

Through another avenue of men, Oka came, shedding his shirt.
His chest muscles were pronounced, and his thighs—familiar to Tengan as opponent and lover both—were like tree trunks. He certainly
resembled a victor, but in a facile, merely muscular way, and Tengan
knew that Oka had no gift for meditation, and that he could not have
prayed very eloquently. Oka made his bow to the referee but, Tengan
saw with hope, he had a near grin on his lips, a betrayal of nervous-
ness.

The referee announced their wrestling names (Wolf and Bear),
and they both bowed to him before taking the ends he pointed out
to them. He carried the usual wooden fan and, gesturing with it,
had them approach each other from outside the opposite ends of the
ring. They stepped over the markings in the dust to be sure not to
obscure them. Reaching each other, they crouched and flexed their
leg muscles right and left, then pumped their legs up and down be-

fore retreating out of the ring yet again. Then, at the next wave of the referee's fan, they again advanced and crouched, facing each other at spots in the dust indicated by the official.

As the referee retired to the corner of the square, Oka yelped piercingly and then let his utterance turn into an ursine growl. Tengan uttered a breathy howl. They contemplated each other eye to eye, and made openhanded feints towards each other. Then the slaps and attempts at grasping began.

Some matches were fast to begin, in that one could get an early hold on the opponent's shoulders after a few slaps and writhings. But that was not the case with Oka. He countered every raid by Tengan, who wanted early contact and could feel in turn the force of his opponent's buffeting attempts to grasp him by the arm, all with the exploratory purpose on Oka's part of finding if it was really possible to drag Tengan over a shoulder and try to propel him down to the dust. Yet Oka could not manage that, and so they went on for minutes, arms tucked under each other's armpits, trying to force the other out towards the margins. One of them would break off suddenly to confuse, and then attempt to lift the other by the loincloth, or to get his left arm around his opponent's neck and his right between the legs, in the hope of a smackdown.

They could both counter like lightning and Oka still had the breath to growl to excite his followers. The skills of both men ensured that they circled and eyed each other for periods of time. Tengan found, however, that his opponent's arms, in reaching for him, sacrificed force for speed.

The contest went on in that way for ten minutes, with the prisoners shouting and roaring with gratitude for such a long-running challenge. But the pernicious instant came when Oka got a grip of both Tengan's shoulders and tripped him from behind. It was so sudden that it seemed to have been done by hypnosis or enchantment. Tengan, on his heels or backpedaling, and trying to find anchorages for his feet, could see the referee circling around them with his fan raised, expecting that this time he might be forced from the ring. However, Tengan managed to achieve a hold under Oka's armpit and slowed Oka down. He realized now, dizzy, gasping from the energy he had used, that he had just escaped the possibility of humiliation—of being forced not only from the ring but deep into the crowd.

But Tengan brought his mind back from indulgence in the fantasy of defeat, and held Oka by the elbow and uttered another howl while he had a remnant of air inside him. He felt Oka trying to lift him and undermine his stability by inserting both hands under his loincloth. Oka's iron knuckles gouged his hips, but Tengan hugged him beneath the armpits and raised him a centimeter into the air. It did Tengan a great deal of mental good to find he could manage such a lift, modest as it was, and as much energy as it used.

It was important for Tengan to show now that he could do what Oka had shown. Tengan moved his own hands and hooked them on either side of Oka's loincloth and lifted, creating the possibility of twisting the hulking soldier onto his back. He felt Oka's arms, suddenly endowed with a new lung-crushing force, attempt to roll him sideways. Neither succeeded in their purpose. Then Tengan felt a great pressure around his shoulders, and the risk was that it might crush him. I can lift him again, he thought.

In fact, as he did it, the pressure eased. From his crouch position he might move Oka suddenly off-balance and out of the zone—this was the way Tengan would assert himself. He owed his forebears this much skill.

He had Oka under the armpit and unbalanced him now, and began to guide him to the edge of the zone. Oka's right hand, however, went under the rim of Tengan's loincloth and lifted Tengan's right leg off the dust, leaving it dangling like that of an unwillingly hoisted child. Tengan spent so much energy trying to retrieve his dignity and his leverage that Oka was now able to take him by the shoulders a last time. Tengan himself slapped resonantly at the big man's ribs, and tried to find solid ground again with his feet.

Now it became apparent that Oka had been doing what Tengan had with some of his opponents—putting on a show for the audience and awarding Tengan a decent time of survival in the ring. Tengan's strength and will were depleted. He had expended all his breath on his earlier lift of this huge animal, and now he felt himself lowered by Oka at an angle that gave him no purchase; and then raised again and lowered closer to the limit of the zone, and again lifted and lowered and, finally, hurled over the line.

He saw the smear of shouting faces as if they, not he, were spinning from Oka's force. Some were hooting. A soldier had made a flier fly. Tengan felt his shoulder strike one spectator. By a massive refusal to land amongst the bystanders like a rejected fragment, he fell to one knee and arrested his momentum. He looked up and saw the pro-baseball hut leader Kure smiling down at him with something worse than scorn—paternal pity. Then he stood in the midst of the howling and cheering spectators.

The rules required that he be expressionless, and having heard the referee shout irrevocably, "Bear's victory!" he knew that he must return to the square. He did it, bile and shame in his mouth. Oka seemed appropriately solemn and humble as Tengan returned, and there was between them a new contest of impassivity. They bowed, side by side, to the crowd. Both of them made a ritual gesture of thanks to the referee. Both left in opposite directions without comment.

They walked towards the showers, the plumbing the enemy had imposed on them, a comfortless cement hut with a row of metal water sprays above head level. They took their sweat- and dust-drenched loincloths off and in a silence that continued the augustness of their duel, they stood side by side. The water came down cold on their shoulders and stung the places on Tengan's body where Oka's heavier slaps had landed and where his hold had tortured Tengan's ribs. Without looking at each other, they washed themselves and rinsed the soap off. Shaking the water from his eyes, Tengan looked up and saw Oka direct an intense yet strangely casual stare straight at him. It was an assertion of dominance—the dominance he had earned. It was also an argument that the pain and energy they had inflicted on each other was part of their private association.

The rumor was that the Australian guards watching the wrestling got erections, excited by the lithe bodies—less hairy and less gross than their own—grappling with each other. Maybe. But what was certain was that some of the prisoners became excited, too, and Tengan himself had secretly felt that excitement. So he knew in what terms he must now pay for his defeat. It was fair, and Oka deserved reward. When the victor took one small step closer, Tengan could see the man's long penis engorged before him. He knelt at once, the water still falling on his shoulders, and took Oka in his mouth. He thought that it would be a wonderful thing to bite into this thong of flesh and not to yield. But the subsequent story would be a humiliation to him, not to Oka, and even worse than failing in the wrestle. He began to apply his mouth with intent.

17

The first cold days arrived, the bush iciness noticeable at dusk and night and dawn, though the days remained as shirtsleeved as summer. By the last days of March, Alice had renounced her Giancarlo mania three times, and relished how natural she could be at table in the evenings with him there and Duncan jabbering away. Should his mood coincide with hers, Giancarlo enjoyed being resolved and calm. But sometimes their spates of appetite overlapped, and her manner or his would become a message, and they would quickly reenter a new season of delirium.

So there were days she blazed, and was once again delighted with this blight, this fever, which attracted somehow the applause of the unthinking sky.

The cooler weather gave them, one afternoon, every excuse to be inside Giancarlo's room. There they took risks of discovery which were in some senses massive in scale, tearing at each other and equal in the contest, no pallid carefulness in Giancarlo's hands but a desire to take and breathe her all in. They operated in a democracy of hunger, though the hunger seemed to belong to another woman—that ferocity, that strange alacrity, that lack of discomfort.

This was worth exile or death, or being pointed out in some plain street.

Nothing could have saved them from an acute humbling, had Duncan visited them. Yet they both knew Duncan was a man of severe privacies. His timid entry was not to be expected as they fell on each other. As well as that, he did not seem to belong to their hours, but to be pottering about beneath an alternative shower of trite seconds, different from their enlarged ones, which rendered him and them parallel and nonintersecting.

That day she was careful of the time—the good sense of her Scottish ancestry came into play in this area, if not across the entire folly. At the close of the visit she managed to leave the room and the shelter of the shearers' quarters with utter and delightful hypocrisy, like a nurse leaving a ward, a teacher leaving a class.

Sometimes, when longing rose in her, an angry contempt for Duncan emerged. Couldn't the old fool see what was happening? Was all that mute signaling, going on with the passing of a knife or a condiment, so hard to interpret? Couldn't Duncan also guess that Giancarlo spoke one grade of English to him and another to her, an improper vocabulary of arousal, sanctified on Giancarlo's lips but originally acquired through the profanity of guards and by way of earnest application in the prison compound to the study of such terms?

She knew, too, at these moments, that she had put Giancarlo himself in a hard situation in many ways, but not least because he felt he had to work himself to the point of near exhaustion—she had seen him laboring like that on the summer wheat, sweating and distracting himself—as if to make it all up to Duncan.

Yes, he would agree solemnly with her, they must try to make an end to it. Resolve might take them through a week of abstinence, perhaps through ten self-congratulatory days. And then evaporate.

Though Duncan praised Giancarlo's mechanical skills, when autumn came it was obvious that, though apparently a townsman's son, he had done some lambing in the past. He required very little instruction. He could lift ewes felled by the gravity of giving birth, could deliver the lambs if necessary, could mark and dock them, and delicately castrate them with a knife. The bravado of using teeth for the purpose seemed far from his earnest style. Sheepdogs seemed to hang around him now for orders, though he was not yet as expert as Duncan was at directing them.

Since Duncan forwent his heavy midday meal at times of demanding activity, Alice beheld Giancarlo's competence when she cycled down with their lunchtime sandwiches and tea thermos. The lambing coincided with one of their periods of mutually resolved abstinence, and Alice was relieved by the self-imposed lie that what was a mere pause was an entire end to the lunacy between her and Giancarlo. So the three of them sat down at the edge of the pasture to hold a brief and primitive picnic, and after a little conversation with Duncan and Giancarlo, in which Giancarlo virtuously avoided transmitting signals, as she did, too, she would ride back along the track to the homestead, occasionally stopping to look at the men resuming work and the movements and energy of Giancarlo. He had turned a plain rural task into a sequence of captivating novelties.

In late April, Colonel Abercare finally took some leave to visit his wife, Emily, at her sister and brother-in-law's property in Tathra on the south coast. Leaving Gawell, he traveled as a husband and private citizen, but his rank made it an easier journey, first class and with a sleeping compartment overnight to Sydney. There he would need to change trains and travel south along a beautiful and seemingly illimitable coastline with notable escarpments crowding in, blocking the afternoon sun and bringing an earlier dusk.

According to Emily's letters, she seemed content there in Cecil's verdant pastures. She got on well with Florence, who never made her feel like a relative who was endured simply because there was nowhere else for her to go.

As for going to pay court to Emily again—its subtleties were such as to interrupt his sleep. During the invasion scare of '41, when he had commanded the militia battalion, he had half hoped for the great intrusion by the enemy to take place and absolve him of his sins by death or heroism. But now that he was a pure bureaucrat, he had no mitigating military perils of the here-today, gone-tomorrow variety to shield him. Demanding forms of truthfulness, diplomacy, penitence were incumbent on him. And indeed he could exercise them with sincerity. Reconciliation was his total ambition.

He had, in barracks in India and elsewhere, seen the faces of men such as he going sour for a telltale second at balls and mess dinners. Men who knew they were sidelined now, that the great military river would never pick them up again, that they would need hereafter to be content, no matter what talents burned unquenched within them, with middling rank and the title it might give them for mild respect in some limited place in England or the dominions.

His own fatuity had not directly altered his military career, as it had altered and destroyed the careers of other officers. He could not blame his never having been given brigade or divisional command, with a major-general's double crown at his shoulders and red lapels, on the fact he'd gone after a senior officer's wife. On the other hand, those who weighed promotions might have sensed in him the possibility of losing proportion. Those submerged tendencies were sometimes instinctively read by the wise. So he had grown out of military vanities. His one ambition was to get Emily back: marriage mending was the supreme task. Occasionally, during the day around the camp, Abercare would be shifted about like seaweed by a wave of grief for his wife; for her orphaned childhood after her parents had died in a truck on some perilous road in Rhodesia, and then her failure—which might well be his failure too—to bear children. Parentless and childless, she'd had only him.

Still, women did not want pity; they wanted the other—the death-less love. He was always puzzled about which of the two operated in him, and did not see them as poles but as two sides of the one entity, one of which underwrote the other. That might have explained his folly back there—that he'd tired of the pity and the politeness and wary tenderness they had somehow come to treat each other with. Now, pity and politeness and wary tenderness looked pretty desirable to him.

Cecil told him in a letter that he'd overheard Emily tell a dinner guest that she must join poor Ewan in Gawell soon, and she gave as an excuse for not having gone earlier the fact that the seasons were so severe out there. He hoped this excuse would give way to another soon—to her excuse for going to Gawell after all. So Ewan Abercare's ambitions ran.

For him, part of the pain of going to Tathra was the surmise as to whether Emily had told her sister about *it*. He imagined that her sister knew something was not right, but would have made no fuss about it. Surely the brother-in-law, Cecil, who was a decent enough fellow and who had in the past sat up with him whisky-bibbing and exchanging anecdotes, and mentioning nothing of marriage, would have suspicions, too, but, Abercare hoped, no exact knowledge.

The slow overnight train to Sydney then, the Western Mail! That title "Mail" stated a priority for envelopes over passengers and meant mailbags must be dropped off at and dragged along the gravel of every larger station throughout the night journey. Even without that, he would have slept badly. He woke frequently to locomotive brakes applied or released, or to carriage doors banging and the inconsiderate shouts of railway yokels. In the sour dawn he was served a cup of tea and an arrowroot biscuit by the porter, and disembarked at Sydney Central, where a military porter carried his bag and took him to the officers' section of the tearoom. Here he read the *Herald*. He had a novel with him, too, but could not read it for more than three minutes at a time. Nothing stuck. Print didn't stick. So come back, Emily, and save me from this fretfulness and from the stupidity of envisaging a fling with a certain Mrs. Galloway, the solicitor's wife, who had glimmered in his direction at a civic reception at the Council Chambers at Gawell.

Mrs. Galloway was extremely pretty in a waspish, disappointed way. What they were beginning to call "neurotic"—a slightly kinder word than "mad" but one he couldn't have defined. One thing he knew: I attract the sick, and the sick attract me.

Now, on the south coast train on a lovely autumn afternoon, he saw the empty Pacific Ocean the Allies were slowly reclaiming. So immediate to the railway line, the sea did its glittering utmost to charm him, and only an occasional marring waft of coal dust from the engine came between it and him. He felt a spell of nausea as the train pulled in at the country station, which lay between the blatant azure of the beach and Tathra's lush, shadowy hills.

Cecil met him in his Buick with a rectangular coal gas bladder in a wooden frame on top of it, an imperfect means of dealing with petrol rationing, and drove him away from the sea through the somnolent town and up the valley of steep, luxurious pastures and fifteen miles inland, where he bred beef and sheep so profitably. Abercare asked after Florence and was told she had had some women's problems but was altogether in good health. "Still a perky talker," said Cecil. "Natter, natter, natter. Emily's company's very good for her."

Cecil's great-grandparents had owned these amiable coastal acreages, and he had met Emily's younger sister on a steamer to England— he had been making his Grand Tour. Florence had seemed pretty and somewhat pathetic after the simultaneous death of her parents. It was true that from the start of Abercare's own courtship with Emily, her orphan condition—even though she had been seventeen when it happened and was thirty when Abercare had first met her—had sharpened his feelings for her.

"And what about Emily?" Abercare asked, blushing beneath his tan. "I mean, I get letters from her. But . . . your assessment. Good health, would you say?"

"Oh, Emily's in great spirits, old fellow. I wouldn't worry too much about that."

Cecil spoke quickly, to get past that giant fact that Emily and Abercare weren't living together. Cecil seemed to prefer to pretend Emily was on a fairly long holiday.

"For sisters," he told Abercare, "they like each other's company pretty well. There's a link between sisters who like each other. You and I don't have a chance of understanding or disrupting it."

"Oh," said Abercare, "I wouldn't want to."

They talked awhile about cattle prices, the world's hunger for wool—in neither of which Abercare was much interested. The drought was years over and there had always been rain here on the coast anyhow. And the war drove up demand. The colonel knew his brother-in-law was minting money.

Abercare got out and opened the gate into the property. Beyond its screen of poplars, the house was long, low, deep-veranda'd, graced in front with a garden full of winter-enduring purple, white, violet, and scarlet. He walked to the house, and his brother-in-law parked the car and got out.

With an uncertain face, Emily appeared with her sister at the door. They had heard the Buick turn up. Her lean, handsome looks immediately roused desire in him and hope of contentment.

"Hello, Ewan," she called.

That was hopeful, thought Abercare. Her sister came out all the way to within feet of him, chattering about how well he looked in his uniform. But was that some weight he'd put on? she asked.

"Not enough soldierly exercise out there," Abercare apologized. "The desk is our only obstacle course."

He smiled across Florence's shoulder at Emily, who nodded. When he went up to her, she let herself be chastely kissed.

They had some sherry in the living room. Again, how much did Florence know? It seemed to him from the friendly style of his sister-in-law and her husband that Emily's reticence had saved him from utter shame here, in this homestead, and that she had laid down an unspoken ordinance that he be warmly treated, without a hint of chiding. Florence was certainly a conversationalist of a kind, and her flow of trivial chat rode like a well-intentioned tide over all that was unsettled between Emily and him. She was interrupted only by her visits to the kitchen. She had had one of the dairy farmers' daughters to cook the meals before the war, she said, but what with the manpower regulations, the girl was off doing men's work.

Emily asked, "Ewan, would you recommend Cecil get an Italian POW? Have you any to spare?"

"Well," said Abercare, as if the question were more than fanciful, "in a general sense, yes. I mean, we've got hundreds out there on farms. We get a number—perhaps half a dozen—returned each month as unsatisfactory or insolent. But I'd suspect in half those cases it's the farmer who's at fault."

"I bet you're right about that one," said Cecil. "Some of these old farmers are sour, grudging beggars."

"Do the Italians behave themselves around women?" asked Florence.

For reasons Emily would understand, the question made him uncomfortable.

"It seems so," he said quickly. "And a number of them are from the Italian countryside and understand livestock."

They moved on from the Italians. Florence chattered about her recent Sydney trip. At the Australia Hotel they have a jazz band in the lounge, not a palm court orchestra. The Americans had altered the nature of things! At the Trocadero it was all about jazz and swing and something called jive, and you'd need an American to explain the boundary line between them all. "Australian girls are queuing up to dance in this ridiculous jitterbug way as if they want to say, 'Look, we can be just as much up to date as you Americans.'"

"Did you queue up to jitterbug, Flo?" asked Cecil. "Is there something I don't know?"

"I don't have the joints anymore. It's still the two-step for me."

Emily reminded her, "There was a time you danced the Charleston in the Muthaiga Club, Flo. Is jive sillier than the Charleston?"

"I thought you were supposed to be my sister," said Flo, in mock chagrin.

The two men both chose to hoot, and Cecil shouted, "Touché! I'd venture to say that it would make sense to you, Flo, if you were still twenty-two and living in a town full of amiable, ambling Yanks. I remember like Emily that fifteen or more years ago you rolled down your stockings and danced! I saw that. I thought, what a girl and what a free spirit! Next thing I knew you were taking me to Mass. It was a pretty nifty piece of missionary work you did there, old girl."

"The interesting thing," said Florence, ignoring Cecil's gibe, "is that white American soldiers are said to hate black ones. But they sing their songs and dance their dances. It's as if we decided to take up Aboriginal corroborees. Highly puzzling."

"There is no accounting for what people do when they're young," Emily asserted, keeping her eyes to herself. She became contemplative then. Her manner reminded Abercare of times in Elgin before the separation, in the era of rumors, when he'd enter a room where she might be talking to other people and see her features lively and imbued with a sort of light till she noticed him, when her conversation became subdued, dutiful, and halting. He had reduced her to that from her true self, in that terrible limbo time on the farm, before he met up with Nola.

But here at her sister's house it seemed her powers of conversation had mended a great deal. She *had* been party to the evening, had thrown in her share of observations.

It was time for bed. Cecil and Ewan sat up for one more whisky, but they could not make it a session, for Cecil was driving to the sales in Bega the next day. When Ewan Abercare got to the bedroom, he found his wife on her knees, finishing with her rosary beads, just beginning to ball them in her fist at the end of saying what they called "a decade." The bedroom was cold. In a flannelette nightdress she rose from the floor, and Colonel Abercare saw her thin ankles and the protuberant balls of her feet. Lovely, lanky English bones were the bones she had. She was good-looking in that Nordic way, a woman whose ancestors came from dim regions where complexions could afford to be white and unblemished, and who had then been dragged off for the Empire's sake to the most blatant sun on the planet.

He thought, I was corrupted by Indian and Sinhalese women before such bones came my way. But it wasn't the women's fault. They were fulfilling the role of servants and bringing to it gifts that Northern Christianity had attempted to suppress in European women.

In this cold, plain bedroom, with a picture of the Virgin on one wall and a framed photograph of a racehorse Cecil had once owned on the other, and with Emily as his sole comfort and hope, it seemed to him an even more astounding, ridiculous thing that rank and hope, recorded diligence, loyalty, and companionship had ever meant, in the balance of his mind, less than the chance of a fifteen-minute adventure, with a possible repeat or two.

He and Emily were of course now inevitably uneasy at the prospect of sharing a bed again.

"Well," he asked, taking off his jacket. "How have you really been, dear?"

Even in his thick khaki pullover he felt the cold.

"No coughs or anything, I hope?"

"No," she said. "The old house up north was much worse than this."

"Yes, it could get much chillier up there," he admitted briskly. That house sold at a sacrifice price and was never to be visited again. She flipped the sheets, blankets, and eiderdown aside and launched herself athletically and girlishly into the bed. A high jumper when she was young. He knew that.

"I have to admit," he said, "there have been some beggars of frosts out Gawell way. The interpreter says the Japanese can't understand why it doesn't snow. We had a brief dusting of the stuff—when was it?—early last winter. But it aches and aches with cold and all we get are these ironclad frosts."

"Ewan?"

"Yes."

"I don't know where it comes from," she said, relaxing her shoulders. "When I go quiet."

"That's no problem."

"You probably think I do it to get even, but it's something older than our problem. It's me. I just wanted to let you know. And I've taken too long to cure. I've been difficult. A reasonable person might say that a reconciliation should have taken place long ago. It's an indulgence, and I feel sorry for you."

"You feel sorry for *me*?"

"Because I haven't known how to do it."

As if to demonstrate that she still felt apartness, she arranged the bedclothes about her functionally, laying definite and discreet claim to part of the territory. "Are you seeing another woman out there? I could barely blame you. My pride would have caused it."

"No," he said. "I thought that was understood. I'm willing to wait for you to come out there and join me. Because you're the only true love I've had."

He recollected Mrs. Galloway. Her gin-inflamed gaze lighting on him, unchecked and hungry; the chance of compounding the mayhem of his life and hers.

"Forgive me for asking," she said. "I know that you're a man and that men have certain needs. But I can't manage it all yet. I have a real phobia, for some reason, of turning up in a new town and . . ."

"No," he said. His face burned beneath his tan. "No, it won't happen."

He stood some feet from the bed. He would not get in with the ease of possession that characterized Emily. He removed his pullover and exposed a crisp khaki shirt—one as issued by the quartermaster, no visits to private shirtmakers as in the old days—and he wore his pants and socks still.

"Look, do you think you *might* consider coming out there at some stage? I know nice people—Dr. Garner and his wife. He and his partners come up and do the rounds in the hospitals now and then. There's an interesting priest out there, a Father Delaney. We've even got an Italian army padre as a prisoner. Father Frumelli. Not sure he isn't a bit Fascist from the songs he lets some of them sing at Mass. Or else he's naïve. But what I'm trying to say is, you'd make friends there. Fairly easily."

He could see the idea of Gawell flicker a second in her mind as a chance. But there'd be no final answer tonight.

Behind a screen, he put on his pyjamas and approached the bed.

"Would you put the light out, like a dear?" she asked. He went across the room and did it. It was an autumn night designed for shared body warmth. Whether he would be given any he was not sure. But he had made progress, he knew that as well.

"So let's sleep on the prospect of coming to Gawell," he suggested as he settled under blankets. He had an erection and turned aside to hide it.

She said, "Very well, Ewan."

She turned her back and settled herself to rest.

That night he was troubled by half dreams of the Urdu-speaking woman who had been his maid and bedmate when he was a callow first lieutenant. He had actually believed, from her knowledge of erotic possibility, that she was a partner to his pleasure. He had not understood it was the habit of submission; that she made the bed and set the table and sat on his prick and that it was all one to her. It was necessary to achieve her take-home pay with a bonus for copulation.

He heard Emily wake in the middle of the night to use the chamber pot. A chaste and—he thought—careful flow.

18

In late autumn there was a visit to Compound C by a Red Cross delegation of two Australian Red Cross men and the vice-consul in charge of the Japanese bureau of the Swiss consulate general. In some ways it was like earlier visits. They all wore solemn suits and plain ties. None of them spoke Japanese; they depended on Nevski. Thus, with Major Suttor and Sergeant Nevski attending them, the officials inspected the huts, the sleeping arrangements, the cook house, the supplies, the sanitary arrangements—all as usual. There was an assembly at which they asked through Sergeant Nevski if there were any complaints, and promised immunity to those who did complain. There was the profound complaint amongst them that they had been captured in the first place, but they did not deign to voice it. In fact, they offered no plea and uttered no dissatisfaction. They saw the Russian sergeant in his ill-fitting uniform turn to the Red Cross delegates to assure them that his translation of their invitations and reassurances had been accurate.

The novelty turned out to be that the officials had brought with them a Red Cross photographer. He began his work in the two Italian compounds, taking photographs for the Red Cross to send to families. That took some days, and then it was the turn of Major Suttor's compound. Nevski and an escort of guards accompanied the major through the gate in Main Road. Sergeant Nevski made it apparent to a meeting of hut leaders in the recreation hall that the photographer was to take a portrait of each prisoner in Compound C and the Red Cross would send the photographs home to families. If any man did not wish his photograph sent home, the photographer was still authorized to take photographs of them, purely for Red Cross records.

Aoki stepped forward and growled, not entirely negatively, and declared that they would need some time to decide this matter with their men. Major Suttor said that he would return with the photographer a little later in the day to hear their decision. But they must have their photographs taken, entitled with their names, to ensure the Red Cross could help them be repatriated when the war was over.

Again, as there had been over the less crucial matter of baseball, there was a quickly assembled hut leaders' meeting, this time in Aoki's barracks. Once Aoki, as camp leader, had spoken, it was apparent there was unanimous feeling against the photography. Goda and Aoki and Tengan were one on the matter, and so were the rest of the hut leaders. They in turn went off to put it to their huts, and no voice dissented, not even the Presbyterian, Ban, who did not oppose the combined will in his hut of the rejects, of stragglers on jungle marches, of homosexuals who made an unseemly show of their love, and of those rendered unreliable because of the shock of battle. The belief was that the photographs would be sent to families who were already reconciled to the individual prisoner's death, and thus confuse, dishonor, and aggrieve.

At two o'clock that afternoon Major Suttor entered the compound again, to the sound of a bell, and saw the prisoners assemble. Nevski stepped up to speak to Aoki. Aoki replied with an uncooperative rumble. Nevski marched back to Suttor and his line of guards. They did not want photographs taken for their families *or* for the Red Cross records, he reported.

Suttor by now profoundly resented having had to organize this meeting. He needed to marshal all his composure to stop himself launching into a furious harangue and threatening these indulged creatures with unlikely punishment. He had not received any photograph of his son in captivity, and it bewildered him, even apart from the insights into the culture provided by Nevski, that these men should debate such an offer, and then reject it.

Tears pricked Suttor's eyes. He said, "Tell the bastards it's required that they submit to being photographed so the Red Cross can attach it to their files in Geneva. That's all."

Nevski said he had already told them.

"Tell them again," Suttor demanded. "Tell them it is compulsory!"

Nevski saluted, turned, and reiterated this. At once every man in the compound dropped to his haunches, crossed his legs, and covered his face with his hands.

"Tell them to fucking get up," said Suttor, and Nevski did, but they would not obey.

"No photographs," called Tengan in English from behind his hands.

Aoki wondered how these fools could not understand that, with their burial services having taken place, men could not now show their faces to a photographer. Suttor told Nevski to inform them they would stay there, in that awkward and ultimately painful posture, indefinitely. He took the photographer and Nevski and the guards out of the gate, and watched the compound for a time from Main Road. When the prisoners did not move from their crouched and face-covering posture, he at last marched away.

I could be writing, he thought. Instead, this bullshit!

After some hours, Nevski visited Suttor in his office and told him they had not moved. Suttor called the Swiss vice-consul, who had by now returned to Sydney, and told him what was happening—that the Japanese were all crouched, their hands in front of their faces. The vice-consul sounded remarkably calm about it. "Oh yes," he said. "There are reports of the same problem in camps elsewhere.

There is regrettably little to be done if they continue to oppose the measure. It will delay their repatriation, but they don't seem to mind."

The sun was getting low in Gawell. The photographer had to leave the next day to go to the camp at Wye, where, except for the Italians—and they had some Germans there, too—the small number of Japanese would likely also resist his work.

Suttor, still aggrieved that his prisoners would pretend to be ghosts, called Abercare and suggested a punishment he considered utterly appropriate. (He did not understand that it was a punishment that would gratify Tengan.) "I want to send a platoon into the compound to confiscate every baseball bat they can find. I'll put men with light machine guns in the towers."

He heard a silence. He knew that Abercare was chewing the insides of his cheeks over the matter, and Suttor found it hard to endure those few seconds. For lack of a photograph of his imprisoned son, forcing these men to be photographed or punishing them for refusing was an imperative that burned within him. It had become more his business than that of the Red Cross.

Abercare spoke at last. "I shan't confirm that order," he said. "There is no regulation that says they need be photographed, and it must be obvious to the Swiss that they are not being brutally treated or starved. If we did what you suggest, then they would grow more intractable still, *and* . . . and we would give them material to use against us."

"Then they'll have won," said Suttor. "They'll have bloody won, sir. As they always do, however we paint it."

"Well," said Abercare contemplatively, "they're only winning in their own minds. They're losing in terms of reality. Look at the war news. Events have shown, though, that it's futile playing games with these chaps. They are not subject to the same set of reactions. No, I would really recommend, Major, that you not enter into direct contest with them. Let them sit there till nightfall if they must. Till there is no light left for photography, till it's damned cold. I bet they'll get up then. In fact, better to send Nevski over. I'm going to tell him to let them know the photographs are off."

Suttor felt bewildered tears burning his eyes again. He wanted more than to deprive them of baseball bats. He wanted a larger and more penetrating punishment, but wasn't even permitted a gesture.

At dusk, the prisoners did rise from their crouched postures and uncover their faces. The next day, Suttor—on his way to the compound and still aggrieved—saw with some bitterness prisoners wearing mitts and throwing balls to each other. In this mode they were like men anywhere throwing a ball, exercising that basic human comfort and duty of not letting the orb, the symbol of the essential egg, fall from your hands and into the dust.

"Can't shoot 'em," he muttered. "Can't punish them."

He was coming to a bitter awareness that the captors are prisoners too.

On Fridays in Gawell, Oxley and Castlereagh Streets were alive with the backing, surging, clutter, and creak of traffic, from buses arriving from remoter parts of the shire, and gas-bladder-topped cars of the better-off townspeople and families who could call themselves "graziers" to the trucks of mixed farmers such as Duncan, the drays of smaller soil scratchers, and the foot traffic of agricultural laborers and their families.

Alice had come in with Duncan, but she had her own tasks: some grocery shopping and the most enlivening of all endeavors—to find a copy of a new book for Giancarlo in one of the gift shops that stocked a modest number of titles. She had read of some of the latest titles in the *Herald* and sought something like *Mrs. Parkington* or *And Now Tomorrow*. She found in fact *The Song of Bernadette*, which Giancarlo would, anarchist or not, study for the sake of his English.

It was in traffic-cluttered Oxley Street, which seemed crammed all at once with every adult and child who populated the shire, that, inevitably, she saw the face of Mrs. Cathcart, who was bound for the School of Arts and her prisoners' women's meeting. Another instant and Alice could have avoided her glance and pretended not to have seen her, and so hurry on with that Friday-afternoon urgency that drove people from one encounter with friends or shopkeepers to another. But she was too late in looking away—there had been mutual recognition which necessitated an exchange of words.

"Alice," called Mrs. Cathcart, moving in, "we've missed you. As I said to some of the others, I hope everything is all right."

She had the power to express concern while making Alice feel like a slack participant.

"Things have been pretty busy out our way," Alice told her, but in a mutter.

"But you haven't given us up, have you?" Mrs. Cathcart asked in a half-amused way that annoyed Alice and brought out in her the determination to be an equal arguer.

"I *might* give up on the whole business," she admitted with a sudden acrimony. "I haven't heard anything from Neville for four months, and even then it was just a postcard saying he was well. I don't think that news would be very interesting to the others, do you?"

"Ah," said Mrs. Cathcart, "but interesting each other is only part of what we do. We support each other too. And there's always that matter of prisoner exchange."

Those overused words—"prisoner exchange"—enraged Alice and made her study Mrs. Cathcart in a new way. She stared directly at the column of certainty and stoicism Mrs. Cathcart was. It was easier for her, beef prices being what they were. Even though people said it couldn't be done—you couldn't send prisoners of war money—she wouldn't be surprised if smug Mrs. Cathcart had found a way to send some to her husband. Though probably not. It may just be that Alice had come to dislike the woman.

"There'll be no prisoner exchanges," Alice said as a challenge. "You must know that too. Stringing those poor women along does them no good."

"I beg your pardon, Alice. I don't believe that's what I'm doing. Hope is a marvelous benefit."

"But half of us know that it's nonsense. Even the Italians up in the camp there are not being let go. And their government's on our side now."

"So, are you fed up with Mr. Herman's Italian and want him returned?"

Alice studied Mrs. Cathcart for signs of a knowing sarcasm. But no, it seemed just to be old-fashioned bullying.

"I don't care one way or another," said Alice. "I'm saying the Nazis will not let our men go. And as for the others . . ."

Mrs. Cathcart, Alice was astonished to see, was partly routed and a tremble took hold of her lips. "There are medical and other benefits the government wants to give us all," she argued. "And our little committee is the only one who keeps the women informed of all that."

"If the government wants to give me something," Alice stated, "I'll wait for it to tell me."

Mrs. Cathcart shook her head. "I am sure that this will be a disappointment to the older women," she told Alice. "They're so comforted by the presence of the younger ones."

"But what is it for, for God's sake?" asked Alice.

"What's come over you? If I have to explain all that over again, then perhaps it's best you don't come." Mrs. Cathcart nodded and, moving on, was done with her. The idea did not distress Alice at all. She was more amazed to find herself a woman who had offered a civic leader a solid talking-to. She was sure it had something to do with the change Giancarlo had produced in her. It had to do, too, though, with forgetting Neville or failing to reinvigorate her memory.

Afterwards she felt ashamed for assailing Mrs. Cathcart's kindliness or delusions, and knew that she would report the incident in her own terms to other prisoners' wives. The thought of this chastened Alice, in the same way her other bouts of frenzy did.

19

Aoki, as a straightforward fellow and a married man, could not help disapproving of the female impersonator, Sakura. Given the conservative streak almost guaranteed by his rural upbringing, he found it inappropriate for an elite soldier to dress the way Sakura did. At least on morning and evening parade Sakura dressed in the weeds of a prisoner. But she took refuge in her identity as entertainer, and perhaps seductress, at first every Friday and Saturday night, then on most nights, except when she professed herself very tired. One or two performances were one thing, but the fabrics had taken over and made the soldier something other than she was in the field.

In her/his childhood, Sakura had pursued for a time a lesser career on stage in Kabuki. His taste was not serious theater, but one-act slapstick plays that enabled him to be outrageous and flaunting. But his true forte was his own amalgam of narrative and improvised and performed ballad—that was how he, or let us say she, had made her living before the army. She had in those days, as now in Gawell, performed to the strumming of the three-stringed samisen and gingered up her quick-witted comic song act with female mimicry, clothing, and makeup.

Sakura was perhaps most popular in Compound C, whose members believed she would have been famous, had it not been for the war, for a play she had written that allowed more natural acting. It was a comedy concerned with reverence for parents and rebellion against them, and was played by prisoners costumed in ordinary modern clothing, the more angelic-faced young prisoners filling the child roles, and Sakura as the handsome mother. Sakura was so far advanced in performance skills, and so talented, that she filled the recreation hall with longing—filial and sexual. Tengan and his clique were appalled by this cheap betrayal of the classic forms, and Sakura compounded the sin by setting her popular play in a warless world. It had been accepted with such joy and enthusiasm by many that there were further performances. Some people in the compound had attended two or three times. Even though it filled them with a near-unbearable nostalgia, it also supplied them with hilarious double en-tendres.

Sakura was unashamedly frank about her promiscuity. "If it was good enough for the warriors of old, it's good enough for me," she had once said during a ballad performance. She did not, however, offer honest warrior-style sex, said the more serious-minded. Not a forti-fying, head-clearing, undisclosed exchange between equals. Instead she flaunted. She flounced.

Her true companion and confidant was a lame little man named Tamura, the costumier for performances staged in Compound C. Tamura did not seem interested in Sakura in any way other than ad-vising her on costume. He had been a tailor, and spent his days in Compound C sewing costumes for which fabric had been requested from and supplied by the captors. He devoted to Sakura's finery the best of the cloth provided by the commandant. Though it was banal material, austerity fabrics, the little tailor transformed it all, and Sakura wore her clothes with an assumption that tended to turn everything to satin—except, of course, the shameful maroon of cap-tivity.

So with the end of roll call and the setting of the sun, she spent her time snaking around the huts in costume, her face made up with arduously collected and blended cosmetics—even with red clay extracted from the earth of Gawell.

When she swayed into huts, the ones she knew she was welcome in at night, she would be greeted by cheers and whistles, by howls and hoots, by the banging of tin mugs and fists against timber walls. There was no chance that she would ever be violated or misused or beaten up for decadence by the dogmatic types from Tengan's hut. She was protected not least by her popular hut commander and his section chief, both of whom she had got on side by means that did not need specifying. As well as that she was muscular and had been a senior private and explosives expert in the South Seas detachment. And now as a prisoner she covered her individual diminished condition under a front of strutting.

Hello, soldier, she might sing—for she was a demon for improvisation and it was different every night—

> *Guess my name,*
> *Or we could play a different game.*
> *Once I've tapped you on the knee,*
> *You'll soon see more than you're s'posed to see.*
> *You've been bowed by battle's grief.*
> *I'll give your spirit some relief . . .*

Each song stuck to that theme: the question of exile, and the momentary forgetting she brought to men. If one of them lunged for her posterior, she'd slap him resonantly on the face. "I have other friends to visit, and my arse must last the journey."

A man unable to restrain himself might come up to fondle the bogus breasts. "Please desist!" she'd roar like an NCO. "I may be a nursing mother soon, and my baby will need those things more than you do."

She was so convincing, so expert in her lewdness, she gave men erections that some were willing to display to her. But she was, by the standards of what might have been possible, relatively chaste, and she had her rules. Sometimes she would walk out of a hut dragging a young man by the hand. Since it was known one of her assignation places was the bakehouse, men might call after her, "Don't get anything in the dough." There were known to be uncomely men she took pity on, this simulacrum of a woman. Perhaps that was how the friendship with the tailor Tamura had begun, before it became akin to that of racy niece to wise uncle. Perhaps only he knew that Sakura felt as bound as anyone else to approach the pit they all confronted and to throw herself in.

Emily Abercare arrived in Gawell on a June Friday at the beginning of the region's bright, frosty winter. She found her edgy, attentive, and delighted husband waiting for her on the station platform. They exchanged kisses on cheeks, chaste and accustomed gestures that implied habitual marriage rather than hard-won reunion. Emily believed that it was no use reuniting on cold or reserved terms. Both of them must risk themselves again, she said. (It was kind of her to imply an equal duty on her side.) But obviously she was not quite ready to deploy all the force of her nature, which was reserved anyhow, at Gawell railway station.

A driver took them in the colonel's car to the house he had rented in Parkes Street—a corner house, in fact, with a garden of defiantly surviving gerberas and daphne, as well as flowering shrubs and a coral tree dazzling beneath the sun.

"You can garden if you wish," said the colonel just before they left the car, "and one of my chaps will mow the lawns for us."

He gestured to the front door.

"Mrs. Cullen's inside with morning tea."

He led her up the path and the steps. The driver was behind them with Mrs. Abercare's bags, and when the colonel opened the door—it was characteristic not to use keys in houses in Gawell—the driver asked, "Do you want me to take them to the bedroom, sir?"

"No, thank you," said Abercare—the private man, the householder who did not want his innermost rooms snooped on, or some indefinable snide tale released amongst the garrison. "Just leave them there," he said.

Emily went ahead of him up the hallway and inspected the living room. Her father and brothers had all been of middling rank in India and East Africa where, in peacetime, promotion was slow and billets were often humble, and one had to console oneself with the fact that at least servants were everywhere and cheap. So she inspected this new billet without any expectation of perfection. She looked at a scene on the wall of a red lane with a stockman and a flock of sheep on it. Parts of it had come loose from its backing board and so it bulged here and remained fast there, further distorting and cheapening the effect. It looked even worse than the picture of Cecil's failed thoroughbred back in Tathra.

"This living room," she said, giving it a reasonable mark out of one hundred. "One could get a few prints, maybe . . ."

He knew she liked prints of distant prospects of the elegant homes of Britain, of a fabled home that, because of her family's service in remoter places, she had elevated to an ideal; the kind of home everyone, the Australians, too, seemed to yearn for in their way, and which she had barely glimpsed while at a severe convent boarding school in Surrey. Indeed, he wondered now, did such a place, incarnate in elegant Georgian houses, seen by way of botanical avenues designed by artful gardeners, even exist? For most Britons, it lived only in prints, a reflection of the imagination rather than reality. Yet was this embedded print in the British brain what we all fought for?

"Next time we're in Sydney," Abercare said, "we'll go to a shop that sells those things. I'm afraid there aren't any art or antique shops in Gawell."

"I wouldn't expect so," she said, with a half smile and stalwartly refusing to bring down any negative judgment on the town.

"You are really a true brick!" he complimented her.

She nodded, but in a way that said, "We'll see about that."

Mrs. Cullen came in from the kitchen, rubbing her hands on an apron. She was sturdily built and she earned her money cooking and cleaning for people around Gawell. She had come recommended by the colonel's friend Dr. Garner. He introduced the woman to his wife, feeling an unfamiliar uxorial pride as he did it, showing off Emily's angular beauty at forty-four to this worn and hollowed former girl, misshapen from labor and rural poverty, who might have been any age between thirty-five and fifty-five, and who had reached a plateau of endurance of which her body was a map. When Mrs. Cullen said she had fresh tea and fruitcake in the kitchen, and would they like it brought into the dining room—the dining room not set for tea yet, she was sorry, the time had got away—Emily said, "The kitchen. That'll be cozier. The Romans had kitchen gods, didn't they? They knew their stuff."

This degree of scholarship made Mrs. Cullen blink. Emily's was not a very Gawell sentiment. "Yes," said Mrs. Cullen. "I've got the old range going. It's warm in there."

Colonel Abercare's heart sang when she chose the kitchen. It said to him that she intended to give staying here, on this corner in Gawell, a real try for as long as her husband had his job with prisoners.

So they sat down to homemade scones, blackberry jam made by Mrs. Cullen, and the fruitcake rich from eggs and butter, to which Mrs. Cullen's laborer husband got access through his work on farms. Mrs. Cullen wiped her hands again in gratification on her apron, excused herself, and left. The fruitcake was so good and such a simple delight that a profession of love for the colonel trembled on the edge of Emily's lips. But her wariness restrained it, and she was unhappy that it did.

• • •

Colonel Abercare declared to his wife at dinner on the night of her arrival, "I thought we might introduce ourselves to Father Delaney, the parish priest here. I hear he's rather a scholar. Trained in Rome, too dreamy to be a bishop. But apparently—so one of the officers told me—he wrote three volumes of theology, all in Latin. Actually, they call him Dr. Delaney. As in, doctor of divinity."

Emily was half-amused that his efforts to win her back had extended to researching the condition of Catholicism in Gawell. "I thought I might just turn up on Sunday," she said. "I mean, it's kind of you. But we don't have to give him notice beforehand, do we? He sounds more interesting than the Irishman down at Tathra, though."

"Mrs. Cullen says he lacks the common touch. But the 'touch' out here is very common indeed. What if I call him? I'll tell him he'll be meeting just one Catholic, and that I'm godless."

Emily declared, with what seemed like artlessness, "None of us is godless. If He's not there in our acts then He's there in our punishment."

Ewan Abercare was of course both made uncomfortable and impressed by this aphorism. But—to be honest—it was delivered the way Emily had delivered her theological reflections before the disaster, easily and without trying to hammer it to his forehead. He said nothing for a while, suppressing the tendency to mar the exchange with yet another of his useless apologies. At last he said, "I'll concede that. Although if it's not God who punishes us, we certainly know how to punish ourselves."

"Handsomely said yourself," Emily smiled. "You're a clever man, Ewan." There was a genuine smile of admiration for him in her eyes. She actually thought he was a professional success, and that compliment elevated him.

He smiled at her. "I could have gone far," he said.

The next morning, from his office at the prison camp, Colonel Abercare called Dr. Delaney's presbytery and managed to persuade his ferocious Irish housekeeper to fetch the priest, who was disrobing after weekday morning Mass. He introduced himself to the priest and said that he had been born a Protestant, but his wife was from an old English Catholic family and he would be honored to introduce her to him. Indeed, he invited Delaney to morning tea in the house on the corner of Parkes Street.

Emily got in Mrs. Cullen, her coreligionist, to help with the morning tea. Dr. Delaney proved thin and wild haired, and had a melancholy, though willing, face. Despite Gawell's climate, he looked far more like the pale English-born priests Emily had known in her childhood than someone from this part of the world. He shook hands with the colonel and bowed to Emily. A professional man's bow. He would in the end come to know, Abercare presumed, by way of the confessional, much of her inner soul—though not, he hoped, her history, since she seemed to have at last recovered from it.

After the three of them had sat down and Mrs. Cullen had served the tea, Delaney said, "I go up to the camp sometimes myself, to say Solemn High Mass with Padre Frumelli for the Italians who aren't out on the farms. As for the Italians who come to my ten o'clock on Sundays, most of them use it purely as a get-together. But in any case, that's a sung Mass. We have an excellent choir."

Abercare was strangely proud of the four-hundred-year-old resistance to the established system that Emily's family had accomplished. He knew Protestantism had ultimately encouraged diversity of opinion and had given men a lot of time to invent the steam engine, and so forth. They weren't distracted by holy days and novenas and too many saints. But he boasted now to Delaney that Emily's family had been Catholics through the age of Henry VIII and Elizabeth I, through the Gunpowder Plot and Act of Settlement. Politics had always been closed to them. But they had crept into the army.

"I've read about families like that," said Delaney when Abercare had finished. "They hid priests in cavities in the wall. That's the case, isn't it?"

"There are stories of that kind," Emily conceded. "We've only had a few generals in the family, of course. If you're Catholic, you need superlative military skills to become a brigadier."

"What is the explanation for my humble rank, then?" asked Ewan Abercare, comfortable for once with his place in all hierarchies.

"But we had other consolations," Emily said. "The thing I have never understood about other Christian religions is how they get by without a mother in them. Just God—who is always a male or shown in those terms. Since I was a little girl I've needed the Virgin Mother, and would feel orphaned without her."

Dr. Delaney said, "Yes. But of course we need to be careful of Mariolatry."

Ewan Abercare let the unfamiliar term flow over him and pursued his normal private puzzlement about how a Virgin could be described as a "mother" and in what sense. But he did not know how to comment and he let this great Catholic contradiction slide by him.

Delaney told Emily, "You'll discover our congregation a pretty hardhanded lot of people. Generous. And very observant. There's not a lot of mysticism there or much *visible* spirituality, you know. Their spirituality is deep, though. It's like Australian rivers that run pretty far down in the earth—to avoid evaporation. I certainly don't get too many of them discussing my book on the mysteries of faith. But they have a strength I don't. It's the strength to lead a normal life. You'll hear plenty of laughing and raucous talk outside the church door."

"You have to take whatever congregation is offered if you're a Catholic," said Emily. "I'm not great shakes as a mystic myself."

The priest nodded and said, "You're a member of a very big club. Colonel, I wanted to say that you are very welcome, too, but that's not an attempt to proselytize you. I'm no good at converting people. It happens if it's going to happen." Abercare could tell that Emily was delighted with this man, and his willingness to descend from his three-volume work to see his congregation as more gifted and virtuous than he was. In inviting him to morning tea, almost by instinct Abercare had done something to reconcile her to this house and to him.

On the strength of the blessings this theologian had given him, Abercare approached her in his bed that evening. His hands reached over her back and took hold not of the breast, but of the ribs below, a lesser claim, he thought, and tolerable. She understood what his ultimate objective was. She allowed him to cup her breast and then she turned and addressed herself to fulfilling the reunion.

Beyond the house was silence—the silence of an achingly quiet room in an achingly still house girt by streets that slumbered as soon as the night came down on Gawell. And no one knew what remarkable shifts of trust and penitence and longing were being acquitted on the corner of Parkes Street.

The colonel came home one evening when Mrs. Cullen was leaving. She had insisted on staying back to cook an evening stew for the Abercares, so the colonel offered her a lift, which she refused. When he insisted, she acquiesced, but, embarrassed by the attention, she told him he could drop her three miles southwest of town. It was a distance which, in these exorbitant reaches of earth, town to town, was minute to drive and considered appropriately walkable. When he offered to drive her to her house, and saw the corrugated iron shack in which she lived, he knew that this was what she was trying to hide. This was but one of many houses on a property owned by a family called the Doyles, and Mr. Cullen was a rouseabout there and elsewhere, and when the shearing came on every spring, a shearer.

This first time Abercare dropped her through the gate and up to the shack in its nest of granite boulders, he did not see the husband. He saw a boy of about sixteen appear in a doorway wearing the uniform of Gawell High School. He had sharp, intelligent features and eyes like his mother's.

"That's my son, Martin," she said. "He's in fourth year high school."

Mrs. Cullen said "fourth year" with a faint emphasis. Most Gawellians had left school by the end of the third year at the latest, and perhaps more than half of them much earlier than that. Fourth year meant a Leaving Certificate and then God knows what! A job in a bank. Or there was a subtler ambition he sensed in Mrs. Cullen, which put a university not beyond her objectives for the boy.

Colonel Abercare said, "Thank God the war is going well. It'll be much better if it ends and your boy is allowed to be a scholar."

"Of course," said Mrs. Cullen. "But we all have to pull our weight."

Pulling our weight to save this corrugated iron shed for the commonwealth of Australia, Abercare thought.

"But I prefer he wasn't put in danger too," she admitted.

The colonel could bet that Martin Cullen was the only fourth year Gawell student who came from corrugated iron.

20

There was an occasion when Giancarlo asked if it was possible for him to go to Mass. It wasn't that he believed much, he told Duncan and Alice, but he wanted to meet up with other men from around the farms of the district. A great deal was happening in Italy, and even if the things other men were saying were half wrong, he said, it meant they were also half-truths. He said he could walk—"She only five kilometers, Mr. 'Erman." But perhaps to relieve his guilt about the extra petrol ration he'd been given and used for other purposes, Duncan suggested that they could take Giancarlo to the Catholic Church, and then he and Alice could go to the Methodist service—it wouldn't kill them, said Duncan, to go to Sunday service. Alice wondered if the straight and dimly perceived God of Methodism could somehow cure what was, within her, a glory and a disease that seemed to belong to another jurisdiction altogether.

She waited by the truck in a dress, straw hat with veil, and brown, heeled shoes, and when the men appeared—Giancarlo in his prison clothes as required—she climbed into the front beside Duncan while Giancarlo vaulted onto the back. And so they set out to their diverse worship.

"You won't tell the priest?" she had asked him, privately, and nearly as a joke. They had been together in his room twice that week and had not yet fully repented. And she had heard the priests of the Catholics were hypnotic in their influence, and sometimes she had a fear that they might glean the truth from Giancarlo, who said he did not believe but who surely must retain some of what he'd learned of these things in his childhood.

"I don't tell the priest," he had assured her with his wryest smile. "I say to God on his own—where this girl of dreams comes from?"

She and Duncan dropped Giancarlo outside the large church, where POWs milled beneath a tall gum tree waiting for the people with names such as Doyle and Hogan and Murphy to enter the church first in their suits and best dresses and hats; and for the young girls dressed in blue and white, the Legion of Mary, to march into the church in a phalanx. Duncan called as Giancarlo walked towards the others, "Keep out of trouble, Johnny." He thought the admonition very funny, and after his chuckle died, he turned the truck and drove to the humbler Methodist church on the eastern edge of Gawell.

Alice had always enjoyed the Methodist hymns. She fancied herself as a passable soprano, and had felt in the days of her vanity and innocence that the Wesleyan anthem "All People That on Earth Do Dwell" was well suited to her gifts. This Sabbath it meant nothing when put beside her incapacity to direct her mind to anything but the thought of Giancarlo, lost for an hour or more in the unimaginable environs of his idol-worshiping childhood faith.

The Reverend Temple's sermon was very different from John Wesley's hymns—a most unmusical rant about the evils of American films and the false glamour with which they imbued improper clothing, smoking, and alcohol. He named Bette Davis and Cary Grant as embodying the flippancy Hollywood brought to issues of courtship and marriage, though he was willing to admit there were worse cases whose names had been reported to him by his congregation.

The service was familiar from her childhood and allowed room for the forefront of her mind to wander. Thought swung, of course, compass-like, to Giancarlo and for the first time, the nearness of Duncan and his redolence of tobacco and shaving cream and soap placed the two men, Duncan and his prisoner, into the one frame and in a new way. Her skin prickled from the idea this evoked. Was Duncan, who she'd assumed was almost perniciously unaware, in fact utterly aware, and putting up tolerantly with the Giancarlo affair until it reached what she now knew must be its conclusion, Alice returned to her chaste vigil, her temporary widowhood? She heard herself swallowing, trying to absorb or choke the idea down. She covered her eyes with her hands as if in an onset of a phase of devotion.

What would be his motive? she then asked herself. Could this simple being really be so immoral as to tolerate Giancarlo and herself? And why would he? Did he do it in a kind of tired wisdom, letting her find out by exhausting herself on the body of another, different kind of prisoner? Or did he let it happen for pure malign enjoyment and one morning soon would call the Control Center and demand they take the Italian back? Was she kneeling beside gullible virtue or worldly viciousness?

The minister spoke relatively briefly and the service ended by ten o'clock. Somehow, Alice stumbled from the church.

Outside again, hauling himself into the truck, Duncan called to Alice, as if he were the target of the Reverend Temple's condemnations, "Haven't been to the pictures since nineteen thirty-seven. Not since Mrs. Herman got ill. She was always more keen on it than I was."

And so Duncan reckoned himself safe from the baleful influence of the flicks.

There was something so completely convincing about this, she decided with a spasm of delicious reprieve. She was convinced again that he had decided at some time, out of fear of the world, not to look beyond himself. And now, from lack of use, he'd lost the ability to do it. A minister spoke of the sins of moving pictures, and Duncan thought at once only of himself and the flickers. So he had—it was obvious again—resigned from all wisdom except the wisdom of running a farm.

But before that pulse of reassurance ended, it was followed instantly by something immensely bitter. While idling her mind in church and being put in a sudden sweat by the idea of a satanic Duncan, even she had thought of an end to the Giancarlo business. It was the first time her mind had alluded to a limit to all that. She was suddenly and sharply conscious of a finish that was part of the unchangeable order, but also that she was the one who must finish it. This did not seem a duty. It seemed something she would do, independently of what she wanted, sooner or later. Bleakness possessed her as she crawled up into the truck. She wanted the end to be later, not sooner. But her crimes, as she envisaged them now, had something like a piece of fuse attached. She knew it spat fire, but she did not know its length.

They drove into town, back to the other, larger church behind the town hall. Incomprehensible Catholic singing could be heard from inside. Duncan left the truck and stood in the shade of the tree where the prisoners had earlier gathered and smoked a roll-your-own cigarette. She got out herself after a while and went to join him.

"I'm going inside," she said. And to anticipate his question, she declared, "To see what it's like."

She wasn't looking for his good advice on the matter. Her going inside and seeing for herself what Giancarlo had believed in before he'd lost his soul to anarchism was the reigning proposition. She felt nervous but was determined not to be tentative while mounting the steps of the strange cult and entering the shadow of the vestibule. She passed the marble font full of water in which people dipped their hands before making their sign, and saw the racks of pamphlets— "The Plain Truth"; "Catholicism—the True Faith?"; "The Papacy and the Faithful"; "The Blessed Virgin and the True Faith"—and advanced into the sinister smell of incense, like the reek of paganism itself, that reached even to the backseat, where a number of thick-necked farmers knelt on one knee. Across from them, on the other side of the crowded church, were the Italian prisoners, in whose numbers she could not see Giancarlo.

She must have arrived at a pause in the ritual. Organ music crescendoed and ceased, the choir stopped singing, and the congregation began hauling themselves from their knees and sitting. She found herself a place to sit. This church is a space like any other space, she reassured herself. Even though it doesn't feel like it, it is part of Australia, and to prove it, all those prisoners our nation has captured are there in their dyed uniforms. Amongst them somewhere the familiar flesh of Giancarlo.

At the front of the church, she saw people milling to receive the wafers of bread in their mouths, and some of the Italian prisoners, when it was their turn, going up to the altar to fetch the snow-white sacrament. As those who had been given it returned to their seats and their queues thinned, she saw Giancarlo, sitting back in his pew, dissenting, and felt no longer threatened by the abnormality of the space with its strange scents and Latin utterances. The choir began to sing again, and she was not alarmed. Other and more important matters swamped the incense.

As Catholics whose faces she knew from around the town, townspeople and farming families, knelt with the wafers in their mouths, the choir sawed on with a repetitive and ancient-sounding chant. Giancarlo was again invisible in the press of his fellow Italians. She rose and left. She did not try that strange bobbing that Catholics managed so negligently.

After the Mass the Italians were allowed to socialize for a little while outside. From the truck, Alice saw they were passing around a newspaper and discussing it excitedly, some laughing as if it were good news. An Italian officer, apparently trusted by the authorities, soon told them to break up and depart, either to walk back to their allocated farms or to the trucks of their allocated farmers.

Duncan, who had shown no interest in her adventure inside, now took to the front seat of the truck and so did she. They watched without a word as Giancarlo separated himself from the vocal group, arrived, and prepared to launch himself into the tray of the truck. Alice looked through the rear window to observe the imminent grace of the vault, but Duncan called, "Hang on! Tell us what all the excitement's about, Johnny."

Giancarlo canceled his jump and moved respectfully to Duncan's window. From her side of the truck Alice could see his face—a liveliness there. He had got it from mixing with his own kind. It made her anxious. "It is a *Corriere di Campo*—a prisoner newspaper made in another camp and sent us. *Antifascismo*. It say in print the British want use Italian mechanic—in factory—and send the young back in the war. Maybe, too, the Australia want that same thing. *Italia antifascismo* now."

He said it so lightly. But the story had not only increased her anxiety but brought out something close to anger. For he was thinking of the end, too, and it wasn't—in her mind—his business to do that.

"But you weren't on our side when you were taken prisoner," she said. He stood, instantly chastened, in the Sabbath light. Within a few seconds she regretted that meanness. It had been there, too, in the supposed honesty with which she'd told off Mrs. Cathcart. She was by some lights proud of that encounter, by others frightened she had somehow become an acid woman. She could feel his confusion too. That she'd so randomly reminded him that she had all the power.

"Well," said benign and stupid Duncan, "we'll face up to losing you when it happens, Johnny. Hop in the back." She heard him leap, one hand on the truck, onto the rear tray. She looked back through the glass behind her and saw his well-made and bemused face and his profound eyes, both young and aged at the same time, and puzzled. She could not continue inspecting him much longer with her head turned—pretense was back, and she wanted her interest to appear casual to Duncan.

The news from the camps rendered her skittish—as she would

have acknowledged to a confidante, if she'd had one. But, if she took a respite from her certainty that he would put a closure to things, the earth, in occasionally allowed mad spates of imagination, had also expanded with new chances—a shift in hemisphere, the contour of foreign earth and new terrain, Italian towns, the taking in of a new language through the pores of her delight. Wife of the *meccanico anarchico*.

The spoilsport within convinced her at most hours of the absurdity of these delusions, but there were also hours on end during which they seemed ordained and definite. In the coming days, which were days of painful abstinence mutually embarked upon by her and Giancarlo, she studied more intently the copies of the *Herald* Duncan got, and scoured the maps of the Allied line in southern Italy, its flanks and its center, looking for that mass of Allied victory that might mean the repatriation of Giancarlo.

Naples had fallen, Giancarlo's parents were safe, she knew, though he rarely mentioned them. The line had advanced to the south of Rome. In its wake, Frattamaggiore and a thousand other places were repairing themselves and looking for nourishment.

The armies of the right side had not yet liberated Neville. But would the whole affair resolve itself into a race between Neville's repatriation and Giancarlo's? Could she let poor Neville be victim of some kind of race? When she was halfway undeluded, she knew matters wouldn't resolve themselves in such a theatrical way.

21

Dr. Delaney had a passion for church music. His congregation thought it an eccentricity in him. The question for many of the Catholic men was, "If you can get to heaven by attending a short Mass, why attend a bloody long one?"

But Emily had joined the choir because that sort of thing was to her taste also. Delaney could not get the farming tenors and basses to swell like those of Italian monks, so he must depend largely upon the voices of their wives. The choir were rehearsing "Ave Verum Corpus" on a Thursday night in the cold church, and the colonel sat in the back pew as a visiting Protestant witness while the clarity of the music lanced the dimness. It was a very simple and pure melody that Mozart had pursued here. It was beyond flamboyance and showmanship. Dr. Delaney was not interested in approximations to perfection either. Occasionally he would mention Roman choirs he had heard, and the Roman pronunciation was to prevail in Gawell. It was "Ah-vay vay-rum," and then the trailing off of sound at the edge of each phrase, so that "verum" died and from its glorious remains arose "corpus natum," and "natum" died and in its turn gave birth to "de Maria Virgine." He was aiming for the standards of that distant independent and eternal city which, thankfully, the Germans had just now abandoned before it had become rubble and its choirs had been stifled.

Mrs. Cullen had tramped into town three miles from her husband and her clever son to learn to sing like a nun of Rome. Listening, the colonel understood the peculiar seduction of Romanism and the mortgage it seemed to have on plainchant and even on Mozart. He saw Emily's pale face shining in a row just behind Mrs. Cullen's gypsy-brown one. His affections soared on "cuius latus perforatum," soared higher than the modestly vaulted ceiling of Dr. Delaney's church, spiraled into Australia's enormous but unpraised night.

It was here, in the Catholic church, under the flutings of Mozart, that the intelligence officer Captain Champion and Sergeant Nevski found Abercare. They had failed to reach him by phone and so had gone to Parkes Street and been advised by a neighbor that the colonel and his lady were at choir practice. Their arrival at the church was exceptional, because it portended some emergency. But they felt the colonel should be advised as soon as possible of some new information that had come their way.

Cheong, the Korean, hand healed, was back clipping grass along the ditch at either side of Main Road and cutting it from around the uprights of each compound, thus preventing it from concealing the lower strands of wire that might then be cut open by enterprising prisoners. On the other side of the inner fence where Cheong worked, parties of Italians in their own compound were engaged in similar work. Some Italian groups raked the earth, for the camp commandant did not want his compounds to look like so much rubble. Sometimes the Italians would call out to the Koreans, "Hello, Japan!"

"Good-bye, Japan," Cheong would cry when the spirit took him—a small utterance of Korean independence.

There was a handsome Italian boy who worked a little separately from his comrades and who, as he moved closer to Cheong, smelled more than them of sweat, as if he were a peasant unused to water.

"Name, Japan?" asked the Italian in English.

"Cheong," said Cheong. "Korea. No Japan. Japan stink."

The young Italian accepted this assessment of Italy's former ally. He told Cheong his name was Franco, and Cheong used the name and they smiled at each other. The primitive conversation had bored Cheong's companions, and they had gone back to grass cutting. Franco got talking at greater length. He was proud of the scatter of English words he possessed. He pointed to the barracks and said, "Hut." He pounded an upright of the fence. "Wood," he said. He touched the barbed wire and uttered its name. "Wire."

Cheong tried to say it—a most difficult word—but Franco nodded and nodded to ease it from him. This boy is simpleminded, thought Cheong, but likeable.

"Come under," said Franco. He dropped to his knees and opened a little wire gate someone—not the garrison, of course—had constructed in an area where the grass at the side of Main Road generally grew highest. By attaching cut wires to little wooden jambs—one dug into the ground, one swinging free like a door—they had been able to make this surreptitious gateway. It was the way some Italians got into Main Road and sold grappa to the men in Compound C for cigarettes. A thin man could imagine scraping on his stomach through the little opening. Cheong did not know afterwards why, apart from amiability and curiosity, he'd obeyed the boy and had separated the strands and rolled clumsily between them into the Italian side of things. This was playing at escape, of course, and to enter another compound, particularly one as neutral of threat and as different as that of the Italians, was itself a small and stimulating exploit.

Franco had been wearing a nondescript canvas hat and, smiling, he took off Cheong's cap and put his own sunhat on Cheong's head so that from a distance Cheong would pass as Italian. They walked across the gravel compound amidst its occasional clumps of grass. A man who had been excused duties sat on a step in the sun and was playing an accordion—their kind of instrument.

Franco, after looking around the compound, led him up into a particular hut. The accordionist called after either the boy or Cheong, "*Cretino!*" But Cheong did not know what that meant.

"No problems," cried Franco cheerily, in the English of the guards.

Inside the hut Cheong encountered, as in his own compound, a smell of creosote overlaid with another smell he was getting used to—some dull exhalation that was peculiar to huts full of imprisoned, thwarted, spiritually foreshortened men. Franco came to his bunk and sat and patted it as a sign that Cheong should sit beside him. Cheong was now deep inside the hut and making ready to sit on an Italian's bunk for politeness' sake. But his enjoyment of the adventure was waning. The plain-minded Franco was unconscious of this and leaned down and brought from under his bed a book. Cheong could not read the text. Perhaps it was one of their scriptures or, by the looks of the heavy print, a dictionary. Franco placed it on his rough bedside table, which he pulled square on to the two of them.

Next, the Italian pulled out a small notebook and showed him photographs held inside it. An older woman frowned at the camera as if it were her first acquaintance with it. A picture of Franco with four girls, all of them quite handsome. "Sisters," he said. "*Sorelle.* Sisters, me."

He pumped his chest proudly. He put all that aside reverently now. Then he winked and leaned down and flexed up a floorboard from which the nails were missing. From the space beneath he extracted, as if it had been lying on a joist, a magazine. A girl with huge flowery bare breasts looked at him from its cover. "Good, no? *Che seni, no?*" said Franco and laughed not like a man, thought Cheong, but a boy.

Then Franco stood for a few seconds, unbuttoned his trousers, and pulled out his pale penis. Sitting down again, he put the magazine picture of the girl across his lap. He indicated that Cheong should follow his actions, but Cheong was little tempted and chose not to engage in such a juvenile scene.

However, he was still sitting there when the sergeant of the compound guards appeared, meaty faced, in the doorway. He yelled a question and a profanation in his harsh English, and advanced across the floorboards on his thunderous steel-tipped boots and waving a baton.

Cheong hurled his Italian cap down on the bed while Franco dropped the magazine to the floor and began rebuttoning himself in a way he absurdly thought was surreptitious.

The remote-seeming Captain Champion, although Australian born, had taught English at an institute of technology in Nagoya. He came to Gawell from Sydney at unpredictable but regular intervals to interview prisoners randomly and see how their self-explanations now compared with the ones they had given in interrogation in the first days of their lives as prisoners. For there were men who did not remember precisely what they had said last time, and who changed their stories subtly. Champion also depended heavily on observation, common sense, and what Sergeant Nevski told him. Abercare and Suttor both noticed that the captain treated Nevski with respect, as if Nevski's academic repute were higher than his own. Champion and Nevski discussed between them the results of new interrogations and passed on their observation to Suttor and the colonel.

Nevski told Champion that there happened to be a Korean in the hoosegow in Compound B who had declared himself to an NCO a Korean patriot and a despiser of the inhabitants of Compound C, and thus defined himself as an ally, not an enemy. Captain Champion thought that it might be worth interviewing this man, and had guards go into the lockup and take Cheong out with roughness and shouts, enough to alarm him. Even so, when Cheong was brought into the office in the administration hut where the interview was to occur, far from being distressed, he was smiling. He saw Nevski, who was at least familiar, and beheld the urbane captain from Sydney. The encounter seemed to delight him thoroughly.

The captain said in Japanese, "We know you were discovered in that hut in the Italian compound. Can you explain why you were there?"

"I was curious," said Cheong. "I had never seen Italians up close before . . . Well, apart from the one we loaded wheat with. I wanted to see what their huts were like and how they lived."

"A cultural tour," said the captain and smiled across at Nevski, who shook his head a little in a way that said, "They'll tell you anything!"

"You see," said the captain, "we think we know why you were there. We think you were there to buy wine or grappa or dirty books to sell to the men in your compound."

Cheong struck a pose of probity and denied he was a dealer.

"I am more a student," he said. "I am inquisitive."

"But we've found bottles of rough Italian grappa amongst the Formosans and some of the civilian internees. You were looking for grappa, weren't you?"

"No. It must be one of the old Japanese merchants in there who buys it. Nothing could have been further from my mind." He beamed. There was something endearing about him; about what Champion would describe to Nevski as "his frank bullshit." It was obvious, meanwhile, to Cheong that they would declare him a black marketeer rather than a mere inquirer. He became concerned now, for the hoosegow was not pleasant, and the cold, with no animal warmth around him and only three blankets to encase him, prevented him from sleeping for more than an hour at a time.

He watched the officer and Nevski talk to each other awhile in English. He hoped that they were agreeing that the idiot boy was not a likely source of commerce and transactions. Why didn't they speak to the ordinary guards, who had a sense of who was up to what in each compound? He said in a rush of inspiration, "There are far more important things than grappa that I know about."

Nevski and Champion exchanged glances. "What could those

possibly be?" said the captain, trying to sneer with a sort of Basil Rathbone broadness.

"You must know we Koreans are different from your true enemy. You separate us from them, you put us in with civilians and Formosans and Tamils. We are like the Formosans but more so. We wear the uniform of a power that is our enemy, the same as it is yours."

He decided to assume an authoritative tone.

"I hope you understand all that, sir. Otherwise there's very little sense in my going on."

"So you pretend you hate your former comrades now?"

"Not only now. I have always hated them. They did me some good by teaching me how to use weapons, that's all. But one day the weapons will be turned on them. That's what I'm interested in. I'm not interested in any black market."

At last Champion conceded that since Cheong had mentioned "more important matters," they might be interested.

"Enough to get me out of the lockup, please, sir?"

And so he told them about the conversation between the senior men and the newcomers—the way the veteran of Compound C had advised them not to be fretful and to be assured that they would all at some time very soon, on a dark night, assault the wire without firearms but with the purpose of suicide and then of taking the garrison's arms and magazine, which they thought of as ultimately the same thing. The sergeant had told the newcomers that in preparation they should do their best to show that their minds were fixed on baseball, wrestling, badminton, and theatricals.

"They are willing to attack those three barriers of wire?" Captain Champion asked, and adopted an air of professional scepticism.

"It is all benefit to them," Cheong insisted. "Given the way they think, if you kill them, it is benefit. If they kill your men and are killed in turn, it is benefit. In killing you they are winning what they want. In letting you kill them, they are winning what they want. That is what you must understand. May I say so, sir?"

It was, he knew, a well-expressed analysis.

Cheong was now let out of the hoosegow and taken back to his hut without anyone in Compound C, or even amongst the Korean demizealots, noticing. "This is good," he told the sentry who escorted him into the open air, and the sentry laughed.

The general idea of an outbreak was a commonplace of Gawell gossip. But the garrison knew better. Once outside the wire, an inhabitant of *that* compound would be both too visible and too surrounded by vastness to make any genuine escape, however temporarily, a reasonable idea. As well as that, amongst the goods Major Suttor permitted into Compound C were copies of the *Sydney Morning Herald* with translations of key articles into Japanese. From 1943, and more so this year, the leaders of Compound C and their fellow inmates must have been aware—even if the alien papers could only be partially believed—that the war was at least in the balance for the forces they had belonged to, if not facing defeat.

Champion and Nevski had already told Suttor and Abercare that the men of Compound C expected to be killed at the war's end. But this was the first concrete news from within the compound of some active gesture being proposed, and that was why Captain Champion and Sergeant Nevski went into town to find the colonel. Because beyond this full phase of the moon, the outbreak might occur, and that gave the garrison only a few weeks of preparation.

Abercare was on the phone to Sydney that evening of the choir practice and was ordered to drive overnight to the city—an indication of medium urgency—and attend a conference to be convened on the matter. He took what sleep he could in the back of the car while the driver negotiated the clear night and the empty country roads and weaved his way over the Blue Mountains and down into the basin where Sydney lay.

The next morning in a bare room at the back side of the army barracks near the Sydney Cricket Ground, the meeting was presided over by General McGregor, a man who had been a British regular like Abercare himself. Once, McGregor had led a brigade against the Italians in Libya. And had the enemy invaded the southeast of this country, as had once seemed very likely, General McGregor might, as might Abercare, have had a great role in resisting the invasion force.

But the thrust never came, and now he was commander of the lines of communication in a tranquil and inviolate New South Wales. He seemed interested in an energetic way, however, when he asked Abercare what the colonel thought of the report from Champion and Nevski. Abercare said he could not see how it could be dismissed. There was a party amongst the prisoners who sought something more decisive—an active death instead of a passive one. Colonel Abercare said he did not wish to imply the active/passive parties were divided down the middle like a parliament. If the general would tolerate a comparison, said Abercare, it seemed many of those in the compound were like Christians who wanted to go to heaven, but not yet.

The general asked, "And are you pleased with the defenses you have in place and the armaments you have at hand?"

Abercare knew the military realities—that generals took no notice if officers beneath them overstated demands. It was more so in this country, which had begun the great conflict undersupplied with martial goods and had never caught up on their lack.

"To begin with, sir," he told the general, "we need two machine guns sited to cover the compound." Because of the contours of the camp fences, these two weapons, he explained, could enfilade both the area within the fences and then, if prisoners managed to get so far, the outer ground beyond. (As he said it, he did not really believe in such an eventuality.) He asked, too, for weapons acclaimed for their impact in the jungle—Bren and Owen guns. And then perhaps, he asked, risking appearing a military Oliver Twist, could each man be equipped with a rifle, since the cooks, the medical orderlies, and the clerks had not been supplied with them?

As he returned to Gawell, starting that afternoon and continuing into the night, he was gratified that the general had ensured the armaments for which Abercare had asked, especially the machine guns, which were being loaded onto the night train and would travel under the care of sentries. As the night deepened, however, he wondered if he should have asked for a further machine gun to place opposite the middle strands of Compound C. But he traced the outer fence in his mind and concluded that a gun so sited and manned by inexperienced gunners could well kill other gunners and garrison members. But should he have asked to be reinforced by another company? Should he have asked for heavier weapons still, and for younger men?

In the car on the long way over the mountains and across the Western Plains, he saw his desire not to be considered panicky by his superiors was the merest vanity. The best soldiers he had known were men who were utterly frank with their seniors, even with those normally affronted by frank juniors. But once in Ceylon he had overheard himself called "a solid chap" by two older officers, and though he knew they thought that because he had done nothing to challenge the even temper of their days, it had been enough to fortify his conceit for a lifetime.

Two days later, an alarm siren was erected near one of the gates into the Main Road and was connected to electricity and tried out—its manic, penetrating howl projecting into the camp from a pole outside the north gate of Main Road. Abercare, who had ordered this trial, watched the arrested faces of Compound C turn in its direction and surmise what it meant. He fancied he could see Tengan contemptuously wondering if this was meant to intimidate the inmates. He and others perhaps felt provoked by it.

A new detachment of guards was stationed in a tent in Main Road where Kelly's Lane intersected it. And Abercare ordered Suttor to bring in extra generators from suppliers in the larger towns to power high-placed lights to shine down on the camp. Every man of the garrison was to sleep with his rifle beside his bed. Yet despite the precautions, still Abercare could not believe that the crisis would arise—Gawell was simply not a credible venue for such dramatic events.

Major Suttor, part distracted by his fictional radio family the Mortons, who were in the process of consoling a family named the Carters, whose son had been lost in the battle at Wewak in New Guinea, went as well into the compound every day and looked into every hut, assessing it for portents. Dark nights came as the moon waned and the machine guns, mounted on trailers, were manned. Foggy predawns wrapped up Gawell Camp. And there was no assault on the wire.

Soon, thought Abercare, the moon would be in the ascendant and too bright to allow any adventure from within the compound. He thought that in any case the lights he had ordered to be set high on poles around the place had settled the matter. The conditions that might permit a great demonstration against the inner wire had been ruled out.

22

As an unconvinced agent in putting a close to the Giancarlo business, she entered a time of abstinence, knowing its allure would wane. When it did, Alice made up the tray of tea and newspaper cuttings for Giancarlo, took it down to his quarters, and found that he was missing. He had recently had a letter from his father in Italy, and her first thought was that it must have distressed him. He shouldn't have been distressed, though. Rome had fallen a month or more before, and his own region had long fallen to the Allies.

Alice set down the tray on his small table and decided she would wait there, in the room. She sat on the bed, but it carried the smell of him. She walked the room and even read a few pages of A. J. Cronin's *The Keys of the Kingdom*, one of the books she had supplied to him. But the words did not penetrate, and she found this a feverish wait. That other crucial virtue of patience, essential in a country woman and a farmer's wife, had been carried away like all her rectitude. So where in the name of heaven was he?

There were credible reasons, though, that Giancarlo might lag behind Duncan in coming home. She walked and walked in the small scope of his room, and felt a rising fury, directed not so much at Giancarlo himself but at the general forces of delay that now mocked her. The afternoon grew freezing without him there. The air went blue gray with the promise of coming dark.

A wise counsel overtook her and urged her to return to the house, and—as if the news might contain a clue—ask Duncan what was in the paper. Where were the Allies located just now in their many-pronged advance towards the core of Europe where Neville was located? That was always a fruitful line of discussion with Duncan. Would the army advancing from Italy, the army advancing through France, or the Russian army from the east be the one who set Neville free? She could discuss Neville in a fever of submerged dread. Poor boy who deserved to be free! She had finally received a postcard: *All good,* Neville had written, *and having some theatricals in camp. Food OK, considering. Lots of love to you.*

History was in favor of liberating him, and yet she wondered again if his release would pull her further down into the life of dreariness her mother had been right to foretell.

On her fretful return towards the house, chickens seemed intent on running between her legs and tripping her. The calf had not yet been locked in the shed—one of Giancarlo's evening tasks. She did the job herself, smelling the complex, earthy aromas of the shed, pollen, fodder, motor oil, all turning cold with the dwindling day. She went out again amongst the chickens, and all at once decided that Giancarlo's nonappearance was serious enough for her to go searching. By the water tank she found her bike with its frayed netting over the back wheel, to prevent her skirt getting caught in the spokes. Surely, even at dusk, riding a bike was an innocent enough exercise, explainable in terms of Giancarlo's nonappearance and apt for a woman used from childhood to cycling on bumpy surfaces, gravels and ruts, and with a friend to look for.

She rode the tracks left by truck and tractor along fence lines, and the failure of the landscape to present him in this half light seemed malicious, a judgment emanating from the darkening fringes of bush. The idea of Duncan's two small dams suddenly tormented her, the chance of a face submerged by some unlikely accident. Now she pedaled without any pretense of casual journeying. She fumbled with the cranky, gimcrack wire fasteners with which Duncan closed his paddock gates. Arriving at the dams, in each case she flung her bicycle from her. But he hadn't come to grief in either of them.

"Giancarlo!" she hopelessly called under early stars. She found her bike again and bounced fretfully back towards the homestead, but then detoured at a fork onto the road that would lead her to the front gate. She knew, though, that he could not have taken to the main road. It was forbidden, and she thought there was something regular about him, something of the rule obeyer. Though he was an anarchist, he had a contradictory respect for Control Center rules, or, more likely, for Duncan. She did not go outside the farm herself—there was no point—but her eyes stretched east-west along the rutted and determined loneliness of the road.

She did not know what destination to choose now and so rode back to the shearers' quarters again rather than confront the kitchen. Giancarlo's neat room with dusk collecting in it was a dead space. And colder still. By his absence he seemed to permit ice to form over the frenzy they'd occupied this space with whenever, afternoons and early mornings, resolve evaporated, as they had clearly planned it would. But she was sweating with fury, too. *She* was the ordained agent who would end the issue. He was trying somehow, by vanishing, to steal that role, and steal it early instead of later.

She dragged her bike back to the water stand and doubled over and straightened again in a rhythm of pain. She gathered herself and went into the bleak homestead to dish up the lamb that was that evening's meal. No meat rationing on Herman's farm!

"How's our Italian friend?" asked Duncan, seated at the table in his slippers, putting aside his thin cigarette into an ashtray. The kitchen had a warmth that meant nothing. Like warmth on the wrong side of a window, it did not benefit her.

"He wasn't there," said Alice, straining for offhandedness. "I just sat there and had a read of a book we gave him. But he didn't turn up. He might have gone for a walk, I don't know."

"Then where do you reckon he is?" asked Duncan.

She said vengefully, "Who can tell with those people?" And then, "Did you two have a row?"

"No," Duncan answered with a little annoyance. "He was a bit quiet. But no row."

She opened the oven and was inspecting the lamb and probing it with a fork as if its tenderness counted for anything when the telephone rang. Fork in rigid hand, she immediately suspended her inquiries into the condition of the meat. Duncan went to the hallway to answer it. After some seconds she could hear the surprised intonation of his speech, though not what he was saying. She began to move after a while, putting the fork down and numbly putting out the plates and knives and forks, the Worcestershire and mint sauces, the salt and pepper and Keen's Mustard. Then the bread Duncan liked to use to attack the gravy with, on its bread board and with its bread knife. God save me from all this—from plates that expect food, from muted flavors, from the endless chewing of animal sinew.

Duncan came back frowning. "That was the Hammonds," he told her before she could ask. "Giancarlo's over on their place. Hiding out with *their* dago. Will our tea spoil if I go and get him?"

She shook her head in what she hoped was a matter-of-fact manner at such inexplicable news. "No," she muttered. "I'll keep it warm."

The kitchen became somehow intolerable when Duncan had gone. Rage unhinged her. She walked to the back veranda, continued out under a trellis where straggly vines grew, found the outer air gravidly dark, the night flopping to earth like a slothful beast. Fretfully, she left it all and went into the house again. An hour and a half passed this way. Long enough for her margin of fear to grow. It could not be guessed what arguments, confessions, humiliations, declaring of intentions, would accompany the two men back from Hammond's place, and how this would enable further men and Control Centers and colonels to take him from her.

When she heard the truck approach the farmhouse, the urge to flee for fear of what she'd see and hear and, above all, say was intense. As she further heard the garden gate creak, she began—like a claim to innocence and command—to slice the lamb and serve the meal onto three plates. He would eat it, she swore—every shred. She heard them both walking around the house towards the kitchen door, and the harshness of their boots on the boards of the back veranda.

Hangdog, Giancarlo entered first in his abominable maroon-colored suit. He rarely wore it anymore on the farm. The fact that he wore it now was meaningful in a way she needed time to think about. And where did the cowardice of his posture come from? Had he learned that from his initial surrender, the North African one?

"There you are, then," the relentlessly jovial Duncan said to her as he followed Giancarlo in. He veered off into the pantry and came back with a bottle of sherry.

"Get two glasses, will you, Johnny?" he asked Giancarlo. Giancarlo glanced wanly at Alice, but a mere second. Then, knowing the kitchen arrangements, what dressers held what, he got two glasses out and put them on the corner of the kitchen table, set as it was for the evening meal. His face grew vacant and his eyes were fixed on the bottle. Duncan poured half a tumbler and offered it to Giancarlo. He immediately accepted it, merely inclining his head.

Duncan said, "That'll warm you. And make you feel more at home."

Giancarlo took it and still looked at an indefinite middle distance. Alice wanted to take him by the jaws and drag his face towards her. She wanted to punish him, the way a cherished child is punished after petrifying its parents with its absence, and to punish him more than that, though all she could think of was hurling the meat plate at him. But she began to dole out the roast potatoes instead.

Duncan began to explain it all to Alice. "Poor Johnny was homesick. That's what he told the Hammonds. Wanted to talk to the Italian they've got over there on their place. I can understand that. You'd expect it. A bit of homesickness."

Giancarlo said, "You need send me back to the *Centro*, the Control Center. Not allowed to wander off. And for certain I wander off."

"Rubbish," said Duncan. "Do you think I'm going to lose a good worker like you? To hell with the Control Center!"

"How would going over to Hammond's help your homesickness?" Alice asked Giancarlo in her cold fury. Why had Duncan accepted it as an explanation? "I never knew the man over there was such a friend of yours. It isn't as if Italy is any closer at Hammond's than it is here."

"If I wander," he told her, his regretful eyes on her suddenly, emphasizing the message, "the *Centro* take me back to camp. That is the true of it."

"The *truth* of it," she told him scaldingly. "Haven't you learned anything from the books I gave you?"

Duncan frowned. "Don't be hard on him. Come on, our tea's getting cold."

They all sat. Giancarlo's eyes were still lowered. They began eating the lamb and roast potatoes and carrots and string beans.

"First class," said Duncan. "Doesn't this do your heart any good, Johnny?"

"I let you down," said Giancarlo as a statement of fact. "You got to send me back. The *commandante* give me twenty-eight-day detention I deserve."

She wanted to reach out and strike him. Here was a renunciation of her, right in front of Duncan.

"Sorry, Missus 'Erman," said Giancarlo softly.

Duncan laughed. "She understands," he said. "She understands homesickness."

"I'm not so sure I understand this version," she insisted.

• • •

On the night of Giancarlo's temporary escape to the Hammonds', Alice made another secret visit to his quarters. She felt calmer now, though still not appeased. Her excursion did seem absurd in some ways, her clothing—army overcoat, nightgown, thick socks within heavy boots—all ridiculous and ungainly. Yet as she skirted the house and slipped amongst the fruit trees, she began to feel sage, like a teacher about to show a student the order of the world. In the hour since the meal she'd served them, she had come to see that it was not a decline in his ardor that had caused his vanishing, but a *heightening* of his feelings, and fear of some vast outfall. These motives could be forgiven. Now the idea that she wanted to soothe and wisely chastise him obscured the other objective—to start up the entanglement again.

In any case, she knew she was in charge now, that she was in a position to question him. Her *rat-tat-tat* on the door was that of a person who expected entry as a right. She heard him move inside his room, as if it were exactly what he had lain waiting for. He answered the door so swiftly that he must have been waiting, his open eyes fixed on a ceiling it was too dark for him to see. She noticed as she edged past him that his body was somehow cowed and uncertain. When the door was shut and she stood there waiting, he went and lit his Tilley lamp in the corner, the one fitted with a mantle to shield the pulsing dim light even more, so that little of its glimmer would penetrate the heavy burlap curtains with which the window was hung. He left the lamp there on the floor, but when he rose it shone upwards against his lowered eyes. He sat at the table where their teas and reading classes had taken place and pointed with a solemnity of gesture for her to take a chair there as well.

The tenor of this meeting was of course different from early ones—everything between them was utterly changed by his attempt to be arrested and disciplined and returned to a prison compound.

"Well," she said, and reached for his wrist and with her index finger stroked the downy hair there.

"Mr. 'Erman," he said, lifting his eyes at last and emitting a small groan. "You know. A good fellow."

She said softly, "Do you love Mr. Herman more than you do me? If you'd had your way, you'd have never seen me again. Did you want that?"

"No," he said. "But it was getting too large. It had got so big there was no room anymore."

"Oh," she said, treading that edge between composure and a sort of acid amusement, yet already, she knew, displaying a meanness, a concealed bullying. "No room left? There was plenty of room when you first lay down with me. It was an adventure, then, wasn't it? To use the lonely woman? *La sposa solitaria?*"

Behind her chagrin, she was crazily pleased to show him how her Italian had come on. To suggest how it might come on if it existed in Italian surroundings.

"It is not a good thing for you, Alice," he told her. "What we do. Better it was just fun, like the girl and the boy in a park. Hello, good-bye."

"Well," she said, "it is not that."

"You understand," he insisted. "Better if it were, you know, *avventura.*"

"Oh yes," she said, "an adventure."

And she did not know what to do with the word, and was caught between scorn, which she sensed was useless but tempting, and stretching her imagination beyond spite and taking it close to agreeing with him. Safer if it had been an *avventura*. And more tidy. And more pardonable.

"Please don't leave me here," she said, suddenly, all her confidence and sense of power gone.

He took her hand. He stood up and leaned over and kissed her. He turned the Tilley lamp out and they returned to their tract of warmth, a bed designed for a single shearer against a cold wall. All questions were suspended or, more exactly, did not apply in that arena.

But it was as she returned later towards her bedroom window at an hour when in summer there would already have been a dawn glow, that the tedious spaces of the house and its skirt of garden and shed and fruit trees reclaimed her, and she felt the authority of her hunger fall from beneath her. If there had been a place where she could have been locked up, as Giancarlo had sought to get locked up, at that hour she would have chosen it herself.

23

Colonel Abercare was driven through the northeast sector of town and towards the training camp, which was set on flatter ground three miles north of Gawell. The Ewan Abercare who approached that installation had never been more at ease with his life, not even when he'd been young and wild in India and itching with ambitions, carnal and military. He had achieved Emily's return. That was a guarantee of contentment. More keenly than ever, he knew the carnal and the military were evanescent. He had a sense from her embraces, which were at first wary, that he had partly to thank Dr. Delaney and Mozart for this thorough and new rapport—Emily was charmed and consoled by Dr. Delaney's superior kind of Mass, which annoyed other worshippers by its length. Mozart, in invoking the true body of Christ so melodically and solemnly, had somehow reconciled her to Gawell and thus, within Gawell, to her marriage.

On the military side of his life, Abercare had himself chosen the positions of the Vickers guns on the perimeter, and even in this Suttor had chosen to quarrel over it, declaring it was his understanding that machine guns should be placed much further back, at least two hundred yards from the fence. Abercare declared that the first of them should be sited close to the wire and on the edge of the camp by the gates of Main Road. It should be left there unmanned and sitting on a trailer so that it might serve as mute discouragement to the prisoners. There, it was nearly two hundred yards from the prison huts, and it was the distance from the huts that counted. So placed, argued Abercare, it could fire down the length of the first of the camp's twelve, nearly circular, sides, three of them owned by Compound C.

The second gun he had set back on the edge of the bush so that it might fire down the midsection of the fence and so that its crew did not run the risk of being killed by the first machine gun. Abercare had seen such arrangements, according to lines of sight, made in the defense of camps during the troubles in Waziristan just ten years before, in another age, when the Fakir of Ipi was innocently considered more dangerous than Hitler and Tojo.

Suttor had registered his own convictions about the placement of guns in a marginally respectful letter. But it was Ewan Abercare's decision, and he made it. He also took the trouble now to go into the Japanese compound every day at four and inspect the demeanor of the inmates—a vain endeavor but one that must be undertaken. Abercare noticed that they seemed a little more prompt than they had previously been—it had been necessary to harry them into the ranks in the past. Did this mean they believed resistance to the process had become less necessary now that they were so sure about their futures? Or, to put it more accurately, their lack of a future. Their faces looked at him emptily, confessing neither hostility nor expectation.

"Do you think they're more tractable recently?" he asked Suttor. "A bit less cheek from them?"

Suttor said, "Perhaps." And then he weighed the proposition. "They go through phases," he concluded almost genially.

When the moon was new and nothing but a shadow, he had slept in his quarters in the barracks, where he could be promptly roused by the duty officer. He slept there four nights while it was still a minor crescent. Despite all the lights he had erected it was the moon that ruled his intentions, and after the half-moon presented itself he went back to town and Emily.

As a means of pacifying Compound C, Suttor had released into the orderly hut within the wire three copies of the *Sydney Morning Herald* for those few who could read and translate for their brethren. There were a few former merchant seamen, Yokohama hands, who had the shaky capacity to write out on toilet paper rough versions of what they saw in the newspapers.

Unlike earlier toilet-paper bulletins, the claim that Saipan had fallen produced the most profound erosion of belief. Many men reasoned that if the enemy were choosing to mislead, to pretend to success, it would have been beyond their gifts to claim a capture so far north in the Pacific as that of Saipan. It sounded so credible, in fact, that Tengan and others honored it with the idea that now, by capturing these islands, the enemy was straining his lines of supply and communication so far that his string would soon run out. This was not the cry of the majority.

Such was the situation at Gawell Camp when Colonel Abercare approached his counterpart at the infantry training camp. He did not know its commander, Horace Deakin, intimately. He knew of Deakin's good repute, but that he had not evaded the chief vice of a training officer—to despise his charges. When he was finished with them, his eighteen-year-olds were either further educated in rainforests in Queensland or else thrown with less decorous preparation into a military adventure—perhaps even the invasion of the enemy homeland, at which task, Deakin was sure, they would, despite all effort put into them, behave haplessly.

On this visit, some days after the emergency meeting at the headquarters in Sydney, Abercare sat in Colonel Deakin's office—Abercare sleek and Deakin hollow-cheeked—passing on the news of a potential outbreak one dark night, and reviewing the signals by which the training battalion would know it had occurred.

Colonel Deakin asked Abercare, "Dark night?"

"Even our informer overheard them say it. A dark night, no moon."

"But," said Deakin, frowning over expressive brown eyes, "if their aim is to get killed, wouldn't any day or night do?"

"No," said Abercare. "Because, again according to our source, they want to capture our company armories. As well as doing themselves harm, they want to do us some. A combination of motives."

They had tea, and while drinking it Deakin made it clear the defense of *his* camp was paramount, because of its substantial magazines. The safety of the town itself was connected to that issue. And if there was an outbreak, the signals from the camp must be clear, for he had a hundred women from the Army Service, nurses and clerks, in the training camp. "It's unthinkable what might happen to them . . ."

Abercare referred him to the preexisting document covering the issue—the arrangement for shots and flares, the siren.

"We can't be expected to necessarily notice them," said Deakin, with a desire to fix the entire issue on his own camp and its integrity. If he had had spaciousness of mind in Syria, had been capable of any broad reading, he had lost the gift now, three years later. "Distance and wind might muffle the shots, and the siren ditto. Terrain might block our view of flares."

"Well," Abercare conceded, "be assured that my duty officer would be straight on to yours by phone. Would you be in a position to send support?"

"I could send out one company of my first battalion as soon as it could be arranged. This would be to contain your perimeter, or if it were breached to round up escapees."

Abercare had hoped for a little more, but a company of more than a hundred was not to be despised.

"And that would be dispatched . . . ?"

"As promptly as it can be arranged."

Abercare passed an intelligence assessment over the table to Deakin, who read it as if it were designed to affront the tenor of his mind. "Well," he said, "this camp here would still be the king on the chessboard. I must employ the mass of my recruits to defend it. At least they can do that without shooting farmers' cows by accident or design. My desk is laden with farmers' complaints about ill-disciplined fire sweeping across their paddocks. That's the problem with sending them out in numbers, you see. Farmers."

A company dispatched promptly would be very welcome, Abercare told Deakin. Then he broached the issues of morality, of diplomatic necessity, and of the risk of brutal retaliation against our prisoners up there, in the indefinite reaches of Asia and Melanesia. Morality dictated patrols should recapture any men who escaped from Compound C and should not shoot them even if they pleaded to be shot. "The diplomatic problem," he said, "involves the good repute we have so far with the Swiss Red Cross and the Japanese section of the Swiss consulate general, to whom the Japanese command listen—if they listen to anyone. In that case, I wonder, might you send me a copy of any relevant orders you now issue? I hope you don't mind my asking." Deakin conceded that that was all right. He looked into the middle distance. It was as if he were thinking, The final battle is close, and this is such a picayune matter. There would be no outbreak. The boys in his camp would be fighting in the streets of Yokohama, and he would still be in this bush camp and nothing would have happened.

Part of Abercare agreed with him.

After his preparations were in place, a comforting signal from the New South Wales headquarters reached Colonel Abercare. Plans were being drawn up in Sydney to split up Compound C, and move the Japanese NCOs away from Gawell to another camp further west. Amongst the officers of the garrison, only compound and company commanders were to be told as yet. Abercare felt an intense lifting of a pressure he had not known he felt so sharply. This would assure it. No outbreak.

Further instructions came as the headquarters marshaled the necessary transport. On the morning of the first Monday of August, the NCOs would be transported to Gawell railway station in a convoy of trucks. From there a train with opaque and barred windows would take them west to the camp at Wye. Bereft of its leadership, the supposed stratagem of self-obliteration amongst the lower ranks within Compound C would be orphaned.

The garrison somehow knew what was to happen—they had seen the new guards, assigned to take the Compound C men westwards, arrive by truck from another camp. The garrison tasks of the guards were banal, but now at last they had found out, under warning of keeping the secret, something exceptional. By lunchtime on the following Monday, after a watchful weekend, there'd be barely more than half the bastards in Compound C.

Abercare understood that secrets escaped almost by their own internal pressure, by the pressure of the vanity of those men who held them. He conferred with Suttor on the issue of informing the prisoners themselves—of finding a sensible mean between the inevitable leakage of the news, which would enrage the prisoners and perhaps make them reckless, and him or Suttor or both forthrightly telling the prisoners. Abercare thought the men should be told on Saturday afternoon, according to the recommendations of the Geneva Convention that men be given adequate time to prepare for being moved.

Suttor suggested Abercare might perhaps have misread the provisions of the Geneva Convention. "I consulted it myself and in Chapter Eight there is a provision the prisoners must be told where they are being sent. But there is no mention of giving them enough time for farewell parties or troublemaking."

Abercare went and got the Geneva Convention from his shelf, and a volume of Red Cross recommendations regarding prisoners. The fact he got two codes, thought Suttor, meant he wasn't sure in which one of them the recommendation was. But Suttor said nothing. To do Abercare justice, he did not look like a man desperate to prove a point. He found the place in a pamphlet on Red Cross recommendations. "Here it is," he said. He read a passage that declared the International Committee of the Red Cross recommended that before prisoners were moved to another camp, they be given at least twenty-four hours' warning, although a longer warning might in most cases be recommended.

Suttor nodded but said, "That doesn't sound very binding. *Recommended?* In these circumstances?"

Abercare surrendered himself yet again to the inevitability of never liking the man, and never being liked. If we were an infantry battalion in the field, Abercare knew, he would need to get rid of Suttor—by organizing his promotion if other means failed.

"Well . . . how long would you give them if you had your way?" Abercare asked, leaching the question of any tone of annoyance.

"A day, if that?" Suttor suggested. "These are special circumstances involving prisoners who have made speeches about suicide and mayhem. I know how much notice the citizens of Gawell would want to give them. An hour."

"With due respect for the citizens of Gawell, the prisoners would not feel kindly towards any of us on one hour's notice. It would be good vengeance but a destructive policy. But a little under two days makes sense for all of us. They must have time to pack and say their good-byes."

Suttor said, "This is an enemy that has refused to ratify the Geneva Convention."

"But we have, and we fulfill our commitments."

Suttor, nakedly aggrieved now, said, "I hope that helps my son. And all the others spread across North Asia."

"Telling them before the men go to town for a drink on Saturday night is wise. And as well as that, the news will cause a lot of drinking of grappa and bombo. It's likely half of them will be tight for the last two nights. And even without the new searchlights, these were wrong nights for any attack from inside the compound—especially if the prisoners had any ambition to capture the armory."

"And we'll get a big tick from the Swiss and the Red Cross," said Suttor, calmer now but still intractable and shaking his head. "For what that's worth."

For his daily inspection of the compound, Major Suttor took three armed guards and Nevski, who never wore a sidearm.

Suttor's instructions had always been not to be overly diligent about searching. Homemade weapons were to be confiscated, but he did not want to find the stills they possessed, which turned their polished rice leftovers into the clear liquor they called bombo. Neither he nor Abercare were concerned if their prisoners stupefied themselves with booze. They did not seem to be aggressive drunks, and bombo, like the news of Saipan, was a means of pacifying the compound.

In the same spirit, Abercare had decided that it would create great suspicion if the captives saw the machine guns permanently manned. It was enough to mount them on trailers with belts of bullets in tin cans arrayed plentifully around their bases. The nights abetted this policy—even apart from the searchlights that drenched the compound with yellow, migraine-inducing light, they were bright, and the moon rose fuller every night. With the searchlights beating down from the outer camp and from within the Main Road, and beneath the vertical eye of the moon, every timber of every hut was delineated.

Nevski, Suttor noticed whenever he entered the compound with him, walked through with his chin high. It had always been thought that the Russian might be able to cultivate some of the Japanese as sources, or at least friends. This hope took no account of the previous war between Russia and Japan, which had destroyed Nevski's life at the university in Harbin. Suttor saw that there existed a special hostility directed by the inhabitants of Compound C towards Russians.

Nevski's clinical and careful behavior had failed to make him a favorite there. He was a true scholar and had a true scholar's pedagogic reserve. He was a good, but not winning, soul.

"'Shitdrip,'" Nevski told Suttor they sometimes called him.

"And, 'fart voice.' And yet," he said, defending them, "they are not a very foul-mouthed people. They are surprisingly fastidious."

The prisoners did not seem to react to the company of new guards that had been introduced, a few truckloads at a time, into the camp. These transfer guards, a little excited to have a break from the arid plains out there at Wye, settled into the mess, and discussed and compared the camp they came from and the one, less monotonous in terrain, they now found themselves in. In the meantime, in the railway yards, which could not be seen from Gawell Camp, the train with the blinded and barred windows had arrived and been located on a siding.

24

Sergeant Nevski and an escort of guards appeared in the Compound C mess hut at lunchtime on Saturday.

"Present yourself at the gate in Main Road at two o'clock," Nevski told Aoki. "Bring Mr. Goda and pompous young Mr. Tengan. There is something of significance you must discuss with the colonel."

"Significance?" asked Aoki.

Nevski declared axiomatically, a little like an annoying scholar, "If I told you the significance now, it wouldn't be significant, would it? Just be punctual."

The three men were at the gate at the nominated time, and were marched up Main Road, through the huts of Suttor's company and so to Abercare's office a little beyond. There Abercare had had chairs placed around the room to accommodate them in the manner of a conference, and he invited them to sit. He offered them some of his Navy-cut cigarettes. Aoki would have accepted if judgmental Tengan had not been there with his automatic and universal rejection of mercy.

For translation by Nevski, Abercare declared that the subject he was about to broach with them was fixed in place and was not open for discussion by them or him. They must accept it, it came from superior authorities, and there was no way out of it. They and other men of rank from Compound C were to be separated from the NCOs and sent west to the camp at Wye.

"It will occur on Monday morning," he explained. "I have told you today purely out of courtesy and based on the recommendation of the Red Cross. I hope this courtesy will be respected. It is granted so that you can say good-bye to your men and to your friends, and attend to whatever possessions you choose to take with you."

The prisoners said nothing. Each of them was astonished, and it was news on a scale one needed to weigh over time. The announcement hung in the room and exerted its weight on Abercare as well.

Aoki gestured for Tengan to speak first, as the first of the prisoners to know Compound C and the one who reached certainty very quickly. Tengan turned to Nevski as if to demand a fair translation, and then spoke in a voice whose level of threat was not remarkable, since it was his normal tone. "This will not be a good thing," Nevski translated him as saying. "Your army might be different. But in ours the bond between NCOs and the men is unbreakable."

Abercare studied them but as ever learned not a great amount, except that the older men, Aoki and Goda, had shown a marked respect for the aviator in letting him state their case. Aoki said then, "Senior Sergeant Goda and I agree with the sergeant that the men will be very angry." Goda made an assenting gurgle in his throat.

"Well," said Abercare, depending on Nevski's translation, "there is no point in anger. It is your duty as one of their leaders to reconcile the men to what cannot be avoided. *This* cannot be avoided and, after all, by the standards of all you've been through in your military lives, it is a small rearrangement. The war will soon be finished and then reunions can occur. You'll have a long sea voyage home to become reacquainted with each other."

All three of them rose and, as they did each morning, bowed to him—performing the respectful concession to his rank even within his army of clowns and savages. It was all so solemn that it could have passed as satire, Abercare thought. He had a sense that the meeting was ending perhaps too promptly, even if everything that could be said had been.

Nevski was appointed by Abercare to escort Tengan, Aoki, and Goda as they marched in a severely dignified file back to Compound C. The sun seemed to be benign at this hour and beneath it men were sitting at pine tables in the open playing cards or Go and mahjongg. There was some baseball practice in progress, and that satisfying *bock!* when bat struck ball full-on. From the recreation hall came the plaint of stringed instruments and Sakura's complaining, ironic voice rehearsing some ballad.

There had been a supposition by Abercare and Suttor that the three might discuss their situation with Nevski and thus give some illumination on their true feelings, their degree of cooperative sentiment. But they said nothing, so Nevski asked before he left them, "How do you feel about all that, gentlemen?" But he knew it was a clumsy question. They did not answer. There was a guttural belch—he could not have said from which one.

Once Nevski had said good-bye to them and begun to leave with his escort, he noticed that they seemed uncertain what first step to take. Aoki bent down and massaged his upper thigh, as if it had been paining him throughout the interview, but he had not wanted to demonstrate that to Abercare and Suttor. Watching from the Main Road outside the compound, Nevski saw them at last strike on an objective, and turn towards the hut in which Aoki was leader. Aoki collected two young prisoners on the way—one was the wrestler, Oka—and set them as sentries at either end of his hut. The three leaders would first summon together their parliament of other hut and section leaders, Nevski concluded. Their parliament, their prisoners' soviet.

Giancarlo's escape from the Herman farm, forgive it or not, continued to have its influence on Alice, and an impulse arose to do what she had condemned in Giancarlo. She wanted to escape the farm and the question of Giancarlo. It struck her that she had every means to do so, at least for a few days. She could leave dutiful stews for Duncan and Giancarlo to heat, and she would visit her girlhood friend Esther Sutcliffe, who was married to an engine driver named Ronnie and lived in Carcoar. Recently she and Esther had not been as close—the things that had drawn them together in childhood, shared grudges against teachers and a sort of enchantment with each other's company, had vanished. But she wanted her girlhood back now, and at the same time had a suspicion there was something fruitful or curative to be learned from Esther about marriage.

Alice had written to Esther earlier that week. Esther wrote back a come-as-you-choose letter, and Alice sent a telegram announcing her arrival time. Then she packed her bag and decided she'd let Duncan tell Giancarlo that she had gone away for a few days. Facing Giancarlo might have changed her mind.

It was the Blayney train she caught, criticized for its snaillike pace and satirized by young travelers, who often jumped off and jogged beside it. With its number of unhurried stops along the way, it took nearly three hours to reach Carcoar. But she enjoyed the fallow time it gave her and even read coherently a few articles from the *Women's Weekly*. When she walked with her suitcase up the road to Esther's little railway cottage of plum-colored brick, she was pleased to see straight off that Esther could not be mistaken for an unmarried woman. She was still good-looking but somehow more solid in a way that did not have to do with physical weight. The established planes on her face and an enhancement of the hips bespoke her as being settled for life, embayed in marriage, in Ronnie Sutcliffe—a pleasant man no more inspiring than Neville.

Alice discovered that Esther lived amongst noise and mess, since she had three children under the age of six. She attended to them with casual efficiency, not letting any of them interrupt her sentences, many of which were devoted to what had befallen other girls they'd been to school with. This is what Alice wanted. Her idea had been to go and more or less take a bath in the normality of that squalling little house in Carcoar. She wanted to calm herself down, get over thinking of herself and Giancarlo as if he and she were characters in some great drama, instead of laughable figures on a plain mixed farm outside Gawell.

In her two days' break with Esther she drank a great deal of tea while, almost as a side thought, looking after the three children. She was especially aware of the heavier and more settled nature of Esther's body, its fullness and its gravity, when they took the five-year-old to school. Alice held the hand of the three-year-old girl while Esther pushed the younger boy in a stroller. Alice wanted a body like that, one that had got safely home and was beyond madness and didn't have to fret itself. She would get one from having children. Surely, given what she knew now about sex, she could achieve them eventually with Neville. Indeed, Esther took it for granted that the only reason Alice didn't have a child was Neville's absence. But Giancarlo had taught her how to achieve a state of delight without necessarily risking pregnancy. With Neville, properly tutored by her, the trick of conception might be completed.

The cottage was somehow not as cold as the Herman homestead—Ronnie could always get coal for the fire, and if not coal then wood, and the rooms were smaller. But Alice's assigned bedroom, very small, grew much colder at night, since nights were, in every way, a different story. During the day she could drench herself in the normality of Ronnie and Esther's house and drink tea to the limit of her bladder. Ronnie got it from an uncle who was a grocer in Bathurst. When billeted in Bathurst railway barracks, he always made a respectful visit and came away with a little more of everything than rationing allowed others.

Esther wanted to know about Neville. Alice told her about his camp in Austria, unless he'd been recently moved. And everyone had already heard, said Esther, of how he'd reached the island named

Chios—way over near Turkey—in a Greek boat and had nearly got away from there before the enemy had arrived. "He was game as Ned Kelly," Esther asserted reverently. "And unlucky, poor bloke."

As she spoon-fed the baby boy some arrowroot, Alice thought, This is life—a spoonful of arrowroot. Giancarlo is something else. He's over there, in a dangerous sphere where no sane girl would want to live for long.

When Alice left the warm kitchen for her bedroom to get the book and the magazine she had brought with her, and discovered her inner cold in the corridor, she would pass the open door of Esther and Ronnie's bedroom. There emerged even in the cold hallway a heavy scent of fertility, and plain but endless affection. There was no scent of frenzy. It was a companionable smell—of the accustomed, the regular, and the unpunished. As she stood there, inhaling, she thought, There it is, I'm cured. I'll take that home.

But she lost her grasp on all that at night. It was disgraceful. Giancarlo still called her "missus" in public and even in private only occasionally said "Alice," to be safe, to make a slip less likely in front of Duncan. She heard his particular ways of uttering the word, in nuances of deception and friendship and lust, and rehearsed them mentally and for hours during the night. At those times it seemed nothing was healed in her, and no lessons had been learned.

25

The lack of normal time-killing activities taking place in Compound C that afternoon was explained by the rumors the senior NCOs had, by their very solemnity, sparked in the compound. Baseball practice or competition was futile now that the teams would vanish overnight. Card games were abandoned, all musical rehearsals, instrumental and vocal, went mute.

The council of three sat cross-legged on two mattresses, dividing almost as they always had: Tengan the flier on one, and Aoki and Goda the commoners on another, but old enough to feel amused rather than outraged by Tengan's assumptions.

"Well," Aoki murmured, "I have to admit, we couldn't get a clearer indication than this."

The two infantrymen lit and began to smoke their thin cigarettes. Tengan made a murmuring and threatening sound to overbear the unease of Oka's nearness as guard at the door, of his defeat by the huge young idiot, and of his sexual submission. "Yes, it has been long enough," he said. "I knew something like this was going to come. I can't deny that sunlight under any sky is sweet. But I've been a prisoner for more than two years, so a neutral party might accuse me of being a delayer."

The extraordinary admission silenced the two older men awhile. This sudden, admitted rawness. It was in its way a preparation for the end—as if Tengan did not care about the accusations and slurs. Because now he was taking action.

"This is why you snarl at newcomers?" asked Goda. "To stop them accusing you of delay?"

"Do I snarl?" he asked, returned to his old severity. He sniffed at their tobacco fumes.

It was characteristic of Tengan, though, to measure the intentions of the whole compound by his personal need, his number one prisonerhood—and thus to declare that this was the ordained hour for everyone else.

Goda said, "Let's not get ahead of ourselves. We have to tell the other hut leaders first. The men should vote, even if we believe we know what their decision will be. I think we ought to have a drink, too, while we all discuss things. It might be the last chance. Get that great lump outside . . . Bear, is it? . . . Oka? . . . Get him to fetch some bombo."

Aoki was a little amazed that the suggestion would come from the apparently dour Goda, though he knew by now that to read Goda as lacking any taste for solace was a mistake.

"Do you think we need liquor to help us reach a decision?" asked Tengan.

"No," said Goda. "But it would be brotherly, and a toast to seal the issue. It will also be, one way or another, the last time the hut leaders meet. Besides, what's it matter if some of us get a bit tanked? It'll create a fiery sentiment."

Goda went to the door to give Oka instructions, and to recruit another guard to replace him. Then he ordered two men playing flower cards outside to go and notify the hut and section leaders.

As they waited, the three counselors couldn't help but continue predebating the outcome. So, returning to his palliasse and dropping to his haunches, Aoki said, "It's hard to get around to carrying out one's obligations here. They put us in a daze by jamming us together and feeding us better than we ever were in China and the islands. We're like neutered cats. But I think they've given us back our balls now."

"*I* certainly refuse to be sent away," the admirable Goda declared. "But others might be willing to be sent. In my opinion, that should not be a matter on which we point fingers, mainly because it is an individual duty. If some men don't face up to it, they have to consider what this will mean for the remainder of their lives."

"They'll all be executed at the end," Tengan asserted, but without dogmatism.

"I don't know that we all believe that anymore," said Aoki. "We must understand, too, that many of the men will want to go along with any suggested action, not because they choose it for themselves, but because they don't want to let us down, or their hut leaders or their brothers inside here. But I know there might be others who will back away despite all that. I'm in accord with my friend Goda. Men should make their free choice. Otherwise, what is suicide worth?"

"Free choice?" asked Tengan. "Have they resigned from the army?"

"I haven't," said Aoki. "But even I feel the world beyond us here is changing, and that under their flesh men's opinions might be changing too. In this matter, I can speak only for myself. I can address only my own obligation. A coerced sacrifice isn't worth a lot here. A voluntary one is a different matter. In any case, let's wait now and talk to the others."

The memory of China rose in him, as it always did when he contemplated death by his own volition.

"There are a few riders to be raised as well," Aoki went on. "An important issue for those of us who survive and get to the outside is what to do with civilians. *They* presume that we are savage towards civilians. But the purpose is to take their soldiers with us, not women and children and old men."

The others both said they were willing to agree to that. The civilian population was an irrelevance, said Tengan.

Around the time Colonel Abercare went to collect his wife to go to dinner with the Garners, the guards in the tower and those in the tent and on the gates of Main Road noticed considerable groups of men going from one hut to another. This was understandable in view of the coming separation, and was considered to prefigure nothing remarkable.

In Aoki's hut, the triumvirate stood at one end with their backs against the wall that sectioned the hut in two. They bowed to the assemblage, who bowed in turn, and then seated themselves on tatami mats and low beds. As Aoki broke the news to the assembled leaders, a few junior men passed around bottles and jars of rice liquor. It seemed to Aoki that some of the hut leaders had already enjoyed a pannikin or two of bombo since roll call and that perhaps Goda's idea that sociable drink should be offered here was a mistake. But if men were fueled by the stuff, they would be more inflamed and ready to commit themselves to the charge.

Whether solaced by rice and potato distillations or not, the hut commanders listened to Aoki assuring them that Abercare's mind could not be changed, and that he claimed to lack the authority to alter the arrangements. The fact that he was pleased not to have the authority was obvious, said Aoki, but any further appeal to the man would put him on his guard.

"So, here we are," he concluded, "and what do we do now?" He declared that men in their various huts must be consulted on any motion passed here. He also spoke of the pressure for an outbreak and declared that would come from men's military selves rather than their shakier private selves. There were men who would do it, even if dubious as individuals, because hut leaders and NCOs—the remaining forms of command under which they had served—voted for it.

All this passed for now without argument. Hut leaders seemed calm. The air filled with accustomed cigarette smoke. "But," he warned, "the decision about whether to plan an outbreak will need to be made quickly, and action must quickly follow. For if it's delayed, all our plans could seep out through the wire, and might become apparent to the camp commander." Or even on prisoners' faces, he thought, some of which, in a new morning, might be hungover. If the long-spoken-of break was decided on, he declared further (and that was what they were to discuss here), it was time to produce their hidden and crude weaponry—the baseball bats, which had from the day of their entry into the compound recommended themselves as bludgeons, and which now were to be studded with nails; the honed knives stolen from the kitchens. All must be brought out ready for the charge.

It was curious to Aoki that when men were faced with this, the ultimate and the unpredictable, they often mentioned something minor, something pebble sized, as a great obstacle. One of the hut leaders said, "But *they* haven't even manned the machine guns yet."

"They will," Goda assured him. "Once we start. I wouldn't be worried about that."

The marine Hirano, leader of his own hut by now, cheered all souls by raising the germane point that the bored garrison got paid on Saturdays and then a third of them were allowed to go to town. They would drink beer and play cards and reel back to camp utterly unprepared. Best, therefore, for those such as him, who had decided to go, to move in the small hours. For it would be more opportune to attack confused men suffering from headaches. By choosing the right hour, the prisoners might not solely achieve their purpose within the wire, but those who were still upright could seize the garrison arms depot.

One of the older hut leaders, Kure—the one whose demeanor had offended Tengan at the end of the wrestling match with Oka—declared that though he would consult the men in his hut, and would do whatever was decided, he did not think he would encourage the hope of overthrowing the garrison or seizing armaments. There would be no cloud tonight and no fog, and the drench of light would favor the machine guns and self-atonement far more than it would any ambition to capture arms and wage a campaign.

Tengan was allowed to rise and state the basic principle: it did not matter if they overthrew the garrison or not. "But to show them we know how to run at their fire—that's the thing. Above all, getting to the immortal shrine where the dead are waiting for us—that's definitely the number one objective."

Again, guttural sounds of assent echoed around the hut and nearly all forty-nine men seemed to be preparing to explode in noisy unanimity.

"I suggest," Goda continued, "you don't yell your agreement or objection. That will be noticeable to the garrison. Let's have a show of hands."

But here their careening intentions were for a moment blocked. "Wait, wait," said a voice. "We haven't been allowed to speak on the motion." It was a hut leader who could not be accused of prevarication since he was a holder of the rare and cherished Order of the Golden Kite. "I don't know if we can achieve much," he said. "It's all such a rush. I think that, purely so we don't make fools of ourselves, we compose ourselves, make plans appropriate to a military operation, and go tomorrow night."

The all-at-once surly Hirano seemed the one most angered by the proposition of delay. He rose to his feet. Even so, he did not direct his fury too specifically at the holder of the Order of the Golden Kite.

"Can't you hear, all of you, daily, our fallen ones," he called, "even those who might sometimes have been tyrannous bastards, calling out to us, singing the regimental songs? I don't see them, but I certainly hear them. Because what else is there to listen to through all the time filling we do here? We've been asked to embroider nothingness here. As well as that, I am in the common situation of knowing that my wife and parents have installed my memorial tablet in the family shrine, and so absorbed my death. Those ashes can't be revived into the shape of a living return. We are caught between heaven and hell, and, I tell you, now this plan of separation has been foisted on us, I know more sharply than ever that we must be released from this state of neither life nor death. I feel sorry for those who cannot run against the wire and the guns. Yes, I know many have valid wounds. But that's where honor lies—to absorb an enemy bullet. And—by the way— to reduce his resources by at least those few ounces. And I know there are many who feel this way. I believe that those who oppose this have let themselves become foreigners in this camp. They are nothing more than vagrants in this middle zone we've let ourselves be stuck in. If we could see our own souls, what would we see? We would see those of baboons with bulging arses. Apes who live for the next banana."

As much as Aoki intended to run—or at least hobble—along with the others, he was somehow annoyed at the flamboyant ardor of this speech, even if it had been much applauded.

"Please," said Aoki, holding a hand up, even though he was aware Hirano's oratory had swept the floor. "We applaud your sentiments. But it is not a time to talk about baboon's arses. If we do this, it is to reward ourselves. And, again, if we do it—"

Cries of, "We'll do it, we'll do it!" arose from the floor.

Aoki held up his hand. "If we do it, that itself will shame those who backslide."

Hirano wanted to say more but yielded to Aoki's seniority and sat down.

One further hut leader got to his feet and said that there were practical issues as well as poetic and religious ones, and he would like to propose a motion. Men who could not charge the wire should be told that in hanging oneself, the belt buckle was meant to be behind the ear. There were other methods, too, of course. There were knives. "Cutting of the carotid is a good method."

The holder of the Order of the Golden Kite, as he alone could, asked, "But what if only a small group wish to attack the wire?"

Aoki looked at the other members of the troika. Almost involuntarily he regarded Tengan, in his way the prophet of self-obliteration, and now strangely withdrawn. No one else knew it, but Tengan was reprising within his own head the changes of engine pitch that had brought him down from the sky and the black party of plant gatherers who had captured him, and the self-amazed issue of his having been here so long.

Goda took up the slack, which would normally have been Tengan's pleasure to address. "If there is no majority for the breakout," he said, "I assume that those of us who still wish to go forward will do it. The vote in the huts does not take away that individual option in our cases."

The unassailable holder of the Order asked, "How are the men to vote—secretly, or before their peers?"

This point about the possibility of secret ballots seemed to annoy many, and some asked satirically what would be used for ballot boxes. Hats? Pisspots? And it was laughable to treat this as some sort of municipal election, said one.

Tengan, revived, now suggested they vote to put the motion to their men, and the assent seemed unanimous. Aoki proposed a further motion should be put to the men about leaving the civilian population alone. There was no dissenter amongst the leaders. For they had no imperial warning to impart to the town of Gawell anymore, no message about the folly of resistance. And there existed the ambition to make an immaculate sacrifice, one that could not be explained away by the enemy as a desire for plunder and savagery.

Aoki therefore concluded the meeting by declaring the vote in the huts should be taken before the bell for dinner sounded. Yes, there might be the remote problem of something being overheard by somebody such as Nevski, but that was a small chance compared to the imperative that men have time that evening to bathe for death and prepare themselves in ways of their choosing.

And so with a few further informal motions and ad hoc amendments, they were the parliament of death, even if their arguments seemed so full of the impulse of life and sagacity and compassion. Not all were vocal on these matters, and—Aoki sensed—there was still some scepticism that the ragtag garrison would oblige them; that it would get around to manning the machine guns.

The hut leaders finished off their rice spirit and moved out, pannikins in hand, in sudden silence, except for the clump of hard-tipped infantry boots the enemy had imposed on them, and went to their huts to institute the lethal voting process.

The committee of three themselves also moved out to conduct a vote, each in his own hut. Aoki's men reduced the enemy's stocks of toilet paper by voting in a secret ballot on scraps of it they had stolen from the latrines, the environs of the hated upright porcelain seats. He saw some men's eyes widen with terror at their own decision. But they all said yes. They sensed his wishes and would not vote against them.

Aoki told the dwellers of his hut to disperse again so that he could now receive the votes from elsewhere in Compound C. Tengan came back first with results—Tengan's vote had been open and all men agreed. Goda had the same result. "The fact it was put to them made them feel they had to say yes," muttered Goda percipiently, as if he, too, had seen the widening eyes.

Waiting for other results, they discussed tactical arrangements. The huts should be set fire to at the instant the outbreak began. Since there was so much light directed at the compound, so much moon above it, the prisoners had nothing to gain by not adding their own light. Tengan ran through the assigned tasks—which hut numbers would do what, based on their geography within the compound. He would lead the rush towards the Main Road gate, and so into open ground.

Goda agreed to wait ten minutes in the orderly room while a series of appointed runners came back—if still living—to inform him of the progress of things and then follow up the charge with any remaining men, calling out to those who might have been initially cowed and still sheltered on the ground to take on the fences and join themselves with the aspirations of Aoki's group to turn the weapons of the garrison against them.

In the case of those who attacked the outer wire—or, in Tengan's case, who led men into Main Road and tried to break through its outer gates—the men who reached the machine guns were to turn them on the garrison, and in their last hour take these old and imperfect enemy soldiers with them into the darkness. Yet should these battles make it possible for prisoners to reach the company magazines, these were certainly to be plundered and a last battle fought along more conventional infantry lines but with the same sacrificial objectives as the original rush.

It had to be faced, said Goda, the steady mind, that machine guns and magazines might not be taken. In that case, it was decided, it behooved any survivors to make off into the bush; to keep to the rocky, forested ridges, rather than the lowland pastures and roads. They could do more damage from these positions, and hide until patrols were close to them, and appear and startle them, perhaps harming some before themselves being shot by the ever-growing parties that would be sent forth against them. The enemy's reserves of men and weaponry would need to be expended in the process of finding and executing them, and thus they would not die without having eroded the strength of their adversary.

Aoki contemplated the end of his world, the affirmed widowhood of a wife whose face he scarcely remembered. There was an impulse to take more of the raw liquor as if he deserved a reward. He resisted it. There had been too much liquor in China. Tobacco would be his companion, then. To the limit of things.

26

The family of the prisoner named Ban had been Presbyterian for the past fifty years—his grandfather had led them into the church founded by Americans on the edge of the prefecture's capital in which the whole clan lived. As the war began Ban was serving in Indochina and he heard that these American pastors had been placed in prison camps, but also that the congregation in the suburb still functioned under the care of one of their own Japanese leaders. Faith endured.

Today he had stood mute in his hut, this hut of second-class people, when others had raged and voted, fists raised, with the battle cry on their lips, oblivious—it seemed—to the fact that as well as "Hurrah" it meant "Long life." Ban knew that not all the young men, and certainly not all the older ones, wanted to die so soon. Yet they were captured by a communal enthusiasm larger than their individual consent, and compelled not solely by the rice-liquor-fueled voices of some, but—as ever—by their sense of the homage of the muted yet perpetually remembered spirits of the inescapable dead, and the fact they must honor the memorial rites no doubt already carried out in their honor by their family, rites from which some thought there was no possible return. In the minds of the mothers who bore them and of the fathers who begot them, they were already gone.

Ban had thought as the meeting proceeded that he must stand up and profess to his faith now, not that the inhabitants of the hut were uninformed of this eccentricity of his. He struggled, through cowardice and genuine issues of stratagem, with the question of whether this would be an empty gesture, to be communicated later to his relatives as proof of his cowardice. Yet another matter as well was delaying Ban. There would have been no memorial service for him, or if there had been he was not permitted to abide by it. The letters from people in Japan that Nevski had brought into the compound might have been seen to throw doubt over the idea that their return would incommode and shame their families. Yet in a few hours, they were determined to make return impossible.

The hut voted yes with an open show of hands. One older man, considered a little touched by having encountered too many close-up explosions in his life, found the courage or contrariness to vote no with a fully, earnestly extended arm. Ban had half abstained and half extended his arm. His apparent assent after the mass of men had already thrust hands in the air was cowardice. A number of them knew he had done enough as a machine gunner in the log-fortified fighting at Buna for them to take him for granted, a strange but unthreatening phenomenon, if not quite one of them.

Ban despised himself for his timid, bent-armed vote. But he chose to believe that his tentative arm would be simply a saving of energy to allow him to invest and summon up all moral rigor and fortitude for a genuine duty of salvation, which he would rather not be faced with.

Discussion began about setting fire to the hut in the moment of escape—they were for it. Now each one of the men grew so intent on his destiny that some of those enduring Compound C under false names wrote their true names to carry in the pockets of their uniforms and to enable those who buried them to do so to a body correctly identified. As the rejected soldiers of Ban's hut worked with ink and paper, they believed they would be transformed into the mass of the perfected dead by the next morning.

Queues formed outside the showers as men went to clean their bodies for death. NCOs began to arrange things so that the lines did not become noticeably long. Others, in fatalistic groups around card tables in the huts, poured themselves more bombo to celebrate or reinforce their decision. They did not give Ban a thought as he sat cross-legged on his bed, a figure irrelevant to the great imperatives of the hour.

He remembered a verse from Ecclesiastes which, curiously, the men around him would have agreed with. "A good name is better than precious ointment; and the day of death than the day of one's birth. It is better to go to the house of mourning, than to go to the house of feasting." He had two daughters who would now be six and four years of age and he remembered them more sharply than his late wife, victim to a brain tumor. For their sake he found the choice Christ presented him to be a dismal and unutterably painful thing, something too frightful to shiver at; something vast enough to render mere sorrow a side issue. He was as desperate as Christ had been in Gethsemane. It was all wormwood, and should he succeed he must barely expect to survive the night.

"I greet my sure redeemer and my king," he declared under his breath as the hut leader appeared and reiterated that the evening meal must be taken and be consumed with apparent appetite, just as on any normal night. "My only trust and savior of my heart."

There had been a deal brokered at one stage between the Presbyterian church in Gawell and the camp authorities for Ban to receive a discreet visit from the Reverend Ian Finlay in a room at one end of the camp hospital, with Sergeant Nevski present to interpret. It would be too much for Mr. Finlay's congregation, as Ban himself could see, for the good man to bring Ban, in his strange and off-puttingly colored uniform, down to Gawell to the Presbyterian congregation, even had the commandant permitted it. The faithful, said the Reverend Finlay without apology, are not ready yet for universal brotherhood—some of their sons are prisoners. He placed a brotherly hand on Ban's forearm and said, "Although the Christian standard is to avoid making cruel judgments, it is a standard that most of Eve's fallen children find it difficult to achieve." Ban knew some of the accustomed prayers in English. "Let all mortal flesh keep silence / And with fear and trembling stand . . ." It was only through these that he could commune directly with the Reverend Finlay, without intervention by the Russian interpreter, the suspect presence towards whom Ban held the usual prejudice of his nation.

Ban could not avoid thinking now, with an edge of futile vanity, that the Reverend Mr. Finlay's congregation, if they knew of it, could feel a fraternal solidarity with his dangerous purpose tonight. It was important to Ban that in the end the Reverend, inquiring into Ban's survival or death, should know that he had stood in the way of the proposed havoc. He might then even pass on the word to Ban's daughters.

"Gather not my soul with sinners," prayed Ban, "nor my life with bloody men . . ."

But a machine gunner such as he had been was, of the nature of his craft, a bloody man, and would exult as he saw the enemy reaped in an enfilading sweep. "Deliver me from the workers of iniquity, and save me from bloody men . . . depart from me therefore, ye bloody men." Depart from me myself!

One man who had often found time to speak with Ban was a tinsmith named Nonake from a prefecture south of the capital—not a friend Ban would have chosen as an intimate himself, but one who had chosen Ban, and who did not feel that the strangeness of Ban's sect disqualified him from all friendship. Nonake was a man of more than forty years of age and he now came up with eyes Ban would have described as bloodshot with doubt. He was walking proof that it is fairly easy to drill young minds—who have not yet invested in extensions of their lives by way of children. It was harder to compel an older man.

Nonake got down on his haunches by Ban's bed. "So what do you think a fellow ought to do?" he asked Ban.

Amidst all the preparations and clumping about, and shouts and laughter from the drinkers, and amidst the bringing of baseball bats and spiked crowbars, knives, and sharpened lengths of wood out of cavities in the floor, and the further hiding of them, for the time being, under palliasses, Ban had liberty to speak to Nonake almost in a normal voice.

"You want my advice?" Ban asked him. "You really want it?"

"Yes."

"You know what my advice is. Men have a duty to live. To tell ourselves we're washing away all our weakness by dying isn't the path of learning. Anyhow, it's all very well for these unmarried men, isn't it? To shout, 'Death! Death!'"

"Why didn't you say that when they were debating?"

"Because I would have been beaten up," Ban admitted. "And to no purpose." But there were other reasons, too, which he didn't tell the tinsmith about.

"No one would've killed you. The hut leader wouldn't have allowed it."

"Still," said Ban.

"Anyhow," said Nonake, losing interest. "This was damned strange. Half the men here who have pledged for death have done it because they don't want the others to think badly of them. Me? Well, I just didn't put my hand up. And I'm an old man the fire-eaters don't notice."

Ban whispered, "When it all happens, why don't you just fall down into the ditch beside the fence and lie there until it's all over?"

"Because at the end of the day I must be a man," said the tinsmith. "And I abide by the majority rule. Even if half the hut are crazies."

"That's a strange case of democracy in a man your age," Ban declared. "But I know you can see through it. Please. You have a family."

"All that," said Nonake, with tears glimmering awhile on the lower rims of his eyes, "is over. It ended the day I was inducted. I knew then, I knew it in my water, that it was the end of my life. That I'd become something else—already a different sort of spirit. A danger-ous one. I intended as a soldier to become dangerous. And the more I managed it, the more I forgot the town and the home. It's better that way. A man in that situation has to become something else again, otherwise it is too painful. My wife's voice is very far off for me now. The voices here are close and they move me more. I know you belong to a sect, but you're a good chap, and I wish you would join me. We could race shoulder to shoulder across the compound."

Despite the invitation, Ban could tell the tinsmith didn't want to do it himself.

Ban said, "My religion prohibits me from suicide. That's how it is."

"But you nearly sacrificed yourself at Buna. You stayed at your post raving with dengue fever. You were raving when they dragged you out from behind your gun. I saw it. I was there . . . Anyhow, for tonight . . . we're all pretty much locked in. And I can't deny that for me there's a sense of relief and peace in it that's worth something."

But Ban felt the man was arguing too long to believe what he was saying.

Ban said, "You can't tell me you're at peace. I just don't believe it."

"Let's give it a break," said Nonake. "All our palaver isn't doing much good."

He must be saved, Ban thought.

By early evening, the hut leaders had reported back one at a time to Tengan, Aoki, and Goda. There had been abstentions in some huts. But no hut had voted outright against the proposition. Two had voted instead to abide by the camp majority. A number of the more doctri-naire hut leaders warned the triumvirate that they suspected some would not run at the wire and instead would hide. Should special squads be formed to hunt out the backsliders before they themselves went running at the wire? Even Tengan thought this impracticable and perhaps not to be desired.

So it was decided the outbreak would occur at three in the morning, at the deepest hour of the garrison's sleep. It would be signaled by a bugle call played by one of the prisoners. Each hut leader was to be vigilant in the unlikely case some dissident tried to warn the garrison.

The bell call for mess time sounded out across the compound. The last supper unforeseen, Ban thought, by the Reverend Finlay and by my Presbyterian brethren in the garrison and in Gawell! Nonake began to get up, groaning, from his cross-legged posture by Ban's bed, where he had continued to sit after their conversation. Ban, also rising, grabbed the tinsmith's arm.

"I can save you," he murmured. "I don't believe for a moment you want to go charging out at the wire and be shot down."

"You're just making it harder," Nonake told him.

"Eat your meal at a separate table from me, and then wander off and I'll meet you on the far side of the recreation hall. Like two friends saying good-bye."

Ban had noticed that, despite the searchlights which had now come on, there was a little triangle of darkness there, not sufficient to protect them from the gaze of the garrison but enough to make them, in all the movements going on around the camp, an unremarkable pair in contrast to far better-lit groupings. Men obeyed the dinner bell as their hut leader urged them. Many were loud, singing couplets of some song or other and breaking off out of ignorance of the lines that followed.

The meal presented to them by the men on mess duty was served, as usual, on china plates, a concession of respect by the commandant, but was the same old stodge of mutton, polished rice, corn, and carrots—unappetizing even by the standards of a normal evening. The hut leaders passed amongst their men quietly urging them to swallow—they must complete this exercise of consumption to make their captors, the enemy lieutenant and his section keeping guard at one end of the mess, think that all was normal.

The tinsmith sat at a far table from Ban but within sight of him. No one spoke to Ban during the meal except for the routine business of asking for condiments to make the dismal meal halfway swallowable. From the kitchen, the enemy cooks and their guards, both of whom would soon be able to withdraw from the compound for the night, casually watched them digest the stuff, and the prisoners at the tables, in the irrelevance of their hunger, acted their part. Prisoner stewards, who served according to a roster that applied to all but senior NCOs, cleared plates and took them to the kitchen counter, and, since many plates were only half-finished, uttered the habitual words of the enemy orderlies. "Ungrateful bastards!"

The men began to rise from the tables and leave. Across the room, Ban saw the tinsmith get up. Ban did the same, wished those around him good night, was largely ignored, and went outside. It was cold already in this country of bony earth where it never snowed.

When he got to the triangle of dimness he had earlier nominated, he was astonished to see Nonake already there, smoking a cigarette. He had not expected the tinsmith's conflict of intentions would allow him to move so fast.

Nonake said, "I just want to hear what you've got to say, that's all."

"Do you need to use the latrines first?" asked Ban.

"What has that got to do with it? Do you?"

"No," said Ban. "I suffer from constipation. I believe it's the camp curse."

"Well, I've got it too."

Ban was delighted to be about the business of garnering this one soul. It might well be the reason he was put in Gawell by God.

"Come with me then," he told the tinsmith. "Just come with me. You can make up your mind when you get there."

Ban led him away amidst knots of men in discussion on a night of understandable after-dinner movement in the compound, which the garrison would interpret as the business of farewell. Other men made for the shower block or latrines. Nonake walked at a distance behind Ban, as if ashamed of the company he found himself in.

From the path they trod, Ban could see the draped machine guns, essential implements in the rite his fellow soldiers sought, shining with night moisture on their trailers. He could see enough to delineate separately the wheels on the trailers that supported them. He led the tinsmith to a shed near the hospital. This building was known to Nonake, and he balked. "This is the incinerator shed," he said in distaste.

"Yes. Have you seen the incinerator?"

They went inside, Nonake following with reluctance. They did not turn on a light but could see from the all-drenching searchlight beyond the wire, which entered by a window in the door of the thing. There was the stench of cold embers, the cooled remains of the compound's detritus.

"You expect me to climb into the cursed incinerator?" asked Nonake.

"You shouldn't dismiss it," said Ban. "It's perfect. No one will come here tonight. And don't worry. It's not lit till four o'clock each afternoon. Some of the ashes in there, by the way, will still have warmth, which should make you comfortable. See, the rake's there." Ban reached out and touched the iron implement leaning against the side of the incinerator.

The tinsmith churlishly admitted that he saw it. "They burn all sorts of muck in there. Dressings from the hospital . . . I don't know what."

"You've lived in muck before. Shit and blood and rotting flesh. You know this is nothing. Besides, I didn't offer you a hotel. And look, you can close the door partway and use the rake as a doorjamb. Then you can't get locked in. But no one's going to come in here tonight."

Nonake felt he needed to manufacture more arguments against taking this admirable chance of salvation. He did not choose to seem a man too anxious to preserve himself.

"Are you going to join me?"

"Perhaps later in the night."

By now, totally won over, Nonake grunted and asked, "When do you suggest I enter the bridal chamber?"

"Now," said Ban.

"But I need to piss," he complained.

"Then do it in the corner. Stop behaving like a child. Anyhow, I must go."

"But I'll see you later."

"I hope so."

The tinsmith, complaining as if Ban were responsible for the fullness of his bladder, went into one of the back corners of the incinerator shed and let go a stream of urine. "You're not thinking of anything ridiculous, are you?" he called over his shoulder. "Making a fool of yourself?"

"Nothing ridiculous."

Ban waited until his friend had climbed into the incinerator, with plenty of groaning because of old wounds. As he settled, swearing, into the thick ash bed, Ban leaned the rake diagonally across the huge door and then eased the door part closed, sufficiently to shield the old soldier from vision. Ban heard him start into a fury of coughing, which then stilled. In a choked voice from the interior he called, "Thank you, then."

After consigning Nonake to his hiding place, Ban went not into hiding himself but back to his own hut. Lights were out but no one was sleeping. There was a musk of frenzy in the hut. Palliasses had been stripped from beds and were heaped on the corners, ready for burning. Ban could see a knot of animated men further along what had once been, until the bedding was heaped, the aisle. He sat to wait on his tatami. His hour had not come and he was left alone by everybody, except a notorious, sometimes amusing, and now drunken incompetent they all called the Clown. The Clown shook his hand dolorously, and Ban could see even by the shifting, sweeping, erratic light the heretical glint in the man's eyes that said death might not be easy and, from its far side, mightn't seem as desirable as it had previously to the more oratorical section of Compound C. He heard his name at one stage and knew that they were discussing briefly his otherness and whether to finish him before they charged the wire. Their retrieved weapons, which lay under the mattresses not needed for tinder, were available for the task. But then they moved on to other issues. Even so, to judge the moment he should slip away was difficult. Some of the men drank more of the bombo and were blessedly distracted by it, and conversations were held with fellow drinkers.

"Behold, he that keepeth Israel shall neither rest nor sleep," Ban recited and tried to fight a drowsiness inappropriate to such a high hour.

Time to go, he decided. He grabbed his maroon overcoat and rose and left the hut as if for the latrines, and was not stopped. He walked to the neighboring hut and stooped and crawled in between foundations onto the mud-smelling earth beneath the floorboards. Here was the only music of the evening—he heard the men above him singing to the plaintiveness of the samisen, on which someone was working with a thumb-lacerating ardor that made Ban want to weep for him.

He spread the overcoat he had brought and lay under the boards and bearers on freezing ground. He decided it was futile for him to try to combat the extra cold of this space, so he decided to embrace it for a while, in the spirit of Christ embracing the leper. Above him the bombo flowed, and he could hear toasts being drunk by men caught in a vast necrophilia. An entire ocean and all its archipelagos had been captured by a cult of death, and he lay shivering on the earth, a dissenter from it all. Yet its soldier as well.

And when should he go? He must wait at least until the traffic around the camp, hut to hut, was at an end. Two o'clock, he decided. He prayed a ready-made prayer about perseverance, which he had known since childhood, before he knew what exactly that virtue consisted of. Lying as a mere insect on the earth he was grateful to feel a strange serenity and resolve grow in him. This was his most solitary moment since his capture a year and a half past. A memory of his wife was like a visitation at that dismal hour. It was a visit of God's own redeemed flower. Her soul had been cultivated and generous and her presence endowed him, at this huge distance of space from her grave, with acceptance. He hoped his daughters would not be destroyed by their orphan status. Surely other members of the church would take them in. But even his uncertainty on that issue became something acceptable and part of the broader plan that is the comfort of Christians.

Though it continued to be awfully cold down where he was, he distracted himself by praying awhile for an unlikely revolution in the souls of the prisoners to halt the coming stampede, and begged that if willfully caught by machine-gun fire, they would die in Christ and not in some vacant boast. One thing he knew as a soldier—there was rarely arrogance after the bullet had gone in. There was the humility of terror, the reduction of the soul to childhood fears and the realization that monsters exist, and then the reflex cry for the mother who was not there to succor or give rebirth.

But they wouldn't need a revelation of that kind as long as his ploy was successful. At this hour, after midnight, he was the loneliest but most soothed man on the planet.

27

Mrs. Garner, the doctor's wife, had promised Colonel Abercare long ago that if his wife came to Gawell she would put on a Saturday-night dinner to welcome Mrs. Abercare. It had taken two months— the Garners had engagements in town and invitations to go to dinner at pastoral properties whose magnates felt they owed a debt to the doctor, and Abercare himself had a mess dinner to which he'd needed to invite the boring mayor. But an evening had finally been arranged. There was always an outside risk, Ann Garner told Abercare, that Dr. Garner would be called out for a medical emergency. "But at the least I'll be here."

Indeed, Dr. Garner frequently enough complained that in the old days you could send out the young practitioners on a Saturday night, but now the young practitioners were in uniform somewhere. He looked forward devoutly to their return.

Emily told her husband she was very grateful to be welcomed by Ewan's friends, who were also numbered, not that it mattered to Emily, amongst the town's potentates. It was only after he had accepted, though, that Mrs. Garner told him, "I've asked the Galloways as well. We all know Thelma can be a bit strange. But Roy is good fun and keeps her in check."

It was at that mayoral reception eighteen months past, when the women drank sherry and the men beer, that he had first seen Thelma Galloway and knew that she had more than seen him—she had seen through him. She was a smallish, well-made woman, with honey-colored hair. He could not deny that she roused habitual appetites. He did not deny that his first thought was, "Here's a goer!" Beautiful, hungry, and endowed with a serious, cosmic petulance.

His reaction must have been enough that night to allow her to think that some compact of possibilities had been established. She had called the camp soon after to tell him that the ladies of the district would welcome the chance to meet him at morning tea at her place and hear him say a few words on the running of the camp. It would be very kind of him if he would consider it. He made excuses, but she called back twice, and had been a little chagrined he hadn't jumped at the chance. When he'd next seen her at a party at the Garners', he was embarrassed, for she exercised a cold politeness which by the end of the evening had almost transformed itself into a chiding amity.

He worried that tonight Thelma Galloway might assert the air of implication she had in the past, and was so good at. The implication, that is, of a small history of private discourse between her and Ewan Abercare. He assured himself he simply wouldn't play the game for Mrs. Galloway's satisfaction.

The Garners lived in a vast corner house raised up on granite foundations and greatly endowed with verandas. It was capable of holding two surgeries in the front rooms, and Dr. Garner had recently recruited an honorably discharged middle-aged doctor from the medical corps to come and share the practice with him.

When the Abercares arrived, Ann Garner met them at the front door and brought them into a living room, where her husband leaned on the mantelpiece and Thelma and Roy Galloway occupied separate lounge chairs. Thelma was drinking gin and Roy had a beer on an occasional table by his elbow. Roy stood up but, Abercare noticed, there emanated from Thelma a suggestion of disdain as she eyed the non-coquettish Emily. It was as if she expected Emily to say something childish at which she could laugh acidly.

Roy Galloway said straight off, "Well, congratulations, Colonel. You'll soon have the troublemakers out of the camp."

"You know about that, do you?" Abercare asked, a little bemused and overtaken by a sudden anxiety. He certainly didn't want the town to be apprised about what was to happen on Monday. It was as if news of the prisoners' removal to Wye were in the air like influenza and the knowledge had been caught like an infection. Garrison soldiers drinking in the pubs, of course; the filament between the town and the camp being so porous.

Abercare's sense of the appropriate was affronted. It was bad taste for Galloway to hit him on the head with this during the introductions. As well, that evening Suttor had phoned through a report that there was a lot of to-ing and fro-ing in Compound C, which could be entirely explained by farewell taking, but which was nonetheless obviously putting Suttor on edge.

The colonel answered Roy Galloway with a banal question about how the law was treating him. He kept his eyes on Galloway, though he could feel the pull of Thelma's, like the cliff you couldn't help looking over.

Dr. Garner held up a whisky in his hand, which also clutched a cigarette, as if he wanted to combine a large swathe of the pleasures of the earth in one fist. "Look what we have," he told Abercare. "Johnnie Walker Black. It's a gift from a publican. Supposedly for curing his wife's lumbago, which would have cured itself."

"Just one," said Abercare.

"Terrible thing is," said Dr. Garner, "I am restricted myself to one or two weak ones, in case I have to go forth into the night."

When Emily was introduced enthusiastically to Thelma by Ann Garner, a moment the colonel had feared, nothing unwanted occurred. No snide message was sent. There was a slight indifference on Thelma's part, which a reasonable person might consider to be due to the level of tipsiness she'd already achieved.

Emily and Thelma began to talk amiably about Parkes Street, and Thelma ventured to say that it was a well-made house. The slightest slip and hesitation in her voice, and a perhaps too-frequent blinking, showed again that this was not her first drink of the day.

"The biggest question people ask when your name comes up," Galloway said in the men's corner of the room, "is whether you will stay on here in town when the peace comes."

"That's jumping the gun a bit, isn't it?" asked Abercare. He could not imagine, without ill-defined fear, what he would do when the war ended and the compounds emptied and he gave up his uniform for the last time and received the pro forma thanks of the authorities. People at home, in Britain, talked about genteel poverty, and there was something about the indoors climate of Britain that allowed people to hide shame and decline better than here, where all seemed exposed under brightness.

"Well, you're liked around here, you know," said Dr. Garner. "You'd be very welcome."

Abercare nodded his appreciation. But his postwar occupations would be unlikely to put him in the company of the Garners or their circle. He had thought intermittently and with some dread of the necessity to parlay his rank into a suburban insurance brokerage, but it remained to be seen whether his separation pay from the army would permit that. Or he could run a little real-estate office somewhere. But a colonel did not necessarily have the liberty to do that. If he expected soldiers to honor his rank, he must honor his rank too. Perhaps it was better to live in obscure poverty in a city than to become a visible struggler in a country town.

"The liking mightn't last if I settled in," he told the solicitor. "Anyhow, sometimes it seems the end might be a long way off, doesn't it?"

"We've got them both beaten," Galloway assured him. "Japan and Germany. Just that they won't lie down and admit it."

Sometimes Abercare considered what might happen when Malaya was invaded—Japan, for that matter. Would his prisoners abound, thousands upon thousands?

The women were still conversing very easily, he noticed with relief. In fact, it was as if Thelma were enlisting them in some grievance against her husband. But Abercare's peace of soul had been disturbed by Roy Galloway, and it struck him again that if the town, or at least Galloway, knew all about Compound C, then that somehow added a volatility to the whole business and meant that he must go up to the camp tonight. And tomorrow night. Just to be on top of things between the knowing town and the knowing Compound C.

The telephone rang in the hallway. Abercare had left the number at the camp. If it were from there, he would have no option but to be gone. It proved to be a medical call. There was a farmer way out at Reids Flat whose wife couldn't breathe, Dr. Garner announced to the company. Ann groaned, but the groan had a habitual quality to it, an acceptance. Reids Flat lay at the end of dirt roads, set by a creek with some notable hills beyond it.

"Do you want company on the drive?" Galloway asked, wanting to escape the emanations of reproof from his wife.

"Roy," Mrs. Garner chided him, "you'll leave the company unbalanced."

"Roy . . . doesn't . . . mind . . . about . . . that," said Thelma in an exaggerated, drawn-out, drunk thespian sort of way.

"Well, I can stay," said Galloway. "It's the same either way. I just thought . . . Donald might like company."

Thelma looked past him.

"All right, I'll go with you, Donald," Galloway decided, since he was to be punished either way and might as well delay it.

"Good night, sweet ladies," said Dr. Garner, "and good night, Colonel. Come on, Roy. I'm very pleased for the company."

They went up the corridor, stopping at Garner's surgery, and Abercare could hear the two men talking in there.

"Christ," said Thelma, "this is so boring and so predictable. Sometimes I think the bugger is a pansy."

Mrs. Garner exchanged a glance with the Abercares. The voices in the surgery receded. They heard the doctor's car start. It would be more than an hour's drive to Reids Flat, and a dreary, winding one.

"Roy's in for a good time," said Mrs. Garner with fond irony. "I know how Donald fills in the time while he's driving. He recites cricket scores to himself. Honestly. First, he argues why Test cricket should date from 1883 instead of 1877, then he starts quoting batting figures. He'll then continue with intercolonial and interstate batting averages and bowling figures. The Gregory brothers and Demon Spofforth matter more to him than latecomers like McCabe and Bradman. He can recite Sheffield Shield matches from 1908. Entire innings, how out, and the bowling figures too. It's astounding. I was very impressed by it all when I first met him. But as a trick, it wears thin after thirty-five years."

Thelma asked, "How do you know he's not making it all up?" It was precisely what she'd suspect a man of.

"Because he's an honest fellow," said Mrs. Garner, bridling a bit. "And it would only satisfy him if it was right. Look, it's going to be quite a time before the men are back, Thelma. Would you like to have a lie-down in the spare bedroom?"

Thelma refused. "Damned Roy," she said. "We go to events and one way or another he gets away. If I'm indoors, he's outdoors. And Reids Flat is about as outdoors as you can get."

She had provided them with a window into a habitual conflict, but the view was stale. She looked very beautiful, Ewan Abercare thought.

"Look," she said. "I think I'll go, if you don't mind. He left the keys with me for safekeeping."

"Are you sure you can drive, Thelma?" asked Mrs. Garner.

"Perhaps you should wait, and the colonel and Mrs. Abercare could perhaps . . ."

"I'm afraid I don't have a car at the moment," said Abercare. "Perhaps I could call the camp for one . . ."

He hoped it was obvious that he didn't want to do that; it would be untoward, an excess where he had forsworn excess.

"We would be delighted if you stayed here, Thelma," he suggested. "And gave us the pleasure of your company."

As if he hadn't spoken, Thelma said, "Everyone forgets I've been driving since I was fourteen."

But she stayed on and set a fast pace of consumption as she ate the roast and vegetables and half the flummery, and then decided to go. She insisted on not being accompanied to her car. "It is so much fuss," she said, waving them back to their chairs with an exaggerated movement, up and down, of her spread right hand.

"Well, at least I'll see you to the door," Mrs. Garner insisted. In the absence of the other two women, Emily looked across the room to Abercare and smiled a private smile. It declared they were no longer in conflict. It confessed a kind of luckiness she felt.

But I must leave you tonight, my one flesh, he thought.

"She'll be all right, I think," said Mrs. Garner when she came back into the lounge room. "The problem is that they live two miles out of town, at her late father's property. Lovely old house, but a few gullies on either side of the track into the homestead."

Abercare was not entirely at ease about that either. He wanted mad Thelma to get home safely, so that he was not distracted from the issue of Compound C. By and large, however, he had enjoyed this evening to which Thelma Galloway had given her own little flavor of unruliness.

"My dear," he said to Emily, as they walked home the short distance to Parkes Street, "I feel I must sleep at the camp tonight, and tomorrow night too. Just to be on the spot, you know."

"Oh?" she asked. It was a neutral question, but a question just the same. The streets were bright under the blatant full moon. You could have played cricket in Parkes Street by moonlight. He had done that sort of thing in India, wearing mess uniform, bowler and wicketkeeper and slips elegant in their regimental mess gear, hooting and tipsy.

"It might not be quite a rational thing," he admitted. "I mean, it's a full moon and nothing is going to happen. But those fellows tonight, Galloway in particular, talking about what's happening in Compound C, with as much information as if they were part of the garrison—that's set me fretting. There is no danger, of course, but I feel I must be on the qui vive, you understand."

"Yes," she conceded. He was aware of her elbow securely locked around his. "I certainly see that. And after Monday morning, you'll be at greater ease."

"That's right," he said.

He knew it was beneath her to have him asking whether she would be all right on her own. Soldiers' women were by definition all right on their own.

He continued to explain, not as a necessity but as a form of sharing matters with her. "Everything seemed calm enough today, but Sergeant Nevski reports there was nobody at the baseball plate this afternoon. A little curious when they're not being moved until Monday and you'd expect some of them would want to get a final game in over the weekend. Mind you, they're probably saying prolonged good-byes to their NCOs—that would be enough to suspend play."

He could feel her shiver suddenly inside her coat. "Are you all right, darling?"

"Yes, tonight is one of the cold ones, though, isn't it? It would be very nice to have you here."

"It would be very nice to be here. I won't be a soldier too much longer. And next week is going to be much easier. We'll be in better control."

They were nearly home. But Ewan Abercare could not put aside the subject of Roy Galloway's opening conversational gambit that evening: it had caused him to make decisions for reasons he felt he did not quite control, ones he could not define. He liked to define things.

"I mean," he asked, "how is it possible that the word gets to Galloway, a solicitor in town? Roy Galloway and the prisoners don't even have the same sort of mind, the same background, the same language, and he has never even visited the camp."

"Stop fretting," Emily told him, "I do understand you'd want to go. It's what I'd do. But Galloway—you shouldn't fret about him. He's the country town god and Thelma's his Achilles' heel. He should be worrying about that."

Emily opened the front door before Abercare could dutifully do so. "I'll make some tea before you go," she offered.

"Thank you. I'll call the duty officer at the camp to send someone for me."

"You'll find fresh flannel pyjamas in your drawer," she called to him from the kitchen. "And remember to take your dressing gown."

28

Soon after the Abercares arrived home, a car turned up at Parkes Street to collect the colonel. The driver was at the rear door to salute him and Abercare returned the greeting with his baton and got into the backseat. The driver took them through the still streets, streets that soothed some of Abercare's unrest by seeming lost in the earth's far south and disconnected from the world's serious traffic, and so far from anguish and untoward events. At this time of night, country towns had finished their society, sportiveness, and excesses. He saw two soldiers of the training battalion weaving in the broad main street, and the car slowed for them and they let it roll past. They were not his task, these schoolboys, these apprentices. If by some false impulse of democracy he had got them to squeeze into the front seat, at least one of them would have been sure to have vomited.

It was a different matter a mile east of Gawell when he saw a civilian vehicle, a Chrysler, pulled up on the side of the road with its hood raised, as if broken down. It looked to be the car of a person of eminence, Gawell-wise, and Abercare knew he must take a moment to see if the wayfarer could be helped. He told his driver to pull over but leave the engine running. By the hooded headlights he saw Thelma

Galloway move out into the road with a wry hope of rescue on her face. She carried in her hand a metal crossbar of the kind designed for inspecting spark plugs or loosening battery bolts. He remembered that Mrs. Garner had said that the Galloways lived out this way, on a property owned by Thelma Galloway's late father. Roy Galloway had a manager in to run the place, which allowed him to keep the farm going and work at his law practice as well.

Colonel Abercare got out. "What's up, Mrs. Galloway?" he called out in solicitude. He could see by the vivid moon and the headlights that her eyes were not fully focused. Her own beaming headlights made it worse, illuminating her in a way that suggested each eye had a different objective. She almost looked fit to bay, as the moon was said to make mad people do.

Thelma said, "I've been inspecting the engine, but I can't diagnose its ills." She shook her head slowly. Her bemusement seemed whimsical—obviously the engine did not upset her as much as other factors did.

"No pipes loose," she said. "The battery cells are all right, the radiator's got enough water, and the fan belt isn't broken. That's all my father ever taught me to do with a broken-down car. If I'd been the son he might have taught me more. God, it's cold, isn't it?"

"I'll get the driver to see what's the trouble," said Abercare.

The driver, carrying a torch, had already got out, and now he set to work under the hood. Since he would need two hands, Colonel Abercare offered to hold the torch for him.

"Carburetor seems all right, sir," he said cheerily. He opined that there might be carburetor problems.

"Do you think you can fix it here?" asked the colonel.

"Don't have the tools for that, sir," the driver told him.

Ewan Abercare looked at Mrs. Galloway. She stood by the limit of the torchlight now, and her eyes looked withdrawn, dreaming of something else.

"I think it'll need a repair truck from the camp, sir," said the driver.

Colonel Abercare peered into the darkness as if desperately hoping a redeeming mechanic might present himself. It was utterly characteristic of Thelma Galloway to break down in such a place, in the path of his pressing business. It was what women like her did.

"Well, we can't have you out here in this cold," he said, trying to keep a trace of blame out of his voice. "I'm afraid I'm expected at camp. I'll take you there with me and you can sit in my living room until we rouse our mechanic. Then you can come back here in the truck with him."

"It is the coldest and brightest night of the year," Thelma told him as he sat beside the driver on the way to the camp. He could smell an unpleasant emanation of gin and perfume coming from the backseat. Gin is a fragrant liquor, thought Abercare, but it was beginning to turn rancid in Thelma. A gate with an armed guard by it stood open at the camp entrance. Most of the sentries were in the watchtowers and in Main Road, and at either end of that great avenue.

As they progressed through the camp it was bright as nighttime at a fair. There were lights around the perimeter, and though it was lights-out in the barracks, the interior of the guardhouse and sundry rooms in the officers' quarters also shone—one from the room in which Major Suttor was up, probably writing his serial.

The car stopped outside Colonel Abercare's quarters.

"I'm sorry I can't drive you straight back," he said. "But I need to keep my car here. I shall organize another . . ."

"Understood," Thelma muttered as he helped her from the car. "Understood."

As he handed her into his quarters, he saw his orderly hustling towards them, woken, he assumed, by the duty sergeant or possibly by yet another mercurial rumor—that his boss had arrived out of the night trailing a drunk woman from town.

He led Thelma into his sitting room while his orderly stooped and fanned into existence a wood fire in the stove in the middle of the room. The fire drew cleanly, and Abercare decided nothing burned so aromatically as Australian eucalyptus. The residual oils released from a dead bough like an ascending soul.

The proposition that he had orders to keep his car by him was not strictly the truth, but it was true enough. If he felt the necessity to come to camp in the middle of the night, then he should have his car nearby. So he called the duty officer, Lieutenant Cook, a slim little fellow with a game leg. Cook was about forty years old and was said to have been the last Australian wounded in the Great War, though he was too modest to press such a claim. Abercare got a report from him. Guard posts had reported that though lights were out in the compound, there was still more movement than usual, hut to hut.

"Have the duty sergeant call for a mechanic and the tow truck," Abercare ordered the officer, "to attend to Mrs. Galloway's car. It's broken down on the road to town. I gave Mrs. Galloway a lift here, and she's in my quarters. I'll meet you at the north gate of Main Road in five minutes and visit the posts with you. In the meantime, call Major Suttor and tell him I'll meet him in a quarter of an hour in my office."

He realized Thelma Galloway was still standing, waiflike, in the middle of the floor.

"Please, sit down," he said, pointing to an undistinguished easy chair appropriate to his rank. Majors had to do with slightly more spartan upholstery still.

"Could we have some tea, please?" Colonel Abercare asked his orderly, after the man had been able to quit the business of fire making.

"I think I'd rather have a drink, if you don't mind, Colonel."

"Oh," said Abercare. "Of course. I just wondered . . . Gin again, then?"

"Come on," Thelma protested, at least in amusement, but implying for the orderly a closer relationship of teasing and reproof than existed between her and Abercare. "I haven't had that much. Yes, gin, thank you."

The orderly, who had some experience as a waiter, went to the plain dresser where Abercare kept the liquor for visits from civilians such as the mayor of Gawell or the Red Cross and the Japanese and Italian sections of the Swiss consulate general.

"Don't worry, Private," said Abercare. "I'll get the drink. If you could check first on what's happening with the mechanic we're sending out to take Mrs. Galloway home and repair her car."

The orderly went. Abercare poured Mrs. Galloway's gin on the weak side, with plenty of tonic, scarce though it was. In the mess, they served it from crushed-up quinine tablets mixed with sugar and water, but here he poured Thelma Galloway the authentic thing, and she took it from him and looked at it blearily, shifting in her seat and with a gloss of sweat on her forehead. "We'll have you on your way soon," he told her, but it was largely a promise to himself. "You won't mind waiting here while I attend to business, Mrs. Galloway, will you?"

"No, no," she growled, and then she smiled a lenient, bilious smile. "I hear there's a war on."

"I'll have you informed as soon as the truck is ready to leave," Abercare assured her. "And even if he can't fix your car at once, the mechanic will drop you home and then tow your automobile to one of the garages."

"Our overseer on the property will see to it," she told him blearily. "If your chap can't."

In the functional, upholstered chair, Mrs. Galloway began to drowse before she had half finished her gin. The orderly returned and suggested tea to Abercare.

"Is the mechanic here?" asked Abercare.

"Not yet, sir. He's just getting back from town. I've left an urgent message."

Thelma Galloway closed her eyes. He went into his bedroom and fetched an army blanket and spread it over her.

"I think you can go to bed now, Private," he told his orderly, who saluted and left.

Abercare stood and reached for his overcoat and gloves and stick. He emerged into the night and walked amongst the huts towards the sentries at the gates of Main Street and saw the extraordinary drench of searchlight across Compound C, turning the earth blue-gray and making the wire glitter decoratively with frost. He met with Lieutenant Cook by a sentry box there, and they visited the sentries at the gates and along the wire. Abercare even undertook a rare visit to the towers, so cramped as to hold only a solitary man. He certainly didn't intend to send a detachment in to forestall the occasional prisoners who still moved across the crusty ground carrying messages of farewell.

"Coldest night of the year," said Abercare to Cook, before asking for a report. Cook responded that there was no exceptional or dangerous behavior, given the circumstances. He told Abercare he was about to visit the guard detail located in the tent within Main Road itself.

"I could just call them, sir. But they feel a little exposed there."

Abercare was cheered by Cook's genial report and by the high, huge moon. He now made his way to the meeting with Suttor. Waiting for the compound commander, Abercare called the orderly in the guardhouse and told him he wanted the guard doubled. This would put half the garrison on the perimeter, but so be it. Suttor arrived, in fact, just after Abercare had entered his office and taken off his overcoat, even though it was still cold enough to wear it. Suttor himself did not wear an overcoat or gloves and when Abercare congratulated him on his imperviousness to cold, he rebuffed the compliment by saying the short journey from his quarters had not been worth the trouble of putting them on.

Abercare, at his desk already, told Suttor to feel free to smoke. Unless events were too pressing for that.

"No," said Suttor, placing a brief written report on the table and bringing out his fashionable cigarettes. "I don't think pressing is the exact word. There are certainly reportable incidents. But the duty officer has no doubt told you this, and some of it you witnessed earlier in the evening for yourself."

The colonel opened the report. As he read, he, too, pulled out a cigarette and lit it.

"So, reportable," he said, and inhaled from his cigarette and continued to read. Then he looked up at Suttor, rather reassured. Suttor looked back at him with those blank, handsome, hostile eyes, and began his verbal report. The feverish walking about, hut to hut, had continued. Nevski, said Suttor, had had the guard take him into the entertainment hall to confirm that there were no play rehearsals going on at the moment. All the costumes were hung up. But that was understandable given that half the cast of future shows would no longer be in Compound C to perform. On a slightly later visit to a hut, he'd discovered that, partially hidden behind a draped blanket hung from a mosquito net bracket, the man they called Sakura was in drag, all queened up, as if intending to perform later. If anything were seriously untoward, Nevski reported, he doubted the female impersonator would have gone to the trouble of attiring himself.

Suttor had delivered the report until this point through lips pursed around his cigarette. Even though the man had been offered the opportunity to smoke, to deliver a report in this way—in a manner appropriate to a recording studio, perhaps—affronted the regular officer in Abercare. This apparently minor gaffe of Suttor's seemed like a case of mockery—was almost certainly mockery. Even so, that didn't worry Ewan Abercare as much as the competing images of a deserted stage but a female impersonator dressed as for a performance. That paradox enhanced a little the unease he'd contracted at the Garners.

Abercare said, "We've given them free run tonight. But we must tell the triumvirate tomorrow that we won't tolerate all this running around tomorrow night, or the next. As far as I'm concerned, they've had their party."

"Yes," said Suttor dreamily. "I think they have. I have to remind you, though, that if they hadn't been told about the move, this would have been a more normal night."

Abercare stared at him. "Would tomorrow have been a normal night, if they found out by accident? There'd be greater unrest still." He broke off, thinking, This is not wise—having a debate with the bugger who had his cigarette cocked upwards like a bookmaker about to write a ticket. It seemed to have gone out, too.

"Do you want the machine guns manned?" asked Suttor. "As a display of serious intentions."

"There's no need," said Abercare, and chose to leave his reasons unexplained. The guard had been doubled, for Christ's sake!

"Machine guns in the wrong place," muttered Suttor, like a civilian. "And unmanned."

Abercare said, "Suttor! None of that."

He was thinking he would contact the training camp, and remembered the two tottering young trainee warriors he had passed in Gawell that night. *Training brigade.* The backup. He got up now, ending the interview with Suttor. Too much time spent on humoring this scribbler! Suttor got his own back by holding that bloody cigarette, which should by now have been ground out in the ashtray, cupped in his left hand as he saluted.

Uneasy that he was working from such imponderables, which seemed most imponderable now, at midnight, Abercare called the duty officer at the training camp. He told the man, a true veteran, minder of boys, to inform Colonel Deakin that the signs in Gawell were ambiguous and that Deakin should entertain for the next three nights the possibility of an outbreak at the prison camp and make his dispositions accordingly.

He felt less restless in his soul as he hung up. He returned now to his quarters and, opening the door into the warm living room, saw that the fire had burned down a little. He smelled an acid sourness in the air. Mrs. Galloway lay on the floor with a spilled gin bottle. She had been sick within the ambit of the spillage. He was appalled, but making jolly pronouncements—"Here we go, Thelma!"—he lifted her from the floor to an easy chair. Her body was firm in his arms, a young woman's body still, asserting its hope for appreciation or even something as fulsome, as un-Gawell-like, as adoration. She opened her eyes and groaned.

"Sorry," she told him. "Came on sudden." She belched and laughed a private laugh. "Madame Garner's bloody hospitality . . . It creeps up on you, doesn't it?"

He hoped none of this acrid smell would attach itself to him. He dumped her in the easy chair again and covered her, and picked up the bottle of largely spilled gin, and then set himself to considering whether to clean up the mess himself. That would create a supposition he had something to hide. He went to his bathroom and got a bleached towel of pale khaki and threw it over the mess. Then he called the guardhouse and demanded to know where the truck and mechanic were.

"There's been a problem, sir, with the tow truck."

"It is broken down too?" he asked incredulously.

"A steering shaft broke," the orderly officer explained. "It wasn't properly reported earlier today."

Like most bloody things, he was tempted—in his impotence—to say.

"They're working on it now with welding tools."

He could not tell the officer the cause of his impatience. It struck him, too, that Thelma Galloway could hardly be transported home, in this state, in a tow truck, even when its steering shaft was repaired. He would send her home in one of the garrison cars and be quit of her. It would reflect badly on her, in that she was clearly well gone. But she could afford that, and he could not afford to have her here long enough for her to recover. He did not care about adverse gossip, except for the way it might reflect on Emily.

"Send me a car and driver. I think my poor driver's already asleep.

I need to drop the person whose car broke down earlier back to her home."

He went into his room to get an extra blanket and took the chance to strap on his Webley & Scott revolver. If he had ordered the doubling of the guard, then he should make this concession to precaution. But he did not know whether to stay with Thelma till the driver came or leave again to inspect the perimeters and have the four machine gunners roused. "You're a bloody nuisance," he told her under his breath. Even if she heard him she would have forgotten it by tomorrow.

He felt an unwarranted stab of responsibility. A potent aftershock from his original culpability. In scalding memory of his crimes he could somehow not avoid uttering a sudden and sharp suppressed gasp of pain and self-condemnation. This sort of thing had happened to him before in private moments. But this one wasn't private. In her half sleep Thelma Galloway murmured, "Come again?"

"Have a sleep," he ordered her, almost gently, as he blazed with memory. The storekeeper's wife at the bush hamlet of Elgin remained with him acutely. He thought it would be wonderful to share the story sub rosa with someone like Delaney. But speaking it—that would be the problem.

29

On his tour of the sentry posts, Abercare had seen the machine guns shrouded by frost-stiffened tarpaulins. Should they now be manned? Was manning them an unnecessary provocation? The sentries along the fences and in Main Road, and the well-armed men in the two towers facing the compound, were surely sufficient to raise an alarm? If the machine guns were manned there was a chance that should a rush be made against the wire, sentries would be shot before they could withdraw to garrison lines. On the other hand, the gunners could be warned to take that precaution. And he should not be influenced by the fact that the odious Suttor had suggested the measure. Abercare told the duty officer that the gunners should be roused to uncover and prepare and take to the guns.

Corporal Headon, the man assigned to fire the crucial Machine Gun A, would have happily been by his gun, his true vocation, with each atom of his being focused on it, and on covering the earth before him from near the gates of Main Road into the innermost hut of Compound C and along the line of the fence, should anyone reach it. His fire, if ever unleashed, would meet interlocking fire from Machine Gun B a little further south, and the enemies of his white race would be caught in that net. Headon thus took on the appointed task with a solemnity no one else in the garrison brought to their duty. He needed that holiness of endeavor.

But he who would have happily been awake was asleep now. He had not been to town and was virtually teetotal anyhow, and his dreams were dreams of being mocked by less conscientious men as he tried urgently to impress upon them the essential function of the fusee spring. As ever he was not taken seriously—his sister having misunderstood his torch morse from the tram on his last leave.

Eamon Cassidy and the two other gunners remained asleep, too, since Abercare's new command that they stand by the guns all night was slow to make its way to their barracks.

Cassidy had begun learning to fire on an earlier model than the one sent to him at Gawell Camp. But all the components were the same ones they had always been. Before the gun had been mounted on its trailer on the site chosen by the colonel, Suttor had assured himself that the two men were competent by observing them fire a short burst at the makeshift rifle range a little to the southeast of the camp. And that, Suttor considered, thoroughly proved their aptitude. Suttor had offended Cassidy somewhat by emphasizing the importance of adjusting the angle as targets got closer to them. And he advised Headon to sweep the ground ahead, since if anything the Vickers was too accurate—its bullets did not deviate, and there was no sense in firing repeatedly into a space whose occupiers had already fallen.

Headon would have preferred a more thorough and serious rehearsal, since he really believed, Eamon Cassidy noticed, that he'd end up using the gun in anger. Cassidy, given his chief ambition to go home and look after his two aging and beloved dependents, was rendered uneasy by that. Headon left no subtlety of the machine unvisited while instructing Cassidy in its wonders. After their first minor use of the thing on the range, and while making sure Cassidy observed, Headon had poured boiling water down the barrel to clean it. He was faintly officious about the seven-and-a-half pints of water the cooling system required and how it was to be emptied and refilled.

He regularly persuaded Cassidy to climb onto the trailer where the gun lay ready on its tripod under a tarpaulin, and unveil it and apply oil to the outside of the barrel. Headon inspected the muzzle cup and the cone yet again to ensure they were free from oil or any obstacle, and then dismantled the thing, looking to all the working parts, emphasizing to Cassidy the importance of the lock and the extractor. He proceeded to oil or add graphite grease to all the working parts, as he had learned as a boy and during the intervening decades, and checked that the connecting rod was adjusted to its correct length. Then he reassembled the gun, giving Cassidy the chance to contribute advice and the occasional correct part. So, such items as recoil plates, handle-block pins, fusee spring, safety-seer, and barrel disks, lifting levers, side levers, and a range of many other magnificently tooled parts became familiar to Cassidy. He did not seem to get the exaltation from it all that Headon did, but he was efficient in loading and feeding the canvas ammunition belt through the belt passage, which was the main order of business.

Headon also instructed Cassidy in the issue of stoppages and the use of the clearing plug. Cassidy wondered if Headon, the priest of the mechanism, by the strength of his desire, would conjure up some accommodating surge of prisoners towards the fence. Nonetheless, he took correction in a very relaxed way. He was a calm, reticent man, and his compliance gave Headon less grounds to be didactic than Headon himself would have liked.

At midnight Aoki ordered the lights to be turned out in the huts, to soothe any garrison suspicion of extreme possibilities. He thought it was his duty now, as a member of the council, to visit the recreation hall, the kitchens, and mess hall, and was amazed by how many men were still moving about, hut to hut, engaged in good-byes. He was a little disappointed by this sign of carelessness, and though he doubted in the circumstances it would cause any dangerous conjecture on the part of the garrison, he ordered these men to return to where, at this hour, they belonged.

By the combined help of moonlight and searchlight, he entered the recreation hall—the venue for plays, music and revues, and, above all, for Sakura. He found on the floor near the stage a sailor who had cut himself open thoroughly. This man had chosen to be a forerunner, to make things certain, not to leave it to the law of chaotic outcome or to risk any intrusion by the garrison. His inner organs were seeping onto the floor. This was one of the buildings intended for burning later in the night and palliasses were already heaped in one corner, and there lay the sailor who had chosen his ritual early, in the knowledge of his own coming cremation. So it is happening, Aoki told himself as if until now he had not quite believed it would. The mind might choose extinction, but the heedless blood kept singing, "Life, life." The sailor's act and the way he lay gave the world an acidic, heightened look. Aoki was stimulated, frightened, and delighted that this young forerunner now compelled him and the others to act.

In the kitchen he found two men hanging from beams—early fruit, soldiers disabled in battle, unfit for a charge. They had believed the vote, the loud majorities, as thoroughly as anyone could. They, too, had established this night's duty for the rest. One of the hanging men was a veteran Aoki knew, and looked very wizened, his hands spread palms out, like a man demonstrating an argument that should be obvious. A young friend dangled beside him in that terrible, contemplative posture of the hanged. Aoki returned to his hut. He would not blare the news. He would tell it softly.

Tamura the costume maker limped into the recreation hall half an hour after Aoki had left. He had said good-bye to Sakura, who understood his situation. He had not wanted to have Sakura present here, despite her domination of the stage he now approached, and the vivid memories her mere presence could evoke. He saw the same sailor Aoki had and paused by the ruin of his body a moment to honor him, and smelled the weight of his blood.

Then he mounted the stage with his usual slowness, tentative about rushing given his old wound, from a bullet passing through a lower section of his right lung. He entered the wings of the stage, where costumes hung on racks or were folded up in naphtha-smelling tea chests. On a table at the back, masks made by woodcarvers and hats made by Tamura himself were stacked. He went along the rack considering which of the garments—ones he'd labored on—to choose. He laid out some of them on the floor, as if he were about to sell them. He was certain it was appropriate that he should not take any of the more splendid costumes Sakura had worn in her Gawell triumphs. He chose a warrior costume, pants decorated with chariot wheels and closed in tight on the lower leg to signify that the wearer was fitted for action. He selected also a spartan, striped undershirt and an over jacket decorated with sails. This was suitable for a mere servant of the theater, a costume pitched between lordship and peasanthood, and an over jacket signifying departure.

He surveyed some of the other costumes for a while—the courtesan's dress from *Sukeroku, Flower of Edo*, and the cocktail dress in which Sakura performed ballads. Having displayed his work to whatever spirits might witness it, he rehung them reverently. Then he approached a beam at the back of the stage and climbed onto an unused chest and made a noose from fabric.

30

A sentry in Main Road, a member of the quarter guard that waited
in the tent Colonel Abercare had placed there, was comfortable
with the balance of things—that his banal and unnecessary watch on
a moon-drenched night would end at two o'clock, that he could then
withdraw to the semiwarmth of the guard tent at the intersection of
Main Road and Kelly's Lane, and that tomorrow night he would not
have to repeat this.

It was a quarter to two when this view of the easy equilibrium
of all elements in the landscape was altered. For without apparent
warning, one of the prisoners was running towards the inner double
gate into Main Road with an energy that threatened to break it down.
He was in the clear space as he sprinted across the rim of the wrestling arena and over the corner of the baseball pitch, or whatever they
called it.

Because the man was clearly more impelled than he himself was,
the guard at first stepped then moved more quickly back with his
rifle at the ready. The Japanese sprinter, meanwhile, had arrived
near the inner gate and raised his hands, and began shouting about
unjust men, and the folly of the wise, in what seemed to be a Bibli-

cal kind of English but was nothing like the sentry's English. Emphasis, intonations were all in the wrong place. The prisoner was athletic and began to climb the first gate acrobatically, lacerating his hands and not noticing it, to yell about unjust men dying by the sword.

His fear of something that was broader than his rant transmitted itself to the sentry too. What this prisoner seemed to be trying to do was sizeable, and the sentry raised his rifle by instinct and fired two shots into the air. This, he knew, was meant to be the first alarm.

No one seemed to stir in the company camps at either end of the prison compounds. No flares were fired, no siren began shrieking. The Japanese babbler was standing expostulating in the space between the compound inner gate and the one by which he could enter Main Road when the telephone placed on one of the uprights rang. The guard, watching Ban's advance and intending to shoot him now that he seemed so close to joining him, answered it nonetheless. It was the corporal of the guard in the tent in the center of Main Road. The sentry told the corporal that a prisoner had run to the gate raving and yelling and was now about to climb over it and jump into Main Road. The corporal told him that if the man did land in front of him, the sentry was to hold him prisoner, and they would all be along from the tent at once.

The prisoner began climbing the second gate like someone looking for the chance to persuade more intimately. From Compound C a roughly performed bugle call was now heard, and it seemed to give license to a sudden uproar, and caused the sentry all the more tightly to keep his weapon and his sharpest attention pointed at Ban's torso, whose body was on the midstrands of the gate's wire. A mass of raging men was streaming from the huts with outlandish threats on their lips; blossoms of fire were glinting through doorways and shattering windows and beginning to reach for the under eaves. Smoke already rose from rooftops, promising they would

go too. The running figures in the compound, who appeared to
be sprinting in all directions including towards him, were not figures stampeded by flames. These were the fire starters themselves.
There were enough of them to take his breath, and they moved
towards him across Compound C's open ground, and some were
very fast.

Now, he was sure, the entire garrison must know that this wasn't
a plain night, but the end of all plain nights. Two other guards with
rifles were jogging towards him along the Main Road from the direction of the quarter guard tent and a little behind them limped Lieutenant Cook. The prisoner topped the wire and, rather than alarm the
garrison, politely climbed down to turn and face them.

Lieutenant Cook and the three guards looked in bewilderment at
Ban's face as he yelled at them words that sounded impossibly like
"For there are murderers, and idolaters, and whosoever loveth and
maketh a lie."

But such an utterance defied belief.

"Escape!" then yelled Ban. "Escape all!"

The men did not know whether it was an announcement of fact
or an order. They noticed that the prisoner had begun shivering and
that there were tears and dirt stains on his face.

"Escape!" shouted the shuddering prisoner a third time, and from
his space by the gates he pointed towards the masses of his comrades shattering the inner gate to the Main Road with clubs and the
weight of their bodies and with such steady determination that the
guards were near hypnotized to find it so easily forced, and its timbers shredded.

To meet this mass, and to be engulfed in it, stood the lieutenant
with a pistol and sentries with rifles from wars past and an informer
who spoke in Biblical riddles.

Lieutenant Cook fired one vain round into the mass and roared,
"Run!" He hoped remotely that the prisoner would scale the last

fence and run with them. It was obvious to him that the man had been his savior.

The sentries on the gate at the northern end of the Main Road—the gate that gave onto a safe, free world—opened it as all four men came running, or, in Cook's case, shuffling along with the raging mass behind them. "Open!"

As Cook felt the stress of attempting to run, he cried, "Bugger, bugger, bugger!" and that, too, was a prayer for mercy. He was the last to the gate, beyond which lay the survivable world, by five yards, and hustled as he could through it, looking behind him for the prophet, hoping to find him beside them. But, no, the man was stuck in place as if bewildered, and for whatever reason had chosen not to run. "Close them!" screamed Cook.

Struggling for breath with the shock of it more than from exercise, he saw a tide of maroon-colored prisoners, undifferentiated, running at insane pace in Main Road, some towards the other outer gate, and a furious howling contingent towards this one. Their ambitions were obvious. They intended to possess the entire night, and he could feel the heat of their intentions. He saw the Bible-uttering informer overtaken by others. A crowd of them stopped and could not deliver enough blows, or hack his body sufficiently with knives to express their rage at him, their disappointment in him. The lieutenant saw his face turned, screaming, but could not hear his shrieks above the general howl.

Cook began to cry out as if the man were taking the attack meant for him. He saw bludgeons raised up above the prisoner and knives, delineated by moonlight, plunging into him. He saw another prisoner armed with a knife tied to a length of wood impale the man's body and someone else kneel and cut open the throat and all the verses that had belonged in it. The assassination party itself, so adroit in its work, soon diffused and, carried on by men pushing from behind, came towards the Main Road gate where Cook was stationed.

Cook ordered his men now to fire at will. A gun from a nearby tower joined. They inflicted intimate death, for the front of the maroon host was perhaps ten yards from the guards outside the gate. No lack of light for marksmen. A positive dazzle from searchlights behind, westering moon above, and blazing buildings in Compound C. And, coming on, these men who intended not to return there! Yet, in the headquarters company in the camp behind him, no siren shrieked.

Colonel Abercare had, however, run from his office, where he had been drowsing, at the very first shots, feeling but shaking off that depression and confusion of head that came from being woken in the small hours. The orderly room officer, having rushed from the guardhouse seeking orders, ran into him at the bottom of the stairs, where Abercare did issue genuine, military-style orders. Siren to sound, all men of the companies on either side of the Main Gate to assemble as arranged in a line to protect the camp. The men from Wye as well to report to Major Suttor. A line to be established between the gate into Main Road, where the sentries were obviously firing at the prisoners running so determinedly toward Machine Gun A.

Hurrying towards the assembly point, he met the captain of the headquarters company and asked him what had happened with the siren. In the abortive pattern of the night, the siren had been meant to startle the garrison but the bloody thing had remained treacherously silent.

"Sir, it seemed to break down," the man yelled, his eyes flicking towards the sights of surging burgundy (so much light there that the tone could be distinctly recognized) within the compound.

"And the red flares?"

"Sir, I ordered them fired but they'd sweated in storage and burst at a low level and mightn't be seen."

"Is everything going to be this ridiculous?" asked Ewan Abercare too frantically.

"Don't know, sir." But the frightened captain gave every evidence he thought it might be.

And the machine guns weren't even in action yet. Hadn't he ordered them manned? Had what he said been ambiguous?

Reality had changed. The remotely possible had manifested itself. The acid taste of culpability flooded Abercare's mouth.

When awoken in his bunk by shots and screaming, Headon got up in bemusement, his head a void of floating items that very soon coalesced into resolve. He could hear the strange roaring from inside the compound. It had happened; he knew at once they were unleashed, those fathomless men behind the wire. A sergeant in the doorway was bellowing about rifles. Headon himself, pulling on his boots, was aflame with eagerness to get to his gun and forestall any risk that at this incomparable instant the mechanism he had devoted such time to might nonetheless be ineffective against those ferocious cries within Compound C.

He was first out of the door—an overcoat on top of pyjamas, boots without socks on his feet—and was pleased that Cassidy was attired in the same manner, as they had discussed, for a night emergency. The surge of noise arising from beyond the fences was a phenomenon now—a storm. The purpose in those voices would have melted steel.

As Headon and Cassidy reached the trailer, the searchlight above it cast a long beam in through to the compound itself, where fires lit Headon's targets more vividly still. Some front-runners were addressing themselves already to the first of the inner fences and tossing blankets over the wire to diminish the impact of the barbs.

He and Cassidy hauled themselves up into the trailer and dragged the cover off the weapon. The second machine-gun team, with more ground to negotiate to get to their trailer, ran past them over open ground as yet sacred to the garrison. Headon was strangely pleased to find the cans of ammunition belts remained within the trailer; that the arrangement had not been altered in some way by the noise and the enlarged reality of this hour. He made the rehearsed movements to prepare the machine, and Cassidy opened a number of the metal cans and fed a canvas belt of bullets with considerable concentration into the feed block. To an observer, the two of them would have seemed utterly undistracted by that dark-uniformed mass raging concertedly across Compound C with the purpose of reaching them.

In addition to blankets, a swathe of deep red figures had now hung themselves like huge fruit bats on the first of the fences, with the purpose of offering their own bodies for others to scale. And others were availing themselves, or else climbing by their own power.

"I always said we fed the buggers too well," Headon called to Cassidy. The range was a little more than one hundred and fifty yards to the ones who had already climbed the innermost fence; two hundred yards to the oncomers behind. The burgundy vanguard fragments topped and then dropped from an inner fence and coalesced again in the intervening space. Across the compound, others hastened to follow, and that all happened without a decrease in chanting and raging and against that further extreme backdrop of a high barrier of flame.

Headon released the traversing clamp without having to look. He worked the elevating gear and looked through the rear and foresights. Like God's elected angel, he held the handles now, thumbs up, knuckles as far back as he could, as he had been taught to do to avoid having them pounded by recoil. He pressed the button.

As he traversed the gun, the parts affected by recoil sang pleasurably in his mind. Immediately, men acting as human ladders for their comrades climbing the inner fence fell or hung on wire like abandoned clothes, and those who had used them as a means of climbing and then dropping into the intervening space between fences, fell and limped, and fell and succumbed.

Major Suttor had presented himself to the colonel early in the attack as Abercare, joined by a signaler with a radio pack on his back, stood watching the line form. Suttor's company platoons deployed creakily and slowly a little forward, and were joined by men from the second company's units whose barracks lay at this end of the camp and who normally lived and slept opposite one of the two Italian compounds. It was an uncomplicated formation, a ragged line near the place where Lieutenant Cook and others had fired into Main Road and apparently made a slaughter there.

They were now joined by a pale Lieutenant Cook, and the three of them assessed the astounding demonstration manifesting itself within Compound C, and Cook reported in brief militarese his adventure in Main Road and his dispositions at the gate. The adjutant told Abercare that the other garrison companies were securing their own sections of the perimeter in case similar phenomena developed there. Later, it would be reported that amazed Italians and Koreans and the rest looked at the flames leaping in Compound C and reaching northwards on the light breeze, and that even the Japanese officers in Compound B had been awed.

The battalion sergeant major, an old self-serious militiaman, called for the platoon commanders at the north gate to present themselves to the colonel, and Abercare told them, "Integrity of the garrison, integrity of the camp!"

It had a nice sound and would have pleased him, had he not already embarked on self-reproach. The moon had been an argument in favor of safety. Now it had turned on him. What clique of fools had argued that a dark night was necessary, when all along these men delighted in illumination and destruction, and had created their own within the compound? What was to be said of men who set their compound afire so that it would mark out their silhouettes and ensure their obliteration?

Stationed behind the line with his signaler and a field telephone, Abercare ordered Suttor to ensure the line was wheeled to the right to take in Headon's machine gun, which had now begun to speak. But the movement was somehow never achieved, being beyond the garrison's experience and repertoire of drill. They stood in a ragged line that tended to clump for the sake of shared certainties. At their officers' orders they began to fire into the compound, some determinedly, some in bewilderment, as if they needed the purpose explained to them just one more time. It was unlikely that they halted the impetus in Compound C in any way. But it halted the garrison itself. A shot from the flank of the line somehow thudded and bounced, singing, off a post near the Broadway gate. It felled a private near Abercare. A medical orderly appeared with angelic suddenness.

At that moment the searchlights were still blazing on the red masses of humped, spread-eagled casualties in the compound and nearer, here, in open country; shapes that seemed to indent the ground, like bodies dropped from a height. Abercare felt he had wrought one of those most shocking of military and spiritual catastrophes: a disproportionate slaughter that was continuing and must, he was sure, do so. He was also aware with part of his brain that soon his superiors would ask him why he'd permitted some of the garrison to go to town earlier, on what had become such a night, and why he himself had been at dinner in town and not locked in permanent study of the omens within Compound C. They would ask him even about the siren. Along from the hecatomb, which made him swallow his nausea and might undermine his reason, they would count him a failed and distracted officer. But not so distracted that he did not see how unlikely the making of a link was between the line of riflemen and the machine gun, now that indeed living burgundy prisoners had energetic hands on the gun trailer. He saw a bald man in army overcoat and pyjamas leap from the trailer athletically, with machine-gun ammunition cans in each hand.

"He's lost," called Abercare to Suttor, but Suttor made the can't-hear-you gesture, hand to ear, half his attention directed to his men ahead of him.

31

Making for the northernmost segment of the wire, towards the machine gun beyond the perimeter, the last cigarette of his lifetime now smoked and its redolence still on his tongue, Aoki found it hard to believe he was not in China, for China had returned to him with the hubbub and the shattering of the night by rifle shots and, above all, the nattering of machine guns. Progressing over open ground towards the inner fence, he had seen the men outside the compound, elevated in their trailer, preparing their gun, and then firing the machine. The cordite smell came to him not as densely as it had in China but sufficiently to evoke his past.

All was brightness, and in it he saw the garrison forming a line that raggedly defended their huts, and firing now and then with casual inaccuracy, uncertain in their drill, facing a duty for which they were spiritually unprepared but for which they might actually be required to act as soldiers. He and his brothers could provide them with some help, could elevate their performance, could evoke from them the skills they might doubt they had. They might already be doing it by the howls they uttered, some of them coherent—"Ten thousand years of life!" He himself, he found, was also bellowing, though he had not realized it, calling upon the imminent machine-gun rounds.

To the left, as he stumbled along, being outstripped in the rush to the wire by younger and less-marred men, he could see men torn by rifle fire and rolling on the ground or driven by the force of impacts into ditches on either side of the road. He was more exultant than affrighted. He had always been calm in action and rowdy only in victory.

Ahead, more young men tossed blankets over the inner barbed wire or prepared to climb over the bodies of those lacerated and wounded men who dangled from the upper strands of the fence. He had forgotten the disquieting, authoritative noise of machine guns, and was amazed how the men around them progressed despite that. The flash of a light weapon from one of the guard towers made more of the climbers sag, eternally safe. Now you could tell from the minute discordance between their fire—the improbably short interval between a round leaving one gun and a round leaving the other—that the machine guns from both ends of the outer fence were in operation. He flinched but welcomed the fullness of sound.

He continued to progress at a fast amble, and looked left and right as other men passed him. It was easier to run towards one's culmination than to walk towards it, and he wished he could be faster. In looking to his right he saw Sakura, moving with a long stride, her head decorated with a fringe of fabric flowers and on her body an underlayer of full-bodied pink top and trousers, and around the lot of it swathes of bright cloth. She ran barefoot. Aoki thought for an instant she had debased the entire demonstration. A partially lame prisoner she passed patted her on her posterior as she hustled along. But then it became obvious that she meant to prove that her pretense did merely clothe a *he*, and the *he* was as willing to be valiant as any of the men who had never left behind their masculinity.

Aoki now saw Sakura as if she were a heavy garment slung on the wire of the fence. A machine-gun round that had borne away the crown of her head had left her suspended there, a great swathe of vivid, blood-drenched cloth. Men were using her shoulders as leverage.

Aoki himself began to climb, at first by way of a blanket. An ultimate respect for Sakura's craft as a balladeer made him avoid the steps of flesh and cloth offered by her body. Higher on the fence, he hauled himself over the body of a young man who proved to be dying, not dead, and who groaned at the weight Aoki put on him. From the top of the fence Aoki looked down into the ground between this fence and the second. Below him men ran and wallowed and fell. He saw the silver of a blade with which one prisoner had cut the carotid of a wounded friend.

He climbed down backwards like a man descending a ladder, expecting the end and seeing other men topple from the top strands and pass him on their descent. He himself reached the bottom still upright amongst these others who had landed dead. A man he recognized was writhing in front of him. As a matter of etiquette, Aoki went down on his knees and asked the man if he needed a final mercy. He could find a knife, he said, or ask someone for one. But the man perished and another fell dead against his back before he had reached his feet again. Between here and the next fence, Aoki assured himself, I'll know what it's like, the whole mystery. He experienced the peculiar feel of air punctuated and knitted by machine-gun rounds, whose buffets made some men clump and, despite themselves, raise a hand as if the way ahead were not transparent to them or could be forced apart like curtains.

When he rose and ran again, other and better sprinters passed him and then fell down. He began climbing the second fence and one of his hands was spiked by a rosette of wire, and clothing caught and needed to be torn away. But the first of the escapees was climbing the outer fence and getting close to the machine gun now, and on the far side of that last wire fence, the crew was working at the thing to depress its angle of fire. These two seemed close figures, and the searchlight that had been a peril to the runners was becoming one to the gunners, since it left them in their own vulnerable, busy cone of glare.

Yet firing in its new angle of depression and at so intimate a range, it was tearing the head, the legs, the arms off those climbing the last wire. There was concerted fire from the garrison as well, in their line in front of the company quarters. They know we want their magazine, Aoki realized.

He knew he had come through the zone of enfilading, crisscrossing fire, but for a second believed he was gone, that he had achieved the desired end. There was darkness before him, but sound continued as before. The searchlights had all died, he realized. Some calamity, which refused to overtake him, had overtaken the electrical system—a line severed by a bullet. The night ahead seemed almost dim, but it was still lit from behind him by the fires in the compound, and Aoki could see, like faces in a theater, the men at that great reaper of a gun, and the ragged line of garrison nearly but not exactly connected to it. It occurred to him that if the gun could be taken, it could be turned on the line.

He was astonished and chagrined at having got this far, and believed it was a symptom of the clumsiness he had expected of them. But as he dropped from the last fence, he was hungry for further acts of war now presented to him. A man was not aware of the existence of such hungers until he launched himself into the storm.

Cassidy fed the gun with a determined concentration, contemplative as a monk, excluding the world. But Headon at the handles knew that he would perish there, that when he had in his training looked down on the parts of the Vickers spread on a tarpaulin, he had been looking at the entrails of his death. The stand did not permit the barrel to be inclined any further than it was. And the garrison line off to one side had not seemed to have the wit or the education to advance and shield him and use him as their anchor. With so many self-liberated figures now massing before him in open ground, he knew that after this belt there would be no time for Cassidy at his most adroit to get the thing reloaded. For an instant he tested himself for terror, probed the skin, but found that there was, above all, a certain anxiety there, different from fear—and peevishness. His fellow garrison troops were piss-poor, timid men, formed up by timid officers. It was in his mouth that he tasted the metallic, ashy, and utterly novel taste of his extinction. They'd take him seriously as a soldier now.

He knew there were further belts in cans on the trailer, and yelled at Cassidy to take them back into the camp.

"Bugger it!" Cassidy roared above the continuing fire of the gun. He was betting he could reload, but there was no chance.

"No, clear off!" Headon confirmed. If these interlopers turned the gun on the garrison, the garrison would not know how to take it. There were prisoners on either flank now, some falling to rifle fire but others not made cautious by it. This horde could be smelled through the cordite—the smell of their ambition and strangeness, of sour liquor and barbarous fervor.

Cassidy stood and, with a canister of belts in either hand, tried to jump over the prisoners' heads. It was an extraordinary vault, he thought, something he didn't know was in him, all to deny the belts to the marauders. His leg was pulled out from under him and he fell amongst them with a great thump that took his breath. These were his and Headon's recent targets. Why should there be any mercy in them? He could not see their individual faces and their shoulders blazed with the reflection of the fires they'd set. The sweatiness of their inevitable fear and strange ambitions encompassed him.

Headon took out the feeding mechanism from the gun and threw it over the heads of those around him, hoping it might find a clump of darkness to lie in. He could hear Cassidy screaming and pleading on the ground and the thud of baseball bats and the descent of knives.

A number of them were on the trailer now and one, standing in front of him, was a tall boy who drew his nail-studded baseball bat back over his shoulder like someone preparing to hit a ball. Rather be killed with a cricket bat, thought Headon.

"Finish me quick, fuck you!" Headon instructed him.

Terror struck now, like a shaft entering him. He did not choose to fall but felt himself going. A tremendous, sudden, and world-ending wallop bore him away, his components of body and personhood flying apart along hectic avenues of yellow and blue light, tearing him away from torches and trams and sisters.

Cassidy, close to finished, bleeding from knife wounds as well as other blows, saw them laying into Headon's body with their clubs, and had the impression that Headon, draped over the rim of the trailer, was dancing under the blows, telegraphing agonies to him. Cassidy had time to see a merciless young man straddle him, knife in hand.

When Aoki climbed up onto the blood-fouled trailer, using the top of one of its tires to ascend, most men lay dead around it or had moved on to attack the line of the garrison, whose fire was more admirably concentrated now. A confidence and a bloody enthusiasm had entered them, and surprised him as much as it might—on reflection—surprise them. He saw some of his comrades sloping away north, having already and reasonably enough despaired of taking the magazine. He knelt across the legs of the pummeled corpse that lay half-in, half-out of the trailer, and inspected the gun. An essential segment of it had been thrown away—he could tell that at once. As well as that, the brave gunner, worthy of a better battalion, had hauled the belt crookedly so that the last few rounds had jammed. All the bravery of the fellow's soul had come together in those two acts of disablement.

"It's beyond hope," he yelled to those still around him, who looked expectant and were waiting for him to turn the gun around and begin the business of damage beyond the wire. The rifle fire from the garrison dropped two prisoners as he spoke. All Aoki could think to do was point the machine gun high in the air and tighten the clamp that fixed it there and jump down. He descended from the trailer and stood considering other options amidst all the havoc. Still bullets maliciously evaded him. Then, he decided in fury, you can outlay your strength in a search. He turned without haste and sloped away northwards up a slight slope to become lost amidst granite boulders. Others followed.

Goda waited in the orderly hut while around him the barracks blazed. He heard the machine guns and rifles, but only one runner got back to tell him some men had crossed all three wire barriers. So he set out, calling to any of those sheltering in ditches or prone on the earth—he could not tell whether from death or cowardice. His mood was somber. He caught up with the tail of the more southerly assault and felt again that half-forgotten peculiarity of advancing into machine-gun fire. He was aware of the surprise of impact that men around him howled forth, yet he remained unhurt.

Extraordinarily, Goda, much nimbler than Aoki, lived likewise and nonetheless through all the phases of crossing the wires, and climbing over blankets and bodies. He dropped from the last fence amongst shredded victims of grenades, which were being dropped from the tower above. He knew that if he stood still he might himself be so torn about, but then he saw men fall cleanly from machine-gun fire and chose that option. Men, as was natural in a battle, which this was more or less, were skirting the span of the gunfire and disappearing into the boulders and the darkness. And then the searchlights went out, and all seemed dim, but only for a moment for the eye was an adjustable organ.

Goda turned towards the garrison and got close enough without being felled to see both that the machine gun there was no longer in action on anyone's behalf, and that, as well, the garrison line had found its military regularity and discipline now, as a line might after it has recovered from its disbelief in what is happening. The option which had presented itself to Aoki, to be gone and to cause disruption as a phantom in the countryside, was the one left to Goda.

Near the gate he could see the frightened faces of the garrison firing and emptying their rifles and searching for new clips in their pouches. He began to climb the wire just inside the gate, gashing his hand, but trying to retain his shaft with its knife blade in one palm, using only fingers for ascent. He was impelled by having seen the commandant calling to a signaler, and his malice towards that fool was illimitable.

He would have been discouraged to know that Aoki and Tengan—even though Tengan had been armed with a stake into which a blade had been embedded, and despite his stopping many times to howl defiance—amongst Goda's section of men in Main Road had been similarly and perversely immune; that there seemed to be a malign plan to save the council of three.

Like most of the men, Goda found his weapon inconvenient and threw it away. It had been hard to climb the three fences and retain it. Now he had only his own intractable and irreducible soul.

32

The young man who dropped ten yards from Abercare was someone he knew, and there was a second's lunatic impulse to greet him. This known fellow held a shaft of wood with a blade stuck in it. He ran purposely, and Abercare saw him coming too fast for anyone to be called on. The rage on his face looked like a mask because of his handsomeness. The fury there was both to be expected but also distorting. He realized this was the hubristic flier, one of the triumvirate—the young fellow with pretty features and astounding eyes.

Abercare nearly addressed him, ordering him to stop. The lieutenant had by now moved away, and Suttor, his pistol drawn, had turned back to support his troops. The signaler near Abercare saw the prisoner and reached for his rifle. The prisoner drew the stern of the shaft down, seemed to assess Abercare's face a second, and then drove the improvised weapon upwards into Abercare's sternum. Abercare breathed in hugely for a second and stood on in searing amazement with the shaft and its knife point fixed in him. The young man was visibly pleased but did not wait there to assess the damage any further. Abercare weighed the strange intrusion of the shaft. It was of a different order from pain, and larger.

"Don't hit our men," he told the signaler, who had found his rifle and was firing after the escapee, who was flitting through the camp. The signaler's shot did not seem to delay him as he streaked north towards the bush.

Tengan had run some way to get to Abercare, northwards along the line of the fence, and of course he expected he would be shot now; now that he had done that hardhanded task, he was full of awe and a desire not to be shot precisely for that but to be shot for who he was—a prisoner. This kept him running. It was automatic, and later he would not be delighted at it. But it seemed to him then that they had failed to stop him from the front, and during his strike against the despicable commandant, and when they did not fell him from behind he simply kept running, with the dawning awareness that given the size of what he'd done, he would draw them away, hunting him, wearying and angering them, giving them motives to finish him in a notable way. Let them go to that trouble, and let them be vicious about it.

The truth at the time, however, was that Tengan couldn't have said why he ran onwards after impaling Abercare.

Back by the gate, Abercare, half turned with the improvised point in him, saw the shots aimed at his assassin miss. Ah, he thought, the arrogance of that young man is profound. He called Suttor, who turned and became instantly attentive.

"My God," he said. "Sir . . ."

Abercare said, "Mrs. Galloway is still in my quarters."

Had she risen and ranted to be let out, or had she by some alcoholic mercy slept through it all?

"The gossips will tell Emily," he continued. "It was a car breakdown . . ."

These words seemed to him each like blows self-delivered against his own trunk rather than items spoken in the ordinary way. He was reduced to placing on Suttor the hopeless obligation to stanch those worthies, that poisonous estate, who would have opinions about Mrs. Galloway being in the camp.

"I'll send a guard," said Suttor.

A medical orderly had appeared and said, "Oh, Jesus, sir."

"Do we take it out?" Suttor asked the medical orderly. For no friend of the Mortons had ever been impaled. Suttor had not even researched the issue. He shouted some orders about guarding the colonel's quarters, that Mrs. Galloway was waiting in there.

"Lie down, why don't we, sir?" the medical orderly suggested. But Abercare was aware that Suttor had—without trying to—released the gossip germ.

"You may be right," he began to tell his adversary. "Vanity . . ."

He wished to make things clearer, but the power had gone from his voice. He fell sideways, the medical orderly guiding him down. His signaler dropped his rifle and supported him.

"Very kind," Abercare, obscenely penetrated, told the signaler and the medical orderly through the wall of noise.

Suttor also knelt and tried to hold him up with a hand under his right armpit. Suttor was crying as if Abercare were his beloved leader. As if this were like the burial of Sir John Moore at Corunna.

"Emily," he told Suttor, and Suttor seemed to half understand and nodded.

Abercare could feel the vitality of all their arms at various parts of his frame, the astonishing corporeal nature of them compared to the mist he was becoming. He was still aware of the huge thing in him, larger than agony, too vast for screams, taking him away before he could get the essential words out. He was washing away in a cold sea. Ah, he thought, the inland sea that once flowed here. It was dragging him up this hill away from the camp. From here he could see below, he could almost count, the burgundy units of his failure.

Where was his breath?

The garrison line became ascendant and there would be murmurs afterwards that its firing went on too long: later-appearing prisoners clumped together; rather than offering a serious charge, they did not seem possessed of the impetus of the earlier wave, and staggered forward as if exhausted by traversing the triple fence. Others, the garrison line firing into their flanks, fled across open country northwards and into the boulders on the low ridge and the kurrajong trees, intending either to continue their defiance there, or else demoralized. These, too, were fair game for the line.

Suttor's duty lay between commanding the men shooting into Main Road, where the merest display of an intention to crawl was now punished by fire, and the main garrison line which, although fortified by an escort that had now arrived from Wye, was in some cases hungover and outnumbered by the captives.

Frightened at first, the garrison grew in self-assertion and vengeance against a population they had been urged, against their better instincts, to treat with abnormal patience. Suttor did not possess the gifts to stop them. He cried, "Cease fire!" but came to know that in this garrison fury he needed to call his platoon commanders and have them visit each man with the command. He sent his sergeant major to do it. Even so there was irrationality and recklessness in him to let the vengeance roll on—for Abercare's sake and for his son's, and in his madness these two poles of affection became entangled on this unspeakable night.

The shooting ceased in the first grayness, and the last of the fires in the compound became embers at about the same time. Suttor noticed that frost had descended and stiffened the earth and its vegetation, and had formed on the bodies of men. In that light the hundreds of blankets and maroon overcoats stuck to the wire, strung out like notations on lined music paper, bespoke a calamitous purpose he felt he could not read, but whose meaning, he was sure, would turn out to be appalling.

At nine o'clock on Sunday morning, accompanied by a detachment of guards, Sergeant Nevski entered Main Road amidst the reek of burned huts and corpses, of all the palliasses, spare clothing, cards and books and keepsakes that had been consumed in Compound C. He could certainly tell that when it came to the huts, men's bodies must have been caught inside those fires, must have killed themselves there beforehand and left their flesh for the flames. Or perhaps they had been murdered as dissenters—he did not know. There was in any case the horrific overlay of burned flesh. Though the bodies in Main Road and in the compound whose gates gaped open had been near refrigerated by the night, there was the odious smell of blood shed en masse.

He noticed men—some subtly stirring—lying in ditches on either side of the road. He was in a grieving mood already, and like many soldiers did not know how to accommodate his grief. He believed that the firing from the garrison line had gone on too long, felling confused and uncertain figures, the aftermath of the frenzy of the front-runners. Nevski was nervous about the control, or lack of it, he could exercise over these guards accompanying him, yet such an entrance into the slaughter zone was necessary. Behind him and his section of guards came the work parties of Koreans and Formosans, detailed to find and lay the bodies in rows for the coroner. One of them, Cheong, said to his friend, but in a shaken voice, "This is what people they are, the stupid pricks!"

Some men now rose from the ditch by the compound fence, and tore their jackets open and exposed their chests and pleaded to be shot. Others simply knelt up and pleaded for nothing; they might at some hour bless their survival. Nevski, knowing the inmates better than the guards did, and appalled by the humps of dyed uniforms scattered everywhere, standing out so vividly on the white-green dust of early light, began to choke at these sights and cried out preventively, "No. Don't fire!"

But sleepless, and having seen Colonel Abercare impaled before their eyes, or seen his draped corpse; having likewise seen Headon and Cassidy pulped near their gun; having always despised the contemptuous prisoners anyhow, two of the garrison soldiers with him accommodated the prisoners. Nevski heard the terrible cracks of rifles by each of his ears, and that cursed cordite smell assailed him again as it had in clouds in the small hours.

At the sound of these two shots, Major Suttor, who had been discussing matters with the commandant of one of the Italian compounds, came running up Main Road with his own escort and entered Compound C and reached Nevski's party. "Sergeant, what in God's name are you doing?" he asked Nevski. He was mad eyed, and spit flew from his mouth. He wrenched the rifle out of the grasp of one of the guards, and then of the other.

"I'll have you charged with murder, you two bastards!" he called. He turned to Nevski. "Did they need to fire? Did they?"

Nevski was surprised by the extent to which he wanted to say they did. "No," said Nevski. "There was much slaughter later last night, too, that needn't . . ."

"Shut up!" yelled Suttor. "I don't want emotional words used. 'Slaughter' be buggered! Don't say it! Don't you fucking say it, you Russian bastard!"

Nevski looked at the two assassins. He saw vengeance cooling in their eyes and their sullen concession to Suttor. They knew, though, they would never be charged with any crime. What did they expect—those people of Compound C—if they tried this stuff on? The enemies of country, Empire, and race, and themselves given to atrocities worse than the cleanliness of the bullet?

Yet Suttor went on roaring at them. "Can't you see that this is what they want? *They . . . They . . .*" He pointed to the dead. "They will kill ten of our prisoners they hold for every one you bastards shoot here. So, go on, kill one of them if you fucking dare, and you can add ten of ours, and so murder eleven at a fucking time! Do you want that, you fucking cut-rate soldiers? When you stand trial? Do you want to face that proposition?"

In any case, through this argumentation—but also because those guards of a mind to take blood for blood had had appropriate vengeance—no more of the living were killed, though further prisoners who had survived came up and pleaded to be. Men who did not offer their hearts as targets, however, were also rising still from the ditches by the fence with their hands raised—dissenters, Nevski knew, from the military ardor of their brethren. There was no misreading the tentative relief on some faces. Those who had wounds had carried them stoically and, wounded or not, it seemed to Nevski by their movements and submission that they had grown out of their previous soldierhood and all its fervor. They had seen battle and now immolation and had concluded either before, or now, that it was ab-surd. With the light of an unexpected morning on their faces, they were willing to be new kinds of men and to await a temporal liberation.

Beyond Gawell's perimeter, wounded prisoners at large in the bush began to be retrieved by patrols from the garrison and even by accidental encounters with farmers or police. Others broke from the trees and exposed their hearts, but the fury had ended and the patrols were under the severest restraint. These retaken arrived back that day, the wounded to the compound hospital, where the garrison med-ical officer and a sleep-deprived Dr. Garner tended them but could not prevent the fatal hemorrhages and expiries from shock and chest wounds. Those prisoners who came back stating their disappoint-ment at not having been slaughtered declared they knew now what they'd merely talked of before—that they could not depend on these people to remedy anything. They were stuck unexpectedly again with the chronic disorder of survival.

A major from the Department of Information, a former journalist and now a regulator of news, arrived by plane at Gawell around one o'clock and reported to Suttor's office, finding him exhausted, bewil-dered, and distrait.

"This has been a frightful business," Suttor told the man. "We can't conceal the numbers. We have to have the coroner in and the Swiss have to be told—if not, they'll ferret it out. And poor bloody Abercare—he was hopeless. Nil nisi bonum and all the rest of it, but just look where the poor silly bugger sited the gun they overran. We had an argument about that. Look, I'm up to my ears but I want to talk to you. To you in particular. But go out and see it all first. It's a literal bloody shambles."

The press officer asked, "Isn't it *their* fault? They're the ones who tried to get out."

"It was to be expected," said Suttor. "I have a meeting with the officer of a patrol I sent off, and I have to talk to Sydney as well. Could I see you after that? I have a huge favor to ask."

Suttor sent him off, a bit mystified, with the duty officer. The major was given a tour of the gutted compound and the survivors and others working at laying out bodies in lines of stretchers, a sheet giving anonymity to the wounds each of the dead had received. He would remark there was near silence over the site. An occasional barked command was like an assault on the solemnity of the day and the sense of bewilderment that hung over the camp and the compound. The victorious garrison seemed uncertain as to their achievement. Then he was escorted back to Major Suttor's office.

Suttor looked still tireder now and was smoking hurriedly and moving urgently. He rushed a chair into place for the Department of Information man and quickly sat to face him.

"I've been waiting to confer with you," Suttor said. "I'm aware that the way this news is managed is crucial. Excuse me, would you like a drink? Tea?"

"Perhaps later, when we've worked this out," the major told him. He gave his condolences at the loss of the colonel.

"Well," said Suttor, gesturing emphatically with his right hand, chopping the air, "I gave a hint of my feelings. But . . . he was determined to give them notice, see. And they gave him notice back. But in everything we did, there was the problem of *our* prisoners. Our prisoners held by *them*."

Suttor crossed his hands on the desk, and the press officer noticed that they were trembling. Suttor asked again, "So how will this be handled? This whole balls-up? I will never say a word against Abercare in public, but I will say 'balls-up' to anyone who asks. I could tell you, item by item."

"Well, we'll use the broadest strokes, I suppose," said the press man. "We've already prepared something for this evening's paper. We say there was an outbreak; we don't specify casualties amongst the prisoners, though we admit there have been some. Of course, we emphasize that they were military prisoners, not internees. In the long run we'll have to say how many. But we don't need to do that yet. We'll talk to the Swiss, of course, about the pace we should proceed at. They're reasonable chaps. How many of the prisoners, do you think, got away into the bush?"

"Figures aren't firm. Men are still climbing out of drains; one of them climbed out of the incinerator . . . Two hundred and fifty or so dead, then some twenty suicides. About eighty at large—out there somewhere."

The press officer said, "I have been asked to state that most of the prisoners are accounted for. Without, of course, endangering the public. But if we don't say that, people will be alarmed, and some members of the public will go out Jap hunting, and end up shooting each other. So it's not desirable to say there are many at large. We'd like to use a term such as 'largely rounded up' or 'only a few still at large,' and emphasize that by now they are in a weakened state. Most of those missing *will* be found before dark, I take it?"

Suttor was all at once on his feet. "Look, say what you like. The bastards are being brought in by the hour. And those who aren't can die out there for all I care, and probably will if tonight is as cold as last night. But the point is, my name must not be mentioned. That's crucial. Not mentioned anywhere in any bulletin or the press. Even in any inquiry, if it comes to that. Or anywhere else the Japanese might see it and exploit it." He stubbed out a cigarette and seemed suddenly cramped by grief. "I have a boy, you see . . . I have a boy in their hands. I'm not even sure where he is. The last I heard was Thailand. I don't want him to pay. Not when it's that old fool Abercare . . ."

The pressman took account of this, writing it down. Even that disturbed Suttor. "Use a capital S instead of my real name."

The press officer nodded. "I understand your concern," he assured Suttor. "By the way, you might need to put up with Colonel Abercare being declared a hero."

"It's like a radio serial," said Suttor, amazed. "You chaps make it up as you go along."

"Well," the man said, "you can depend on me in that regard. The world can get stuffed. This is our business, not theirs."

When the man left, Suttor felt an ease of soul and the capacity to command return to him. He called the coroner's office in Orange, and was told that a gentleman should be there within the hour. Then, at Major Suttor's urgent orders, the recaptured were quickly fed, sitting on the floors of the washrooms and laundry. Let the buggers be confused by charity. He was concerned for their warmth, and requisitioned as many mats and mattresses and blankets as he could from the quartermaster, and ordered from a depot in Wagga truckloads of clothing and towels and soap to replace those they had willfully incinerated. Let them know these were unlimited resources and they could not fight off the tide of mercy.

Rice and stew were served on the Saturday night. Yet for men so hungry, many of them were listless at their food. It was another form of emptiness that assailed the accidental survivors. Some asked themselves why they were entitled to nourishment, and others felt they must act the same way. Even the hungry who had secretly wished for survival ate warily, uneasy to confess to their appetite. The remaining zealots felt they themselves were ghosts and that the dead lain in lines along the wire with a sheet over each of them and being visited one by one by the coroner now lived in the truer sense.

Suttor's fear of being held responsible by his sons' captors had, through its very weight and intensity, become muted by Sunday evening. The pressman had inspired him with confidence, managing to place the emphasis on numbers recaptured than on numbers slaughtered. He had been relieved to receive assurances from a man sent by headquarters that there would be no news release in which his name appeared. That was the sole great comfort of the day, but a light enough to see his path by.

He realized it was now time for him to take the garrison's, and indeed the army's, condolences to Mrs. Abercare. His sense that the slaughter was all Abercare's fault had by now also moderated enough to allow this to happen, though he knew he would have to tell any official inquiry that he had been opposed to the extended notice Colonel Abercare had given, and to other flaws in the preparations.

But he saw now the fault was shared by a number of men, from Sydney to Gawell, and that it had all been dealt with too casually, even by himself. In his earlier arguments with Abercare, he had never imagined the hecatomb that had in fact taken place; the stench of blood and cordite and shit from torn intestines and the dead. The very idea that being the father of a prisoner qualified Suttor to manage Compound C seemed now a fatuous decision by his superiors, a sort of addlebrained attempt at neatness on their part and motivation on his. Though it was true, as the press officer had said, that the overriding philosophy within Compound C had been the true killer, that fact would not be judged as severely as the military errors of the garrison.

So surely, despite what the press officer had said, Abercare would be damned by the military. And he himself might be reproached as an accessory. Just the same, the formalities of the day required he visit Mrs. Abercare and pretend to more admiration of the poor skewered man, the chief of the night's fools, than he had ever felt.

When he arrived at Parkes Street he was met at the door by Mrs. Garner, who ushered him into the living room. Mrs. Abercare, tall and pale, sat on the end of her lounge. She was an active griever, her face bruised with tears. There were other women there—not bloody

Mrs. Galloway, who should have been here (though thank Christ she wasn't). She had been found whimpering behind a chair in Abercare's quarters and driven home at last. She was probably still sleeping off her disreputable night.

Two other women seemed to be out in the Abercare kitchen, murmuring at the business of tea and cake—tannin and sugar as stiflers of grief. Mrs. Abercare rose to meet him, and he found himself adopting the manners of an earnest consoler, taking her hand in his as he spoke about her unimaginable loss. Mrs. Garner got up from her chair and said to another woman, "We should let Emily and the major speak alone for a while."

Suttor wanted to utter a panicked, "No need." But the other woman and Mrs. Garner left.

Emily told him to take a seat. He did, and she took her place on the lounge again.

"I got here as soon as I could," said Suttor. "There has been so much damage to attend to."

"Of course, Major," said Mrs. Abercare in a still, low, compelling voice. "Did you know the body was brought to town by ambulance, and I've already visited him?"

"I . . . I had heard it had been moved from the camp. He didn't suffer, you know. It was a near-instantaneous mortal wound."

"That's a mercy," said Mrs. Abercare, though as a soldier's daughter she was well aware they always said that. There must have been at least seconds of mortal bewilderment, she knew, and she had not been there to soothe him. And after putting him through so many hoops for so long . . .

"He was a fine man and a first-class soldier," Suttor found himself continuing. At this compulsive lie, tears appeared on his lids and he was puzzled at where they came from. But no man deserves to be impaled.

"One thing. You may have heard Mrs. Galloway was in the Colonel's quarters."

"I believe she called Mrs. Garner today and filled her in on her little adventure."

"She had been nothing but a nuisance to him, you know. He was driving to camp, met her broken down on the road, and took her to his quarters to wait so she could return to her vehicle with one of our mechanics. So, she was just waiting for a lift, that's all. As for Colonel Abercare, he was behind our line with a signaler the entire time. He confided in me," Suttor lied, "that he thought the world of you."

"Thank you," she said. That was the information she seemed most grateful for. That was what she seemed to trust most. This utter fabrication.

"I knew he loved me," she said, in a sad and evenly expressed certainty. "This was our happiest time, in Gawell. I thought, of course, like all foolish humans, it would last much longer. But I won't be leaving. I want to be close to him."

"You're taking it so bravely," said Suttor in genuine admiration. She looked at him when he began to tremble.

"You've had a shock," she told him.

33

In the town there was a considerable cluster of police cars outside the police station, and policemen entering and leaving the station, and moving in a hurry between station and courthouse, where no court could be sitting at this hour. This activity was at odds with the town's somnolence. Beyond that the gardens of the town slept under frost, but as the sun mounted and the police moved out to keep watch at the edges of Gawell, the streets seemed habitual again.

At the training camp, the noise of the crisis of the night before had been three miles off and, traveling there through veils of bush that muffled the battle and soaked up many of the cries and terrors, it had barely dented the sleep of young recruits. Sentries reported that fires burned along parts of the eastern horizon. But no flares had been seen.

When a telephone call came from the duty officer up at the prison camp to his counterpart at the training camp, distant noise could be heard over the line. The duty officer at the camp said it was urgent—some of the prisoners had got away—but the officer at the training camp did not awake irritable Colonel Deakin with the news until four in the morning. Colonel Deakin was accustomed, because of the campaigns he had taken part in, to sleeping through distant thunders.

It was obvious, his officer told him, that the outbreak or demonstration was being well contained, since there had been no further call for help. But, he said, prisoners were at large.

The colonel now called the camp and heard from a dazed-sounding Major Suttor that Colonel Abercare had been fatally wounded and was lying under a bloody sheet in the garrison hospital. "As for them, it has been a slaughter," Suttor confessed in a rattled voice. "They wanted it to be a slaughter."

Deakin promised Suttor some aid in finding or repelling the escapees and Suttor sounded like a man in need of such promises. "They have had time to walk five, ten, or more miles," said Suttor. "But they've had to sleep too. They're not supermen." He added, "They should be like stray cattle." At least he hoped so, Deakin could tell.

Suttor suggested sending patrols out to a perimeter to the northwest and then moving them towards the prison, hunting for the strays. "They should be arrested and not killed," said Suttor in a tone of frenzied insistence. "There have been too many killed."

Deakin agreed. But the sanctity of his camp and local farmers were still on his mind—certainly, the farmers would call Sydney and condemn him if they or their stock were in any way harmed by the chase after the prisoners. He had no doubt headquarters welcomed such calls, which in their eyes proved his incompetence.

After the conversation with Suttor concluded, Deakin issued orders that two companies, about one hundred young men in all, should be roused, fed, and sent out on patrol towards the prison camp under the direction of their officers, who were also their educators. If it was true the escaped men were a rabble, the companies sent out would gather them in. If they had designs, however, on the brigade's magazine, then the troops on the perimeter of the camp must battle them.

In Deakin, age, middling rank, an undue sense of persecution by his superiors and the rural population combined to generate a decision that would later amaze authorities. Believing that in broken country and amongst screens of trees and boulders his young men could not be trusted to avoid shooting cattle, farmers—even themselves—in crossfire; or would become so overexcited as to shoot the prisoners all dead instead of acting as police; or else, on the other hand, lose their rifles to those at large, the colonel decided that the men of the company he intended to send out should be issued only with bayonets, while the officers, who had experience of such things, would carry their sidearms. Thus six-sevenths of his troops would guard the camp with rifles against the predators and one-seventh would be sent forth as good as unarmed to round them up before they could threaten the place.

"It comes from the highest quarter that they're to be arrested not slaughtered," a veteran captain told his veteran lieutenants as they waited all morning and into the afternoon for trucks to arrive. "This is diplomacy, we're told, not warfare." The officers stood examining a map of gullies and ridges to the north, amidst them the branching bush roads, then the points where each patrol would be dropped and the bearing each should take. And the distance to be maintained between each man-child as they advanced, searching.

The trucks arrived in the end. It was afternoon.

Aoki found himself amongst an informal group of eight men fleeing, as ordered, for the ridges. The number grew to perhaps sixteen. A few carried bludgeons of baseball bats and dowel sticks, and some must have knives hidden, but he had nothing except his rank, which attracted men to join him.

They found streams in gullies and drank from them. At midmorning he called that they should rest. Yes, they might be overrun as they slept but that meant nothing, did it? They obeyed as if they were still campaigning—they liked to think they were—and Aoki and two others offered to keep watch. After two hours, he was relieved and settled to sleep himself. He dreamed of China and headbands.

Traveling on the roads out of Manchukuo at the start of that campaign, the youths of the regiment had worn silk scarves on which were painted national symbols, charging steeds, chrysanthemums, or tidal waves. By the time they had reached central China, their silk scarves—his, too—were ones they had stolen from Chinese merchants, and were of a particular kind, portraying sexual obscenities, hairy-cunted girls and heedless, multiple pricks. The headbands of Aoki's dream were—if anything—more extreme, and demonstrated that he and his comrades had become the forces of lust as well as the forces of the nation, an idea that did not enthuse him.

One of the lookouts woke him, and on still air came the sound of a truck grinding to a halt at some place within a medium distance. Some of the men were peering around rocks to see what it meant. On a rough track below them an enemy officer jumped from the truck and a number of young men followed. There was a signaler with a radio of some sophistication, a kind Aoki had not seen before and that seemed to come from a new or even future age. Yes, he thought, by the sight of that thing, that back-carried square device, they are probably winning.

A scuffling of grass showed that three of his party were running back over the ridge, fleeing the enemy whose machine guns they had last night faced down, but expecting the young soldiers standing in the road to be handed previously unimaginable weapons. These absconders felt they had tried hard enough for validation's sake, Aoki surmised. You could imagine feeling that way.

But to the bemusement of every one of the remaining escapers, the men in front of them weren't given weapons at all. The officer gave his final instructions, showing them a map of the hilly terrain. At the officer's orders they formed a line, then spaced themselves out and began to advance with nothing but their bayonets in scabbards flapping against their upper thighs. Aoki felt exasperation, a sort of insult.

The enemy officer led off the line. He climbed through some fence rails and, turning, watched his young soldiers, or whatever they were, do the same and then form the desired line that would bring them uphill to Aoki's hidden party. After open ground they embarked on a sparsely forested slope. Under long shadows from the shafts of the eucalyptus trees, one of Aoki's party crawled to him and gave him a baseball bat and saluted.

The young men came on, as if more bewildered by this familiar ground than Aoki felt. When they were thirty or so paces off, Aoki rose with a roar. The other men also revealed themselves, howling amongst the granite rocks that caught the northwest sun and shone a genial gold.

Two of them knelt and opened their tunics to expose their undershirts and the hearts they harbored. The rest had seen what Aoki had, that the young soldiers did not have adequate weapons, and thus they screamed and advanced in threat and fury, calling on the enemy officer to fire at them. The man who was the object of these furious pleadings, Aoki saw, had the face of a veteran, a face leathered by a variety of suns. It showed a strange, blunt knowledge of the kind Aoki shared in, and he was thus, in his way, Aoki's peer. He took out his pistol. He called on his line to draw bayonets and stand. He withdrew his own pistol and fired a shot in the air to halt the demonstration of Aoki and the others. The sky above seemed to be shivered by the noise. Again prisoners fell to their knees, opened their jackets, pointed to their sternums. Aoki remained upright and tried to lock the enemy officer's eyes on his own.

But before that the enemy officer yelled instructions to the pale signaler, who began reporting frantically into his radio.

Aoki screamed in defiance, the others screamed with him. The signaler turned, receiver in hand, wireless on his back, and, appalled by their strange utterance—or so Aoki surmised—began to run downhill. The veteran officer became aware that the youths on his flanks were beginning to waver and abandon him, leaving these howling, crazed figures to some other regiment, turning and vaulting indentations and rocks on their career downhill.

So his next bullet is for me, Aoki believed, and then someone will move in and finish him off in turn. Two old-timers perishing together. His eyes were directly on the officer's, and the officer saw that. He aimed his revolver at Aoki's chest. Aoki was amazed when the revolver misfired once and then a second time. He watched as a young man still remaining on the hill near the officer approached the man and with eyes aghast and purpose trembling on the edge of self-sacrifice, suspended on that filament between valor and selfishness as armies defined both, seemed to be consulting him on whether his faithfulness was required. Then grief and sudden regret won over the boy's eyes and he, too, fled.

The officer seemed unsurprised and inspected his pistol as if to discover its problem. Aoki limped forward towards him, no longer screaming war cries, though the others continued as they closed in. Everyone knew what was necessary—Aoki and the man with the failed sidearm in his hands, one in which a round had jammed. The man raised the revolver and hurled it far downhill, beyond finding—or so at least he clearly hoped. He was naked to assault now. He was about to turn and retreat but seemed indecisive, as if he, like Aoki, had had enough of the world.

Aoki drew back the baseball bat earlier given him and struck the man with a force that surprised even him—the gravity of it and the dense impact on the flesh and bone of the man's head was so unfamiliar, as if he had never delivered wounds before. He knew what it was like for the poor fellow as he toppled—the real, diminished, all-at-once-beloved world plummeting away from him, and on its surface the young men running like antelopes, hurdling shrubs, unencumbered by heavier arms.

Aoki, his leg aching, stood back to let one of the younger men slit the officer's throat. Others came in and dug knives into the man, and one fellow bludgeoned him again. When the officer had received enough damage to have died over and over again, Aoki's party of men looked at each other as if to say, this is too small a triumph. Except it did give them a reason to expect a desired vengeance against them. The man had bled amidst the stalks of rough grass. Little had been achieved except that Aoki had at least proved himself to the enemy as a killer, and thus surely should be granted an inescapable death as a matter of course. But the coming freezing, alien, and unprovided-for night seemed a tedious veil he must pass through first, and an unexpected one since he and his companions had not foreseen it, and had not imagined that adolescents would be set against them with mere bayonets.

Aoki sent them looking for the thrown revolver. This was the second time within a day he had seen a valiant man throw away a mechanism. He himself stepped around the scarlet mash of the man's head and found some loose cartridges in his pocket. If retrieved, the revolver could serve, with these few bullets, equally for taking further life or for self-destruction.

Now he limped downhill himself, joining the search. The crass landscape had turned subtle in the dying light, full of rock niches and crevices, rank grass and concealed animal holes, and the sort of shrubs that deeply hid objects.

When full dark came on and the moon had not risen, he called the searchers together again. Where were the followers, some of the men asked, the better-armed patrol? Did these people not speak to each other? Weren't they connected by reports?

Aoki's party set out to stumble across country, leaving the valorous corpse behind them.

In Carcoar, where Alice had found refuge, Ronnie Sutcliffe was back that Sunday night, coal dust embedded in his overalls. He hauled the dented metal tucker box he carried by a huge strap around his shoulder onto a kitchen bench. He was full of news.

"They reckon there's been an outbreak over in Gawell," he told them. "The Japanese. Not the dagos. They know when they're on a good thing."

A strange pulse, not without its side-pleasures, went through Alice. A call to the colors. To duty. "I'll have to go back in the morning," she said.

"What?" asked Ronnie, grinning. "To protect Duncan Herman and his POW? They're big enough to look after themselves. Though the radio says they've accounted for most of them."

Ronnie escorted Alice to the cold phone box near the post office, which seemed to be set at the deepest point of the valley, under a rising moon that cast sharply delineated shadows. Before this expedition, Ronnie had called on an ageless bachelor gatekeeper who lived within shouting distance of the cottage to bring his shotgun and sit with Esther. Even though Gawell was so far away, the Japanese could move like the devil. Remember Malaya?

"Haven't seen a thing, Alice," said Duncan when Alice got through to him.

"No, you haven't seen a damned thing," she was madly tempted to tell him.

"Don't you worry. They reckon they've got most of them back anyhow. I hear our blokes got the machine guns going at them. Hammond came round and told me some of our fellows are dead just the same. The colonel, he reckons. People say he's not a big loss."

She wanted to ask, Is Giancarlo all right? What does he think of it?

Duncan unwittingly supplied as good an answer as he could. "Johnny and I—we're just going about our business. I've got the .22 in the truck and the .303 in the kitchen."

Where, apparently, it would by its very presence deter Japanese.

"You're better off in Carcoar, just in case any strays turn up round here. Johnny says he knew some of them. He's not very scared of them."

But, Alice told him, she was determined to come back first thing. He told her to be careful on the train. But he reckoned there'd be soldiers aboard, just in case.

The phone went dead, and she had no more pennies to buy time. Ronnie took her back to the house under the honed, cold stars. He said, "Friends of mine want to drive over there with rifles in the morning and sort them out, the ones at large. But if they're so keen, let 'em join the army. I'm not going to leave Esther."

Alice said, "That colonel . . ."

"Brutes!" said Esther, with a shudder.

Alice could hear that Ronnie did not sleep that night, but moved about the house. When she crept out of her bedroom to the toilet, she glimpsed him resting in an armchair with a small-bore rifle.

Nothing happened, and there were clear reasons for that, of course. Gawell. Why would the Japanese want to walk so far when there were so many farmhouses around Gawell to tempt them into plunder and mayhem? And there were houses, too, in Gawell, full of women and children. Alice hoped troops were out to screen the town. She hoped that the streets were guarded. She tested herself to see if these phenomena gave her grounds to hate Giancarlo, a former ally of these unspeakables. Was there in him some obscure responsibility for all this?

Giancarlo wasn't very scared of the escaped men, Duncan had said. In the dark she clung to her strange anger about this. She was alarmed at how her even-tempered self had been borne away so easily. As she failed to sleep in her cold room, under Ronnie's protection, joy at her coming return to Gawell, and desperation and anger and fascination all swept through her, like a succession of low, intimate clouds. Giancarlo could afford not to be very scared. He had even tried to learn their language, sharing barracks with them in the early days of Gawell prison camp.

She let the rage at his unconcern, his alliance with them, keep rolling on above her so that it might submerge desire. He made no pretense these days about his lack of skill in English. He had read her mother-in-law's novels and borrowed Duncan's papers and any magazines that came her way, and circled phrases of which he had dubious knowledge with indelible pencil. Cunning bugger he'd been, cunning bugger he was. As if preparing for something she wasn't privy to, some deep connivance with what had happened.

Yet her rage at last shattered. His studiousness seemed by a calmer light to be praiseworthy. So the memory of his bent head, the dark hair, the sculpted mouth, the boyish down on his cheeks set her off aching again, and pain and anticipation kept her awake until dawn, and she was delighted that in a few hours' time she would be on her way back again, fleeing the failed antidote of Esther and Ronnie.

The party of escaped prisoners that had met the line of boys with bayonets and called for the officers' blood fragmented overnight, as men made their excuses, said good-byes, and dropped, exhausted, to sleep on the comfortless ground. Aoki limped on, to show it could be done, until late—the enemy would have to travel a distance to find him, and the idea of being a nuisance comforted him. Three younger men accompanied him, and he told them not to be so polite as to lag to keep pace with him but to make their own speed. They stood by him, though. They took a few hours of freezing sleep in a core of cold amongst granite boulders, and then progressed, according to orders, along a ridge, this one running southwesterly. The idea of ridges, though—that if they were spotted by an army patrol, they would put the enemy to the trouble of climbing a hill and scuffing boot leather, and that this itself was a sort of victory—seemed a little fatuous now.

As morning came on and the comfort of the sun shone on their right shoulders, seeing a patrol would, in this light, be welcome, and Aoki would descend with the murder of the officer on his shoulders to welcome the retribution they must surely by now have learned uniformly to take. And if not immediately so, he had three young men who could testify to his killing of the officer the day before.

Morning advanced and he was grateful almost to tears to the young men who'd stuck with him. But then . . . where did these three men who had attached themselves need to go? They were weaker than they would admit. Their mood was contradictory, a little like Aoki's. They could not help envisaging a future. It was simply human to do that. It was something the brain did. And they stuck to him for comfort too.

They stopped again in an embayment of stones and slept for some hours, now that it was warm, and slowly woke. They knew there was water over the ridge but one of them dared to talk about hunger, and duckling and pancakes, almost in a philosophical tone, as if he were interested in them as very essences. Just the same, the chief complainant about food had been a barber until two years ago. What further could be expected of him?

Aoki himself ached to resolve this tension between escape and the pain of his progress in this alien and indifferent country, country so hard on his damaged leg and so unrelenting in its emptiness that it almost revived the concept of a future, and thus sparked hazy images of his wife—particular endearments, or instances of coupling.

It was afternoon by now. They pursued the hill's spine in this country of eroded, stone-scattered spines. Aoki was afflicted with a temptation to absolve the others of all duty. The further they went, the more wanly young they looked. They were not urgently hunted, that was it. The enemy had failed its duty of pursuit and fury. Couldn't Aoki say, "Take the risk. Give it up. We've missed the chance and the air's out of the balloon. Will they really shoot you? Young men with such wanly fresh faces, such increasingly bewildered eyes? If they do—a good farewell and an escape from this unreadable terrain. If not, go back to the pancakes. Go back, at least, to the mutton and rice." He wondered again about the sort of army the enemy possessed. It did not send urgently and by thousands after its escapees, but dispatched young ditherers and shitheads, who stumbled off to peep behind trees. The hills and pastures were not ruthlessly scoured by any force he had seen. Yesterday's encounter had been a jaunt, a children's outing. The young men might go. But he would stay out here, surely worth their while chasing, with the blood of the machine gunner and of the fellow with the seized pistol on his uniform.

There were definite reasons he should pursue his lonely search. He wanted to die for women's sake, though not in any romantic sense. He did not think of women as these young men, unrelieved of their juices, so often did. He had not overcome the normal problem of veterans in summoning the face and outline of his wife, whose pictures he'd lost. But Chinese women taken as revenge, and seen at times of berserk drunkenness and conquest, often recurred cruelly and with acid clarity. China had confused the focus of clear desire, had muddied love by offering supposed rewards—those of sexual rapine. In copulating for the Empire and the Greater East Asia Co-prosperity Sphere, in driving home the lesson between the thighs of a dazed or screaming Chinese woman, he had become unfit for the higher fulfillment, the devotions of a monogamous bed. He had forgotten love's husbandry.

The party waited where they were. They were very tired. They watched a search plane drone above hills on the other side of the valley. It did not seem energetic. "They have contempt for us," one of the young men decided. "They're mocking us by not trying to find us."

And, Aoki could have said, there is the contempt this landscape, so empty of meaning, exudes. He had nearly given up movement, but at his suggestion they did move on through the huge stones and the tall trees until they saw a farmhouse below them.

Did it offer opportunities? And for what?

"Should we go down, Senior Sergeant?" one asked.

"Staying up here means nothing," said another with a sullenness alien to military discipline.

"We'll go down to the fields, yes," said Aoki, losing faith now in his own orders about ridges. "As you say, Private, nothing to be lost going down there. Our prospects might lie down there."

He guessed that serious hunts must be occurring elsewhere. There was activity in the air of that inert day, the occasional and distant sight of a plane. But its reverberations gave him no consolation. It was hard to maintain a martial soul when the enemy refused to present himself.

34

After sleeping late on that Sunday morning, Beefy Cullen, perversely nicknamed for his extreme thinness, approached his clever son, Martin, who was doing trigonometry at the kitchen table. Mrs. Cullen was away, sitting with Mrs. Abercare in town and waiting for the coroner to release the colonel's body. Martin and his mother had been to Mass earlier that morning, transported in Mr. Doyle's car—the grazier whose property the Cullens lived on. Mr. Doyle had explained that he was carrying his shotgun in the trunk. He probably should have carried it inside the car, but he didn't want any accidents with it on the bumpy road and he doubted any escaped prisoner could outrun his Buick anyhow. Mrs. Doyle asked him with gentle whimsy if he was going to run over them, or run away from them.

"The first, if possible," said Mr. Doyle, clean-shaven and with the gloss of sanctifying grace on his cheeks.

Two Knights of the Southern Cross, however—Catholic worthies of the town—patrolled the church ground with rifles that morning to ensure the congregation was not interfered with. Mrs. Abercare arrived with Mrs. Garner, who had become a temporary churchgoer to support the widow. Dr. Delaney preached on the tragedy—the incomprehensibility of it, God's mercy in sparing the town, and his feelings for the bereaved. He had somehow sensed by former meetings that Mrs. Abercare would not welcome a specific mention and the resultant turning of eyes to her.

Now, Mass all done with, Martin was home working on his diagrams, which were as eternal as, or even more so, than the mysteries of faith. His father interrupted him by slowly expressing a decision to shave. Then, he said, they were going rabbiting.

"Are you up to a bit of common man's fun like that?" he challenged his son, jealous of the boy's cleverness and coming, unimaginable chances.

His son had indeed hoped to occupy the rest of the day with his scholastic ambitions—a long Honors English essay on Julius Caesar as its climax. The exegesis of Shakespeare's texts came naturally to him. It seemed to him that he had stumbled on them the way Keats had stumbled on Chapman's Homer, and he had evidence that he was a once-in-a-decade delight to his English teacher, and cherished that role.

"Isn't dusk the best time to go rabbiting?" he asked his father.

"Well, you never know what you'll find if you go about now. Run us up some of the mutton sandwiches, will you? Don't spare the pickles. And you can take the rifle."

Martin got up resignedly and started working on mutton pickle sandwiches. He knew his father liked pickles and so did not skimp on them. He had always been an accommodating and obedient child, but he knew that if the sandwiches weren't up to scratch, it would be taken by his father as a sign of Martin's fatal bookishness, unworldliness, and awkwardness. Yet Martin was reaching an age when he'd begun to see as much of the pain as the malice behind his father's commands. In his soured ambitions, his father sometimes declared to Martin's mother that he was a failure in life and might as well shoot himself. This called up a pity, a tremble of love, in Martin, who wanted to enter the corrugated iron kitchen and enclose his father in his arms the way a three-year-old might dare to. Except that none of them could imagine such a gesture, and it might well make things worse.

Beefy's cry always brought a pathetic response from his wife, who cherished him to the point where, for a second, Martin could feel jealousy as well as that awful, thwarted tenderness. At that point he was tempted to ask his mother, "Aren't I the clever one? Haven't I satisfied all you want?" He did not dare think of Beefy, the lover—of anything other than his mother's endurance, and her belief in the Church's version of marriage—as an explanation for what held her there, on Doyle's place in a rouseabout's cottage.

As his father finished shaving, Martin found ammunition in a drawer and fetched the rifle from the shed. It was a light, well-tooled, slim device. He kept it oiled because not to have done so would have produced the normal reaction. That's what he hated about the excursion. It had unsure motives in most regards, but the chance of parental mockery was certainly one of them. Did his father have a fantasy about running into some of the Japs from the camp? The idea had no attraction to Martin, but he knew Beefy had been starved of moments of glory.

They walked in silence towards the hill behind Doyle's, until his father called to him in a whimsical voice, "You've got the rifle loaded?"

Martin said yes.

"Well, if you see any really big rabbits, let me know." Thus it was confirmed to Martin what this expedition was for. They were hunting prisoners. He could not think of anything more vain or alarming. His father had heard from someone that morning, possibly from one of his army mates who'd come through in a truck and who might have stopped at the gate and honked, that the escapees had no firearms. They were out in the bush without means of retaliation except for their well-established, legendary, hypnotic, and illimitable cunning.

"We're not going to shoot them, are we?" asked Martin.

"Depends on what they do," said his father.

"I'm not going to shoot them. I'm going home."

"Oh yes. Be a bloody pansy as usual."

Thus Martin was stuck with him, as if the insult had its own magnetic field. Father and son crossed over the ridge and into their neighbors the Macintoshes' place, and sat on a log and ate sandwiches and drank the tea Martin had brought in a thermos. Martin ate his sandwich quickly, as if getting it down would speed up this silly expedition.

"You're hungry there, tiger," said his father.

"Why do you want to look for the Japs?" the boy asked.

A glint, the desire of warrior conspiracy, entered his father's eye. His smile was narrow lipped. "It'd be good for both of us to get a bit of a reputation around this place. Everyone thinks I'm a boofhead and the rest think you're a ponce. Wouldn't you like to show them a thing or two? Take a few of the buggers in? That'd make people sit up a bit."

Mr. Cullen assessed the trees at the end of Macintosh's paddock, where men might be concealed. He sifted the trees with his squinting, alert vision. Meanwhile, Martin felt sick. He didn't give a toss whether Gawell people thought he was a ponce; he did not intend to live amongst them long enough to incur their habitual contempt. He did not believe anyhow his father's story of achieving new value.

They finished lunch and rose and went through another wire fence, at least using the normal safety arrangements—one of them holding both guns as the other parted the barbed wire and slid through.

They crossed a badly eroded gully, a groin of dust, a wound in the earth of the kind the Department of Agriculture blamed on both the farmer and the drought—which had by coincidence ended in the summer the Japanese expressed their ambitions against the British and the Americans in unarguable ways. The Cullen men could not get round this gully and had to cross it, getting dust into their boots. Climbing out, Martin saw over the rim a burgundy-colored figure running uphill through the trees ahead. For some reason he was utterly unsurprised. Was this, he wondered, a sacrificial decoy from those hiding in the woods? His father spotted the figure too.

"Hey, look at that!" he cried out loudly, a man who was not frightened of his quarry.

The figure disappeared amongst the great rocks and tall eucalypts. Martin was riveted by the sight. It was like a permanent burn on his vision. The world was transformed now that he had seen the enemy of his people, the enemy of Keats and Shakespeare. That fleeting creature was his new objective and, to his own astonishment, he was ready to chase. He ran lithely ahead and found himself, still with reserves of oxygen, up high on the uneven ground, looking around and then downwards at his father, who seemed to be losing breath as he climbed, and losing certainty as well. A little regretfully, he waited for his father to catch up.

"We ought to be a bit more careful now," Beefy panted. "I ought to send you back for help."

"No," said Martin, "I'm not going back."

His father had seen it, too, that Martin was no longer led but had an equal part in the ambush. The flash of burgundy had altered the balance between them—Martin was in fact the leader; his father the offsider who must be persuaded along, his ambitions diminished. That figure, the Japanese one who had captivated Martin, had brought to Beefy Cullen the awareness that he was not a true hunter.

"We've spotted them," said Beefy. "Now let's go down to Macintosh's place and call the army."

"If we go that way," Martin said, ignoring him and pointing out a screen of trees and rocks on the crest to their right, "we can come on them from the side."

"You reckon?" his father asked. Mr. Cullen sounded fretful. They heard a yelp from above, designed to direct them.

"Maybe they are armed," Beefy Cullen said.

"They aren't moving anymore," said Martin, ignoring him.

"They're waiting. I think if we duck around those boulders we'll have them."

He heard his father gasping and wished Beefy wanted to have

them as much as he did. Part of his brain asked why he hankered to find those helpless creatures up there, but chiefly his mind asserted they were not helpless. Would Julius Caesar be soft on them? Would Hamlet, who had finished off Polonius and Rosencrantz and Guildenstern with such a light mind? The men up in those trees had the entire weight of a vicious empire behind them, and Caesar would have been merciless for his own sake and his people's. Gawell High School's English and Latin curriculum left him in no doubt.

Screened by long grass, Martin and his father came round the huge rocks, left—according to the geography teacher—by glaciers, and reached the spine of the ridge where trees and the huge boulders still shielded their quarry. A sudden wind began to blow and combed the grass through which they crept, Martin looking back to his father occasionally.

"What do you reckon now?" Beefy whispered, wanting guidance. Martin was no longer the ponce and the smartarse. There was only their common breath and the scene they were about to invade.

"One of us ought to go around the base there," Martin told him, nodding to a huge boulder. "So I'll go round it to the right, and you climb up it and get on top."

Beefy asked, "Do you want the shotgun? You'll be on the level with them."

Martin raised his .22 rifle. "You can shoot anything up to sixty yards with this."

He gave his father a hoist up to a crevice in the rock. As his father ascended, panting, Martin edged around the granite, almost stringing out the crazy, frightful joy of the seconds before confrontation. He had one round in the spout of his .22, but he knew it was a dominating shot.

He came on two neat groups of three, each set squatting in natural groins of rock. They had been talking quietly, but with an urgency of a peculiar kind, as if they'd been waiting to be found.

"I'm here," he yelled for his father's sake.

The alien men looked up. They seemed even to him to be stupefied. Escape had not left much in them. They were ready to be dominated by his small-bore rabbit-killing gun.

"Look up!" he told them, gesturing, and they clearly saw above him Beefy atop the rock, with his shotgun pointed. Martin was gratified to see that his father resembled a figure of some power.

"Get back a bit, son," Beefy nonetheless advised. "Don't get too close to them."

Martin took a delight in asking, "So what now, gentlemen?" For he had become a figure from a noble play or a Saturday film, and he loved it—the chance for oration.

"And what of all the men you shot in Malaya and the Indies?" he asked. "What did you think when their blood incarnadined the oceans of Asia? Tell me!"

His rifle designed for banal bush purposes now empowered him in front of the six men, who all stood up. They had been surprised but were not cowed. One called to the others in a hacking, commanding voice. Another of them made a motion with his hands, like a man explaining a dance move.

"Watch out, Martin," called Beefy.

The escapee who had first spoken stepped forward now, ripping the front of his tunic and his shirt and trying to tear open the woollen singlet beneath. From the top of the granite, Beefy continued to yell warnings. The Japanese advanced on Martin, screaming at him in gutturals. The huge ear-ringing blast of his father's shotgun split the argument apart, but no pellet seemed to enter this man striding towards Martin with such a fixity. In the stunned air the man was still mouthing and growling. Mr. Cullen's shot had torn apart the upper body of one of the others beyond the men advancing on Martin. After doing such damage Beefy would need to reload. Four ran forwards as if replacing their riddled comrade in a line of battle.

The fellow unhit by Beefy, his shirt open, his demands gusting in hot breath, carried on advancing towards Martin and, though wearing a grotesque face as if he were theatrical, could not redeem himself in the language of Shakespeare. His threats were outrageously remote from Martin's powers of interpretation. When he was seven paces away, Martin shot him in the throat. Martin judged that to use his poor weaponry on the man's trunk would not serve the purpose. He was awed to see the Polonius-like volumes of blood surging from the wound and over the man's lips. It was shocking to see, but he did not repent of the act.

Above him, his father and comrade had reloaded. He, too, was ready to stand, to defend Macintosh's stony hill against the enemies of Wordsworth and Coleridge.

Two of the four men still left alive opened their jackets with more pleas to be shot, yet after a time sank on their knees to the ground as if expecting nothing. The other two began to engross themselves in disposing the limbs of the man killed by Beefy. Martin's enemy had sunk back into the stones of the ridge. He was gone. As for the others, father and son owned them now and need not threaten them further.

"Better go down now to Macintosh's," called Beefy, "and get them to call the military people."

Martin, however, was determined not to let the power revert to his father.

"No," he said, "I've got them under control."

"But I've got the shotgun. Give me the rifle, too, and hop along, son."

His father, for whom Martin now pulsed with love, had indeed issued thunder to the enemy of his people, and, Martin saw, wasn't afraid at all now it had happened. He could see no vainglory in Beefy. The four Japanese were all tearing at their jackets again and crying on the Cullen men to fire. A sudden revelation for Martin was that these fellows were not enemies in the Elizabethan play. They were enemies of themselves. At that revelation, the fever began to die in him.

"Kill," pleaded the men, the ones with faces that had come from a different poetry.

"Shut up!" Beefy yelled at the escapees. "We're not fucking bar-barians, you know!"

Martin had begun to shiver for some reason. He reached the rifle up to his father so that on top of the granite Beefy Cullen possessed an arsenal. The prisoners still pleaded.

"Go to buggery!" Beefy called at them. "Get on with it, Martin." Martin looked a second at the corpse of that guttural and demanding fellow whom he'd finished and shawled in blood, and who now lay as if he had been placed there by a third party as a surprise and a parable. He lost all his vanity in an instant. He felt the map of the world he carried in his head could not be read anymore. His own self, so dominant in the version he'd possessed until now, had vanished amongst the parallels. How could he invent the remainder of his hours and years?

"Go on, Martin," called Beefy in paternal pride and determination. "Cut along now."

Martin consoled himself that he would never again be mocked for knowing cos and sine and the Hittite Empire or Tennyson's "In Memoriam." He ran downhill, bounding and adhering by skill to that line between sprinting and falling. He ran for the sake of his father's safety and to honor the savagery they had been forced to in an attempt to protect the holiness of the iambic pentameter.

As he reached the farmhouse and told Macintosh what had happened, he began weeping from this sense of being lost in his own geography. Macintosh held him by the shoulders and assured him it was all right. He sat him down with sturdy Mrs. Macintosh in the kitchen, where that good lady had a firearm of her own in the corner, and the woman comforted him, not knowing that he had paid himself over to save their rimes from the yellow horde. Macintosh himself rang the police and then set off on horseback with his own high-powered rifle, and, by some counsel of mercy, a canister of water for the prisoners. As soon as he saw Beefy dominant on top of that boulder, he cried, "Why in the bloody hell did you take your boy out today, Beefy? Of all days? You're a total bloody idiot!"

Soon after, Macintosh and Beefy, who was chastened but refused to appear so, saw army trucks mill at the main farm gate, and the troops left the bodies behind for collection and drove the four recaptured prisoners down the slope in front of them. Beefy was anxious to see Martin, and wondered if the army might think more of him than Macintosh did.

This was not Aoki's group. Aoki and his polite companions were on another ridgeline to the north. And so, though separated by some miles, was a party led by Goda. But Goda and his squad of harder-line young men had heard the shots and moved with a new enthusiasm in their direction.

35

On another spur of the low ranges outside Gawell, Aoki and his party were descending into the pastures. The grass was rough and tussocky and they were surrounded by cattle who seemed indifferent to them. "Here's meat," said one of the avowedly younger men.

Another asked derisively, "And so you want us to slaughter and bleed it, make a fire, and cook fillets? It'll be morning by then."

They came to a reservoir dug into the earth with a bank of soil on the far side to protect the water from the prevailing wind. From it an electric pump drew water into a concrete tank with a tap. They drank from the tap and then sat by it to hold council. They saw beyond reddish, gnarled trees a light come on in the farmhouse that was then muffled by a briskly drawn curtain. "The house," said one of the younger men with yearning. The light was a huge, mothering temptation.

"Will we go there, Senior Sergeant?" one of the young privates pathetically asked Aoki.

"We should have a look to begin with," Aoki decided.

Advancing towards it, they saw chickens pecking, and somewhere dogs began barking. These homely signs seemed absolutely to seduce the thirsty and hungry. The three younger men turned their tormented eyes on Aoki. He felt a surge of brotherly affection for them. They had charged machine guns. They would have charged one now if it had only presented itself. But for the dispiriting lack of one, they wanted to go in there. They wanted to be given their food, even if it were bread. And—when it came to it—why not? It was up to them.

"You all go," he said. "And don't hurt the farmer or his wife. We've got no lesson to teach them. They're unteachable."

He saw relief and doubt on the three young faces. But they lingered. They could not understand why he could not commute his own case.

"You've all done your best," he told them. "Go, that's my order." His leg howled and vibrated with pain.

One said, "With your permission, Senior Sergeant . . ."

Aoki said, "No, you're not excluded from the order. You go too."

Allowed to relax their determination, their spirits eased and rose; it was almost like looking at birds freed. Aoki found that he was somewhere beyond warmth or refreshment. He had worked far enough through his history of appetites to be beyond them now. But the men still looked at him. They knew he intended to end it by his own hand. They knew it was unsoldierly to leave him too quickly. One by one they came up, the hungry one first, and extended their hands solemnly. The last said, as if he intended simply to have a sandwich and then seek death, "I shall see you amongst the heroes, Senior Sergeant."

The three privates saluted and walked off, continuing with a decent show of reluctance. Left alone, Aoki flopped to the earth to thrust out his tormented limb. He felt the throbbing and the agonizing numbness release itself a little. Then he hauled himself up. With them gone, he could limp more frankly. He retreated amongst the cattle and back into the hill of rocks towards the crooked-limbed trees. He stopped a little way up the slope and could see the three young men nearing the house and its radiance. Somewhere in there the inscrutable wife would at least be an identifiable being, the eternal provider of meals.

He watched from a height. When the trucks appeared, soldiers surrounded the farmhouse and advanced on it, but a young woman came out on its veranda waving handkerchiefs to them, and quickly behind her the three young soldiers came out, hands raised. This was it, the test by which they would live or die. The young men dropped on their knees by the farmhouse gate, inviting execution, but were raised up by the armpits and dragged to the vehicles. Would they be shot out of sight of the woman? He suspected they would not be; as the trucks drove off and made their way up the dirt road beyond the farm, he listened. Nothing was heard except the last mournful predictions of the birds at dusk and the steady grind of the trucks. Whether it was strange politics or strange mercy that seemed to be delivering the young men, whole and breathing, back to Compound C, he could no longer take an interest in.

Like others, Aoki had created a special belt, sewing together two lengths of leather, sufficient to provide a noose and appropriate hanging material. He took the belt off his waist now, let his trousers drop, took off his jacket and boots, and stood there in his shirt and woollen underwear. At some cost in pain he began to climb a tree, using near-forgotten rules of ascent for snipers. He reached a branch that was far above his height. He made a noose of the buckle end and tied the other end of the belt to the branch. He put the noose around his neck and placed the buckle in the recommended position by his right ear. There was no delaying. He threw himself off the branch. He descended through the air and felt a vast, hopeful jolt, which then insidiously released its force on him. He landed on his arse. He looked up at the broken noose, stitching rotted by sweat, the buckle broken asunder from the rest, the split ends dangling.

Had there been a noise as he fell? There had certainly been. A horse stood above him with a farmer on it, a man his age, holding a rifle.

The farmer spoke like a crow, in purest mockery. "Give it up, sport!" he said.

Unlike Aoki's party, whose followers after all had been fairly anonymous and unremarkable soldiers, Goda's group seemed to consist of a pack of young ultras. Goda himself was sick of the question—to live or to die? At this stage, he was willing to die to escape the debate. Their deep-dyed uniforms were designed to make them stand out in this country innocent of the color maroon. Yet by Sunday afternoon they had still not been tracked down.

Goda's traveling party included the zealous boy-soldier Isao; the excellent tenor from Aoki's hut named Domen; the marine and hut leader Hirano; and Omura, the bomber wireless operator. Despite their rigor of soul, these men were also in a state of moral bewilderment. Like Aoki's group they were famished, and had begun to doubt the proposition about keeping to ridges. Their morale revived when they heard the shots and went looking for their source but, arriving, they found nothing except some blood-soaked stones. To varying degrees they were exhilarated—whoever's the blood was—at this sign of resolution, but disappointed in equal measure that they had not been here at the essential moment.

From here they saw a wheat field, the characteristic mark of all farms except the largest in this region. They could also see sheep, and Domen suggested the possibility of a final feast. It would be marked by a fire the enemy could surely see and approach, perhaps even before the food was cooked. If they were permitted to dine before dying, then so much the better.

It had been hard to cross the three wire fences carrying weapons, though some had succeeded. Domen, who still carried a knife, approached the sheep and caused them to run, but he was a farmer's son and knew how to catch animals. He had a lamb all at once sitting up, seemingly quite tranquil, between his knees. He cut the throat smoothly with one swipe, then raised the animal by its back legs as its blood went flowing onto the grass.

In the meantime, Goda and the others found their way through a nearby wire fence, an exercise evoking memory of other wire. With impunity, they collected the ears of wheat nearly ready for harvest and filled their pockets with them. The exercise cheered them, Goda noticed. It cheered him too. Gathering the grain gave them a taste of purpose on this aimless Sunday.

When they considered they had enough grain, they climbed through the wire again and joined Domen, who still held the carcass upwards by its hind legs. Then they crossed the sheep pasture and dealt with further wire and so began to ascend their ridge, where their cooking fire should surely serve as a beacon for their enemies.

They placed the grain on a long stone, and Hirano and Omura pounded it with alternate blows of rocks, and threatened each other with vengeance if either hit his companion's thumb. Goda descended from his high status and gathered wood, which was not hard with these abnormal trees that shed branches and bark summer and winter and, like everything else here, without reason. He piled the tinder branches and interspersed them with sheets and twists of bark and began the fire. "If it brings a search party in," he dared to say to his set of diehards, "I hope it's not before the lamb's cooked."

The wood burned fast and settled to the earth, radiating a robust heat that stung his eyes with its pungent smoke even as the cold of the day bit at his back. They should perhaps keep this blaze going later, after dark, when fire glow could be seen an even further distance than by day. They put the ground-up grain on a flat stone on top of the coals and waited for it to roast. Then, with one sheet of bark, they scraped the cracked wheat off its rudimentary dish of rock onto another platterlike sheet. They sat around this, reaching in and eating the wheat one ear at a time, while their nostrils flared at the acute savor of the lamb haunch Domen was roasting and turning now and then on the glowing bed of eucalyptus tree coals. There was no time, sadly, Domen apologized, to dig a pit and set up a spit, but the lamb would be good even with ash on it.

Lamb was a questionable dish—to prepare it like this was barbarous—but Goda and the others were willing to excuse the indelicacy of this last meal. They would be welcomed by the spirits of men who had—in their last campaigns—eaten snakes and insects and even human flesh for want of a supply line.

When the haunch was ready, Domen, yelping at the heat of the joint, hauled it onto a wide basin of stone. They all behaved with less elegance now, and tried to tear the meat too early, and laughed, and shook the burn out of their fingers. Domen began to cut the meat in long strips from the bone, and to give one to each of his comrades, but they still found it hot, moving it from hand to hand—as if in a day's time having a blister would matter one way or another.

Goda asked Domen to keep the fire up as they gorged themselves. The meal passed, the ultras were surfeited, and no soldiers arrived. They drank from a canteen one of them had somehow decided to bring. Torpor set in. Goda watched a sated Isao stretch himself by the fire. Soon he was asleep.

"Good way to spend the afternoon, Sergeant," Domen suggested, nodding at Isao, after Goda and the others had thanked him for the banquet.

Goda watched the fine-featured Isao, the mask of his strict young soul, as his breathing became that of tranquil sleep. It was peculiar, but also somehow rational, to rest before death. Goda asked Hirano and Omura to heap more wood on the fire, for the sun was beginning its descent.

Goda awoke in late afternoon. He was cold and needed to shit. Like all of them, he was surprised and even alarmed by how Gawell Camp life had softened him. Shivering, he went behind one of the trees. He suddenly knew this was one of those fitful hours when the Chinese came to haunt him. Without knowing it, he was like Aoki in accepting that his self-destruction must atone for them as well. By day he deserved his death for failing ancestors and his emperor. But in odd hours the Chinese intervened between him and the cleanliness of all that. No one expressed repentance for China. It was left unsaid, and—in terms of conquest—rightly so. For it could be argued, when seen with the eye of a god, that these punishments were required as a tribute paid to history.

When he was finished, he wiped himself clean with forest debris. He rubbed his hand on the rough bark of the tree and got out his rag and went to the canteen, emptying some water on the cloth. Then he took the eucalyptus leaves and split them open to rub their pungency on his fingers. From their strong vapor, tears stung his lids but very correctly refused to fall. He was a little cheered to think that hygiene did not matter as much as the actual indignity of shitty hands. He was certain he did not have enough time left to develop gastroenteritis.

In China they had rounded up hiding soldiers, including ones who had changed into street clothes and pleaded they had never served, and they'd tied them together in batches of fifty and shot into the tethered mass of curs—bad soldiers from a crumbling army. This was not an act for which Goda accepted any guilt. He would have expected the same if he'd been them.

But things he had done with liquor in him were distorted in his memory and shivered apart like a painting on a vase, a very large one that is dropped and shatters, so that only a fragment of the tale reproduced on the glaze can be seen. Officers, severe in battle, had quite rightly given their soldiers free play in captured cities, as a motive for men to capture more cities still, and to allow them to prove their ruthlessness to the enemy.

But had he really selected a quaking Chinese porter, a stunted, ageless little man, and loaded him up with scrolls and silk robes and a chest of drawers and mats, and then had him carry them all to the regimental trucks—where they would never have fitted anyhow? And when this stunted man had successfully delivered the load, had he really, in the madness of plum brandy and eminent power, plunged his bayonet up under the little man's ribs and lifted him off his feet with it, exulting in the applause of fellow soldiers and in the cascade of the Chinese heart's blood flowing down over him? Had he actually and in the fullness of fact been the first to find a woman in a shop and drag her away from the door into the light to see that she was handsome, and then covered her mouth and flooded her with the force of their military triumph? And when other men arrived—figures in his crazed dreams, shards from his shattered urn—had one soldier, perhaps the eighth, distracted by the screaming of her baby indoors, gone and dealt with it at the cost of a last animal child scream at which none of them was shocked? Kill the enemy in the womb, and if that is not possible, then kill it in its cradle. It was her face, flat but well made, that remained through all the shattering fumes of the plundered liquor. Features seen in the heat of inebriation he remembered better than he did the features of those to whom he was connected by blood and affection. It was this woman and her infant's ghost who waited also in the shadow world. She, too, must be appeased.

Now, leaning against a tree trunk, he surrendered his crimes up to the gods, under whose aegis he had not extended pity. For this was the war of the world, and he had been a force in it, an arm of the warrior god, in whose name he had been blessed before taking to the transports sailing from Rabaul. His crimes were his crimes but were also the harsh-edged whispers and the declarations of the gods. On these grounds he suppressed his occasional pulses of torment.

Above them, a search plane with the enemy's rondelles on its wings appeared. What did it think of the smoke of their fire? They were fully woken by its engine and waved and roared at it, but the pilot seemed blind to them. When the plane passed, it passed like the day's last offer of extinction.

So it was clear, at last, they had better stop dallying. Hirano, who wished to wash before the end, went downhill looking for fresh water. He came back up and reported a stream down there. They went down and stripped naked. When they entered the water it took their breath. Each washed himself with his rag or undershirt.

They emerged from the water and put their loincloths on again. Isao was a handsome kid, Goda noticed academically, and there was still a sort of unsullied quality to him despite all his fervor. He had done barely more than garrison duty, supervising native bearers. His sins were few. The erection that had just appeared was probably an unexpected reaction to nakedness, the stinging water, a remembered girl. Others found the innocence of the thing was nearly an affront.

"Someone pull him off!" said Domen, the country boy. Goda stared at him for debasing the moment.

Back up on the ridge, they saw the countryside was still vacant and thus even more so the fiasco could not be permitted to continue. The day was going. The young men knelt to compose themselves and recite a final prayer. While still standing, Goda mentally recited what he had been taught at home.

"For heaven and earth are yet separated, and the purer and clearer part has not yet lifted from the squalid and fleshly part. But the brave passage of a soul will unite them. Thereafter a man becomes a venerated ancestor . . ."

Omura stood up and removed his prepared belt and asked if they would help him.

"Are you sure you want to do this right now?" asked Isao. "You might just be being impetuous."

"Well, I can be pretty impetuous," Omura admitted, as he finished putting on his uniform. "But not in this case." Beneath a thick branch of a river gum, Hirano and Domen lifted him, one leg each, and he tied the belt to the branch and knotted it hard. Then he adjusted the buckle.

"Are you ready?" asked Hirano.

"Yes, let me go at the count of three. And after a few more seconds, haul on my legs." That was how it was done. Hirano and Domen jumped aside. Omura kicked in the air. Hirano and Domen pulled on his legs with sudden and ferocious intent and heard the neck go. They kept pulling as if to squeeze the soul from him and then let him hang.

And so Omura was safe, had led the way as an aviator should, and certified their own purpose.

Hirano, panting a little, asked, "Me next, Senior Sergeant?" The river gum was abundant with branches, and Hirano chose one on the far side of the tree from Omura. Isao joined Domen in lifting Hirano so he could tie and adjust his belt exactly as Omura had.

"When I say 'Yes,'" he told them, and then took only a second to say it. This time the crack was instantaneous with the fall, but they dragged and dragged on him until they were certain his spirit must have vacated him.

Domen then came back to the knife with which he'd killed the sheep, bowed to Goda, and knelt and drove it into himself, all without speaking, making of it a private act.

"Well now, my young friend?" Goda asked Isao amidst the dangling bodies and fallen Domen.

One last look out over the plain. In this dimming light Isao saw what he had not seen before. Steel tracks far off—three miles perhaps—shone with the exactly angled late sun. The intervening country was vacant of all but sheep and cattle and the drowsy fields of grain.

"Anyone can slit their throats, Senior Sergeant," said Isao, and he turned eyes brimming with ambition and certainty towards Goda.

"Can they?" asked Goda. But the parallel tracks drew him, too, the straightest and purest and most demonstrative of things in a chaotic emptiness. Isao had obviously caught fire at the idea of an eminent demonstration.

It took them an hour, tangling with a number of farm fences, to get down to the railway line and shelter in the culvert awaiting a train.

But when they made it, and hid in a log-buttressed ditch beneath the line, no train came in the last light or throughout the entire freezing night. In the camp, they had dressed to die rather than spend an inglorious night in a culvert like this. Once again they endured sporadic, dismal sleep. All night the rails above them ached and ticked in the cold which, they noticed when light came, had put a crust of ice over small pools of water nearby.

In early light, young Isao wondered aloud why the tracks had been built if they were to remain untroubled by traffic.

36

Hundreds of prisoners remained in Compound C, which meant that some had chosen to hug the ground or lie in ditches rather than complete their charge. Yet it seemed all blame and accusation had been purged from the air, except in one case. Men were astounded to see the wrestler Oka brought in on the Sunday morning, from a truck that had delivered a scatter of other recaptured survivors. Most of them wore their obvious shame, but Oka's attitude was hard to read and could have been interpreted as blithe, even though that had always been his manner.

The word was passed around that he had slit a man's throat during the escape, a man who had fallen and needed a brisk end. Those of the survivors who still promised themselves another attempt at self-obliteration, another charge against the wire at some as-yet-unappointed time, began to assure themselves of the improper nature of this behavior. If Oka believed that death was appropriate in the case of a wounded man, why did he now choose to walk back into camp like a man who had suffered a defeat, certainly, but in an apparently unrepentant mode? His appetite at the rudimentary table in the mess hall on the first night of his return would be cited as a cause why men should look askance at him and concentrate their anger at

341

their own failed attempt at self-eradication upon this hulking, brazen remnant. There were rumors that Aoki had done a similar service for a fallen comrade, yet himself survived and vanished into the bush. But, unlike Oka, Aoki could be trusted to court his own end out there.

It was Oka's bulk, apparent appetite in the mess, supposed lack of self-disappointment, unnatural easiness of soul, and (at least as those who disliked him chose to see it) jauntiness that grew so offensive to the small minority of reimprisoned zealots. No one chastised him directly—his size and a reaction from him could reduce a great question of propriety to the level of a brawl. He conversed with some about the charge, and he did at least reflect on the perversity of the odds that had left him and them untouched through all that. The true believers would not speak to him, however.

When Aoki was brought back through the gate into Main Road on Monday at dusk, he fell to his knees and wept, and kissed the earth for the blood that had been offered up. His escort of guards were at the time completing some paperwork at the gate so for the moment he knelt without molestation from them. The black timbers of Compound C were, he thought, a reflection of his burned-out soul—the soul, as he saw it, of a man the odds had made both a clown and a murderer.

News that he was there spread through the remnants of the compound, and an instantly formed deputation of the party of certainty approached him from within Compound C and spoke to him through the wire. Their attitude was respectful since many had seen him advancing over the fences in his slower gait but with the correct ambition. They called out to him, but he had little to say. He could not tell them that the leather of his belt had let him down. He was a buffoon, and it a comic excuse. It was a skit appropriate to the now-burned recreation hall in the days it had heaved with laughter.

They were complaining to him not about his own unscathed return, but Oka's. That the man had come back and settled in just as if he had not executed one of his fellow escapees. Aoki groaned—to the limits of the groan, just before it passed into a howl. "Leave him alone now," he said. "If you are right about him, then being left alone is what he deserves."

At least Oka's buckle hadn't broken and made an ass of him.

"You'll be tried as leader of the outbreak, Senior Sergeant," one of them consoled him, "and be shot. But he's just a dumb ox and will live."

They were, he was certain, correct about his coming execution. Even they, that army of irrationals and fools, couldn't leave him untouched now. But that would require a wearying delay and a formal death, which in fact, in the privacy of his soul, he found more frightening a prospect than the haphazard and more familiar nature of a charge against machine guns.

Aoki was collected by guards and frog-marched down Main Road into the hoosegow in Compound B. Cheong saw him pass, and Koreans of the imperial party saluted him as he went by. Cheong yelled after him, "Idiot!" For the balance had tipped his way he felt—the balance in Gawell, in the world—over the last few days.

At an informal meeting in a corner of the canteen in Compound C, Aoki's advice was discussed, and two of the firmer souls argued it should be respectfully rejected. "Aoki's just exhausted," one said indulgently. Others of the group began to be persuaded, and so a small liquidation squad developed. That night, as the wrestler slept on the canteen floor, they grabbed him, six men to one, and dragged him towards a noose they had already prepared and fixed to a rafter in the remnants of the showers. They lifted him to a bench they intended to knock out from below him.

"Your opponent, Tengan—he's gone," one of them said, in an offhand version of reading the prisoner his rights. (In fact, they did not know whether Tengan was living or dead. But they were certain of his principles.) "He did the right thing, we can guarantee. But as for you, you great beast, you took a life—you took a life and didn't have the rigor to take your own." Oka argued he had asked the soldiers who retrieved him to shoot him. Still, for their own obscure but convinced purpose, the party wrestled him to the scaffold. He went limp now, like a child resisting its parents. But they were powerful enough to hold him up and, as he grunted and spat, the noose was fitted, and then they kicked out the bench and dragged on his robust legs until the thing had been settled and the balance restored and the most blatant survival punished.

Some of them would have confessed they then felt the hollowness of men who had slain the demon and found a tribe of others emerging, not from the outer air but from within themselves. They left him dangling, and guards, on regular patrol, found him early the next morning. Another apparent suicide to go with the ones that had preceded the outbreak, Suttor declared in his report. He was nonetheless frightened by this death as by all of them. Even one like this seemed slated to his account, and thus to that of his own poor David, who had known no normal home, found happiness briefly in a barracks of young men, and lost it in a heinous defeat.

The sun invaded the long line of trees and glimmered on a fence of barbed wire, from which condensation soon dripped, and on the wet flanks of two cows with whom—unknowingly—Goda and Isao had shared the night. The pastures all around, Goda saw, remained malignly empty of searchers. Go a few miles from Gawell, and you were a lonely figure in a ghastly and disordered landscape in which only steel lines had a direction and a rational straightness, though not yet a sufficiently meaningful one. While squatting in the culvert, Isao almost comically moved, still crouched, from one foot to another, warming up like a midget wrestler. Goda said, "In an hour—no, two hours—we should move on and try something else. The bastard train will never come. I think this is a spur line. There must be a main line somewhere and a train on it." As if manufactured by light and the debate about moving on, there was a minor steel vibration in the rails above their heads. Soon the full, though in this case modest and rustic, voice of a locomotive could be heard. Minor as it might be, and sluggish in sound, it made music adequate to their purpose. In the culvert's shadow, Goda took the time to take out and study his wife's photograph awhile, something sentimental he had not risked doing in the purgatory of Compound C. It was easy to confront her features now that she was not a reproach. Isao squatted beside him and glanced across his shoulder to see a pleasant-faced girl in a sec-retarial college uniform. He felt a last futile pulse of blood. The cry of his loins was a whisper from a ghost.

As the sound of the train began to swell and reveal itself as indeed a slowly moving branch-line machine, Goda said, "We mustn't go up there to the lines too soon."

He rose, though, to snatch a look around the flank of the culvert. "A kilometer still," he told Isao and went down again on his haunches in the culvert's shadow.

When Goda gave the signal, and nudged Isao's upper arm, they ran up out of the culvert. This itself was an escape from squalor, from shelter worthy of animals. The locomotive was seventy meters away. They could feel its coming heat as they knelt and laid their necks down on the cold rail, which throbbed against their throats.

The train carrying Alice Herman on Monday morning to what she called "home" had left before five, and had now reached the country around Gawell and its paddocks and crops owned by people whose names she knew. There, after too-eking a journey, the engine took on for the first time dramatic movement. It was not one of speed but of a frantic reach for deceleration. Yet in its urgency and strenuousness it all seemed faster somehow than any pace the engine had achieved that morning. She could hear shouting even before the skidding, shrieking wheels achieved an eventual stop.

She reached the window, which in these trains was—as the girls had said in her childhood—like a guillotine. Once pushed up, it could thunder down on your neck or knuckles again at any second. She opened it upwards and looked out into the bright air. The train was a few feet above the surrounding countryside—the earth sloped away on either side—but she could see soldiers jumping down onto the graveled flank of the embankment and one man lowering a rifle from a carriage door to give it to another.

The train moved again, but backwards from the point to which the soldiers and civilians who had alighted were running. Then the engine gave a hiss and sound of reduced power, which meant it intended to stand where it was awhile. So she opened her compartment door and jumped down to the ground herself. She landed crookedly. She was wearing flat-heeled shoes and happily did not turn an ankle. She made her way unevenly along the sloped embankment. The cold sniped at her bare legs beneath the skirt. When she got close to the front of the engine she saw the driver standing by the track vomiting while the fireman held his shoulders.

"What happened?" she demanded.

"We hit two Japs, miss," said the fireman. "You ought to go back to your carriage."

"I've seen accidents," she argued, a bit like a schoolgirl. She had seen Mr. Archer when his tractor had fallen on him and Mrs. Archer had come screaming to their place asking for their help. Men had lifted the tractor off Archer's body and out of politeness for Mrs. Archer's furniture they'd put him on the sorting table in his modest shearing shed. So she'd seen accidents.

The fireman lost his fragile temper at her. "Go back, for Christ's sake, miss. They put their necks down on the line."

A sergeant major appeared from the front of the engine with the same but politer advice. Awed by their male consensus, and after a delay in which she contemplated the extreme Japanese intentions, she obeyed them.

The train was delayed an hour by those men who had insisted on decapitation. She waited in her carriage, her mind licking like a small hungry flame around what they had done, their utter resolve. She had never thought like them before. Now she could imagine each step they took to the glittering, smooth rail. How they would have bent themselves to its steel, and endured the intervening time full of the shriek and grind of the train. It seemed apparent to her that the hardihood of that act meant she could adopt a similar steeliness and finalize her mess of appetite for Giancarlo. The reasonable and genial single-mindedness of Esther, unblighted by any excess, fortified her and seemed to her the state in which from now on she would manage life.

Duncan met her train at Gawell station, and she sat upright in the truck and explained the delay.

"Must be just about the last of the blighters then," Duncan murmured.

"Then there aren't any more of them wandering around?" She wondered what other gestures of iron determination she might see. "The radio says if there are, they're nothing to worry about. Now, the thing is, I've got to take some fat lambs into the sales this afternoon. The sales wait for no one. Maybe you'd better come with me, just in case."

She remembered her earlier journey for the lamb sales, just after Giancarlo's arrival. She'd gone because Duncan didn't know his Johnny yet. This Giancarlo, who now had the hide to try to escape the two of them.

But the suggestion—Duncan and the saleyard auction of lambs to slaughter; the dust and bush tedium of it—shook her, and she said she believed she was safe to be left alone on the farm. And, she thought, it was in any case a good test of what she had learned from Esther and the train incident.

"I've got a lot of cooking to do," she added.

"Well," Duncan conceded, "I can leave you the rifle and tell Johnny to be on the old qui vive, eh."

"I think that's best. He can stay down there at the shearers' quarters and read."

Giancarlo, captive to a book. She sounded offhand, but hoped offhandedness could become her true style—indifference to all that had compelled her a week back.

She opened the gate for Duncan to drive onto his land and up to the farmhouse. Inside, the news on the radio informed Duncan and Alice that the prisoners guilty of the outbreak were all but accounted for. Alice had of course seen two of them account for themselves.

So, in case of any unexpected apparition—a last wandering prisoner of war—before he went out to the fields with Giancarlo, Duncan left an old but favorite rifle with her, a heavy one with a big brown stock, designed to fire bullets of a very robust caliber and to kick like a mule.

At lunchtime Alice left it at the farmhouse, this defense against phantasmal Japanese, and loaded up her bike and took the men their thick-crusted beef and pickle sandwiches and black tea. There was no sense in the air that weapons might fall into the hands of the rumored enemy. In view of Giancarlo's recent escape and her period of reflection and calm life with Esther, she decided what her face might signify to him—caution or annoyance, which she was tempted by. Certainly not limitless desire, anyhow. She wanted her look to be similar to the one Esther took shopping—a comfortable look that said this was a woman whose contentment filled out her body; that she wasn't an arena for gusts of anger and peevishness and hunger.

Down in the paddocks, she saw Duncan letting Giancarlo whistle up the wheeling sheepdogs, intervening himself only when they failed to respond to the Italian's signals. As she got nearer, it was Giancarlo who first turned and saw her. Duncan then noticed her and moved forward. Giancarlo remained where he was, one eye on her, one on the activities of the dogs harrying fat lambs into a raceway that led to the truck; letting the ewes into another that presented them with a dead end and eternal separation from their weaned young. Giancarlo frowned, unable to give the required brotherly grin, unable to know what her recent absence from him meant, and not knowing what he wanted it to mean.

Duncan suggested she lay out the lunch on the back of the truck and launched himself up quite youthfully to sit on the right-hand side of the cloth. Giancarlo easily hoisted himself, hip first, in a way that teased all resolve in her. It was as if he had declared, "Find someone who can move better than that and you're welcome to him." He continued to study her closely. She knew he was wondering if she showed a sign of renewed welcome, or was terminating all that secret trading of breath and flesh. Alice, meanwhile, felt both strengthened and forlorn, but the strengthening would do her for now.

"So I'm giving Johnny the afternoon off, like I said," Duncan informed her. "You stick close to the house and the rifle."

"Won't you need to take the rifle yourself?" she asked Duncan.

"If I see one of the blighters," Duncan said in an unlikely boast, "I'll grab him and put him in the back."

"Why would he stay there?"

"Because I've got lengths of bailing wire I can use on him."

"No," said Alice. "Drive past him and tell the coppers in town."

Weighing this proposition, Duncan inspected the meat in his sandwich. He turned to Giancarlo.

"So you can read all afternoon if you like, Johnny. You're a beggar for the books."

"I might take some reading," murmured Giancarlo almost sullenly.

"*Do* some reading," Alice suggested neutrally. And then, to show she could give a normal compliment between acquaintances, she said, "Yes, you are really doing well at novels, Giancarlo."

She did not dwell on it. They were finished, and she gathered the leavings, the pannikins, the thermos, and the cloth. She loaded the bike basket up, seated herself on the saddle, and rode away with a casual wave. The impulse was to stop and turn back towards the truck. But she consoled herself that the more normal mere politeness became with her, the more it would become the tenor of the extended if dismal days.

37

Tengan, alone by the second morning, unaware of the demonstration Goda had made on the Carcoar line that same morning, was still traveling the ridges, from which he could watch the country and the roads. Earlier he had seen two of the enemy's aircraft creeping across the sky; underpowered craft, looking for such as him but unable to perceive him, though he waved his jacket. Earlier still, he had encountered and left behind two small groups of men who seemed to have lost their spirit and who lingered amongst the trees on the slopes within reach of farmhouses and roads, ready for surrender. Amongst these men, there was such an air of acceptance that it was likely the enemy, when they came, would take them in with an abominable, forgiving disregard.

Certainly they must be hungry, he acknowledged, but the creeks between the ridges and the dams down in the pastures on the farms would provide them ample water, and with the right spirit, even given the cold nights, they could have gone on for days. But they had lost the right spirit. One young man had asked him, without naming him by rank, whether he was fed up with the farce yet? The farce! Disciplining him, even had one the means, was pointless, but Tengan stared at him as if he were diseased, and then kept on his way.

Tengan met up with food soon after leaving them—a large lizard planted vertically on a tree, waiting as if part not of the animal but of the vegetable reality of the place. At noon he made a small fire and roasted it. The infantrymen had told him stories of the nourishing, almost succulent meat of the more muscular lizards of the jungle, and he adjudged this meat—possibly his last—very superior to the tedious mutton of Compound C.

In the wake of his lizard meal, a sharper understanding arose in him that he had been on the loose for a day and a half now, and that it was an absolutely unsatisfactory span by the standards of the plans laid out in Aoki's hut before the breakout. Could he also believe that in this huge, indifferent landscape he was undermining the enemy's fiber and causing them discomfiture? He did not feel himself to be the inconvenience he had expected to become. He understood that this was a factor that had dispirited the two parties he had separated himself from. It was hard to resist the concept that he could wander this rind of barbarous earth eternally. He wanted to force the issue, but in such supine country he could not find the elements to bring it about. He must go looking actively for trouble, but could not be sure he would find it.

Below him were all the same wheat and fodder crops, the same grass-guzzling beasts, but beyond a track of red and yellow clay within the limits of a farm lay a long white building. Here he could see a man sitting on a wicker chair in a sunny segment of the veranda that ran along the side of the structure. He appeared as young as Tengan, raw looking and sinewy, in a frayed khaki sweater that looked like the ones issued in camp, and old gray pants. The man he saw was the most hopeful omen he had encountered on this second day out of Compound C. The place was a farm utterly according to the pattern of their uncouth agriculture. But the man amidst it excited him. For this might be his man. From a distance the fellow did not look ferocious, and the hour was not good, an hour when the bush and the bright day began to turn violet and serene.

Tengan decided to reconnoiter the man he saw below, who—after putting his book down a number of times and as if distracted—stood up and went to a wood heap near some fruit trees at the corner of the building. He picked up an ax and, having been a scholar a few minutes before, now became a menial.

The clean sound of the ax made Tengan exultant. He is my man! When the fellow had finished, he fetched a barrow from a shed, loaded it with wood, and took it through the fruit trees to the farmhouse. Here he stacked it an armful at a time against the back door. He returned then to his table outside his room and picked up his book. He was in reach of the ax even as he sat back at the outdoor table and began to read again, lifting and lowering the book.

An ax seemed promising. Two days ago, Tengan would not have chosen the crudity of such an instrument as desirable for his purpose. But the passage of the empty hours since he'd broken the outer wire and impaled the colonel had reduced his chances of more conventional death wounds. Tengan also decided that this figure—servant and reader at once—was a contradictory one. This paradox further justified a hopeful investigation.

So he descended the side of the hill where the faded tint of his uniform suited the shade of trees and the tone of granite rocks. Soon he was out of the line of sight of the woodchopper. He was hidden by the winter wheat crop and—climbing through fences, approaching by way of the flank—worked round it to near the barracks from its rear. He passed through a screen of trees and edged along the side of the barracks and took a glance around the corner. He saw the man was again distractedly reading his book, raising his head regularly as if dissatisfied and searching the afternoon—still golden down here—in expectation of something, perhaps someone arriving. Me, Tengan thought.

Tengan estimated that he and the reader were the same distance from the wood heap, and Tengan knew he could run and take up the ax before the man drew breath. So he simply sprinted across powdery earth to the heap and grabbed the labor-smoothed handle. Then, under the duty of directing his own death and impressing his killer by emphatic action, he jumped forward into a stagey stance—legs bent, ax raised—and howled.

The woodchopper stood up and dropped his book so that its first half lay on the veranda planks and the second half hung over the yard's earth. And then all the choreography went out of Tengan. He knew this man. The Italian he'd swapped words with and shared a small pool of English terms. His name escaped Tengan's memory, but this was the sourest climax to his absurd life as Number 42001. His plan had flowered into a most noxious accident—this man would not wrestle him for the ax or use it on him. Tengan's stance slackened under the confusion of the instant. The man was a little shocked but smiling. His mouth assumed a smooth, long-lipped smile of recognition.

"*Numero Uno!*" he cried. "You escape? You bugger off, is it, my friend? Bugger me! You are hungry?"

"Not hungry," yelled Tengan. "No tucker," he pleaded. He advanced to Giancarlo and pushed the shaft of the ax towards him so that the Italian's hands rose by reflex to receive it. "*Morte, ti prego,*" he pleaded. "Do me the death, *Italia.*"

Giancarlo frowned and would not take the thing. "*Uno,* I get you bread. Then maybe you go back . . ."

"No!" Tengan begged at such a volume that it sounded like a threat. "Do me the death!"

In almost playful mood, Giancarlo received the ax and studied it as if Tengan were selling it to him.

"What you mean?" asked Giancarlo. "All this ax bulldust?"

Tengan said, with pride in his more exacting English, "You are my enemy and I will kill you."

Giancarlo laughed and shook his head. "You kid me," he said. He fell back on a phrase of Duncan's. "You act the goat, mate."

But Tengan ran towards Giancarlo again, and the Italian raised the handle of the ax to block him. Giancarlo was strangely submissive even in doing this. No wonder there were two thousand of them in Gawell Camp. Giancarlo dropped the ax and tried a half embrace, a playful hug. They tussled. When Giancarlo pushed him off again, Tengan was breathless. Two years of captivity, two days of hunger, two nights in the open. He felt a weak vessel now.

"If we are friends," gasped Tengan, "then you give me the death. They thank you for it! They send you home!"

Giancarlo still wore an appalling smile, more residual, though, and half-fearful. "You tell me bloody pig's arse," he said.

So Tengan, gathering strength, reached out and struck Giancarlo on the left of his jaw. Surely fury lay somewhere inside that body.

"*Bastardo!*" yelled Giancarlo and struck Tengan a blow that stunned him and made his head ring.

"Now you stop the horsefeathers!" yelled Giancarlo. "Now no more!" A hundred yards off in the kitchen Alice heard the noise—a foreign battle, not one like a yelling match between local men, its cadence somehow different. She felt an electric expectation, not unpleasant, and utterly engrossing. Duncan had said that Giancarlo wasn't worried about the Japanese. Now there was an edge of worry in the intonations she heard.

She was not yet too concerned for Giancarlo, but got the heavy rifle Duncan had left in the pantry corner and, while still in the kitchen, leveled it and worked the bolt and brought a bullet up into the chamber. She left the safety lock on and went quickly out into the late afternoon, carrying the gun by its strap over her right shoulder. It pulled her gait crooked. The day was burning itself out brilliantly over the ridges. She heard further shouting and began to stumble forward.

Then the possibility struck her. What if a rouseabout or a manager of one of the other farms had somehow found out about her and the Italian, and was now seeking to punish Giancarlo as if for woman theft? Or what about another Italian with a grudge? The escapees had owned her imagination since this morning's decapitations, but it might not at all be them.

These new possibilities made her faster. She tripped in the back garden and felt the shock and pain of landing sharply on her knees. She hoped she had not been heard and rejoiced that the safety had not been released and let the gun fire by accident. Once she reached a screen of bushes, she followed them in stealth, emerged into open ground, and ran towards the shearers' quarters.

A fight was on. It had moved inside Giancarlo's room, the former center of all hope. An escapee in burgundy pants and jacket came reeling out of the interior of the room and across the rudimentary veranda, just like a nameless cowboy in a film scene of a barroom brawl. Except that he was Japanese.

Giancarlo appeared from inside, advancing on the man, hands up, palms forward. It was a gesture not of surrender, but of pleading—for moderation. The escapee stood still, his head lowered, and half ran against Giancarlo's chest, half blundered into him.

"Now," said Giancarlo, calmingly. "Stop it and we have tea." His tenor of appeasement all at once sickened her. He is a weak man, she decided. Whereas Neville had given up his place on a caïque to a sick comrade.

The Japanese escapee had suddenly got hold of Giancarlo's throat, and apparently with a measure of success. It would have been clear to anyone that Giancarlo could break the hold. It was, however, Giancarlo's neck. It was the neck of the Hermans' Italian. She raised the rifle to her shoulder.

"Hey," she yelled. "Let go!"

The escapee saw her for the first time and let go of Giancarlo's throat. He hadn't expected that cry. Giancarlo stepped back, shrugged, smiled at her beneath his messed-up hair and over the assailant's shoulder, and spread his hands again like a man saying, "Don't human beings amaze you?"

She would have liked to have yelled, "They don't bloody amaze me!"

The attitude of the escapee as he turned to Alice—gasping, yet his face locked into an unkindly purpose—was very different from Giancarlo's. Here was a fellow to reckon with, a sweat-stained and harrowed young man, furious on one hand and presenting, on the other, large familiar eyes.

The day of the lemonade! An unforgettable man. No pleading hands in his case. Though he gulped air, no doubt was visible in his face. He spread the neck of his jacket open. His flesh was not bare beneath. He wore a khaki sweater. He seemed greatly to admire her rifle.

"Shoot me!" he ordered her and at the same time pleaded.

"Give me the death or I give you."

Alice took the safety off. Her blood itched. No human had offered himself to her in such a way. These people who had started it all. All the madness. The madness had been contained within the wire fences of Gawell, but it had by its force and insistence broken the bounds, and stained the bush with its dangerous expectations. And now it wanted to be shot, and the temptation was close to engulfing her. She trembled on the edge, a fury working up her body towards her shoulders.

"No, no," Giancarlo kept on saying with that reasonable voice. All the children of the earth, he implied. All holding hands in their march to the brotherly resolution some mad teacher at a technical college had called up in his mind. Some of her anger at the escapee therefore spilled in Giancarlo's direction again. His crowd had started it too. His crowd had invaded Greece but been incompetent, and that had brought their masters in, and their masters hadn't been incompetent and had bombed their way southwards and then trapped Neville, the man she'd swapped her vows with, in an island without even a caïque to take him to Egypt.

"I'll shoot you all right!" she called to the handsome foe, like a reassurance.

It was the wrong thing to say. He ran a few steps and picked up the ax. There was a distinct joy in his eyes as he came forward slowly, like a butcher with a particular cut in mind.

Alice was not afraid. She knew Giancarlo could catch him from behind and drag him into a hold. She knew that the prisoner was trying to force her hand. Otherwise he would have come at a rush. Thus she ought to wait for Giancarlo to clamp him. The man should not be accommodated.

But she possessed also a primal hatred and respect for the prisoner. He had not thought of the railway lines, as his two resolute brothers had, but he was resolute just the same. He continued to come forward with the ax. His face was frightful—he had composed a mask for it, a mask of provocation. Without him, she believed, there would be none of this world that had taken Neville away and none of this tearing of her soul and none of this unleashed and merciless hunger in her. So when he was some ten paces away, advancing at a measured but threatening pace, and Giancarlo was moving from the side to grab him yet again, she shot the prisoner through the chest and saw him fly backwards. As she recovered from the recoil, she saw he left a mist of his blood in the air.

After he was knocked onto his back, he raised himself sideways for an instant. Then he fell down again and began a conclusive tremble.

"I can shoot a rabbit through the eye," she yelled at him in the ringing of the ears. It was an outright boast and a late warning. But she was awed by what she'd done and the size of it. Her blood was still up as Giancarlo knelt to the man, who had some slight movement in him. His mouth frothed with blood. Giancarlo's knees were sunk in the bloodied dust. He looked up at Alice and yelled, "He didn't mean . . . He didn't mean . . ."

"How would you know, Giancarlo?" she howled. "You know nothing!"

He watched the man's face as if it were the face of a friend. He rubbed blood off the man's cheek—first aid, anarchist-style. But the prisoner had gulped one last time and died.

Giancarlo had the arrogance of tears in his eyes. She couldn't believe his simplemindedness.

"He was coming at me with an ax, you idiot!" she screamed. But, just as she had never fully believed in her own peril, neither had Giancarlo. He looked up at her and yelled, "*Strega!*" Witch! "*Cattiva,*" he said. "I was come to grab him."

It struck her for the first time. I have used this handsome Japanese to rid myself of handsome Giancarlo, and Giancarlo will use him now to get rid of me.

Giancarlo stood up and grabbed the ax, bloodied not on the blade but along the handle. He turned his back on her and, as an opening to his frenzy, smashed the window of his room with the blunt end, and then walked to the doorjamb, hacking into it with blows repeated at what she thought was an impossible rate. He was breaking out. It was an act of escape. He was smashing his cell and saw her as his gaoler and didn't give a damn what she might do now. The blows, repeated and repeated, caused the wood of the walls to fly in the air. She would let him do it as long as he wanted to, she decided.

She began to shudder but still, in spite of all, did not repent of the dead enemy five steps away. Her dress was splashed with his blood. "My dress is ruined," she murmured to herself. Her shoulder had been pummeled by the heavy rifle, too, and ached. Then, still carrying that rifle, she moved inside to call the camp. From within the house she could hear Giancarlo hacking at his walls.

The Fallout

In September 1944 a broadcast from the enemy's English-language shortwave news service was broadcast and picked up. A transcript was sent to Gawell and appeared in Major Suttor's letter tray, freezing his blood.

Bursting with indignation at the cold-blooded murder of Japanese civilian internees, we demand to know the true story of the midnight murder of these 300 innocent men, belatedly reported more than a month after the incident occurred. It is perfectly clear to the Japanese people that these unfortunates who were murdered in the prison camp cannot have been prisoners of war. They were internees: the Japanese soldier never permits himself to be taken prisoner. The unfortunate victims of the midnight mass murder had lived in Australia for years before the war. They had become accustomed to the Australian way of living and had Australian friends and girlfriends. Then, why should they uprise without cause? And why has there been no statement by the Vatican authorities or by the protecting power or the International Red Cross regarding these killings? It should be obvious that these authorities have been prevented from making a thorough investigation. We appeal to Archbishop Gilroy of Sydney and the Apostolic Delegate from the Vatican, who have repeatedly deplored anti-Axis brutality, to insist on a thorough investigation of the matter.

The idea of the chastisement of an archbishop and an apostolic delegate played, along with so much else, on Major Suttor's already grieving mind. He grieved for the lost men of Compound C as for the lost of the garrison, and, in the latter case, above all for Warren Headon, whom he'd barely known and whose disabling of his gun had saved many of the garrison and perhaps others.

He grieved because Abercare and he and all of them had lived by habits of unvigilance. They had spoken to the garrison about the virtues of watchfulness, but the garrison had taken its cue from Abercare and Suttor's own disbelief, and from their style of life as functionaries.

He grieved most intensely for his son, and all other sons. Abercare was blameworthy but had paid for any crime of negligence. Suttor had not yet, and did not need the archbishop's counsels on top of all else. He was already the chief penitent, and would be so for the residue of his life.

The character of Compound C was changed now. New prisoners arrived, younger men who had not been fully transformed into soldiers because they had been rushed into battle. These boys were critical of generals and the way they themselves had been let down by them and by criminal deficiencies of supply. The surviving party of certainty, the ultras, no longer had the authority they once did.

When the military inquiry was appointed by Headquarters, Suttor was able to tell a reasonable story, the sort of story he related in his nightly serial. He had been told by his legal adviser that there would have been no deaths unless the prisoners had willed them. Abercare was let off reverently by the court, and his early notice to the prisoners of Compound C was construed as an act of civilization to which the inmates had reacted with barbarism.

Though Colonel Deakin of the training battalion was much questioned as to why he had armed his sentries but sent out searchers with mere bayonets, he was ultimately excused with a mild reprimand. For the proposition behind the inquiry was—at least in considerable part—that it could find the three officers culpable or not. If it found the men culpable, they certainly did not merit gaol terms, and mere reproaches and demotions would be mocked internationally as inadequate. So all of Gawell's garrison, and Deakin, had to be exonerated.

Colonel Abercare's grave in Gawell cemetery remained honored, Colonel Deakin still commanded the trainees, and Suttor was soon after given a job in information at Headquarters in Sydney, and was delighted to leave Gawell. A new commandant was installed and a new major for Compound C. Suttor the public man remained with all his visible surfaces intact, and was treated with some sensibility by a creaky military machine. He continued to write about the Mortons, which was considered the most important job he had.

No archbishop's or apostolic delegate's letter ever arrived at Gawell. As for the protecting power, the Swiss, its representatives had, by the Sunday following the outbreak, stood with him in grievous Compound C, in the atmosphere of putrefaction as first one corpse and then another was taken from the outer compound into the canteen block for examination by the coroner. The Swiss and he shared that companionable horror.

There had been a few distractions. A woman on a Gawell farm had killed a Japanese escapee who had threatened her with an ax, and then the Italian prisoner on the farm had inexplicably "gone troppo" and attacked his own quarters with the same ax. He was put in the hoosegow of one of the Italian compounds and quickly forgotten by Suttor.

Aoki was charged within a few hours of his advice to some of the prisoners concerning Oka. He found himself in the high-security corridor of a prison somewhere near Sydney. Other Japanese prisoners came and went there, but he was awaiting a major trial.

Over three days of testimony, he told—through his translator—the truth. He claimed he had murdered Lieutenant Healy, the officer who had accompanied the recruits who'd carried mere bayonets, but there was no conclusive evidence of that—the fleeing militiamen's backs had been turned—and it was thought he was indulging suicidal tendencies in saying it. In the end the court found him a mere accessory, an abettor and not a prime cause, and condemned him to a ten-year sentence in a military gaol on the outskirts of the city named Sydney.

This, in effect, meant that he was sentenced to the haunting, phantom reproaches of the immolated ones of Compound C. His guards watched him to prevent his suicide. They confiscated cutlery after every meal, sent him an army barber to shave him once a week, and otherwise deprived him of all sharp objects.

It may have been that his sanity was saved by a remarkable young diviner, a man of striking eyes, of ascetic tendencies, who could meditate for three hours at a time without moving.

In one of the camps west of Gawell, he had killed a fellow prisoner at the man's intense pleading. Even though his powers of divination were frowned on by many established Shinto priests, he himself had an ambition to be a priest, if he could ever manage it.

Bewildered by the accident of his relentless survival, Aoki inevitably sought the striking young man's help. Sadly, the prison authorities had confiscated the plaques with symbols on them that were one of the essential tools of divination. Aoki's companion was thrown back onto other stratagems of his craft: He counted the footsteps of guards in the corridor and observed over a period the height and direction of birds above the exercise yard. He consulted cups as well. This took him days of assessment, calculation, and reflection. When, during their recreation hour, he was at last ready to speak to Aoki, he told him that all the tools of divination to which he had had recourse indicated that Aoki was by some spiritual force excluded from chasing death. This much was evident from his history alone. He must bear his grief and wait for death to approach him. That was the formula of his life.

In the derangement of his mind at that time, the proposition was like a revelation. The news that there were definite forces ordaining his survival was a comfort at last, and explained why his desire to attain death had been thwarted at every turn.

His sentence was commuted five months after the conflict ended, and he was shipped home in the middle of 1946. By then, Neville Herman had been eight months returned and was farming again and living with his father and his wife. He was a mature man and ready for life, not closed to it like his father. He and Alice adopted a child, and then another. They seemed an exemplary couple and had many friends in the Gawell tennis club. Neville bought out the Hammonds, on whose farm Giancarlo had once sheltered, became a shire councillor and a member of the board of the New South Wales Country Cricket Association. Baseball had been extinguished in the region.

Young David Suttor came home, too, after a stint in Changi and another on the Burma railroad and then in Changi again. He weighed, on arrival at the quay in Sydney, 45 percent of his weight at capture, but while weight was susceptible to remediation, it took four months in what people called a mental hospital to make him ready for life on the streets. At the end of 1946 he left his family for London and became the popular novelist Major Suttor never was and took lovers amongst the most famous of British painters and actors.

It was only later in life that Aoki wondered if the diviner had diagnosed his symptoms of survival to save his mind and his continued life. But such had been the force of the young meditator's character that these doubts did not enter his mind until he was nearly sixty years of age.

Acknowledgments

I must gratefully acknowledge the help of Professor Michael Lewis of the University of Sydney, an expert on Japanese history and culture. If in various instances even his good services do not prevent me from errors, that is not his fault.

Other sources include:

Teruhiko Asada, *A Night of a Thousand Suicides* (Sydney, 1970).

Charlotte Carr-Gregg, "Japanese Prisoners of War in Australia, the Cowra Outbreak, August, 1944," *Oceania*, vol. XLVII, no. 4, p. 253, June 1977.

Hugh V. Clarke, *Break-out! The Japanese POW Break-out at Cowra, 1944* (Sydney, 1964).

Harry Gordon, *Die Like the Carp: The Story of the Greatest POW Escape Ever* (Sydney, 1978).

————, *Voyage from Shame: The Cowra Outbreak and Afterwards* (Brisbane, 1994).

National Archives of Australia, "Cowra POW Outbreak," A1066; A1608; SP1714/1; A373; A430; A7711; SP 112/1; A5954; SP 1048/7.

Seaforth Mackenzie, *Dead Men Rising* (Sydney, 1951).